Pelican Books
Islam in the World

Malise Ruthven was born in Dublin in 1942. On his father's side he is descended from a military family of Scottish ancestry, on his mother's from a line of Irish Protestant clerics and scholars. After leaving school Malise Ruthven spent a year doing relief work in Jordan, where he began learning Arabic and spent several weeks travelling among the Huweitat beduin. He read English Literature at Cambridge University before returning to the Middle East to study Arabic. After several years as a staff writer and editor with the BBC's Arabic Service in London he became a freelance journalist specializing in Middle East affairs. His previous books are *Torture, the Grand Conspiracy* (1978) and *Cairo* (1980). He has contributed regularly to the BBC and the *London Review of Books*.

Islam

MALISE RUTHVEN

in the World

PENGUIN BOOKS

Penguin Books Ltd, Harmondsworth, Middlesex, England
Viking Penguin Inc., 40 West 23rd Street, New York, New York 10010, U.S.A.
Penguin Books Australia Ltd, Ringwood, Victoria, Australia
Penguin Books Canada Ltd, 2801 John Street, Markham, Ontario, Canada L3R 1B4
Penguin Books (N.Z.) Ltd, 182–190 Wairau Road, Auckland 10, New Zealand

First published 1984

Made and printed in Great Britain by
Cox and Wyman Ltd, Reading
Photoset in 9/12 Linotron Palatino by
Rowland Phototypesetting Ltd,
Bury St Edmunds, Suffolk

TO TIGGY WITH LOVE

Contents

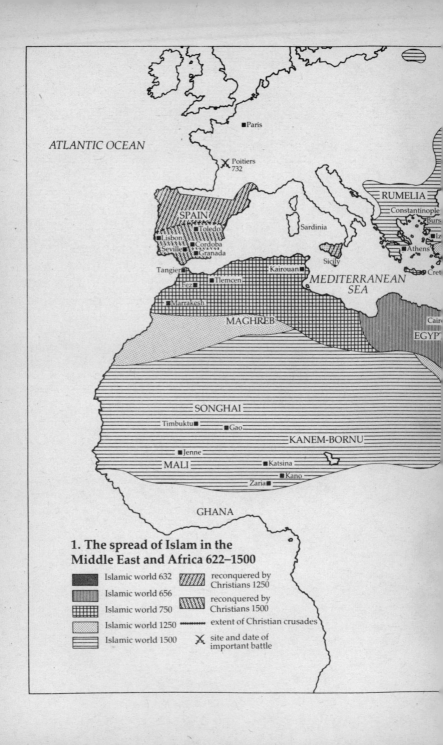

ATLANTIC OCEAN

■Paris

X Poitiers
732

SPAIN
■Toledo
■Lisbon
Seville■ ■Cordoba
■Granada

Sardinia

RUMELIA
Constantinople
Burs
■Iz
■Athens
Cret

Tangier■ Kairouan■
Fez■ ■Tlemcen
■Marrakesh
MAGHREB

MEDITERRANEAN
SEA

Sicily

Cair

EGYPT

SONGHAI
Timbuktu■ ■Gao
KANEM-BORNU
■Jenne
MALI ■Katsina
■Kano
Zaria■

GHANA

1. The spread of Islam in the
Middle East and Africa 622–1500

Islamic world 632	reconquered by Christians 1250	
Islamic world 656	reconquered by Christians 1500	
Islamic world 750	extent of Christian crusades	
Islamic world 1250		
Islamic world 1500	X site and date of important battle	

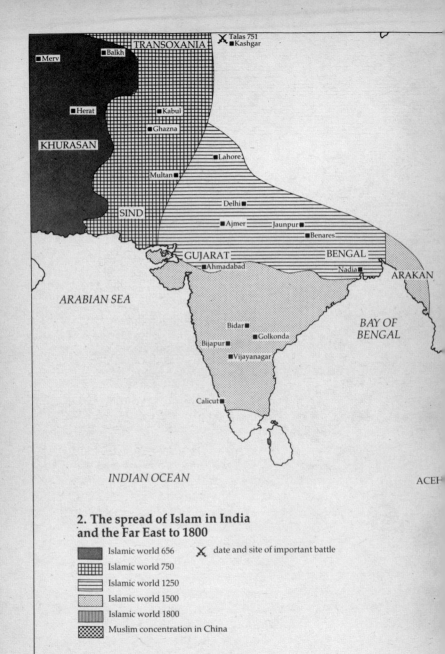

2. The spread of Islam in India and the Far East to 1800

Islamic world 656
Islamic world 750
Islamic world 1250
Islamic world 1500
Islamic world 1800
Muslim concentration in China

X date and site of important battle

CAUCASU[S]
NAQSHBAND[I]
Imam Mansur 17[..]

NAQSHBANDIYA

Istanbul ■
Ankara ■
■ Konya

■ Damascus ■ Baghdad
NAQSHBANDIYA

ALGERIA
1832–47

Jaghbub ■ ■ Cairo ■
KHALWATIYA

NAJD
Wahhabi Sultanate
1740

FUTA TORO
1776

■ Mecca

MASINA
1810

■ Gao

■ Jenne
Sokoto ■   ■ Kano

Khartoum ■
Sudanese Mahdiya
1881–98

■ Lagos

SOMALIA
Muhammad 'Abdullah H[..]
inspires rebellion against
British Ethiopians
1899–1920

SULTANATE OF
SOKOTO
1804

KAARTA
1852–93

FUTA JALLON
1725

BONDU
1680

KASHGAR
NAQSHBANDIYA
1820–77

KANSU
NAQSHBANDIYA
'New Sect'
1761–1877

Tashkent ■

Samarkand ■

Lanchou ■

N.W. FRONTIER
■ Balakot

PUNJAB

Delhi ■

Karachi ■   *NAQSHBANDIYA*

YUNNAN
1856–73
Yunnan-fu ■

■ Bombay

IAQSHBANDIYA
DRISIYA
alihiya

ACEH
Naqshbandi-led *jihad*
against Dutch
1873–1910

MINANGKABAU
Jihad against Dutch
1803–37

Sumatra
NAQSHBANDIYA

Java
Dipa Negra's *jihad*
against Dutch
1825–30

3. States created by *jihad* movements and reformed *tariqas*

      Islamic state established through *jihad*

      extent of influence of the Sanusiya

NAQSHBANDIYA: main centres of *tariqa* activity

Salihiya: militant subsects of larger *tariqas*

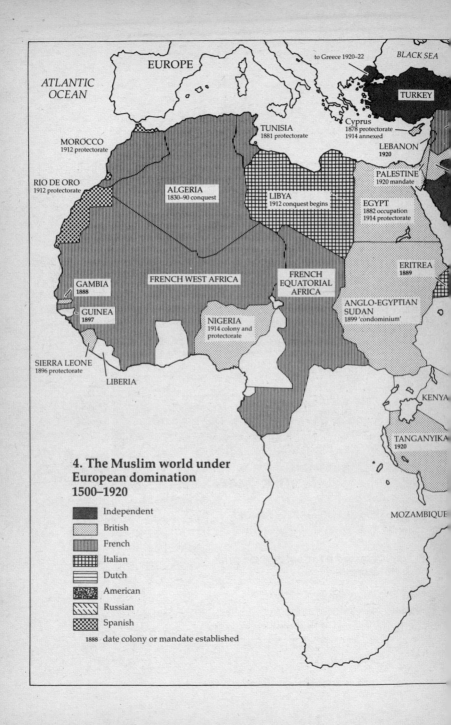

ATLANTIC
OCEAN

EUROPE

to Greece 1920–22

BLACK SEA

TURKEY

Cyprus
1878 protectorate
1914 annexed

LEBANON
1920

PALESTINE
1920 mandate

TUNISIA
1881 protectorate

MOROCCO
1912 protectorate

RIO DE ORO
1912 protectorate

ALGERIA
1830–90 conquest

LIBYA
1912 conquest begins

EGYPT
1882 occupation
1914 protectorate

ERITREA
1889

FRENCH WEST AFRICA

FRENCH
EQUATORIAL
AFRICA

ANGLO-EGYPTIAN
SUDAN
1899 'condominium'

GAMBIA
1888

GUINEA
1897

NIGERIA
1914 colony and
protectorate

SIERRA LEONE
1896 protectorate

LIBERIA

KENYA

TANGANYIKA
1920

MOZAMBIQUE

4. The Muslim world under European domination 1500–1920

	Independent
	British
	French
	Italian
	Dutch
	American
	Russian
	Spanish
1888	date colony or mandate established

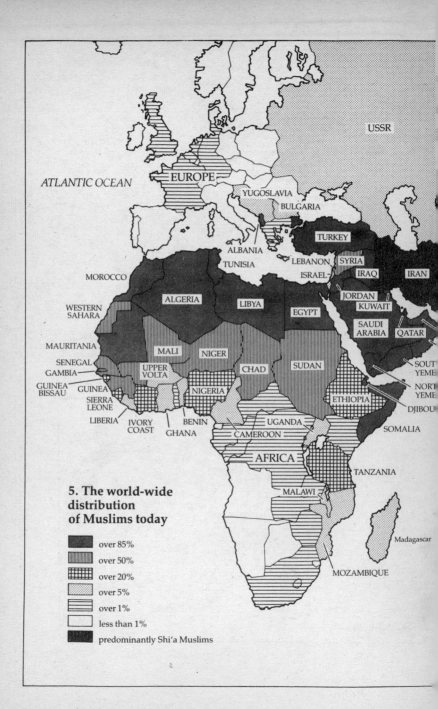

5. The world-wide distribution of Muslims today

- over 85%
- over 50%
- over 20%
- over 5%
- over 1%
- less than 1%
- predominantly Shi'a Muslims

ATLANTIC OCEAN

USSR

EUROPE

YUGOSLAVIA

BULGARIA

ALBANIA

TUNISIA

TURKEY

LEBANON

SYRIA

ISRAEL

IRAQ

IRAN

MOROCCO

ALGERIA

LIBYA

EGYPT

JORDAN

KUWAIT

WESTERN
SAHARA

SAUDI
ARABIA

QATAR

MAURITANIA

MALI

NIGER

SENEGAL

UPPER
VOLTA

CHAD

SUDAN

SOUTH
YEMEN

GAMBIA

GUINEA
BISSAU

GUINEA

NIGERIA

NORTH
YEMEN

SIERRA
LEONE

ETHIOPIA

DJIBOUTI

LIBERIA

IVORY
COAST

BENIN

UGANDA

SOMALIA

GHANA

CAMEROON

AFRICA

TANZANIA

MALAWI

Madagascar

MOZAMBIQUE

Preface

Most books about Islam – at any rate those worth reading – are written either by Muslims or by non-Muslim specialists in the field of Islamic or anthropological studies. As a writer who is neither a Muslim nor a specialist, and who has a very imperfect knowledge of the subject, I should perhaps explain my impudence in trespassing upon such well-tended property.

It is, I hope, no discourtesy either to Muslim writers or non-Muslim scholars to point out that, despite the voluminous literature on Islam, there are practically no works in English that satisfactorily explain how it has become a political force in the modern world. There are excellent one-volume summaries of Islam's origins and doctrines by eminent scholars; there are several more recent books by journalists who seek to explain the significance of Islamic reassertion in the nineteenth and twentieth centuries; there are anthropological studies which build up a picture of Islamic faith and practice by close observation and description of its manifestations in particular regional or social milieus; and there are the more or less apologetic works by writers who try to explain Islam in terms of their authors' particular religious standpoints.

All these books have their value, but none of them will, I believe, be of much use to the general reader or novice student seeking a comprehensive account of the Islamic *Weltanschauung*. The books which describe Islam as an ideal system or set of beliefs pay too little attention to its actual role in history. Those which focus anthropologically on particular regional aspects fail to integrate them within a more general pattern; while those concerned mainly with recent developments fail to demonstrate how Islam's contemporary political manifestations fall within a tradition of political activism going back nearly fourteen centuries.

In this book I have tried to combine aspects of all these approaches. In investigating the Quran and the teachings derived from it I have tried to show what Muslims believe about God and about mankind's duties in the world. I have also tried to show how, historically, Muslims sought to put their beliefs into practice by observing the divine law and sometimes by attempting to re-create the ideal community of Medina founded by the Prophet.

In tackling such an ambitious subject I am very conscious of my shortcomings. I am not trained as a scholar, and as a journalist my opportunities for travel have been very limited. Nor do I hold the religious beliefs that often inspire the efforts of those who seek to understand a different religious tradition. My approach has generally been that of an interested agnostic, not so hostile to religion as to hold the beliefs of others in contempt, but unable to share them. My personal experience of the Muslim world is confined to Egypt, Jordan and the Levant. My knowledge of Islam has been mainly acquired from reading books and articles in English and French, though I have taken the trouble to study the Quran in Arabic and have used some Arabic sources. In some respects, however, my ignorance and lack of formal qualifications may have been an advantage. I have not been afraid to blunder into controversial areas which specialists may have avoided for fear of becoming enmeshed in complicated or esoteric disputations. Today, when knowledge has become so specialized and carefully husbanded, the amateur can sometimes undertake tasks which the experts are too busy to perform themselves.

Any author requires expert guidance for a project of this kind. A list of the most important works consulted may be found at the end of the book. It could never have been written, however, without the generous help and cooperation of many people. To Albert Hourani, who read the manuscript, I am indebted for his wise advice on reductions and for putting me right on many points of emphasis or detail. I would also like to thank Jim Piscatori for reading through the manuscript and for making some useful suggestions, especially with regard to the later chapters. I have generally tried to follow the advice of both these scholars: neither, however, is in any way responsible for errors remaining in the text, or for my essentially personal, and sometimes idiosyncratic, interpretation of Islam and its history. My special thanks are also due to Louise Hosking, who helped with research into Arabic texts and edited the manuscript according to the system of transliteration we devised together, a modified version of that used in the new edition of the *Encyclopaedia of Islam*.

Others who read parts of the manuscript, who helped me develop my ideas in the course of interviews or discussion or who otherwise contributed to this book include the following: Muhammad Asad, James Buchan, Mick Czaki, Omar el Farouq, Abdul Wahid Hamid, Russell Harris, Derek Hopwood, Sayyid Sadiq el Mahdi, Peter Mansfield, Edward Mortimer, Fathi Osman, Terry Povey, Elizabeth Rodenbeck, John Rodenbeck, David Rosser-Owen, Muhammad Salahuddin, Michael Yorke. I wish to thank them all, but would emphasize that none is responsible in any way for matters of fact or interpretation.

Source material for the maps was drawn from Francis Robinson's *Atlas of the Islamic World since 1500* (Phaidon Press, Oxford, 1982).

This book could only have been written with the unstinting moral and material support of my family. My wife, Tiggy, I thank for her continuing support and encouragement; Pamela and Derek Cooper for allowing me the use of their homes in London and Gloucestershire; Wendy and Hugh Hodgkinson for letting me stay in their house in Dorset. Finally, a word of thanks to Derek Alvey of Lloyds Bank, whose sympathetic treatment of my case helped ease the financial pressures under which this book was written; and to my agent Caroline Dawnay and to Peter Carson of Penguin Books for their continuing support and patience during the many delays and postponements before the manuscript was delivered.

1 ✿ Introductory: Pilgrimage to Mecca

And proclaim unto all people the [duty of] pilgrimage: they will come unto thee on foot and on every [kind of] fast mount, coming from every far-away point [on earth] so that they might experience much that shall be of benefit to them and that they might extol the name of God on the days appointed [for sacrifice] over whatever heads of cattle He may have provided for them.[1]

Every year during the season of pilgrimage or 'Hajj', about two million people converge on the holy places of Mecca, Mina, Muzdalifa and 'Arafat to participate in rites whose origins have been lost in the mists of antiquity. About three quarters of them come from abroad, from more than sixty countries where there are Muslim communities. In recent years the largest contingents have been from Nigeria, Pakistan, Turkey and neighbouring Yemen (many of whose nationals are resident in Saudi Arabia), followed by Iran, Indonesia and Iraq. The countries most notably under-represented are the Soviet Union, which with 50 million Muslims ranks fifth in the table of states containing them, and China, which has a community of about 40 million. Both governments allow only a hand-picked selection of officially recognized dignitaries loyal to the Communist Party to attend the Hajj, in order to provide proof that Islam is tolerated. The governments of Vietnam and Laos, both of which have sizeable Muslim minorities, did not, in 1982, allow any of their nationals to make the journey.

Pilgrimage is one of the five *rukns* or 'pillars' of Islam, a religious obligation which every Muslim must observe at least once in a lifetime if he or she is able. According to most religious scholars, substitutes may be sent by those who for reasons other than poverty cannot make the journey. The very poor are exempted altogether. In the past the hazards of travelling restricted observance to a very small number. The trip to the Holy Land took many months and sometimes lasted years: it was not unknown for a man to spend the better part of a lifetime on it, setting out as a youth from one of the distant fringes of the Muslim world and arriving back half a century later, having worked his passage as an itinerant craftsman or labourer. Returning pilgrims have long borne the honoured title Hajji, and are accorded the reverence normally given to religious dignitaries – a factor which may partly account for the pilgrimage's continued and growing popularity.

In the past the hazardous journey exacted a high cost in human misery. Ibn Jubair, who made the pilgrimage early in the thirteenth century CE (Christian Era), noted the skeletons of those who had died of thirst in the desert. Later, well-organized 'caravan cities' were established, leaving Cairo or Damascus under the command of a specially chosen Amir, a practice originally instituted by the 'Abbasid caliphs. The officials charged with the pilgrims' safety included judges empowered to punish violations of the Shari'a law and to advise pilgrims on their religious duties, medical officials, including doctors, surgeons and oculists, and a public trustee to deal with all the legal problems arising out of a pilgrim's death. Practically speaking, the most important officials were probably the lawyers who scrutinized the contracts made between the Amir and the beduin from whom he hired his camels, and the numerous functionaries in charge of food, water and fodder. Despite these precautions, however, the pilgrims often suffered appalling casualties. Those who survived the extremes of heat and cold, hunger and thirst or attacks by beduin marauders often succumbed to the plague. An Austrian sold into slavery early in the seventeenth century, who accompanied his master from Cairo, recorded that by the time the Egyptian caravan had reached half-way across Sinai, 1,500 men and 900 camels were already dead. In 1824 about one fifth of the 20,000-strong Syrian caravan died from heat or thirst; two years later 12,000 are said to have died from the searing blasts of the hot *khamsin* wind. When the Hajj, which like all Muslim festivals follows the lunar calendar, fell in winter, cold was also a serious hazard. In 1846 500 pilgrims, 1,200 horses and 900 camels died on the return journey from Medina to Damascus.

Cholera also took a fierce toll of pilgrims, especially after steamship navigation had led to a huge increase in numbers from places like India where the disease is endemic. Between 1831 and 1912 some 27 epidemics are thought to have started in Mecca, whose insalubrious valley has been described as a 'breathless pit enclosed by a wall of rock' (Eldon Rutter). The dangers of disease were eventually reduced by the adoption of drastic quarantine procedures and fumigation – measures which considerably added to the ordeal of the Hajj. According to a Moroccan gentleman who made the journey in 1897, sea-borne pilgrims were made to wait for up to three weeks in the Gulf of Suez with the bare minimum of food and water, for which they were grossly overcharged, before the authorities would let the ships enter the Canal. They were then disembarked and had to wait out the rest of the quarantine period in conditions scarcely better than those of a prison camp. As recently as 1927 Muhammad Asad, a Jewish convert to Islam, described the appalling overcrowding of pilgrim ships as greedy ship-owners sought to make the most of the short but profitable season:

> There were only pilgrims on board, so many that the ship could hardly contain them. The shipping company . . . had literally filled it to the brim without caring for the comfort of the passengers. On the decks, in the cabins, in all passageways, on every staircase, in the dining rooms of the first and second class, in the holds which had been emptied for the purpose and equipped with temporary ladders, in every available space and corner human beings were painfully herded together . . . In great humility, with only the goal of the voyage before their eyes, they bore all that unnecessary hardship.[2]

Although the number of pilgrims has always fluctuated with the vagaries of war and other international factors, the age of the charter jet has seen a dramatic increase in numbers. Half a century ago about 30,000 people made the pilgrimage each year – a proportion of roughly one Muslim in 10,000, given an estimated population of 330 million. With the present Muslim population estimated at nearly 1,000 million (about one fifth of the human race), the proportion of Hajj attenders has risen to almost two in 1,000 – a symptom not only of improved transport opportunities, but of a general increase in Islamic consciousness.

In response to this increasing demand, and to reinforce the legitimacy of the Saudi ruling family as guardians of Islam's holy places, the Saudi government invested some $5 billion in developing the new King Abdul Aziz International Airport near Jedda, which occupies an area of some 100 square kilometres (35 square miles) – larger than the international airports of New York, Chicago and Paris. The airport's most spectacular feature is the new Hajj terminal, two vast tented halls making up the world's largest fabric structure enclosing its largest covered space. The tent clusters forming the ceiling, which are suspended from cables and steel pylons high above floor level, resemble the great tented city of 'Arafat where the pilgrims forgather at the high-point of the Hajj ceremonies. The fabric itself, a spin-off from space research, is made from an insulated fibre which reflects back most of the sun's heat and retains enough of its light to make artificial illumination unnecessary during daytime. The Hajj terminal can 'process' about 5,000 pilgrims each hour, or just under one million during the season. As impressive an example of contemporary design as can be found anywhere in the world, it is an apt symbol of the Saudi rulers' ambition to bolster traditional values with the latest technology.

However, neither Saudi money nor the know-how they can afford to buy with it has yet been able to solve the problem of moving such large numbers of human beings in the confined spaces of the holy places within the time-limits specified in the Hajj rituals. With its complicated ceremonies lasting almost a week, in conditions that are often far from comfortable, the Hajj still has the aspect of an ordeal undertaken in the spirit of faith. It has yet to become, like so many Christian festivals or pilgrimages, a mere adjunct to tourism. Indeed, in contrast with that of many European cults, the commercial importance of the Hajj has declined with the advent of air transport, stricter passport controls and governments which try to control the movement of people by shepherding them in and out of airport lounges. Though Meccan rentiers and hoteliers still depend on the Hajj for their livelihood and are often accused of charging exorbitant prices for private accommodation, the Saudi government spends more on servicing the Hajj than it receives back in revenues.

In so doing, the Saudi regime is, of course, acting in its own interest. In the history of Islamic ruling dynasties the Saudis are comparative parvenus, descendants of an eighteenth-century desert *shaikh* who formed a military alliance with the Hanbali reformer, Muhammad ibn 'Abd al Wahhab. Like other reformers throughout Islamic history, 'Abd al Wahhab sought a return to the 'purity' of the original Islam of the prophet and his companions. Employing the military power of the Saudis and their tribal allies, he created a state which, following the precedent established by the Prophet of Islam, aimed to reunite the whole Arabian Peninsula. Although this aim was frustrated by the

Ottoman suzerain Muhammad 'Ali, who occupied the Hejaz, opening the way to the replacement of the Saudis by the pro-Turkish Rashids, Saudi fortunes revived under the remarkable leadership of 'Abd al 'Aziz ibn 'Abd al Rahman al Sa'ud (better known to the world as Ibn Saud). Starting out from Kuwait in 1902 with a band of about 40 followers, he regained the stronghold of Riyadh from the Rashids and proceeded, by war and diplomacy, to recover all the former Saudi dominions and much else besides. By 1913 he controlled the Gulf coast from Kuwait to Qatar, having eliminated the Turks from Hasa, now the Eastern Province, where, in the 1930s, the world's largest oil deposits were discovered. In 1924 his ablest son, Faisal, added Asir on the Yemeni border to the Saudi dominions. By 1926 Ibn Saud had realized his final ambition, the conquest of the Hejaz. The way had unwittingly been smoothed for him by the British, who had helped the local ruler, the Sharif Husain, to remove the Turks.

In creating his dynastic state Ibn Saud had followed the classic medieval pattern, exemplified by his own ancestors, of combining military force with religious enthusiasm. The storm-troopers on whom he relied for his victories, known simply as the Ikhwan ('Brothers'), were former beduin from the Mutair, 'Utaiba and other tribes who had been settled into *hijras* or military cantonments, where, when not actually fighting, the Ikhwan observed a spartan and puritanical regime closely modelled, as they supposed, on the first Islamic community established by the Prophet in Medina. The Ikhwan were extremely rigid and literalistic in their behaviour: they cut their *thaubes* (or gowns) short above the ankles, trimmed their moustaches to a shadow while letting their beards grow freely, and eschewed the black *aghal* or rope-ring which secures the Arab head-dress, all because it was said in certain *hadiths* (traditions) that the Holy Prophet was thus attired or trimmed. Above all, they were utterly fearless in battle, and brutal as well, having defined themselves as the only true Muslims in a world of backsliding heretics. 'I have seen them hurl themselves on their enemies,' wrote an Arab witness, 'utterly fearless of death, not caring how many fall, advancing rank upon rank with only one desire – the defeat and annihilation of the enemy. They normally give no quarter, sparing neither boys nor old men, veritable messengers of death from whose grasp no one escapes.'[3]

Though acknowledging 'Abd al 'Aziz as their leader, the Ikhwan refused to recognize any territorial limits to their power. The Saudi leader's northern and eastern frontiers were controlled by the British, whose officials were invariably impressed by his charm and intelligence. Eventually his international undertakings (not to mention his personal inclinations) obliged him to deal with his over-zealous followers. This was particularly the case after his conquest of the Hejaz. During the campaign some 300 people had been massacred in the city of Taif, and Muslims throughout the world were alarmed at what the 'Najdi fanatics' might do in the Holy Places. Their fears were far from groundless: during the previous conquest of the Hejaz in 1802 the Wahhabis had smashed up the Prophet's tomb in Medina and destroyed the remains of most of the saints who had been buried near the Holy Places. When the pilgrim caravans arrived from Egypt and Syria they were turned away as idolaters. After his family's re-occupation of the sacred territories, 'Abd al 'Aziz did his best to reassure the inhabitants that he was no bloody iconoclast. He had to intervene personally to prevent the Ikhwan from slaughtering the official delegation of Egyptians bearing the *kiswa*, the black silk covering of the Ka'ba, renewed every year at the Hajj season. About forty pilgrims were killed in the incident, after which the Saudis decided to supply the *kiswa* (traditionally a gift from Egypt) themselves. When the Ikhwan attacked the British-held Iraqi territory and two of their leaders revolted, 'Abd al 'Aziz disbanded them. Most of their units became absorbed into the Saudi National Guard. For the moment, the genie was back in the bottle – Islam reverted to its more familiar function, a prop to the social order, not a force to threaten it. 'Abd al 'Aziz, who already held the titles of King of Najd and its Dependencies and King of the Hejaz, gave himself a new one – King of Saudi Arabia (the only state in the world whose citizens are labelled with their ruler's surname). In the eyes of the religious militants, it was a classic case of the ideological 'sell-out': instead of being allowed to restore the Islamic government of their dreams, the Ikhwan, like so many of their predecessors from the time of the early caliphs, had been used to further the ambitions of a worldly dynast.

In a sense the problem, a classic one, had existed from the beginnings of Islam. The Prophet, like Ibn Saud, was a realist who recognized that an accommodation would have to be made with the Quraish, rulers of Mecca and once his bitterest enemies, because they were the only power in Arabia strong enough to maintain the tribal alliances upon which the infant Islamic state depended. Before the conquest of Mecca, the Prophet and Abu Sufyan, his former enemy, came to an arrangement which guaranteed that Islam would have a brilliant future in this world, but at a price. The generous terms Muhammad granted his former enemies placed them at the head of the new Islamic community, thereby laying down the basis for the Umayyad dictatorship which presided over the first great era of expansion. The first schisms of the community, which have lasted to the present, were caused by a mixture of ideological and personal factors. However the fact that the 'losers', the party (shi'a) of 'Ali and his heirs, the Imams of the Prophet's house, retained their hold over the affections and imaginations of the more pious and radical elements, was largely due to the sense of betrayal that accompanies any attempt to translate an ideal into reality. Christians had shelved, not solved, this problem by proclaiming that since Christ's Kingdom was 'not of this world', obedience to secular authority, however corrupt or wicked, could be mitigated or atoned for by an essentially private piety or morality. For Muslims there was no such easy way out: the Prophet had been his own Caesar, a temporal ruler as well as the bearer of a divine message. The Quran had urged the faithful to 'obey God and His Prophet': there was no possibility that the two might contradict each other, since the Prophet's utterances were God's speech, not an imperfect human rendering of it. The sense of betrayal must always, sooner or later, rouse a significant portion of the faithful to action, in order to restore the purity of an Islam deemed to have been corrupted. If *imitatio Christi* meant renouncing worldly ambition and seeking salvation by deeds of private virtue, *imitatio Muhammadi* meant sooner or later taking up arms against those forces which seemed to threaten Islam from within or without.

Thus the Hajj, the most central event in the Islamic calendar, cannot be described as a purely religious festival. With so many Muslims gathered together from different parts of the world, it contains a political message and the potential for political action. The political ideals of Islam – universal justice and equality, regardless of tribe, nation or race – are implicit in the rituals themselves. They are performed in the the state of *ihram*, ritual purity, in which all men (and most women) wear the white *kaffan* or seamless shroud which they will keep for their burials, a uniform which removes all outward signs of distinction between them. The potentialities for action are in the opportunities presented by Mecca as the universal Muslim city, where Muslims from distant parts of the world have the right to congregate at all times, not only in the Hajj season. Many of the revolutionary and revivalist movements which swept through Africa and Asia, creating, albeit temporarily, new 'Islamic' states, originated there in encounters between men of God and men of the sword. At the present time, the role of the pro-Western Saudis as guardians of the Holy places and administrators of the Hajj puts them in a very delicate position. Religion is, of course, constantly employed to legitimize their government. As rulers of the Hejaz and major financial contributors to Islamic institutions all over the world, the Al Sa'ud enjoy a quasi-caliphal role: in a sense they are non-titular heads of an increasingly politically conscious pan-Islamic community. This gives them a moral influence within the most important bloc of Third World states which complements their economic weight in the West. But it also makes them especially vulnerable to attacks from religious quarters. This was shown by the armed occupation of Mecca's Grand Mosque in November 1979 by a group of extremists led by Juhaiman al Utaibi.

A child of the Ikhwan who grew up in the shadow of its defeat, Juhaiman and his two hundred followers (who included Yemenis, Sudanese, Kuwaitis, Iraqis and Egyptians as well as Saudis) consciously imitated the style and behaviour of the original Ikhwan and called themselves by the same name. In a pamphlet published in Kuwait which was circulating inside Saudi Arabia at the time of the seizure of the Grand Mosque, Juhaiman denounced the royal family and explained that, according to Islamic law, the people are not obliged to obey impious rulers: 'They worship money and spend it on palaces, not mosques. If you accept what they say they will make you rich; otherwise they will persecute and even torture you.'[4] During the occupation he broadcast similar attacks over the mosque's tannoy system, enabling the message to be heard all over central Mecca. He denounced the scandalous personal habits of the Saudi princes (drinking, gaming, visits to the fleshpots of the West), mentioning by name the Governor of Mecca, Prince Fawwaz ibn 'Abd al 'Aziz. After two weeks of fighting, allegedly under the direction of special forces flown in from France, the Saudi authorities gained control of the mosque and most of the surviving rebels were executed. The great majority of Muslims approved the verdict, agreeing that by bringing in arms the rebels had committed a sacrilege. Partly for this reason, no doubt, the Ayatollah Khomeini, Iran's revolutionary leader and a vitriolic critic of the Saudis, himself denounced the rebels, intimating that they must be US or Israeli agents. 'It is not beyond guessing', he announced on Tehran radio, 'that this is the work of criminal American imperialism and international Zionism.' For the zealots, a hint from Khomeini was a statement of incontrovertible fact: there were anti-American demonstrations in the Philippines, Thailand, Bangladesh, India, the United Arab Emirates, Kuwait, Turkey, Nigeria, Libya and even some western capitals. In Islamabad the military government of General Zia ul Haqq astutely allowed rival student gangs of Muslim militants and supporters of his recently executed rival Mr Bhutto to unleash their feelings against the US embassy, which they burned to the ground.

Although Juhaiman's revolt failed, the Saudis and other pro-Western Arab governments remained vulnerable to criticism from religious radicals, especially the Ayatollah Khomeini. Indeed, while most of the world's attention was centred on the siege of Mecca, a potentially more serious crisis had erupted in the oil-bearing region of Hasa in the Eastern Province, where most of Saudi Arabia's Shi'a Muslims, including many workers in the oil industry, are concentrated. Unlike the Meccan siege, the troubles in Hasa were a direct result of Khomeini's propaganda.

Since 'Abd al 'Aziz ibn Sa'ud conquered the region from the Turks in 1913 the Shi'a of Hasa had been subject to varying social, economic and religious restrictions under the rule of their Wahhabi overlords. The province has a history of unrest. Strikes at Aramco (the US-owned company which originally exploited and marketed the bulk of Saudi crude) in 1953 and 1956, as well as purges of Arab nationalist sympathizers in the late fifties and in 1969, were related to resentments among the Shi'a, who had been ruled since the Saudi conquest by the Ibn Jalawis, a cadet branch of the Saudi royal house.

A special cause for resentment had been the banning of certain Shi'a rituals, in particular the 'Ashura processions commemorating the death of the Prophet's grandson Husain, third of the Twelve Imams or spiritual leaders venerated by the sect. In 1979, inspired by the success of Khomeini's revolution in Iran, the Shi'a leaders announced that they intended to hold the 'Ashura processions during the last week of November. The authorities, preoccupied with the crisis in Mecca, thought better than to make more trouble by banning the march, hoping, no doubt, that the demonstration would pass off without incident. They were not to be so fortunate: after a fracas between a demonstrator and a Saudi policeman, a riot ensued in which seventeen people were shot dead and the offices of the Saudi–British bank were attacked. The government sent the deputy interior minister Prince Ahmed Ibn 'Abd al 'Aziz to calm the trouble. He offered generous terms, including better schools and hospitals, if only the Shi'a leaders would support the kingdom in its hour of need. However, the collapse of the revolt in Mecca shortly afterwards strengthened the government's hand, and at a press conference subsequently called by Prince Naif, the interior minister, no mention was made of the proffered reforms.

The gravity of the crisis in the Eastern Provinces could scarcely be exaggerated, for although previous episodes of Shi'a unrest had been suppressed without much difficulty, none of them had occurred against the background of a militant Shi'a regime in Iran, led by a patriarch whose unofficial title of 'Imam' conveyed a message of messianic expectation. According to Shi'a doctrine, the last of the Twelve Imams of the Prophet's family, Muhammad al Muntazar (the Awaited One) is not dead, but merely in concealment, ready to return as the Mahdi (messiah) at the end of the world, to bring peace and justice to a mankind beset by turmoil and corruption. Though institutionalized and spiritualized by centuries of doctrinal refinement, this chiliastic message had proved its potency as an essential component of an Islamic revolutionary ideology directed mainly against local tyranny and western influence. The mahdist idea, which is also present in Sunni traditions, was used by Juhaiman, who claimed that his confederate Muhammad 'Abdullah al Qahtani (a young theology student who died in the siege) was the expected Mahdi, and timed his action to coincide with the beginning of the new Islamic century (a traditional time of mahdist expectations). It is not improbable that Juhaiman was deliberately trying to exploit the general atmosphere engendered in the Muslim world by the fall of the Shah and Khomeini's accession to power, the first successful 'Islamic revolution' under modern conditions.

As Muslim rulers with their own history of direct action conducted successfully against the 'backsliding infidel' (represented in their case by the Ottoman-backed Sharif Husain), the Saudis hardly needed reminding of Islam's revolutionary potential. The problem for them, and for other Muslim rulers in the Gulf, was whether the appeal of Khomeini's particular brand of Islamic radicalism could overleap the traditional sectarian divide between the Shi'a minority and the Sunni majority. Were Khomeini's charismatic appeal and his radical, anti-western, anti-materialist message universal enough to arouse the masses in the Arab Sunni states to overthrow their mainly pro-western leaders, as Nasser's charisma and his message had been for the previous generation? At the time of writing, this question was still unanswered. The revolutionary republic had become embroiled in a long and costly war with Iraq; and while it had succeeded in clearing the Iraqi aggressors from its soil, it had manifestly failed in its declared aim of overthrowing the secular national-ist regime of President Saddam Hussein and installing an Islamic gov-ernment in Baghdad. Moreover, it had failed to achieve this in a country where a majority of the population were Shi'ites who were resentful at years of Sunni domination. Despite its universal appeal, the Islamic revolution had remained confined to Iran, a country, unique in the Muslim world, where Shi'ism runs in harness with nationalism.

At the same time, the Saudis remained understandably nervous. Khomeini continued his verbal attacks on them, which was hardly surprising in view of the extent to which they contributed financially to Iraq's war effort. Moreover the Ayatollah was not above using the Hajj for his purpose. In 1982, for the second successive year, the Saudi authorities accused Iranian pilgrims of trying to disrupt the Hajj and exploit it politically. They accused Khomeini's representative at the Hajj, Hojjat ul Islam Mousavi Khoiniha (deputy speaker of the Iranian parlia-ment) of organizing a march in Medina, traditional assembly point for Shi'ite pilgrims, at which posters of Khomeini were carried along with banners and political slogans. Khoiniha was said to have 'made a speech containing political references that were outside the rites of pilgrimage, and that disturbed the pilgrims of the House of God and visitors to the Prophet's Mosque'.[5] According to the Saudi statement, the security authorities intervened to disperse the demonstrators and remove their slogans and placards. Twenty-one people were arrested. The Iranians complained that the Saudi police beat the demonstrators and confiscated what they called 'religious literature'.

The Saudis, it transpired, had tried to persuade Khoiniha to cancel the planned demonstration, which he termed a 'march for unity'. According to Tehran radio's account of the incident, the Saudi Minister of Pilgrim-age Affairs and Endowments had intervened personally, saying that any action which violated order and created discomfort to other pilgrims should not take place. Khomeini's representative replied:

> Do slogans such as 'Death to Israel' and 'Death to the USA' create disorder? Do such slogans bring discomfort to Muslims? Today, by taking part in Friday prayers, we want to silence those voices that call us infidels . . . We do not intend to violate security, rather we intend to invite the Muslims to unite against the USA, Israel and

the Soviet Union. We are surprised [he added] that you oppose
this action, as we expect you to lead the way.[6]

Western newspapers reported that Khomeini had been aiming to
'politicize' the Hajj. The Iranians saw things differently: since Islam
made no distinction between religious and political activity, the Hajj was
inherently political, and those who had tried to make it a purely spiritual
occasion had deviated from the true path laid down by the Prophet.

> 'Revive the great divine political tradition of the Hajj,' Khomeini is
> reported to have told his representative. 'Acquaint Muslims with
> what is taking place in dear Lebanon, in crusading Iran, and
> oppressed Afghanistan. Inform them of their great duties in
> confronting aggressors and international plunderers.'[7]

Like most other Muslim governments, the Saudis had a vested interest
in the politico-religious status quo. Their 'Islamic revolution' had come
to an end in 1929, when the last beduin rebels had finally been defeated.
For them the Hajj has become a 'religious' festival more or less in the
western sense, an occasion when people suspend their worldly concerns
and concentrate on God. For the Iranian revolutionaries and other
Muslim activists who sympathize with them, the annual gathering of
Muslims in the cradle of Islam is a symbolic re-enactment of its beginnings that must lead on to the creation of a true Islamic order, a world
free from injustice and oppression.

In Islam the spectrum of interpretation ranges from the ultra-symbolic
to the infra-literalistic. This intersects with the spectrum of activity,
which ranges from passive acquiescence to militant activism. The traditionalists lie near the literalist end of the interpretative spectrum,
believing that in performing the Hajj they are literally re-enacting the
birth of the primordial Islam of Ibrahim (Abraham), the 'first monotheist', his bondswoman Hagar and his son Isma'il (Ishmael), ancestor of
the Arabs. Those who perceive the drama symbolically see these figures
as human archetypes; the significance of the rituals associated with
them, like that of all rituals, lies in the manner in which they link man
with the cosmos. The traditionalists only become activists when they feel
that their comfortable world of fixed references is threatened by outside
forces. Among the symbolists, the quietists or Sufis content themselves
with ritual participation. The activists, however, see a revolutionary
beginning in the Hajj:

Hajj is the antithesis of aimlessness. It is the rebellion against [accepting] a damned fate guided by evil forces. The fulfilment of Hajj will enable you to escape from the complex network of puzzles. This revolutionary act will reveal to you the clear horizon and free way to migration to eternity . . .[8]

Like the Quran itself, the Hajj's meaning depends upon the exegetical activity of the participant.

On arrival at Jedda, pilgrims who are not already 'packaged' into a travelling group are usually divided into parties on a national or regional basis, each of which is placed in the care of a guide known as the *mutawwif*. Many of the *mutawwifs* are from Meccan families which have been in the business for generations: the success of an individual's Hajj will largely be determined by the honesty, influence and resourcefulness of the *mutawwif*. An efficient *mutawwif* will secure decent food and reasonably priced lodgings, better transport and good camping facilities. A dishonest or incompetent one can make the Hajj a misery.

At some point on the road to Mecca the pilgrims will be stopped at a police checkpoint to have their passports examined. For them, this, and not the Saudi entry-point, is the real frontier, for it marks the boundary of the holy territory which no non-Muslim may enter. The Saudi consulates in their home countries will have issued them with special pilgrim visas, only granted against proof of Muslim birth or conversion. In the past, people suspected of being Christians or members of extremist sects outside the Islamic consensus have been done to death for entering the holy places.

By the time the pilgrims arrive in the Holy City, the streets will probably be jammed with its characteristically eastern confusion of motors and pedestrians – for despite its dependence on oil, in Saudi Arabia, as in other Middle Eastern countries, the motor vehicle is still treated like the animal it only recently replaced. Pilgrims from industrialized countries are sometimes shocked by their first encounter with the Holy Land. An Anglo-Indian who made the Hajj of 1968 wrote:

Many people could do well, to begin with, by realizing that cleanliness is part of the faith. No doubt the huge crowd suddenly converging together does create problems of waste disposal and so on. But the behaviour of many pilgrims themselves reflects the low standards of hygiene in their countries of origin . . . Just outside the Haram Sharif [Grand Mosque] itself, the smell is extremely offensive. There are not adequate toilet facilities for the thousands of people and the existing lavatories are therefore always in a shocking state. Many are even forced to answer the calls of nature in the open.[9]

As they approach the Haram area, the pilgrims shout the traditional slogan, 'Labbaika, Allahumma, labbaika!' ('Here I am, O God, at Thy command! Here I am!'), also used as a greeting or password during the Hajj. The huge white-clad crowd converges on the Haram like a mighty roaring torrent. Suddenly, as they pass the sign designating the Haram, a hush descends on them: this is the sacred territory, where from the earliest times all fighting, hunting and killing, even the uprooting of plants, have been forbidden. The goal towards which the throngs are moving through the vast portals of the Haram is the Ka'ba, the small square temple at its centre, the physical and symbolic pole of Islam. To the forbidden infidel eye, the little black box, made of rough-hewn stone blocks covered with black silken drapery, must look strangely incongruous: a tiny square island standing at the centre of a swirling human pond surrounded by tiers of pompous colonnades expensively clad in marble and stucco, the whole overlooked by seven monstrous 300-foot minarets which brood over the Haram like watch-towers. For Muslims, however, the Ka'ba's very simplicity and lack of aesthetic pretension enhances its significance as the House of God and the *qibla* (direction) of every Muslim's prayer.

It would almost appear that he who first built the Ka'ba . . . wanted to create a parable of man's humility before God. The builder knew that no beauty of architectural rhythm and no perfection of line, however great, could ever do justice to the idea of God: so he confined himself to the simplest three-dimensional form imaginable – a cube of stone . . .[10]

Each pilgrim makes the *tawaf* or ritual circumambulation of the Ka'ba, a ceremony that has changed little, if at all, since pre-Islamic times. He will make seven circuits of the building, in an anti-clockwise movement, during which he will try to kiss, touch or otherwise greet the famous Black Stone which is set in a silver casing in the eastern corner. Muslims are taught that this is a fragment of the original temple, for the Ka'ba is said to have been rebuilt several times, before, during and after the Prophet's lifetime.

The 'Abrahamic' origin of Islam is a controversial subject on which there is little agreement between Muslim and non-Muslim scholars. For Muslims it is an article of faith that the patriarch, helped by Isma'il, built the Ka'ba as the first temple to the one true God on earth; that he also willingly prepared to sacrifice Isma'il until rescued at the last minute by divine intervention. The Quranic account of the sacrifice (which in the Bible, of course, is told of Ibrahim and Isma'il's half-brother Isaac, father of Jacob) does not mention Isma'il by name, a fact which led some western orientalists to argue that Isaac was understood as the intended victim in the original Quranic story, while the figure of Isma'il, supposed ancestor of the northern Arabs, only emerged in the course of Muhammad's polemics with the Jews of Medina. References to Ibrahim, however, occur in several Quranic passages accepted as belonging to the period of the Prophet's residence in Mecca. It is related that Ibrahim attacked the idol-worship of his father Azar and his people, and advocated belief in the one single God. The non-Muslim or sceptic will take the story of Islam's Abrahamic origins symbolically rather than literally. A semi-tribal society, such as Mecca's during the time of the Prophet, expresses ideas in terms of tribal formations or lineage groupings. The northern Arabs ('Ishmaelites' to the Hebrews) naturally conceived of all authority in patriarchal terms, and could never have accepted reforms as far-reaching as those undertaken by the Prophet unless they were seen as a restoration of the religious order instituted by their own patriarchs. Muslims object to being called Muhammadans because they believe that Muhammad restored an old religion, rather than inaugurating a new one.

According to the Islamic tradition, which continues where the Hebrew tradition recording in Genesis leaves off, Abraham brought Hagar, the Egyptian bondswoman who had borne him a son, incurring the wrath of his wife Sara, to the barren rocky valley of Mecca, and there abandoned her and their child under a solitary wild *sahra* tree with nothing to sustain them but a waterskin and a bag of dates. (According to Genesis, God is supposed to have reassured him by saying: 'Let it not be grievous in thy sight because of the child and because of thy bondswoman . . . Of her son will I make a nation because he is of thy seed.'[11]) After two nights and a day alone in the valley, Hagar began to despair. The dates were almost finished and there was no more water in the skin. As the child sat on the ground crying vainly for water, Hagar ran to and fro between the hillocks of Safa and Marwa, pleading with God: 'O Thou Bountiful, Thou Full of Grace! Who shall have mercy on us unless Thou hast mercy!' The answer came with the spring the child miraculously uncovered with his hand. 'Zummi, zummi!' she cried, imitating the sound of the water, which duly became the sacred well of Zamzam.[12]

Shortly afterwards a group of beduin from South Arabia passed by the valley and, seeing some birds circling overhead, concluded that there must be water. Arriving at the well, they asked Hagar's permission to settle, which she granted on condition that the land should for ever remain the property of Isma'il and his descendants. Isma'il grew to manhood and married a girl from one of the South Arabian tribes. Eventually Abraham returned, and with Isma'il's help built the Ka'ba, the first temple to the One True God. While the work was still half finished, he stood on a small rock and called out to heaven, uttering for the first time the traditional pilgrim cry: 'Labbaika, Allahumma, labbaika!'

The Islamic tradition furnishes several clues about the possible anthropological origins of the Ka'ba. Like several other shrines in Arabia, it was part of a *haram*, or sacred area, where inter-tribal fighting was forbidden in order to facilitate trade. The temple was evidently at the centre of a cult involving idol worship. The presiding deity was Hubal, a large carnelian statue kept inside the temple; 360 other idols were ranged outside. The three goddesses described in the Quran as the 'daughters of Allah' – Allat, 'Uzza and Manat – were also worshipped in the vicinity. By the Prophet's time Christian influences were making themselves felt. When he entered the Ka'ba after the 'conquest' of Mecca in 8 AH (630 CE), Muhammad is reported to have found two icons depicting Jesus and Mary, which he ordered to be preserved. The rest of the idols he destroyed 'miraculously' by merely pointing his staff at them.

According to the early Muslim authorities, the Quraish, hereditary guardians of the sanctuary, venerated the idol in the Ka'ba and offered sacrifices to it. A number of early monotheists apparently objected to these practices, including the circumambulation of the Black Stone which 'could neither hear, nor see, nor hurt, nor help'. They are described as having believed that their people had 'corrupted the religion of their father Abraham' – the same charge that Muhammad himself was to make not only against the pagan Quraish but against most of the adherents of Judaism and Christianity among his contemporaries.

The report cannot be dismissed as legend based on later Muslim piety; its significance is that veneration of the Black Stone is mentioned explicitly in the condemnation of 'idolatry'. However, during the Farewell Pilgrimage in 10 AH (632 CE), when he laid down the Hajj rituals as they are observed today, the Prophet was recorded as having gone out of his way to venerate the Black Stone. Some of his companions were evidently shocked by his attachment to the old ritual. 'Umar, the second caliph, is said to have once remarked upon greeting the Stone: 'I know you are nothing but a stone, have no power to do either good or evil, and had I not seen the Prophet greet you, I would not do so.'[13]

Another clue to the origins of the cult is the fact that although the Black Stone was venerated as a fetish, it was not directly associated with any particular deity. There seems to have been a general cult of stone-worship in the peninsula. The early Muslim sources suggest that it developed in imitation of the cult of the Ka'ba:

> They say that the beginning of stone worship among the sons of Ishmael was when Mecca became too small for them and they wanted more room in the country. Everyone who left the town took with him a stone from the haram area to do honour to it. Wherever they settled they set it up and walked round it as if going round the Ka'ba. This led them to worship whatever stones pleased them or made an impression on them. Thus as generations passed they forgot their primitive faith and adopted another religion instead of that of Abraham and Ishmael.[14]

The inference from this passage is clear: the cult of the Black Stone was intimately connected in the minds of Muhammad's contemporaries with the 'original' cult of Ibrahim and Isma'il.

What was the nature of this original 'Abrahamic' religion? The Quran refers to Ibrahim as a *hanif*, a term used by Muslim writers to indicate a pagan monotheist, Muslim in the religious but not the historical sense. Like Muhammad, he rejected the idols worshipped by his tribe; interestingly, he turned for a time to the worship of the astral bodies – first a star, then the moon, then the sun – and finally to the One God. The Quranic passage is significant:

> And lo! [Thus] spoke Abraham unto his father Azar: 'Takest thou idols for gods? Verily, I see that thou and thy people have obviously gone astray!'

And thus We gave Abraham [his first] insight into [God's] mighty dominion over the heavens and the earth – and [this] to the end that he might become one of those who are inwardly sure.

Then, when the night overshadowed him with its darkness, he beheld a star; [and] he exclaimed, 'This is my Sustainer!' – but when it went down, he said, 'I love not the things that go down.'

Then, when he beheld the moon rising, he said, 'This is my Sustainer!' – but when it went down, he said, 'Indeed, if my Sustainer guide me not, I will most certainly become one of the people who go astray!'

Then, when he beheld the sun rising, he said, 'This is my Sustainer! This one is the greatest [of all]!' – but when it [too] went down, he exclaimed: 'O my people! Behold, far be it from me to ascribe divinity, as you do, to aught beside God! Behold, unto Him who brought into being the heavens and the earth have I turned my face, having turned away from all that is false; and I am not of those who ascribe divinity to aught beside him.'[15]

Like Muhammad, Ibrahim regards the idolatry of his fellow-tribesmen not as a sign of backwardness or primitiveness, which would not have been their fault, but as wilfully perverse. He himself arrives at the concept of the One God by a gradual process, highly suggestive in its imagery: the three astral bodies are in turn rejected because they are not dependable, disappearing as they do at certain intervals. But their rejection as suitable objects of worship leads to the perception of the Creator's 'mighty dominion over the heavens and the earth', since their regular motions are evidently part of a process brought into being and sustained by him. The God of the Quran is much closer to Aristotle's Unmoved Mover than to the anthropormorphic deities of the Old and New Testaments.

The association of Ibrahim and Isma'il with the Meccan cult has led some western scholars to suggest that Islam really originated in a Jewish cultural milieu among the partly Judaized Arab tribes of the Peninsula, who applied certain Judaic ideas to Arab customs. During pre-Islamic times there appear to have been many *haram* areas in the peninsula where the tribes could enter into trading or other negotiations under a form of truce. Originally these *harams* were cultic centres devoted to a local deity and usually presided over by a hereditary 'holy family'. (Similar functions, up to the present time, have been performed in North

Africa by hereditary Muslim 'saints', whose tombs, presided over by the saint's descendants, are often the centres of trucial zones located on the borders of tribal territories.) Thus at ancient Taif there was a shrine devoted to the goddess Allat under the control of the Thaqif clan; there were other, originally pagan shrines at Nakhla, north of Mecca, and at Najran and Sana'a in Yemen, which later became centres of Christian worship. Although originally under the aegis of the pagan god Hubal, the Meccan *haram*, which centred round the well of Zamzam, probably became associated with the ancestral figures of Ibrahim and Isma'il as the Arab traders, shedding their parochial backgrounds, sought to locate themselves within the broader reference-frame of Judaeo-Christianity without abandoning their distinctive identities.

Like the Quran itself, the earliest Muslim sources suggest that the pre-Islamic cult of the Ka'ba had some astronomical significance. The historian Mas'udi (896–956) stated that certain people had regarded the Ka'ba as a temple dedicated to the Sun, Moon and the five visible planets (making up the mystical figure of seven, the number of circumambulations required for each *tawaf*). The story that there were exactly 360 idols placed round the temple also points to an astronomical significance. Among the votive gifts said to have been offered to the idols were golden suns and moons. Such an astronomical cult may later have been associated with the story of Ibrahim, as is suggested in the Quranic passage already quoted. It is thought that the 'place of Ibrahim', a stone near the Ka'ba, now covered by a gilded cage, where the patriarch is supposed to have stood when completing the building of the temple, was a name originally applied to the whole *haram* area, having been adopted from the Hebrew tradition surrounding the 'place' where Abraham was visited by God. A similar borrowing, it has been suggested, may have occurred in the case of the Black Stone, lodged in the south-east corner of the Ka'ba. In the Hebrew tradition the stone 'pillow' on which Jacob, son of Isaac, had his dream of the heavenly ladder becomes the corner-stone of the Temple, the pivot on which the whole world is balanced. The first ray of light which illuminated the whole world issued from it; it is said to have come down from heaven, being one of the few objects of heavenly origin on earth.

There are very similar traditions about both the Black Stone and the stone known as the 'place of Ibrahim'. One of the commonest traditions about the Black Stone is that it once shone so brightly that if God had not effaced it, it would have illuminated everything between the east and the west. In Muslim tradition the stone's blackness is attributed to its pollution by human sin, or by the various fires which have engulfed the Ka'ba. Whether these are really borrowings from Jewish traditions or parallel traditions from a common source cannot, in the present state of knowledge, be finally determined. It is tempting, however, to give primacy to the Muslim tradition, for several visitors to Mecca, including Sir Richard Burton, who made the pilgrimage in disguise in 1853, have suggested that the Black Stone is really a meteorite. Could this have been the 'Star' originally worshipped by Ibrahim? What more natural object of adoration than a fragment fallen from outer space, which may once have lit up the sky with a trail of blazing particles? Such a possibility is strongly suggested by the Quranic account of Ibrahim's spiritual progress from the worship of the stars to that of the one Creator. In ritualistically imitating the primal motion of all heavenly bodies, around a temple incorporating an extra-terrestrial object, the Muslim, like Ibrahim, is expressing his allegiance as a subject of a universal cosmic order. For this, in its own distinctive manner, is what Islam demands as the primary religious duty.

The late Ali Shariati expressed the Ka'ba's cosmic significance in a long poem entitled 'One and an Eternity of Zeros':

> God was the Creator . . . He created clouds and freed them to float in space, clouds from particles, each particle a tiny universe called an atom . . . The clouds began to move, luminous, spiralling, a whirlwind, a whirlpool, rotating fire . . . A Ka'ba, pilgrims going round, from Black Stone to Black Stone.[16]

Elsewhere he likens the sensation of joining the circling crowd making the *tawaf* to that of jumping into a river:

> As you circumambulate and move closer to the Ka'ba, you feel like a small stream merging with a big river. Carried by a wave . . . you lose touch with the ground. Suddenly, you are floating, carried on by the flood. As you approach the centre, the pressure of the crowd squeezes you so hard that you are given new life. You are now part of the People; you are now a Man, alive and eternal . . . The Ka'ba is the world's sun whose force attracts you into its orbit. You have become part of this universal system. Circumambulating around Allah, you will soon forget yourself . . . You have been transformed into a particle that is gradually melting and disappearing. This is absolute love at its peak.[17]

Many people, carried round and round by the human whirlpool, fail to reach the Black Stone at its centre. An Indian pilgrim described how a group of beduin with wild, matted hair would 'form themselves into a tightly knit ring and, with the action of a battering ram, would charge through the cluster of people around the Black Stone, regardless of whether there were old people among them', after which, having achieved their objective, they would indulge in wild, ecstatic frenzies, 'the coarseness of which [was] quite repulsive to the dignity of the occasion'.[18]

After performing seven circuits of the Ka'ba, the worshippers proceed to the other rituals of the *haram* area. Near the corner of the temple housing the Black Stone they leave the circling human mass to offer two prostrations at the Place of Ibrahim, now covered by a gilded cage. They may then drink and fill their jars with Zamzam water before proceeding to the *sa'i* – running between the hillocks of Safa and Marwa, in imitation of Hagar's plight. The whole distance, some 460 metres, has to be covered seven times at something between a walk and a jog. The pilgrims start at Safa and end at Marwa. Shariati sees the progression as symbolizing the active, purposeful life in the world, as contrasted with the self-immolation of *tawaf*, since Hagar, in her search for water, never lost hope: 'Searching for water symbolizes searching for material life on this earth. It is genuine need which shows the relation of mankind to nature. It is the way of finding heaven in this world and enjoying its fruits on this earth.'[19] The strain of performing the *sa'i*, in which the pilgrim must travel some 3.5 kilometres, has been to some extent relieved by the architects who have enclosed the whole passage inside a long air-conditioned gallery. The marble-flanked walkway includes a special corridor where the old, infirm or disabled can be pushed along in wheelchairs.

The performance of the *sa'i* after the *tawaf* completes the *'umra*, or lesser pilgrimage, which can be performed at any time of the year. The pilgrim who continues to make the Hajj, which only takes place at the appointed season, leaves the *haram* area after performing the *sa'i* and makes for the plain of 'Arafat, a vast natural amphitheatre surrounded by hills about 11 kilometres from Mecca. For the Hajj to be valid the pilgrim must reach 'Arafat before sunrise on the ninth day of Dhu al Hijja – the so-called 'Day of 'Arafat'. The problem of moving some two million people in less than one day through the narrow pass between Mecca and 'Arafat is not an easy one. Before the Saudis banned the use of private cars the journey could amount to ten or more hours of nightmarish struggle between traffic and pedestrians. In recent years the Saudis have tried to alleviate the situation by banning vehicles carrying less than nine passengers, but the confusion is still considerable. Nevertheless, despite the distractions of traffic, noise and fumes, the Station at 'Arafat – high point of the Hajj ceremonies – is a most impressive occasion. The sun rises on the Day of 'Arafat revealing a vast tented city which has grown up the previous day in this normally deserted valley (where, according to legend, Adam first met with Eve after their expulsion from Paradise). Each *mutawwif* will have a group of tents assigned to him where his party will spend all the daylight hours in prayer and contemplation. There is room at 'Arafat for everyone, but the crowds are thickest around the rocky prominence known as the Jabal al Rahma, the Mount of Mercy, and the huge Namira mosque immediately below it. It was here that the Prophet preached his famous last sermon during the Farewell Pilgrimage of 632, a few months before his death, which set the final seal on the teachings of Islam and laid down the sequence of the reformed Hajj rituals, every detail of which has been meticulously followed by the believers since that time.

The most impressive moment arrives with the call to prayer. As the thin nasal voice of the muezzin rises from the loudspeakers in the Namira mosque, echoing across the empty spaces of the valley, the serried masses of people turn towards Mecca and with a single movement begin their prostrations – in the streets, in the car parks, under the lee of buses, upon every available surface among the jagged rocks. Prayer in Islam is never an act of purely private mental activity. The sequence of bodily motions – standing, bowing, kneeling, touching the ground with the forehead – are performed with care and precision, like the gymnastic displays beloved of totalitarian states. But unlike these secular rituals which can only be performed to order when the people have been specially drilled together, the movements of Islamic prayer have been fully internalized and assimilated from early childhood. When Muslims who have never met before pray together, their prostrations are usually perfectly timed, through the drilling of fourteen centuries.

The setting of the sun at 'Arafat is the signal for the *ifada* or 'Onrush', when the pilgrims make for Muzdalifa, the narrowest point of the pass between Mecca and 'Arafat. During the Farewell Pilgrimage the Prophet led the multitude on his camel. For thirteen centuries the pilgrims used to ride their 'finest mounts' at a thundering gallop across the plain, each one of them a 'tiny particle of that roaring, earth-shaking, irresistible wave of galloping dromedaries and men' that once conquered the better part of the known world for Islam. For in that fractious world of Arabian tribalism, where warlike energies were fruitlessly dissipated in inter-necine strife, the new solidarity brought by the Prophet and welded into a universal brotherhood at 'Arafat was the prelude to the *jihad*, or holy war. Nowadays most people have to make the six-mile journey on foot, or inch their way in the traffic as two million pilgrims and 50,000 vehicles compete for space in the narrow funnel of the hills. At Muzdalifa they are required to 'remember Allah by the sacred monument' – once a place of pagan worship dedicated to Quzah the thunder-god. Here two evening prayers, the *maghrib* and *'isha*, are performed together: the pilgrims, now cleansed of sin, are expected to purge themselves of all resentments against others. The narrowness of the passage makes it densely crowded.

At Muzdalifa – 'the place where one makes oneself agreeable' – the pilgrims collect the small pebbles, 49 in all, to be used in the most complicated and arcane of the Hajj ceremonies, the ritual stoning of the three pillars, or Jamarat, at Mina. The pebbles, each of which is supposed to be the size of a chick-pea, are thrown in sequences of seven at each of the three pillars situated about 300 metres apart along the road between Mina and Mecca, where a huge two-tier walkway has been constructed enabling the people to stone the pillars from either level. The ritual is purely pagan, and there is no reference to it in the Quran. The pilgrims perform it only because, according to the *hadith* traditions, the Prophet himself did so during his Farewell Pilgrimage. There is no mention in the canonical texts of the popular belief that the ceremonies involve the 'stoning of Satan'. Nevertheless the belief is held universally throughout the Muslim world, and is said to account for the violence with which many pilgrims attack the pillars. Ali Shariati, the Iranian radical, gives the ceremony an unabashed revolutionary symbolism:

> These pebbles will be used as your weapons to kill your enemy . . . What does the pebble represent? It represents a bullet . . . Each soldier in Ibrahim's army has to shoot seventy bullets at the enemies in Mina. They are to be fired at the head, trunk and heart of the enemy. Only those which hit the enemy will be counted. If you are not an expert select more bullets to compensate for your lack of skill . . . If you hit one less than the recommended number, you are not considered a soldier nor is your Hajj valid.[20]

Some Muslim authorities suggest that the three pillars – whatever their symbolic function – mark the route taken by Ibrahim when leading Isma'il to the place of sacrifice. For Mina, as well as being the place of the stoning ceremonies, contains the killing-ground where the animals are sacrificed on the 'Id al Adha, the final day of the Hajj. All pilgrims will wish to perform it, but it is not obligatory for the very poor, who will benefit from the largesse of the more affluent, since it is stipulated that some of the meat must be given to them. The Feast of Sacrifice is celebrated all over the Muslim world. Even in densely crowded cities, fattening sheep can be tethered in the streets or courtyards in preparation for it. Some agronomists have even suggested that the natural cycle of sheep-production has been interfered with in order to provide sacrificial victims for the 'Id. At Mina the wastage of meat has up till now been appalling, since most of it has had to be destroyed in lime-pits soon after the killing. Today the Saudi authorities are investing in freezer-plants and other ways of preserving the animal products. The animals are counted in 'sheep-units', rating from one for a sheep or goat up to seven for a fully grown cow or camel. In 1981 about one million 'sheep-units' were sacrificed, seventy per cent of them during the first day of sacrifice, and of these, about half between morning and midday.

The idea of up to 350,000 sheep being slaughtered in the space of a few hours in honour of the Almighty is somewhat unappealing to Christians, who celebrate the Sacrifice of their founder by a purely symbolic act of cannibalism. Along with the physical movements around the Ka'ba, it demonstrates the concrete factuality of a faith which, at its core, is strongly resistant to the observance of rituals in a purely symbolic manner. This inner core of literalism and factuality is the source both of Islam's power over its adherents, since in the last resort social practice must be moulded to conform to it, and of most of the problems it faces in adjusting to contemporary realities, since that very social moulding leads only too often to a stultifying literalism which sees all change as the enemy of the good: such is the dilemma facing Islam in the World.

The pagan background of all these rites, from the standing at 'Arafat to the Feast of Sacrifice, is still obscure. Muslim authorities are understandably reticent on the subject, while, for obvious reasons, archaeologists are unlikely to be admitted to the area in the forseeable future. What information there is has to be gleaned from the earliest Muslim writers and measured against comparable data from other parts of the world.

Some anthropologists have seen in the standing at 'Arafat relics of an ancient rain-making cult. Before Muhammad abolished the intercalary month by which the Meccas adjusted their lunar calendar to the solar year, the Hajj probably occurred in autumn, coinciding with the great fair at Ukaz held to celebrate the date harvest. The 'ifada from 'Arafat to Muzdalifa, which in pre-Islamic times began before nightfall, may have represented the 'persecution' of the dying sun. The stone-throwing at Mina, according to the earliest Muslim sources, only occurred after the sun had passed the meridian, suggesting a ritual pursuit of the sun-demon, whose harsh rule ends with the summer. Similarly the halt at Muzdalifa, home of Quzah the thunder-god, accompanied by shouting and other loud noises, may have been a ritual attempt to call forth the thunder and bring on the rain. Rites such as these are found all over the world at the beginnings of the four seasons.

The significance of the anthropological background, however sketchy the evidence, is that it points to the subtle adjustments by which the Prophet accommodated his vision of a single transcendent deity within the prevailing symbolic structure. Just as the Quran did not suddenly appear out of nowhere in a strange and incomprehensible language, but was assembled from existing verbal materials, so the central ritual of Islam, the Hajj, was arranged out of existing cultic practices. The actions themselves were almost unchanged, but their meaning was transformed to fit a new, vastly expanded, cosmic vision. The result was a religious and ideological *tour de force*.

By abolishing the intercalary month, Muhammad freed the rituals from their seasonal connections: from now on the Hajj could fall at any time of the year, for the cosmic deity to whom all the rituals were to be addressed was the same God in autumn and spring, summer and winter. Similarly, the sanctuaries associated with particular localities were not abolished, but included within a set of rituals covering the whole area. 'The whole of 'Arafat is a place for standing, the whole of Muzdalifa is a place for stopping, the whole of Mina is a place for sacrifice,' the Prophet is related to have said on the Farewell Pilgrimage.

Similar effects were achieved by subtly adjusting the timing of the ancient ceremonies. Ancient taboos associated with the rituals were deliberately violated to demonstrate the impotence of the pagan gods and the inefficacy of the rituals when dedicated to them. But the forms of the rituals were preserved because the Prophet was fully aware of the importance they held for his people. Beyond that, he knew that the rituals formed part of a universal language composed of bodily move-ments as well as verbal utterances, by means of which human beings express their deepest needs and apprehensions. The remarkable expan-sion of Islam, especially in the Far East and tropical Africa, long after its initial political and military impetus had exhausted itself, was in no small measure due to the ease with which it absorbed local cults and then directed them towards the broader social and cosmological purpose of the monotheistic vision.

2 ✤ The Muhammadan Paradigm

Muhammad ibn 'Abdullah of the Banu Hashim of Quraish was born in Mecca in about 570, at a time when the ruling tribe of Quraish were increasing in wealth, power and prosperity. The caravan-city of Mecca, probably the 'Makorba' mentioned in the writings of the second-century geographer Ptolemy, had long been an important commercial centre. The shrine from which its name derived, and the surrounding *haram* or sacred area, was a place where the beduin tribes who controlled the traffic in spices and other goods between South Arabia and the Mediterranean could exchange goods without fear of attack. The pilgrimage to the Ka'ba, in addition to its religious functions, encouraged trade, especially during the four sacred months when fighting was forbidden. Other *harams* in the Peninsula similarly combined religious with commercial functions, but Mecca seems to have been the most important of these sanctuaries, lying as it did on the strategic road between Yemen, seat of an ancient if declining civilization, and the Mediterranean. In the decades before Muhammad, the volume of trade had increased, partly as a result of the continuing warfare between the Persian and Byzantine empires which disrupted the northern land routes. The tribes who controlled the Hejaz trade were becoming not only more powerful but increasingly civilized as they came into closer contact with the regions of high culture.

Unlike South Arabia, whose higher rainfall and ancient systems of irrigation had led to the development of forms of feudalism in combination with a tradition of divine kingship, the aridity of Northern and Central Arabia was such that society was entirely organized on tribal lines, while anything resembling the state was virtually non-existent. Although the sedentary people outnumbered the nomads, the prevailing ethos was determined by the beduin, whose superior mobility and fighting skills enabled them to subdue the settled pastoralists, semi-nomads, peasants and small merchants, extracting from them payment of taxes similar to the protection money demanded by urban gangsters. Actually, no hard-and-fast distinction can be made between 'nomadic' and 'sedentary' peoples in the Peninsula: there was rather a continuum extending from the camel-herding beduin aristocrats, through the humbler sheep- and goat-herds, to the agriculturalists and date-farmers who lived in permanent settlements (usually in individually fortified households) around the oases. Tribalism was the only mode of social organization. Each individual saw himself as belonging to a kinship group claiming descent from a real or supposed ancestor. Solidarity increased with ancestral proximity: the most immediate loyalty was to the family; then to the clan, a small group of closely related families; beyond that to broader groups of increasingly distant relatives who could sometimes be called upon for support, up to the level of the 'tribe', which can roughly be defined as the largest group capable of providing effective social solidarity.

The beduin camel-breeders were a military aristocracy in the sense that they dominated the more sedentary folk, to whom they felt superior by birth and professional skills. But they were far from wealthy, and in bad years were obliged to prey on the sedentary folk to avoid starvation. Normally, they survived on camel milk and the few staples such as dates that they were able to exchange for their own meagre products, including hides, leather, cloth or livestock. With little surplus to accumulate, every member of the group was directly involved in herding to some degree, so social organization, though hierarchical for military purposes, was relatively egalitarian. Chiefs were usually chosen by their peers as being the fittest in battle and most knowledgeable in the ways of the desert.

In certain cases, however, the mobility of the camel-breeders enabled them to engage in, and ultimately to monopolize, the long-distance trade in such luxury commodities as slaves and spices. The Quraish had gained control of Mecca and its shrines some time during the fifth century under their leader Qusaiy. By the time of Muhammad's birth their caravans were converging from the four cardinal points – north and west from Syria and the Mediterranean, south and east from Yemen and the Persian Gulf. In the manner of other beduin leaders the Quraish buttressed their power by forming alliances with neighbouring tribes. In effect, as well as being the leading merchant traders in the Peninsula, they were the rulers of an important military confederation.

A caravan city such as Mecca was unusual, even by Arabian standards. Most of the important cities of the region were situated either in mountainous areas such as Taif, south of Mecca, or in oases such as Medina or Khaibar. In such cases the city formed the nexus between the nomads and the cultivators, where animal goods were exchanged for agricultural products. Mecca was different. Apart from the brackish well of Zamzam, whose output was barely sufficient for the citizens and their stock, it was situated in a waterless valley where cultivation was impossible. Its wealth was therefore purely commercial and its inhabitants were more closely tied to the beduin tribal structure than those of other cities. The *haram*, with the well at its centre, was, in effect, the city's only *raison d'être*.

It seems probable that, in addition to their possibly astral significance, the 360 idols placed round the Ka'ba represented various tribal totems, signifying adherence to the sanctuary, rather as the flags of member states are ranged in the UN Plaza in New York. The god of Mecca, Hubal, represented by a statue of red carnelian, is thought to have been originally a totem of the Khuza'a, rulers of Mecca before their displacement by the Quraish. Some accounts state that Qusaiy, who conquered Mecca from the Khuza'a, imported the cults of the goddesses 'Uzza and Manat from Syria. There is little evidence that by Muhammad's time the pagan Arabs were particularly attached to idol worship, though in the war which followed Muhammad's proclamation of Islam the pagans carried some of these idols as standards into battle. For most of the Arabs, a vestigial attachment to one's tribal totem would not have seemed incompatible with a general monotheistic belief. There is evidence in the earliest written sources that monotheistic views were widely held. (Indeed, the name 'Abdullah – 'servant of the god or Allah' – was in general use and belonged, among others, to the Prophet's father.) Monotheistic ideas may have been diffused among the Arabs by Christian and Jewish converts, since anyone with a serious interest in religion, as well as a desire to raise his cultural standards, would have drawn close to one or other of the scriptural communities. But it is highly simplistic to suppose that 'monotheism', and the scriptural lore associated with it, was necessarily a 'monopoly' of these two communities. The logic of the prevailing social system – the patrilineal kinship group – led inevitably from monolatry to monotheism once the tribal totem had ceased to be the only available cult object. The presence of a multiplicity of symbols round the inter-tribal forum of the Ka'ba must have focused the attention of the tribes on the things which united rather than divided them – in particular, their supposed common ancestry from 'Adnan, Isma'il and Ibrahim, the original *hanif* or 'pagan' monotheist. By Muhammad's time Allah – meaning simply 'the god' – was certainly understood as a concept. What he lacked was a cult and a ritual, and above all a scripture in a language the Arabs could understand.

The pagan Arabs (the word originally means 'nomad') may have lacked the formal qualifications of a 'people': that is to say, a community owing common cultural and religious allegiance to one of the recognized scriptures. But they had ceased to be mere barbarians. Though without writing, they had developed poetry into a refined and sophisticated art form. Though none of it was written down before about A D 700 – after the earliest recensions of the Quran – much of it had been preserved for hundreds of years by professional *rawis* or reciters, who passed on their knowledge from father to son for generations. Although a certain amount of spurious matter may have found its way into later collections of pre-Islamic poetry, enough of the original corpus has survived to provide a convincing picture of the beduin values which were to be transformed, modified or rejected by the Prophet of Islam.

A key concept in the beduin value system was *muruwa* or 'manliness'. It has been described as meaning 'bravery in battle, patience in misfortune, persistence in revenge, protection of the weak, defiance of the strong'. In the absence of any central authority, tribal solidarity was the only source of individual protection. The 'virtue' of a tribe was conceived of as something inherited: a man would act nobly because of the noble blood that ran through his veins. The extent of individual freedom – defined in terms of choosing between different courses of action – was severely limited. The tribe's honour, and adherence to its norms, were imperatives to be followed at all times. Generosity, a highly praised virtue, was expressed in the lavish hospitality extended to anyone who placed himself under a tribe's protection – less for reasons of pure altruism than for the prestige such lavishness accorded to the tribe and its chiefs. The power of a tribe was due to its wealth and prowess in battle, both of which were commensurate with its size and the number of its dependents. A large and wealthy tribe like the Quraish would have numerous 'clients' or weaker tribes (often previously defeated enemies) dependent upon it. Inter-tribal warfare was endemic – being, as it were, an essential part of the ecology. But it was subject to certain customary limitations. Apart from the ban on fighting during the four sacred months, the beduin warriors deliberately sought to avoid unnecessary risks and casualties. The aim of the traditional *ghazwa* or raid was to detach the enemy tribesmen from their flocks or camels, and to carry the latter off as booty. If the defeated tribe found itself facing starvation, it would have no alternative but to place itself under the protection of a stronger tribe. In such a manner major confederations, such as that led by the Quraish, were built up from smaller units or clans.

The organization of tribal life was aristocratic in the original Greek sense. The chiefs of the tribe derived their authority from 'noble blood, noble character, wealth, wisdom and experience'. A hereditary principle was acknowledged, but only insofar as it pre-supposed a fitness to lead rather than rule. The leader of a tribal group would, of necessity, belong to its kin. But there was no formal system for electing leaders or for passing the chiefship down from father to son. A chief emerged and retained his leadership by a consensus of his peers – the tribal elders. Success would strengthen this consensus, failure or bad luck would undermine it. The absence of such consensus would lead to bloody internecine disputes; but the elders would always be conscious of the dangers which internal strife would pose to the whole community. Thus the Arabian chief had authority, derived from his superior personal fitness, but little power to give orders or punish his fellow tribesmen. The latter governed themselves according to a moral code developed over generations, based on a highly successful adaptation to the economics of stock-breeding in a desert environment.

Politically, the beduin were conservative and egalitarian. They understood that safety lay in observing the ways of one's ancestors. No man could be regarded as inherently better than his fellows, except through his actions and the demonstrable superiority of his blood. Generally this world-view, in which formal religious observance played only a minor part, has been properly described as 'tribal humanism'. The tribe's survival and growth was a sufficient end in itself, the only standard against which human excellence could be measured. The attitude embodied a certain element of fatalism: the tribesman depended not, as the peasant-cultivator did, on mastering his environment, but on adapting himself to suit it: in short, he submitted to the laws of nature as he understood them. Fate determined his sustenance, the term of his life and the number of his children: in effect, his happiness or misery. In desert conditions, such matters lay beyond human control. Within these parameters, however, he was bound by the knowledge that prosperity was enhanced by social harmony and cohesion and diminished by strife. Such an austere, and ultimately pessimistic, world-view offered little comfort for the individual. There is scant evidence of a belief in the after-life. Though the Day of Judgement is referred to in at least one pre-Islamic poem, this was probably a borrowing from Christian sources. Belief in individual survival after death was kept in subjection to the practical task of ensuring that the social collectivity of the tribe expanded and prospered in this world.

As for the individual, there were plenty of worldly pleasures, including wine and women, with which he could console himself:

> Roast meat and wine: the swinging ride
> On a camel sure and tried,
> Which her master speeds amain
> O'er low dale and level plain;
> Women marble-white and fair
> Trailing gold-fringed raiment rare:
> Opulence, luxurious ease,
> With the lute's soft melodies –
> Such delights hath our brief span;
> Time is Change, Time's fool is Man.
> Wealth or want, great store or small,
> All is one since Death's are all.[1]

In Mecca, as in other populous parts of northern and central Arabia, many of the old assumptions of beduin society were beginning to give way. The increase in trade was producing a new social environment in which the cash nexus was replacing the simpler bartering arrangements of the old system. As they retained their profits in order to finance further ventures, the beduin traders were becoming merchant capitalists. The new dynamic of economic expansion began to replace the older dynamic of tribal growth. The new commercial values superseded the older communalistic ones, as disparities of wealth became increasingly apparent at an individual level. In the tribal society, poverty, like wealth, was shared. In a lean year, everyone went hungry, from the chiefs down to the household slaves. In a good year, when flocks were plentiful, everyone ate meat and benefited from the largesse of the chiefs. Now, in the emergent social order of Mecca, something approaching class divisions had begun to appear. The rich were getting richer, but many, including former household slaves, widows, orphans and people who for one reason or another owned no stock or exchangeable goods, were becoming destitute. A harsher, more individualistic society was coming into existence. For the wealthy and 'upwardly mobile' the range of social and cultural opportunities had never been greater. For the poor, or those who were in the process of becoming impoverished, the tribal system was ceasing to provide basic social security.

The tensions in Meccan society were reflected in the rivalry between the clans that made up the tribe of Quraish. At the time of Muhammad's birth, the competition for influence and prestige was strongest between the clans of Hashim and 'Abd Shams. Muhammad's grandfather, 'Abd al Muttalib, was the leader of the Banu Hashim, and a man of considerable importance. He had dug out the well of Zamzam, having inherited from his uncle the responsibility of providing food and water for the pilgrims. He also inherited from his father, Hashim, the franchise of the lucrative Syrian trade. However, by the end of his life he had lost much of the Syrian trade to the rival clans of 'Abd Shams and Nawfal. Muhammad's father 'Abdullah took over what trade was left to the Hashimis, but he died comparatively young on a journey from Gaza. 'Abdullah's wife, Amina bint Wahb, of the clan of Zuhra, was either pregnant at the time, or had just been delivered of her son Muhammad. Her husband's death left her with very little: according to some accounts, one slave, five camels and a few sheep. She herself died when her son was only six.

We know little about the Prophet's early life that is of historical value, as distinct from mythical or theological significance. The latter category includes stories of impressive encounters with holy men who instantly recognized the young Muhammad's spiritual destiny, and tales about the angelic surgeons who opened his breast and 'cleaned his heart' before replacing it. In accordance with Quraishi custom, Muhammad was farmed out with a wet nurse from one of the beduin tribes: the pure air of the desert was considered to be good for the health of children, while the ties of fosterage (a custom practised by other pastoral peoples, including the Irish), like those of marriage, became a means of strengthening tribal alliances. More importantly in Muhammad's case, his sojourn in the desert at a formative age made him familiar with that special elliptical quality of beduin speech (known as *i'jaz*) which characterizes the style of the Quran.

Many Muslims who accept uncritically the dogma that the Quran is the 'speech of God' are reluctant to admit that literary influences have any part in its formation. The mature Muhammad is supposed to have been illiterate when he received his first 'revelations' at the age of about 40, a tradition enhancing the miraculous character of God's 'messages'. Actually, it is not certain that Muhammad was illiterate, though his knowledge of writing, like that of his contemporaries, was probably rudimentary. The term *ummi* used in the Quran and *hadiths* (reports of the Prophet's deeds and sayings) can mean 'unlettered' rather than illiterate, in the sense that Muhammad was a 'gentile' Arab having no knowledge of the Hebrew or Christian scriptures. The fact of Muhammad's illiteracy, however, would in no way constitute proof of the Quran's miraculous origin. As has already been mentioned, the great pre-Islamic poets were illiterate, and so were the *rawis* who transmitted their verses. Muhammad, who, for reasons to be explained, hated the pagan poets and disclaimed any similarities between their verses and the Quran's, must, consciously or otherwise, have absorbed some of their techniques and facility of expression. Along with the rest of Mecca, he must certainly have attended the annual fair at Ukaz, where the poets competed for prizes, as in a Welsh Eisteddfod.

Thus we may be reasonably sure that Muhammad, though born into one of Mecca's best families, had experience in the early years of his life both of poverty and of the special intimacy of beduin life, in which human affection acts as a kind of insulating blanket against the harsh realities of the desert. He had learned the pure speech of the Arabs from the beduin and their poets. He was probably familiar with monotheistic ideas, as well as with much of the biblical and talmudic folklore which the pagan Ismaelites shared with the scriptural peoples of the settled regions, including the Christians of Najran and the Jews of Yathrib, the oasis-settlement north-east of Mecca.

After his mother's death, the orphaned Muhammad was taken into the household of his paternal uncle, Abu Talib, who became leader of the Hashim clan on the death of 'Abd al Muttalib, when Muhammad was about eight. According to some accounts, Abu Talib sometimes took his young nephew with him on trips to Syria, where he came into contact with Syrian monks. But there is no evidence from the Quran or the traditions that Muhammad was at all well acquainted with Christian beliefs or practices. Like everyone else, he probably participated in the pagan cults around the Ka'ba. The story that Abu Talib, despite his affection for Muhammad, refused him permission to marry his daughter Umm Hain on account of his poverty, is quite plausible.

Despite the hagiographical tendencies of Muhammad's biographers, a convincing personality emerges from the earliest sources. He was evidently physically well-favoured and mentally astute. He was about average height (which for beduin Arabs is around 5 feet 9 inches) and sturdily built. His forehead was large and prominent, his nose curved, his eyes large and black with a touch of brown. His hair was thick and slightly curly. His skin was lighter than is usual for an Arabian, and a vein could be seen throbbing in his temple when he was angry or otherwise upset. His mouth was large, and he had a pleasant smile. He walked at great speed, and when turning to look round did so with his whole body. He conveyed the impression of great energy, but his contemporaries found him unusually taciturn and self-controlled. When he spoke it was briefly, to the point and without elaboration. He seems to have been a serious-minded introvert in a society where it is usual for men to be excitable, exuberant, boastful and loquacious.

It may have been this quality of seriousness beyond his years that earned Muhammad the nickname Al Amin – the trusty one. His tact and discretion would later show themselves in his political career. Doubtless it was awareness of these qualities, together with an intuitive recognition of his exceptional talents, that persuaded a Quraishi widow of means, Khadija bint Khuwailid, to make him her steward and later her husband.

Khadija is supposed to have been about 40 and already the mother of several children when she married Muhammad, then aged about 25. Since she subsequently bore him four daughters and several sons (the sons all died in infancy), one finds this hard to believe. At a time when girls were usually married at puberty, 30 was considered more than mature. Perhaps the early biographers exaggerated Khadija's age in order to emphasize the unusual fact that she was older than her husband and that – as a woman of means – she had chosen him for herself.

Muhammad and Khadija seem to have been content together for the 15 years of their marriage, despite the loss of the infant boys. In the patriarchal society of the Arabs, a man's prestige, even his identity, was to some extent dependent on the number of his sons. His *kunya* or nickname came from his first-born male. Muhammad's was Abu Qasim, father of Qasim. The death of his boys must have been a considerable blow. In other respects, however, the outward circumstances of Muhammad's life seem to have been prosperous. The family, if not wealthy, was comfortably off and highly respected. The marriage was evidently happy: Muhammad, who travelled regularly on the Syrian route, appears to have availed himself neither of the slave-girls nor of the temporary marriages permitted by custom. It is conceivable that Khadija, who had been in a position to dictate terms, had insisted that he remain monogamous.

It seems useless to speculate about the psychological causes which inspired Muhammad, when he was about 40, to spend increasing amounts of time in solitary contemplation, in the manner of a Syrian monk or an Arabian soothsayer. In all societies artists and intellectuals are to some extent people apart, who find it necessary and desirable to spend time on their own. Muhammad may well have been such a man from his birth. But only after he had reached a satisfactory level of material prosperity would he have been free to indulge his taste for solitude. In a mainly non-literate society, without a high cultural tradition in the visual or plastic arts, the main outlet for individuals with creative imaginations was necessarily limited to poetry. Muhammad – if, as non-Muslims must, we credit him with 'authorship' of the Quran or of a substantial portion of it – was unquestionably endowed with poetic genius. If he chose not to become a poet, this must have been because he rejected the social and artistic values of the poets of his day. As panegyrists or satirists, the poets were the propagandists of the tribal chiefs who employed them – a role not wholly unlike that of many Arab journalists today. Though still credited with supernatural powers (they were believed to be inspired by devils or jinns, depending on one's attitude towards their paymasters), the poets must have seemed increasingly frivolous and out of touch with the needs of a changing society to people like Muhammad, who sought a unifying principle in their culture. The poets helped foster the contentiousness and disunity that were the curse of beduin life.

For a thinking man, of course, there was the alternative of religion. There is evidence that some of Muhammad's contemporaries, or near contemporaries, adopted Christianity. At Yathrib and Khaibar, as well as in Yemen, many former nomads had adopted Judaism, though it is not certain how much access they would have had to the Hebrew scriptures, or whether the rabbis regarded them as Jews in the strict sense of the term. Both Christianity and Judaism, however, entailed adherence to scriptures in foreign languages, involving an admission of cultural inferiority which most Arabs, who were rightly proud of their linguistic heritage, found unacceptable.

There was a further possible outlet for a man of Muhammad's temperament, though not perhaps of his cultural background and social status. This was the traditional role of *kahin*, or soothsayer. The *kahin* – a word etymologically related to the Hebrew *kohen*, or priest – was a shamanistic figure common enough in the Arabian peninsula. The *kahins* believed themselves to be inspired by familiar spirits, made repetitious invocations to natural and physical phenomena, such as the morning or evening stars, or certain plants or animals, and were often consulted as oracles in both public and private matters, such as the loss of camels or the interpretation of dreams. When prophesying in this manner the *kahins* would cover their heads with their cloaks and give utterance to their visions in breathless, rhythmic cadences known as *saj'*, or rhyming prose. *Saj'* was, in fact, the earliest form of Arabic poetry. Its use by the *kahins* suggests that the latter were operating within the most ancient of all oral traditions, in which the rhymes were preserved for purely mnemonic purposes. For a man of Muhammad's more sophisticated background and broad intellectual outlook, to have become a simple *kahin* would have been unthinkable. But it is significant that the first revelations which he uttered resembled the *saj'* of the *kahins* in both form and content. The earliest *suras* (chapters) of the Quran consist, in the main, of shamanistic invocations of natural phenomena in short, ecstatic breaths of rhyming prose. This was the very core of the Quranic message, and it conferred upon the 'speech of God' a demotic and directly inspirational quality which was lacking in the higher style and more finely wrought language of the poets.

Muhammad's favoured retreat was in a cave in the hill of Hira, a few miles from Mecca. It was here that, according to the earliest accounts, he received his 'call' to prophethood and the first of the revelations which, assembled into chapters or *suras* (a Hebrew loan-word meaning 'row'), make up the Quran (literally the 'discourse', or 'recitation'). According to his widow 'Aisha, to whom the prophet confided his story in later years, 'the beginning of the revelation for the Messenger of God was true vision. It used to come like the breaking of dawn.' For this gifted and intelligent man, these first intimations were enough to set him, temporarily, on the mystic's path. We are told that 'solitude became dear to him', and that he returned to the cave for several days and nights consecutively, taking provisions with him, in order to engage in devotional exercises (which he may or may not have learned from Christian monks). He was evidently expecting something dramatic, and may have felt such despair when nothing happened that he contemplated suicide.

At last, unexpectedly, he became aware of a presence (identified, in later Muslim tradition, as the angel Gabriel) who told him: 'Muhammad, Thou art the Messenger of God.' Subsequent alternations of certainty and despair may have been repeated several times before divine communication finally came in the form of words.

According to Muslim tradition, the first revelation 'came down' on the night of 26–27 Ramadan, the so-called Night of Power which the Quran says is worth a thousand ordinary nights, and when to be born, or to die, is still seen as a special mark of Allah's favour. The presence was with Muhammad and said to him: 'Read! [Recite!]', to which Muhammad answered: 'What shall I read [recite]?' Variants of this tradition, conforming to the dogma that Muhammad was illiterate, give his answer as 'I cannot read!' The presence then shook him and crushed him until all the strength went out of him. 'Read!' came the command once more. Twice Muhammad refused, twice he was shaken by the presence. But finally the words came to him which would later form the opening of the 96th Sura, regarded by the great majority of scholars as the first of the Quranic revelations:

> Read [recite] in the name of thy Sustainer who has created –
> Created man out of a germ-cell
> Read, for thy Sustainer is the Most Bountiful One
> Who has taught [man] the use of the pen –
> Taught man what he did not know![2]

Was the presence which spoke to Muhammad something from outside himself, or an irruption from within his unconscious, the result of severe stresses brought on, perhaps, by his religious devotions? Muhammad's experience appears to have been both ocular and auditory: he *saw* the angel, and *heard* the words that were spoken to him. But whether or not the traditional version is accepted, the story of the angelic presence does conform to certain conventional assumptions about the forms of both prophetic and poetic experience.

Within the traditions of prophecy, the encounter of Mount Hira has obvious parallels with that of Moses on Mount Sinai when he received the Torah from the god of the Hebrews. Surprisingly, there are no references to this incident in the Quran, although Moses figures prominently as one of Muhammad's predecessors. The story of the angel seizing Muhammad and shaking him has, however, several precedents among the tales of the Arabian poets. One of them, Hasan ibn Thabit, who later became a Muslim, was assaulted by a female spirit who pressed him to the ground and 'forced' him to utter three verses when previously he had never been able to compose a single line. This and other legends about the supernatural origin of exceptional eloquence embodied the same cultural assumptions as beliefs in the magical powers of poets and soothsayers. With the coming of Islam they were not so much abolished as translated into a broader framework. The language of the Quran, more perspicuous than that of the soothsayers, more eloquent than that of the poets, could not be other than the speech of God himself, transmitted through an angelic intermediary.

The belief that God speaks through the mouth of his prophets is central to the Irano-Semitic tradition. Leaving aside the question of whether this claim is 'true' or 'false', it can be said with reasonable certainty that the Night of Power represents the moment when Muhammad assimilated this tradition to himself. Henceforth he would see himself as a Prophet charged with a special mission for his people and, through them, for mankind as a whole. He conceptualized this mission in a manner appropriate to the times and circumstances in which he found himself. Convinced that the source of this overpowering sense of purpose, which gave his existence a new meaning and coherence, came from outside himself, he not unnaturally identified it with something with which he and his contemporaries were familiar. The Source could only be the same God who had spoken through the other prophets about whom he had heard. His mission, like that of the prophets who came before him, must be to convey the communications he received from the Source to his fellow human beings, regardless of the cost to himself and to others.

For believing Muslims, the externality of the Source must be accepted without question. After the Night of Power Muhammad was the recipient of the revelations which make up the Quran at more or less regular intervals. At first, before he got used to them, the experience of revelation could be agonizing. We are told that he became covered with sweat, was seized with a violent shuddering, and lay unconscious for hours as though in a drunken stupor. At other times, the revelations were accompanied by ocular visions of angels who spoke to him. It is clear that he was unable to summon the revelations at will, and that when they did come, the messages sometimes contradicted his personal judgements or criticized his actions. Sometimes they 'came down' when he was least expecting them, when he was in the middle of a conversation or as he was riding on camelback.

For the non-Muslim, the externality of the revelations may or may not be admitted. Most believers in the existence of God, whether or not they are members of other faiths, would probably find acceptable the distinction that the Quran, taken as a whole, has two messages, one special and the other general. The special revelations were directed at Muhammad's auditors and, by extension, to the whole Muslim community which came after them. The general revelations were applicable to mankind as a whole. If this distinction is accepted, Muhammad can be recognized by members of other faiths as the Muslim Prophet, a man who genuinely received messages from God and conveyed them to his people. Atheists or agnostics, on the other hand, will tend to argue that, while Muhammad may have been perfectly sincere in believing that the messages came from outside himself, there is no way of proving that the Source was really external to himself. No modern scholarly writer seriously claims, as used to be argued by some Christian as well as some anticlerical writers, that Muhammad was an impostor, well-intentioned or otherwise, who faked his 'revelations' in order to persuade his unwilling countrymen to accept his social and political programme. His sincerity is universally admitted. Nowadays the sceptics' case consists either in undermining the historicity of the Prophet, or in arguing that, while acting in perfectly good faith, he was nevertheless the victim of some form of mental delusion.

That Muhammad's mental state was abnormal when he experienced visions upon receiving revelations goes without saying. His recent Marxist biographer, Maxime Rodinson, argues convincingly enough that these visions emerged from within his unconscious:

> One has only to dip into psychology text-books to find a hundred perfectly bona fide cases of people in a state of hallucination hearing things and seeing visions which they claim quite genuinely never to have seen or heard before. And yet an objective study of their cases shows that these are simply fresh associations produced by the unconscious working on things which have been seen and heard but forgotten. Facts of this kind we now take for granted. It is therefore conceivable that what Muhammad saw and heard may have been the supernatural beings described to him by the Jews and Christians with whom he talked.[3]

However, only if we regard the unconscious as a discrete entity comparable to the conscious self can this line of reasoning be made to conform with atheistic assumptions. Freud's famous pupil C. G. Jung challenged the idea of a discrete unconscious after analysing the dreams of his patients and finding that many contained the same symbols and archetypes as are to be found in medieval gnostic texts with which the patients could not possibly have been acquainted. From this evidence he inferred the existence of a 'collective unconscious' transcending the boundaries of individual self-hood. He wrote:

> I have to admit the fact that the unconscious mind is capable at times of assuming an intelligence and purposiveness which are superior to actual conscious insight . . . Since modern research has acquainted us with the fact that an individual consciousness is based upon and surrounded by an indefinitely extended unconscious psyche, we needs must revise our somewhat old-fashioned prejudice that man is his consciousness.[4]

If we take a Jungian, as distinct from a Freudian, view of the unconscious, Rodinson's argument that Muhammad's utterances irrupted from his unconscious cannot be made to support an atheistic version of the origins of Islam.

Perhaps we should say that Muhammad believed that the irruptions from his unconscious mind which he experienced from time to time, and which were subsequently included in the Quran, were the products of an 'intelligence and purposiveness' superior to the conscious insights of which he believed himself capable. Having drawn from this unconscious reservoir, he continued to distinguish the words in which he formulated these perceptions from those of his normal everyday speech. In this respect he was probably conforming to the shamanistic practices of figures with which he was familiar – the *kahins* or soothsayers. But the message he believed himself to have been entrusted with was infinitely grander and more majestic than anything contained in the oracular pronouncements of the soothsayers. It was a message about the unity and purposiveness of the universe, and the special destiny of humanity in relation to it. It was a message which, like the messages of earlier prophets in the Iranian–Semitic tradition, stated that a coherent and rational universe, resulting from a divine act of creation, or 'decree', must needs find its human expression in a harmonious social order, in which extremes of wealth and privilege should be minimized; it was a message, in short, that demanded the creation of the good society, in order to provide men and women with a positive reason for living, to sustain them in times of difficulty, and to moderate their natural urge towards excessive self-indulgence when times seemed good. The message did not, of course, come to him all at once. His mission would be to create for himself an environment suitable for its safe delivery. He knew he would have to make use of all his strength, cunning and ingenuity to achieve this purpose. At times he would be utterly ruthless, resorting to war, assassination, even massacre, to achieve this purpose. Some Muslims shrink from facing up to these actions, many of which run counter to contemporary western ideas about morality. But Muhammad was not a god: at no point did he identify himself with that inner voice prompting him to action. Every pronouncement he made drew attention eloquently and forcefully to the impassable gulf between God and man, between the Creator and his creatures. It was because he never ceased to emphasize the distinction between his own human self-hood and the Source which inspired him that of all the men in history who have wielded political power, he was one of the least corrupted by it.

Muhammad's first converts were members of his household – his wife, Khadija, 'Ali ibn Abi Talib, his young ward and first cousin, and Zaid ibn Haritha, a freedman from the mainly Christian tribe of Kalb. For three years Muhammad expounded his messages privately, mainly to his family circle and a small group of others who joined them. Centuries later, when the oral traditions were committed to writing, it became a matter of the greatest importance to the political families of the day to have had an ancestor among the earliest converts. The evidence was probably tampered with, so we cannot be absolutely sure who they were. One of them was certainly Abu Bakr, a merchant who succeeded to the Prophet's political authority as caliph in 632. Two other young cousins, Sa'd ibn Abi Waqqas and Zubair ibn al 'Awwam, joined early on, as did two younger members of Mecca's ruling clans, Khalid ibn al 'As of 'Abd Shams, and 'Uthman ibn 'Affan, the future third caliph, then a somewhat dandyish young man of about 30 who is said to have embraced Islam after falling in love with Muhammad's daughter Ruqaiya. Khalid was eventually joined by his brother 'Amr, future conqueror of Egypt.

Other early supporters included younger men who, like Abu Bakr, came from less aristocratic and influential clans, such as Talha ibn 'Ubaidallah of the Taim, and 'Abd al Ka'ba (later 'Abd al Rahman) ibn

'Awf of the Zuhra. The majority of early supporters, however, came from lower down the social scale: some were members of minor clans affiliated to the Quraish, others were artisans, freedmen or actual slaves such as Bilal, the famous Abyssinian whose stentorian voice was to be the first to announce the call to prayer. Most of the first Muslims were young and independent-minded. When they began performing their prayer in public and Muhammad started preaching in the open, the group met with indifference and occasional ridicule from upper-class Meccans because of the lowly status of most of its members. But in the early years they were tolerated, since they were not yet seen as a threat to Quraishi power.

Most of the Quranic passages dating from this period concern the miraculous character of God's creative power, its durability as compared with the transitoriness of mortal existence and the need for human beings to show their gratitude in worship. All references to God, as well as those concerning the Day of Judgement when men and women will be punished or rewarded according to their merits, imply a knowledge of these doctrines on the part of Muhammad's auditors. There is little emphasis on God's unity and the denunciation of idolatrous practices such as occur in the passages of the Quran dating from a later period. The message does, however, have important social implications. The Day of Judgement will be 'a Day when no human being shall be of the least avail to another'.[5] That is to say, people will be judged on their merits as individuals, not in accordance with their 'inherited' virtue as members of one or another tribe. The accumulation of wealth as an end in itself is attacked: '[Woe unto him] who amasses wealth and counts it a safe-guard, thinking that his wealth will make him live forever!'[6] The rich are denounced as complacent, considering God's bounty as being no more than their just deserts. If they find themselves in straitened circum-stances, they think God is being unfair and turn away from him. 'You are not generous towards the orphan,' proclaims the Quran, 'and you do not urge one another to feed the needy, and you devour the inheritance [of others] with devouring greed and you love wealth with boundless love!'[7] Even the Prophet himself is reproached for frowning and turning away a blind man who approaches him while he is giving his attention to some of the Quraishi chiefs.[8]

There seem to have been three main reasons for the opposition to Muhammad's teaching that now began to develop among the leaders of the Quraish. His attacks on the private accumulation of wealth almost certainly struck a raw nerve because it was partly couched in terms of traditional tribal values. It is not wealth as such that is condemned, but rather the meanness of tribal leaders who no longer dispense largesse in the manner of the desert.

A second reason may have been that the leaders of the Quraish realized, perhaps before Muhammad himself, that the new allegiance he was beginning to acquire from his followers must eventually represent a threat to themselves. A man who claimed to speak directly for God, and whose followers believed him to be so speaking, was hardly likely to submit to any purely political authority. Mecca's 'merchant republic' was governed by a Council on which all the leading clans were represented. Muhammad, though of aristocratic birth, was neither wealthy nor important enough to be part of the city's 'Establishment'. There is evidence that the Quraishi leaders tried to 'co-opt' him, offering money and power if he would stop attacking them.

A third and related reason had a religious dimension. If we accept the chronology of the *suras* as developed by such scholars as Theodor Nöldeke and Richard Bell, none of the earliest Meccan passages contain overt attacks on the pagan idols around the Ka'ba. The real source of religious opposition appears to have had a much more problematic character. The Day of Judgement announced in the early passages of the Quran implied a doctrine of individual resurrection, something which the Quraish, like modern atheists, regarded as self-evidently ridiculous. While it can be accepted rationalistically as a metaphorical way of expressing the notion that man is individually responsible for his actions, the idea that dust and bones can somehow be reassembled after death is not especially convincing. Muhammad's opponents saw this as a weak point in the Quranic message, and made the most of it. The Quran itself deals with their objections in rather general terms. In the miracle of God's creation, it says, all things are possible. If God can create human life out of a 'germ-cell', 'Is not He, then, able to bring the dead back to life?'[9] This was evidently not enough to satisfy the critics. Those who challenged Muhammad's message were told that they would burn in hell. The implication was that their fathers and grandfathers would burn likewise.

It was probably at this point that the issue of idolatry came to the centre of the argument. The new teaching emphasized *individual* moral virtues in a society where virtue was still thought of as inherent in group lineage. The basic values of honesty, generosity and courage preached by Islam may not have been so very different from the social virtues prized among the beduin. However, from the earliest passages in the Quran it was clear that these values were now to be applied universally, regardless of lineage. Even the disreputable elements surrounding Muhammad would be judged according to these standards; like the beduin aristocrats, they would be expected to live according to them.

Such a doctrine was more than the pride of the Quraishi leaders could be expected to bear. Muhammad was implicitly passing judgement – as they saw it – on their ancestors, and on the deities of their clans. In this they rightly perceived a threat to themselves: for in demanding unqualified recognition of the one true god, Muhammad was now creating around himself an allegiance which superseded the ancient loyalties to the clans of which they were the heads.

The leader of the opposition to Muhammad was 'Amr ibn Hisham of the Banu Makhzum, known to his supporters as Abu al Hikam ('Father of Wisdom'). The Muslims nicknamed him Abu Jahl, 'Father of Ignorance'. His chief supporter was the prophet's uncle, Abu Lahab, a younger brother of his former guardian and protector, Abu Talib. The persecution to which these men and their followers subjected the Muslims mainly took the form of ridicule and petty harassment. The junior and low-born Muslims suffered most, having no one to protect them. Many who had previously joined the movement were intimidated into renouncing their allegiance. Muhammad was sufficiently alarmed to send about 100 Muslims, including his daughter Ruqaiya and her husband, 'Uthman, to Christian Abyssinia, where they found protection from the Negus.

During the lifetime of Abu Talib, Muhammad's own position was still fairly secure. Though Abu Talib never embraced Islam, family honour demanded that he continue to protect his nephew. The price of this loyalty, however, was the complete isolation of the whole Hashimi clan. No one was to do business with them, or to form marriage ties with them or their allies. It seems doubtful if this boycott, which lasted two years, was particularly effective, since most of the clans who were persuaded to join it must have realized that it merely served to increase the domination of the Banu Makhzum and 'Abd Shams. The fact was that the split in Meccan society was transcending clan allegiances: Muhammad's uncle Abu Lahab, though a Hashimi, was a keen supporter of the boycotters, and broke off the proposed marriages of two of his sons with two of the Prophet's daughters; while the principal meeting-place of the Muslims during this period – when their numbers had been reduced to about 40 men and 20 women – was the house of Arqan, a member of the Banu Makhzum. A notable convert at this period was 'Umar ibn al Khattab, the future second caliph and the man who, after Muhammad, probably achieved most for Islam. Like St Paul, he began by being an avid persecutor of the new sect, which his sister Fatima and her husband, Sa'id, had secretly joined. He is said to have been converted after reading a sheet of paper containing the opening verses of Ta Ha – the Quran's 20th *sura*.

During the persecutions of the later Meccan period, Allah's messages became more strident and denunciatory. The Quran alludes frequently to earlier prophets – such as Salih, Hud, Shu'aib, Noah, Lot and Moses – who were sent to warn their peoples, only to be rejected by them. Inevitably those who failed to heed the warnings were punished, like proud Pharaoh and the people of Sodom, 'Ad, Thamud and Korah. Speaking as he was with God's voice, Muhammad identified himself completely with the earlier prophets. The same fate as befell these earlier peoples would overtake the pagan Quraish if they failed to heed God's messages. Sometimes these punishments were administered externally, the forces of nature acting as God's executioners. The people of Madyan and Sodom are destroyed by earthquakes, the people of Noah by the flood which his family alone survives. In other instances the idea of punishment presents itself in an altogether more sophisticated form: those who deny the truth are *wronging themselves* by rejecting God's messengers. Socially and politically, the message reaffirms the teachings of earlier prophets in the Hebrew–pastoral tradition: abandonment of the traditional morality of the patriarchs leads inexorably to communal disintegration and the suffering associated with it.

Generally speaking, attacks on idolatry dating from this period are relatively mild, confirming a story preserved in tradition that at one point Muhammad was tempted to compromise with Quraishi belief in the intercessionary power of the three female deities Allat, 'Uzza and Manat. The idols are merely represented as powerless, incapable of interceding on behalf of those who worship them. On the Day of Judgement they will themselves bear witness against man's folly: 'It was not us you were wont to worship,'[10] they are made to declare, indicating that such deities are merely projections of men's imaginations or subconscious desires. There is little of the feeling of 'abomination', of almost physical nausea, that accompanies the Hebrew attacks on idolatry in the Old Testament.

Despite the failure of the boycott, in about 619 the Prophet and the small Muslim community suffered a double blow. Within a short period Muhammad lost both his wife, Khadija, and his uncle Abu Talib. Khadija's death was a heavy personal loss: he had leaned heavily on her during the early days of revelation and despair, and she had been the first of his followers. Soon afterwards Muhammad married Sawda, herself a widow, from among the faithful. About the same time he was betrothed to 'Aisha, the child of Abu Bakr, who evidently wished to strengthen his personal ties with the master.

The death of Abu Talib deprived the Muslims of the protection which, despite the boycott, they had hitherto received from the head of the Hashimi clan. His successor Abu Lahab at first extended his protection to Muhammad, despite his earlier opposition to him: not to have done so would have reflected badly on his prestige as the Hashimi leader. Muhammad's other enemies, however, reminded Abu Lahab that the Prophet's teaching implied that their common ancestor, 'Abd al Muttalib, must be burning in hell. When Muhammad confirmed that this was indeed the case, Abu Lahab felt free to abandon his nephew without loss of face. The deterioration in Muhammad's position was evident from the insults he was now forced to tolerate, such as having a sheep's womb thrown at him during prayer, or having sand cast in his face.

Up till now Muhammad had probably seen himself as the Prophet of the Quraish – a role which he was to assume again at the end of his career. He may already have realized that any chance of long-term success depended on getting the backing of this, the most powerful of all the Arabian tribes. For the immediate future, however, he realized he would have to look outside Mecca for protection. He thought first of Taif, the cool hillside town where some of the wealthier Quraishi merchants had their summer residences (just as Meccan merchants and Saudi princes have today). But a ten-day visit to members of the Thaqif tribe who held their lands from the Quraish produced nothing but ridicule. Muhammad also tried to enlist beduin support; but when the Quraish denounced him they answered back, 'Your family and your clan know you better than we do, and they do not follow you.'

These were depressing times for the Muslims. But there began to be a glimmer of hope. Around 620 or thereabouts, Muhammad was approached by some members of the Khazraj, one of two tribal federations controlling the oasis of Medina (then usually known as Yathrib) about 200 miles north-east of Mecca. The previously dominant Khazraj had been in bitter conflict with the rival federation of Aws, who had recently defeated them with the help of three Jewish tribes, the Quraiza, the Nadir and the Qainuqa'. Clearly the situation in Medina was tense, for although some kind of equilibrium had been established, it was probable that civil war would soon break out again. The problem of clan rivalries and tribal feuding seems to have been much more acute in Medina even than in Mecca, since no one had unchallenged supremacy there, nor managed, like the ruling Quraish, to maintain a precarious consensus among the ruling clans. But the root causes of the malaise in Medina were probably not dissimilar from the ills affecting Mecca: the incompatibility of nomadic values with life in a settled community, especially at a time when population growth may have been exercising increasing pressure on food resources.

The Jewish influence in Medina was strong. Though the fully judaized clans were smaller than the Aws and Khazraj, they had the cultural prestige of being a 'literate' or scriptural community, and this gave them a social and political influence out of proportion to their numbers. Some of them may have been of original Israelite descent. However, there is no evidence from Jewish sources that Medina was a recognized centre for studying the Torah. The Judaized Arabs, some of whom may have been immigrants from South Arabia, were unlikely to have had a full or detailed knowledge of the Mosaic law. The pagan Arabs worshipped the goddess Manat, who possessed a shrine in the area.

Muhammad was related to the Khazraj through his father's mother. This, together with reports of his persecution at the hands of the Quraish for preaching monotheistic doctrines, may have been enough to recommend him as a possible arbiter by those Medinans who were seeking a way out of the bloody vendettas that had been affecting life in the oasis for decades. In 620, six members of the Khazraj who were visiting Mecca for the pilgrimage sought an interview with Muhammad. After hearing an explanation of his teachings and a recitation of the Quran, they accepted Islam. Back in Medina they made some more converts, and the following year they brought along some of the newcomers, including two members of the Aws. Muhammad sent one of his followers back with them, to teach them to pray and recite the Quran. These contacts culminated, in June 622, with a secret meeting at 'Aqaba, close to Mecca. 75 Medinese, including two women, were present. Here, in the presence of the Prophet, they pledged themselves to defend any Muslims who should come among them, including, of course, the Messenger of God.

Twelve delegates – nine from the Khazraj and three from the Aws – were appointed guarantors of the pact.

The departure of the Muslims from Mecca took place gradually over the following three months. For the most part, they met with no opposition from the Quraish, who were generally glad to be rid of the dissenters in their midst. However, some of the leaders, including Abu Jahl, saw that the exodus would sooner or later mean trouble, given that Medina lay on the route to Syria. There seems to have been a plot to assassinate Muhammad before his departure, including the provision that a representative of each clan was to take part in the killing, in order to make it impossible for the Hashimis to take revenge effectively. But the plan probably foundered for lack of agreement. A few Muslims decided to remain in Mecca for family reasons. Muhammad and the faithful Abu Bakr were the last to leave their native city. In September 622, they slipped out secretly with a guide, travelling south at first to avoid pursuit. After three days spent hiding in a cave, they decided that the coast was clear and headed north for Medina. A new era in history had begun.

When Muhammad arrived in Medina, he simultaneously had the role of Chief of the Emigrants and umpire of the fractious and divided community which had chosen him as their arbiter. Some of the members of this community – known to the Muslims as the Ansar, or 'Helpers' – had already accepted him as Prophet. But he knew that his position, and that of the Muhajirin ('Emigrants'), was vulnerable. One false move on his part must put an end to the precarious alliance between the Aws and Khazraj, the Jewish tribes and the Muhajirin which had been temporarily stitched together.

Muhammad the Prophet continued to receive God's revelations. If the style of the Quranic verses changed, the passages becoming longer and more sustained, the language more fluent and less breathless, the content more concerned with establishing a positive doctrine with a specific moral and legal content, this was hardly surprising. The Source – like the small but determined community inspired by it – was having to adjust to new conditions. It was no longer enough to fulminate against the Quraish and their iniquities, to proclaim the Day of Judgement and to marvel at the infinite majesty of the Creator and all his works. The new situation demanded a coherent formula for living as well as the will to put this formula into practice. Whether or not Muhammad became more adept at 'calling up' revelations in order to deal with the demands of the moment, the Quranic passages dating from the Medinese period are mostly of a different character from that of the ecstatic utterances of the early Meccan years. The Quran becomes more conscious of itself as a source of law and as a commentary on current events.

Muhammad's first move on reaching Medina was characteristically astute. Instead of risking offence by accepting the hospitality of one of its many clans, he left the choice to Allah – through the ambulations of his camel. On the spot where the camel settled herself, the Emigrants helped him build the house that would become, after the Ka'ba, the foremost mosque of Islam. It consisted of the simplest of structures, a courtyard overlooked by a number of flat-roofed rooms or huts, sur-rounded by a sun-baked mudbrick wall. It was here that he received petitioners and visitors and conducted the thrice-daily prayers at which the whole of the Muslim community was present; it was here that he organized and directed the affairs of the infant Islamic state, whenever he was not actually campaigning in the field (which took up most of his time); it was to be in one of these rooms – beneath the floor of that occupied by his favourite wife, 'Aisha – that he would be buried on his death, ten years after arriving in Medina: the ten years of his active career that would transform Arabia and shake the world.

Having established his headquarters, Muhammad set about defining the relationship between the Muslims and the tribes of Medina. Accord-ing to one tradition, each of the Ansar swore an oath of brotherhood with one of the emigrants. A detailed agreement governing their relations, however, has been preserved in a written document considered auth-entic by most western and all Muslim scholars. According to this docu-ment, subsequently known as the Constitution of Medina, 'the believers and Muslims of Quraish and Yathrib [Medina] and those who follow and are attached to them and fight alongside them . . . form a single community [umma] distinct from other men.' The Jews are specifically included in the Umma: 'Those Jews who follow us are entitled to our aid and support so long as they shall not have wronged us or lent assistance against us.'

The Umma or community referred to in the agreement – which follows the lines of a *hilf* or tribal pact such as traditionally formed a nomadic confederation – is composed of groups (rather than individuals) consist-ing of the Muhajirin, the Arab clans of Medina and the Jewish clans attached to them. Each group formed a single unit for the purposes of paying blood-money. Pagan allies are evidently admitted, since they are specifically mentioned. Muhammad must already have been anticipating conflict with the Quraish, so his primary concern was the political one of preventing them from making common cause with the Meccans: 'No pagan is to give protection to any person of Quraish, either his goods or his person.' The Muslims themselves, however, were bound by stronger obligations. They were to help any of their number seriously in debt over blood-money or the payment of ransom; they were never to take the side of an unbeliever against a Muslim; all Muslims, however humble, were to be entitled to aid and protection; in the event of war, no one was to make a separate peace with the enemy. They must maintain internal law and order, punishing the wrongdoers among them.

Muhammad's own role is primarily that of mediator: 'Whenever there is anything about which you differ it is to be referred to Allah and to Muhammad . . . for Allah is the most strict and faithful guarantor of this document.' In all other respects, Muhammad appears to be just one tribal chief among many – the Muhajirin constituting, as it were, his own tribe.

The Muhajirin had no means of subsistence: they had little in the way of stock, and could hardly be expected to live on the charity of the Medinese farmers for long without coming into conflict with them. The solution adopted by the Muslims was a traditional beduin one: to prey on the merchant caravans proceeding from Mecca. Other tribes, had they been strong enough, would have done the same in similar circumstances. What made for a radical break with custom was that as Quraishis themselves, the Muhajirin would be preying on their own kin. From a superior moral viewpoint they were justified in this, not only because their pagan relatives had treated them badly, but also because they had a legitimate interest in what, after all, constituted Quraishi property.

The earliest raids seem to have been small affairs, without booty or bloodshed. The first blood was spilled during the second year of the *hijra* (in January 624) when a Quraishi was killed in an ambush at Nakhla, south of Mecca. The caravan, which must have been a small one since it was attended by only four people, was captured and triumphantly brought back to Medina. Muhammad had misgivings about the raid, which occurred towards the end of the sacred month of Rajab, when, according to custom, bloodshed was forbidden. He withheld distribution of the booty until a revelation came down justifying the raid.

The Nakhla raid greatly helped the Muhajirin, for, in addition to the booty, they received 1,600 dirhams in ransom for the three prisoners. More important, perhaps, was the boost it gave to their prestige in the eyes of the Ansar. The Medinese, who had not taken part in the raiding so far, now became anxious to gain a share of the booty. In March 624, two months after the Nakhla raid, news arrived of a very large caravan returning from Gaza to Mecca, with goods estimated at 50,000 dinars. It was accompanied by about fifty merchants, representing all the Quraishi clans under the leadership of Abu Sufyan of 'Abd Shams. Every family in Mecca had an interest in its safe return.

Aware of the danger posed by the Muslims, Abu Sufyan called for reinforcements from Mecca. A huge force numbering nearly 1,000 men, just about every able-bodied man available, was sent under Abu Jahl to escort the caravan home. The relief force continued to advance on Medina after Abu Sufyan's caravan had passed out of danger by staying close to the sea. Forewarned of Abu Jahl's approach, Muhammad made for the strategic wells of Badr with about 300 men, most of them Ansaris. Muhammad had three of the four wells filled in, forcing the tired and thirsty Meccans to fight for water on ground chosen by their enemies. The Muslims spent the night in prayer. At dawn Abu Jahl's army advanced to be greeted by a hail of arrows from the Muslim archers. After a period of combat, Arab-style, between individual champions, a mêlée ensued which turned into a general rout of the Meccans, 49 of whom, including their leader, were killed. The Prophet watched the action from a palm-fronded booth behind the lines. After the battle he asked one of the Emigrants to see if Abu Jahl's body was among the slain. The man found the Quraishi leader mortally wounded. 'You have climbed high, little shepherd!' he said with his dying breath. The Emigrant cut off Abu Jahl's head and brought it to the Prophet, who gave thanks to Allah.

The political and ideological implications of Badr, the first major victory for Islam, were more important than the military ones. Like the Cromwellians after Naseby, the Muslims now had proof that their steadfastness had been vindicated. As the Quran proclaimed afterwards, 'It was not you who slew the enemy, but God who slew them.'[11] Before Badr, Medina had been little more than a place of refuge for a group of persecuted outcasts. After Badr, the feeling that God was on their side would carry the Muslims forward toward those much vaster victories that would culminate in the defeat of Byzantium and the collapse of Persia. Though mostly young and inexperienced in battle, they had shown that unity under the Prophet's leadership and the moral purpose engendered by the sense of absolute justice in their cause could defeat the bigger battalions of their enemies. They had learned that solidarity was the key to success. The Quraish – so the earliest accounts suggest – had been reluctant to kill their own relatives among the Muslims for fear of giving rise to a new round of vendettas. The faithful had had no such inhibitions about despatching their kin among the polytheists. The new solidarity of faith had triumphed over the older loyalties of kinship.

If Badr vindicated Muhammad the Prophet, it also greatly strengthened his hand as a political leader. Acting on a revelation received after the battle, he established an important precedent by distributing the booty equally among the Muslims. Resisting the demands of 'Umar that the 70 or so prisoners should be put to the sword, he kept all but two of them for ransom. The two he allowed to be executed had incurred his wrath in Mecca by comparing passages in the Quran unfavourably to parts of the Persian and Jewish scriptures, casting doubt on the authenticity of the revelation. Muhammad readily forgave his physical enemies, but rarely, if ever, his ideological opponents. It was about this time that he arranged for the assassination of the woman poet and satirist Asma bint Marwan, who had written verses ridiculing the Medinese tribesmen for obeying a leader not of their kin.

With the immediate threat to Medina passed, Muhammad was now faced with the most formidable source of ideological opposition – namely, the Jewish tribes. Although he had a high regard for the Jews as monotheists and had needed their support during the first embattled days in Medina, he must soon have realized that conflict would be inevitable. The Jews could hardly be expected to recognize his claims to prophethood without abandoning their own religious assumptions and their distinctive scriptural heritage and identity as God's chosen people. At some point, even before the battle of Badr, the break appears to have been formalized, when the direction of prayer – the *qibla* – was changed from Jerusalem to Mecca. The first of the Jewish tribes to be attacked by Muhammad after Badr was the Banu Qainuqa', a clan composed mainly of goldsmiths and other craftsmen. A market-place row involving the wife of a Muslim provided the pretext: a Jew and a Muslim were killed in the fracas and the Banu Qainuqa' withdrew to their quarter. The Muslims laid siege to them till they surrendered unconditionally.

Muhammad wanted to massacre the Jews but was dissuaded from doing so by 'Abdullah ibn Ubaiy, chief of the Khazraji clan, of which the Qainuqa' were clients. Instead they were given three days in which to quit the city, leaving their goods behind them. The spoils were enormous, and Muhammad kept one fifth for himself, in accordance with tribal custom. The two most powerful Jewish tribes, however, remained to be dealt with.

At about this time the Meccans, smarting from the defeat at Badr and from further raids upon their caravans, were preparing a new, more powerful expeditionary force. They assembled an army of 3,000 men, including dissident members of the Aws and clansmen from among their tributaries in Taif and among the beduin. They were led by Abu Sufyan, who had succeeded Abu Jahl as leader of the Quraish. As the army of the Quraish advanced on Medina, the Muslims and their allies had no alternative but to withdraw into their fortified dwellings, leaving the horses and camels of the enemy to gorge themselves on their freshly planted crops. The Medinese clan leaders held a council of war and decided at first to sit out a siege behind the defensible stone walls linking the different quarters. However, some of the younger Muslims who had missed the action at Badr urged the Prophet to attack the enemy. For a time Muhammad prevaricated; then he put on his suit of armour and decided to launch an offensive. Of the thousand or so men he had with him only one hundred had armour, and there were only two horses. The Jewish tribes, who had begun the sabbath, remained in their homes.

Half-way towards the hill of Uhud, where the Quraishi army was encamped, Muhammad sent back some of the younger boys whom he felt might prove a liability. At this point 'Abdullah ibn Ubaiy decided to retire with a third of the army, on the dubious pretext that the Muslims did not seriously intend to fight. As a clan leader, he was probably within his rights. He may, however, have hoped that a defeat for Muhammad would strengthen his own position, which had declined considerably since Badr.

The engagement at Uhud proved a disaster for the Muslims. At first things seemed to be going their way until Muhammad's archers, posted on the hillside, abandoned their posts in the expectation of booty and were mown down by the Meccan cavalry under the brilliant command of Khalid ibn al Walid (later to become the most outstanding of all the Muslim generals). About 70 Muslims were killed, including the Prophet's uncle Hamza. The prophet himself was badly wounded and at one time was even reported dead. The Quraish celebrated their triumph in the barbaric manner of the times, the women who accompanied them fashioning necklaces from the ears of their dead enemies.

Despite his victory, Abu Sufyan decided against trying to occupy Medina. The defeat of Badr had been avenged: he was still thinking in terms of traditional beduin warfare. Muhammad, for his part, lost no time in trying to regain his lost prestige. His wounds had scarcely been dressed before he set out in pursuit of the Quraish, a purely symbolic action which nevertheless boosted the morale of his supporters. The lesson of Uhud was not to be lost. If the victory of Badr had constituted proof that Allah was on the side of the Muslims, the defeat of Uhud had been ordained in order to test their faith, and to sort out the steadfast believers from the 'doubters' like 'Abdullah ibn Ubaiy and his followers.

The experience of Uhud and the defection of 'Abdullah now made it essential to deal with all possible sources of dissent, especially the remaining Jews. Convinced that the Banu Nadir were plotting against him, he presented them with an ultimatum. They must leave the oasis with their goods and chattels within ten days: otherwise they would be massacred. 'Abdullah ibn Ubaiy urged the Banu Nadir to resist. The Muslims began felling their palm-trees. After about a fortnight, the Jews surrendered. They were allowed to leave with such goods as they could carry on their camels, barring weapons. Most of them went to Khaibar, a mainly Jewish oasis settlement about 70 miles north of Medina.

After his failure to intervene successfully on behalf of the Banu Nadir, 'Abdullah ibn Ubaiy's prestige began to decline. His downfall came with the so-called 'Affair of the Slanderers', an incident in which Muhammad's youngest and favourite wife, 'Aisha, was accused of being unfaithful with one of Muhammad's men on the way home from a military expedition. 'Abdullah and his party, who included those Medinese who had become thoroughly disgruntled at the take-over of their city by the Meccan prophet and his followers, seized on the episode to impugn Muhammad's honour. For an Arab to have an unfaithful wife is a social disgrace. For a prophet, such a thing is unthinkable. Fortunately for Muhammad, after a period of suspense in which he was distinctly cool towards his young wife, there came down a revelation clearing her of all scandal. The faithful sighed with relief, while Allah himself turned on the slanderers. From this episode date the Quranic provisions stipulating that charges of adultery or fornication (punishable by 100 lashes) must be supported by four adult male witnesses, or eight female witnesses, to the act of copulation. About the same time Muhammad received further revelations demanding special protection for his wives.

Although Muhammad's warlike expeditions had led to a signal increase in his prestige among the beduin tribes, Abu Sufyan and the Quraish had not remained idle. A new hostile coalition was in the making, encouraged by the exiled Banu Nadir. Muhammad, on the advice, it is said, of the Persian freedman Salman al Farisi, decided to reinforce the Medinese defences by digging a ditch along the unprotected northern perimeter of the settlement. The invaders, who had no siege engines and despised manual work too much to build any, swore impotently at the ditch, which they considered some kind of outrage. A few individuals were killed by arrows and stones flung from either side. After a few weeks, the Quraishi army ran out of supplies and decided to withdraw.

Despite the victory of the Battle of the Ditch, Muhammad still did not feel safe. He suspected, with good reason, that during the siege the Jews of the Banu Quraiza had been in contact with the enemy, who were trying to persuade them to attack the Muslims from the rear. The Jews had apparently debated the idea, but little, if anything, was done. Nevertheless Muhammad decided to eliminate them once and for all. After a siege lasting 25 days the Banu Quraiza surrendered. They agreed to accept the arbitration of their leading ally, Sa'd ibn Mu'adh, chief of the Aws, who had been fatally wounded during the siege. He was brought on a donkey, surrounded by his fellow-tribesmen urging clemency. Unmoved, the dying man made everyone present swear that his sentence would be carried out. Only when this had been agreed did he pronounce it: all 600 adult males were to be killed, the women and children sold into slavery and the tribe's property divided among the Muslims.

Muslim writers tend to accept the massacre of the Banu Quraiza as the judgement of God for their treachery. Be that as it may, the ideological and political implications were paramount. It was not simply a question of eliminating the Banu Quraiza: the new allegiance to Islam must be seen to triumph over ancient loyalties. Politically the sentence, though harsh, was judicious. The Banu Nadir had been a menace since their expulsion to Khaibar. There was no alternative between massacre and exile. If permitted to survive, the Banu Quraiza would probably have joined their co-religionists, despite the ancient rivalries between them. Who knows if, in the course of time, Judaism might not have become the ideological standard of the Quraish, with very different historic consequences? The fighting men would never have submitted to Islam. But, to underline the fact that this was an ideological, not a racial, matter, the women and children were spared, to be eventually assimilated in the Muslim Umma. As if to demonstrate this by personal precept, Muhammad took one of the widows as his concubine.

Increasingly, Muhammad's thoughts were turning to Mecca. He continued to consolidate his alliances with neighbouring tribes. Still too weak to make submission to Islam a condition of any pact, he concentrated on persuading the beduin to disrupt the Quraishi trade, thereby isolating the Meccans and their allies, the Jews of Khaibar. For their part, the Meccans were becoming thoroughly demoralized. Their continuing ideological poverty was demonstrated at this time by the conversion to Islam of two of their most outstanding soldiers, Khalid ibn al Walid, future victor of Yarmuk, and 'Amr ibn al 'As, future conqueror of Egypt. No doubt opportunism as well as faith played a part in these conversions. The more far-sighted members of the Quraish were beginning to realize that since there was no beating Muhammad, the next best thing was to join him. This was probably not the first time that the Quraishis had thought of compromise. But they would find in due course that the terms of a compromise would be surprisingly generous – so generous, indeed, that the concluding phase of the Prophet's career and the subsequent period from his death in 632 to the 'Abbasid revolution of 750, could be described as the victory of the Quraish over Islam.

Towards the end of the sixth year of the *hijra* (March 628), the Prophet announced his intention of visiting Mecca in order to perform the *'umra* (lesser pilgrimage). He took with him about seven hundred men and four women. The men were armed only with their swords, which they kept sheathed according to custom. The Meccans, however, were alarmed, and deployed their armed men to prevent the Muslims from entering the Holy City. Muhammad headed for Hudaibiya on the edge of the sacred territory, where he received several emissaries from the Quraish, who returned impressed by the discipline and peaceful demeanour of the Muslims.

After discussions, a ten-year truce was signed between Muhammad and the Quraish, according to which the Muslims agreed to forgo the right of pilgrimage until the following year, when the Meccans would evacuate their city for three days, during which the Muslims would be allowed to perform the rituals. Many of the Muslims, including 'Umar, the future second caliph, protested vigorously at what they saw as a 'sell-out'. But Muhammad and Abu Bakr were more far-sighted: the Quraish had recognized the Muslims as equal parties and had given them a free hand to tackle the still pressing problem of the Jews of Khaibar. Muhammad returned to Medina and soon afterwards set off for the oasis with 1,600 men. The Jews were abandoned by their beduin allies and were gradually forced to submit, household by household. Muhammad spared their lives, taking half the date-crop and the better part of their possessions. The men were kept as slaves, the women distributed among the Muslims. Muhammad chose for himself a beautiful girl of 17 named Safiya, whose husband had been killed in the fighting. After the fall of Khaibar, the other Jewish colonies in the region submitted without a fight and were allowed to keep their goods on payment of the *jizya* or poll-tax.

The following year Muhammad set out on the pilgrimage, in accordance with the terms of the Hudaibiya treaty. Accompanied by 2,000 Muslims, he entered the empty city, performing the *tawaf* on his camel, as well as the *sa'i* between Safa and Marwa. Bilal, the former Abyssinian slave, made the call to prayer from the Ka'ba roof. While he was in Mecca Muhammad is related by some traditions to have married his cousin Maimuna, daughter of his uncle 'Abbas, and to have consummated the marriage in the state of *ihram*.

With the elimination of their last remaining Jewish allies, time was running out for the Quraish. The fickle beduin tribes, always opportunistic, were beginning to flock to Muhammad's standard. The Hudaibiya treaty no longer reflected the true balance of power in the Peninsula. Incidents over blood-money and clashes between beduin clients of Muhammad and the Quraish were making it unworkable. Abu Sufyan decided to confront the coming crisis by visiting Medina and making terms with the Prophet. The true picture of what took place has probably been distorted, since the earliest accounts date from the 'Abbasid period and were written by historians concerned with discrediting Abu Sufyan, ancestor of the Umayyad caliphs. It appears, however, that the Prophet and the Quraishi leader negotiated what followed. In January 630 Muhammad marched towards Mecca at the head of an army which eventually swelled to more than 10,000 as his beduin allies joined him on the way. They halted outside the *haram* area, where Abu Sufyan came to the Prophet and formally embraced Islam. The Quraishi leader then returned to Mecca, where he delivered Muhammad's terms to the people: there would be no danger so long as the city surrendered peacefully. (A very similar arrangement occurred in 1925, when the city fathers came to 'Abd al 'Aziz al Sa'ud, who offered almost identical terms.)

On 30 January 630 Muhammad entered the now deserted streets of the Holy City. Only a few pagans offered resistance in one quarter, where they were soon rounded up by Khalid ibn al Walid. The Prophet made for the Ka'ba and touched the Black Stone with his stick, proclaiming 'Allahu Akbar' (God is Greater), the traditional war-cry of Islam, in a loud voice. After performing the *tawaf* on his camel, he ordered the idols to be thrown down from their pedestals. Then he called on the pagan Quraish to make their homage to him, which they did by filing past him as he sat on the rock of Safa.

An amnesty was proclaimed for most past offences; only a few individuals were proscribed. Characteristically, they were intellectual enemies. They included the composer of some satirical verses against Muhammad, as well as the woman singer who had chanted them. Another was a former scribe who came to doubt the absolute authenticity of the Quranic revelations, when the Prophet had allowed him to include a statement of his own in the Quranic text. His life was spared, however, after the intervention of his foster-brother, 'Uthman ibn Affan.

Muhammad had not been long in Mecca before he was confronted with a new danger. The tribal confederation of the Hawazim, traditional enemies of the Quraish, were amassing against him, in conjunction with some anti-Quraishi elements in Taif. Within a fortnight of the conquest of Mecca he had taken to the field once more at the head of an army of 12,000. He defeated the tribesmen at Hunain, but failed to take Taif. The women of the Banu Hawazim were shared out among the Muslims, but returned to their menfolk when the latter embraced Islam. In distributing the spoils, Muhammad infuriated some of the longest-serving Muslims by outrageously favouring the newly converted Quraish. Abu Sufyan and his sons, including Mu'awiya, future founder of the Umayyad dynasty, were each given one hundred camels. Even members of the Quraish who had not yet been converted received some of the spoils. The Medinese became seriously alarmed that Muhammad, now 'King of the Hejaz' in fact as well as in the appellation of his enemies, would settle permanently in Mecca. They were greatly relieved when he returned to Medina.

The Prophet Muhammad was now approaching the end of his life. He must have been about 60 at the Battle of Hunain, when his personal resolution in the face of the enemy's cavalry converted what might have been another Uhud into a major victory. Among the beduin tribes, the bandwagon effect, already building up before the 'conquest' of Mecca, had become a landslide. Delegations from all parts of Arabia came to Muhammad asking to be included in his system. The tribes which made the pact with Medina promised troops and pledged themselves not to attack any other tribes in the alliance. Many, however, embraced Islam only in a nominal sense while remaining attached to pagan practices. Muhammad understood – as his more zealous followers did not – that it would take several generations to 'Islamize' the new adherents. What counted for the present was the protection they could afford the fledgeling state he had succeeded in creating in Medina: the state which must outlive him in order to become the vehicle for Allah's purpose.

The problem to which the Medinese system was primarily addressed was the maintenance of social cohesion. The new solidarity of the Umma, the Islamic community, replaced the old solidarity of the *qawm* or tribe. The doctrine of the Day of Judgement proclaimed in the Quran implied that individuals were primarily responsible for their actions, regardless of birth. This was a reflection on the psychological plane of material changes in Mecca itself, where a society of beduin traders was being transformed into one of merchant capitalists. Similar tensions between individualism and group identity had been occurring in Medina, where the clan system of formerly nomadic tribes was proving increasingly ill-adapted to the needs of an agricultural community. A clan system which helps maintain an overall ecological balance under desert conditions breaks down when applied in an environment necessitating a much higher degree of cooperation between different social groups.

The old tribal system had been at the root of Arabia's problems, barring the road to future development. What had once worked well in the desert was becoming unsuited both to the caravan-city and to the oasis. Yet tribalism could not be eliminated overnight, or even abolished altogether. What was required was a new field of loyalty which would smooth the transition to a more individualized society without, however, exposing the individual to a feeling of utter helplessness. The new solidarity provided by Islam was the Umma, a super-tribal entity whose loyalty was to Allah, the super-tribal deity. All other allegiances, symbolized by inferior deities or tribal totems, were either abolished or so subsumed within the new allegiance to the Prophet's community that in due course they could be expected to 'wither away'. Naturally, none of these changes came about spontaneously. They occurred as a result of a carefully worked-out social and ideological programme.

This programme came under five heads. Known to Islam as the 'Five Pillars' of the faith, it is still the basis of belief and practice common to all Muslims. The first pillar is the *shahada*, the profession of faith by which the Muslim acknowledges his allegiance to God and His prophet: 'I testify that there is no god but Allah, and I testify that Muhammad is the Messenger of Allah.' Utterance of the *shahada* before witnesses is sufficient for full conversion to Islam. The second pillar is *salat*, or prayer, a basic duty performed both individually and publicly. In its public or congregational form performed on Fridays and feast-days, prayer is a means of reinforcing group consciousness and expressing social solidarity. Muhammad probably chose Friday as the day for public prayer because this was the time when his Jewish allies were themselves preparing for the sabbath. But the Quran explicitly rejects sabbatarianism. Apart from the congregational prayers usually held at noon, Friday was traditionally a normal work-day in Muslim lands, and indeed one which provided special opportunities for business.

The physical movements of Muslim prayer were, in addition to any spiritual dimension, a means of promoting group solidarity. The old kinship groups of Arab society had been reinforced by all sorts of subtle physical traits: an individual's membership of a particular tribe might be determined by a special gait or gesture. By subjecting itself at regular daily intervals to a series of identical and repeated physical actions, the Umma subsumed the particularisms of tribal or racial identity in a common physical discipline. In the original context of beduin Arabia, and in parallel conditions elsewhere, the Muslim prayer had an effect similar to the discipline of the parade ground: the new recruits were welded into a single uniform body under Allah's generalship. The psychological impact of prayer was also effective at an individual level: by insisting on the interruption of ordinary mundane activities at least three times each day, it continuously reminded the believer of the superior claims of God and the community.

The social obligations of Islam are made most explicit in *zakat*, third of the five pillars. The word has evolved semantically from its primary meaning – 'purification' – to its current definition of 'obligatory charity'. The implication is clear enough: personal property must be 'purified' by payment of one's dues to the community, for the upkeep of its weaker members. Zakat introduced a rationalized form of social security in place of the largesse formerly administered by tribal chiefs. Traditionally it consisted of a two and a half per cent annual levy on income and capital – reflecting, like the Muslim inheritance laws, conditions in a society in which wealth consisted in stock or merchandise rather than land. The distinction between capital (i.e., land) and income (i.e., crops) is much less evident in pastoral than in agricultural conditions, since herds are continuously increasing themselves.

The fourth pillar of Islam is *sawm*, the annual fast of Ramadan, the ninth month in the lunar calendar, during which all food, drink and sexual activity are forbidden between dawn and dusk. The arduousness of the regime varies according to the time of year in which Ramadan falls (as well as the geographical latitude). In general it can be said that the fast confers on the community many of the benefits of asceticism, such as self-discipline and mental control over bodily needs, without falling into the excesses of the eastern churches, where 'spiritual athleticism', by separating the ascetics from ordinary lay believers, tended to undermine group cohesion.

The fifth pillar of Islam, the Hajj, was not instituted in its final form until the Farewell Pilgrimage of 632. While directly connecting the new community with the traditions of Arabian paganism, it also reinforced Islamic cohesion by making the Umma aware of itself as a physical entity.

In addition to the 'five pillars', the community was enjoined to observe certain Quranic injunctions, most of them adapted from existing Arabian customs. Marriage was contractual and polygyny (one man and up to four wives) permitted. The provision was realistic in a warrior society in which women had always been considered part of the booty. In time the practice of marrying non-Muslim women would facilitate the breaking down of ethnic barriers within the community, contributing to Islam's multi-racial character: thus the Hui Muslims of China, descendants of Arab traders, are Chinese by race, just as the Senegalese Muslims are black. The Quran's insistence that every wife should be treated equally should have meant that captive women were accorded the dignity of wives, ruling out concubinage. This law, like the ban on wine-drinking, tended to be observed in the breach by the Muslim ruling classes. The laws on inheritance, by which the sons shared equally in the property of their parents and the daughters received half the portions of the sons, accorded with the needs of a pastoral community organized on patriarchal lines. Unlike agricultural holdings, livestock can be subdivided without becoming less productive.

The dietary rules of Islam were simple and practical ones for the region, and generally reflected existing Arab practice. The ban on carrion is obviously necessary in a hot climate. Pork contains dangerous bacteria and parasites if not properly cured or cooked, and is not generally economical to produce in non-forested, arid regions. However, its general prohibition by the Hebrews and Arabs may also have reflected the prejudices of pastoralists against the eating habits of peasant-cultivators. The insistence that no one must eat meat over which any name other than that of Allah had been pronounced – usually converted into a positive injunction by adoption of the Halal dietary provisions – was obviously aimed at discouraging idolatry. The progressive prohibition on wine and other intoxicants, while aimed at promoting social decorum, may also have had a religious basis, since wine played an important part in Christian and some pagan rituals.

The Quranic rules were not always clear in themselves, and in later centuries they would receive much elaboration from the scholar-lawyers. There is no way of knowing how strictly they were applied during the Prophet's lifetime. Where they involved a simple adoption or modification of Arab custom it seems reasonable to suppose they were generally adhered to. Some rituals, including prayer, may have been observed more strictly by the pious of later generations: it seems that in the Prophet's time it was considered sufficient to pray three times each day, instead of the five times stipulated by the lawyers. The Quran hints at certain sexual practices – including temporary marriages – forbidden in later times. Apart from this, however, there can be no question but that the Prophet allowed himself, and was permitted by the Quran, to have wives well in excess of the four permitted under Islamic law.

According to the earliest sources, Muhammad married at least eleven, possibly fourteen, women after Khadija's death. Most of his marriages had a political significance: like any beduin chief, he cemented his alliances within or outside his tribe through marriage. Thus, nine of the Prophet's wives, including Khadija, were from the Quraish or clans allied to them. Three more were captives, two of them from the defeated Jewish tribes: this again accorded with prevailing custom. They included Juwairiya, daughter of the Chief of the Banu Mustaliq, defeated by Muhammad in 626, Raihana, whose husband was a member of the Banu Quraiza massacred in 627, and Safiya, taken captive at Khaibar in 628. In addition, Muhammad had one Christian wife, Mary the Copt, a concubine sent to him by the ruler of Egypt in 628. Mary bore the Prophet a son, Ibrahim, who died in infancy. None of Muhammad's wives came from the Ansar, perhaps because he did not wish to favour any one Medinese clan above the others.

However, although political motives could be found for most of Muhammad's marriages, personal desire definitely played a part, as is made clear by the earliest accounts of his life. Modern Muslim writers who show very Victorian attitudes towards sex find his voluptuousness embarrassing, and try to explain it away. His near contemporaries, however, evidently found nothing unusual in his amorousness, or in the multiplicity of his wives. Again, there are parallels with that other great Arabian tribal chief, 'Abd al 'Aziz al Sa'ud, who, like the Prophet, boasted that he loved 'prayer, sweet odours and women'. In pastoral societies prestige and virility are often closely linked, not least because the human community shares many of the features of the animal society by which it lives.

The problems caused by Muhammad's multiple marriages are alluded to in the Quran, which offers his wives the choice between the claims of this world and those of God and His Prophet. Having chosen the latter, they are ordered to conduct themselves with the dignity of their position.[12] In the same *sura*, the Prophet is told that he may marry no more women, 'even though their beauty should please him greatly'. However, it is also made clear that, because of the purity of his heart, Allah has allowed him sexual privileges denied to other men.

For the ordinary Muslim, the Quran laid down certain norms governing sexual conduct. No sexual relations were to be permitted outside marriage. *Zina*, meaning both adultery and fornication, is punishable by flogging – one hundred strokes for each partner, irrespective of whether they are married. Marriage itself is a civil contract and may be terminated by either party. If the wife terminates the contract without offence by the husband (*khul'*), she is obliged to give back her marriage portion. If the husband initiates the divorce by declaration (*talaq*), she retains it.[13] Men are allowed up to four wives at one time, women are permitted only one husband. This is consistent with the twofold aim of ensuring that all women from puberty onwards have the option of marriage – which the Quran insists upon as a duty, and of ensuring the paternity of children, essential to the maintenance of the patriarchal structure. Since the husband is responsible for the upkeep of his children, it is absolutely necessary that he should know that they are his.

Modernist writers have argued that the right of polygyny, which is clearly discriminatory, is effectively negated by provisions insisting that all four wives be treated equally – a provision which, in its broadest interpretation, would be impossible to fulfil. However, it is clear, from both the Quranic rules of marriage and the Prophet's own example, that equality of treatment refers strictly to legally enforceable matters such as a woman's right to her own household or to an equal share of her husband's property. The Quranic marriage-laws, as with other provisions, took over and modified existing beduin custom, in this case by strengthening the legal and personal property rights of women. In the context of a mainly pastoral society, polygyny acknowledged an important biological fact: a woman can only be pregnant with one man's child, while a man may father several children in the course of a single pregnancy. It also assumed that the purpose of sex was purely procreative. To allow a surplus of unmarried nubile women meant wasting an important human resource. A tribe's women, like its mares, ewes and she-camels, were an essential part of its capital.

In the long term, Muslim women would suffer a progressive loss of social and sexual rights *vis-à-vis* men. This probably had more to do with the situation prevailing in the conquered Byzantine and Sassanid territories during the period, at least two centuries after Muhammad's death, when the Islamic law was being formalized and consolidated, than with provisions explicitly outlined in the Quran. For example, the verse enjoining the faithful to address the Prophet's wives from 'behind a screen' (*hijab*), originally a matter of protocol, was later invoked to justify such radical forms of sexual segregation as the complete veiling of women. Similarly, in matters of dress generally, the Quran leaves vague the character of the garments considered suitable: it merely enjoins the women believers to 'lower their gaze and be mindful of their chastity, and not to display their charms [in public] beyond what may [decently] be apparent thereof'.[14]

Another aspect of the Medinese Umma which would have important implications for the future was its economic life. The collection of *zakat* (compulsory charity), as well as the voluntary donations known as *sadaqa*, provided for the poor and needy. In addition to these funds, the Prophet had at his disposal the fifth share of the booty which, according to tribal custom, was reserved for the chief. In practice this portion, which the Prophet received in his capacity as chief of the Umma, came to be the basis of the Muslim treasury – the *bait al mal* – from which the Muslim state financed such activities as the purchase of horses and other war material and the subsidies or bribes paid to secure the friendship of allied tribes. In addition to retaining his fifth share of the booty, mainly for military purposes, the Prophet appropriated certain lands for the common pasturing of horses, establishing a precedent for common ownership that would be extensively used by Caliph 'Umar in the conquered Byzantine territories.

Riba or usury, as prohibited in the Quran, is generally equated with the lending of money or goods at interest: 'O you who have attained to faith, do not gorge yourselves on usury [*riba*] doubling and redoubling it, but remain conscious of God so that you might attain to a happy state!'[15] Later generations of scholars would interpret the prohibition so strictly as to cover any form of profit or unearned gain, and elaborate tricks (*hiyal*), such as the double contract of sale, were invented to get round the ban. Modern Muslim authorities see the ban as applying to interest rather than profit: where money is earned on money, it is *riba* and therefore forbidden. Where it is earned through trade or productive investment, even if this involves buying cheap and selling dear, *riba* is avoided. Generally, the Quran does not condemn wealth as such, but only its pursuit as an end in itself which can interfere with social concern or spiritual awareness. It is in this spirit that modern Muslim economists have interpreted he prohibition as applying to risk-free interest rather than profit. Where the lender exacts his payment regardless of the borrower's circumstances his action may be exploitative and socially irresponsible. But if he stands to lose as well as to gain by the borrower's enterprise, he becomes not an exploiter but a business partner. Thus modern Islamic banking is based theoretically on equity participation or profit-sharing, rather than on lending at fixed rates of interest.

From the historical viewpoint, the polity created by the Prophet at Medina represented the germ of a system rather than a fully realized ideal. Compared with the flowering of Islamic civilization that would occur in the great riverine valleys, it was a rudimentary and primitive society. It would take several more centuries for this embryonic system to reach maturity. During the Prophet's lifetime the model was incomplete and far from monolithic. Many Muslims look back on the Medinese polity during the time of the Prophet and his immediate successors as a sort of desert utopia, where a state of perfection had been reached which could never be achieved by subsequent generations, like the Garden of Eden before the fall. Historically this view is nonsense; religiously it resembles the fetishistic attitudes against which the Quran so eloquently inveighs. The Medinese polity was born in blood and violence. The decade of the Prophet, its midwife, was a time of almost continuous warfare and armed struggle. What Medina offered was not a final solution to the ills of mankind, but rather a distinctive approach to certain crucial problems in the life of the Arabian peninsula. Because these questions were accurately perceived, the solutions proved generally successful – so successful, in fact, that later generations of Muslims never cease to imitate them.

In 632 Muhammad the Prophet embarked on his last ('Farewell') pilgrimage and finalized the Hajj and 'Umra ceremonies described in Chapter 1. He returned to Medina stronger than ever. If not actually ruler of a united Arabia, he was now, as the *de facto* head of the Quraish, its virtual master, as well as being a widely acknowledged religious leader. For the first time in its history, Arabia had been unified. This unprecedented political unity was the first fruit of the new religious system, under which allegiance to Allah and his Prophet overrode all prior allegiances based on tribal or family ties. The new solidarity of the Umma opened the way to what would become the most remarkable of Islam's historic achievements – the conquest, almost overnight, of the whole of the Sassanid empire and the southern Byzantine provinces of Syria and Egypt. No doubt the internal weaknesses of the empires, their exhaustion after years of mutual conflict and the religious and class divisions affecting their populations played a part in their defeat, among the most sudden in recorded history. But the decisive factor was the new religion. The greater mobility and superior fighting skills of the Arab warriors was – for the first and last time ever – directed towards a common cause. The energies that had previously wasted themselves in bitter tribal feuding were welded into a new, irresistible power.

The conflict with Rome and Persia was inevitable. Muhammad's system was a dynamic one, depending for its stability on continuous outward expansion. By the time the dwindling stock of Arab pagans remaining outside the *pax islamica* had become absorbed, the only avenue of expansion lay northward and eastward, beyond the Byzantine and Sassanid frontiers. Already, about ten months after the fall of Mecca, Muhammad had mounted a great expedition consisting of 20,000 to 30,000 men, which breached the Byzantine frontier at Tabuk, about 250 miles north of Medina. There he received tribute from a number of marcher lords, including the Christian king of Aila (modern 'Aqaba) and Jewish settlers from Jarba and Udra in Transjordan. He had then turned back, partly because his men were exhausted from the heat, partly in order to deal with opposition from a group of Muslims resentful at the privileges accorded to the recently converted Quraish.

Now, on returning from the Farewell Pilgrimage, he was preparing to launch another expedition against Syria when he fell ill and died suddenly on 8 June 632, in the arms of his beloved 'Aisha. He was buried on the spot where he died, in what is now the Prophet's Mosque in Medina.

The death of Muhammad caused an immediate crisis. The alliance he had created depended largely on his prestige as a great tribal chief who was also the bearer of divine revelation. Now the Message, incomplete or otherwise, had been delivered. Allah had ceased to provide his people with day-to-day guidance. The community must stand on its feet, or disintegrate.

In the half-century following the Prophet's death, disintegration seemed imminent. The infant state was disrupted by internal discord leading to civil war. The divisions have not yet healed, and account for the major sectarian splits in Islam. The survival of the new community was assured, not, as in Christianity, by the religious devotion of its martyrs, but by the military successes of its rulers. Survival on such terms was to prove problematic: whether as a result of Muhammad's foresight in 'coopting' them to lead the new community, or because they themselves 'sold out' on the original message, the first leaders of this new Muslim empire were to be the former pagans of Mecca, the Quraish.

The first task after Muhammad's death was to find a leader who could act as his successor (khalifa or caliph) in his purely human capacity as military commander and head, both spiritual and temporal, of the Umma. At first, some of the Medinese Ansar proposed that they should choose a leader of their own, leaving the Emigrants under the leadership of the Quraish. But the Ansaris soon realized that their own dissensions made it impossible to agree on a leader, and that the best prospects lay in following a Quraishi, who alone would have the prestige to maintain the fragile tribal alliances. After some deliberations, Abu Bakr emerged as the obvious choice: a Quraishi, one of the first converts to Islam and father of Muhammad's favourite wife 'Aisha, he had béen chosen by the Prophet himself to lead the pilgrimage of 631 and to act as Imam (or leader of the congregational prayers) during his final illness. The ablest Muslim general, Khalid ibn al Walid, was sent to quell the 'apostates' – Arab tribes who had renounced their allegiance to Islam on Muhammad's death and who, in some cases, were rallying round new leaders claiming to be bearers of divine revelation, like the 'false prophet' Musailima. The defeated tribes were bound more closely into the system and forced to pay *zakat*.

Abu Bakr's death in 634 thus saw the Islamic state ready to embark on the extraordinary expansion which, within less than a century, would bring it from the shores of the Atlantic to the Indus valley. Before he died, Abu Bakr, after consultation with a few of the Quraishi leaders, had designated 'Umar his successor as being 'the best among the Muslims' and therefore the man most fitted to be caliph. During the reign of 'Umar the sporadic raiding of the tribes gave way to a full-scale war of conquest. The governments of the territories surrounding Arabia collapsed like ninepins.

In 635, Hira, capital of Iraq, was occupied and forced to pay tribute. In 636 the Byzantine army in Syria was defeated by Khalid at the Yarmuk, opening the way to the conquest of Jerusalem and the fertile Palestine littoral. In 637 the main army of the Sassanids was defeated at Qadisiya on the Euphrates. After this most of the cities of Mesopotamia, including Ctesiphon, the imperial capital, surrendered to the Muslims. In 641 'Amr ibn al 'As entered Egypt; the following year he occupied Alexandria, the Byzantine capital, having founded a new city on the Nile near the old Persian fortress of Babylon. By the time of 'Umar's death in 644 the Arab raiders were reaching as far as Barqa (Tripolitania) in the west and the central Iranian highlands in the east.

The collapse of the Byzantine and Sassanid armies was hastened by the defection of their Arab auxiliaries who, sensing defeat in the air, went over to the invaders. The morale of the Arabs was, like that of the Muslims after Badr, greatly encouraged by these successes, which proved once again that Allah was on their side. (Even today the rapidity of these early successes is adduced by some Muslim writers as 'proof' of Islam's divine origin.) But the military weakness of the Romans and the Persians was also indicative of wider social and religious discontent in the conquered provinces. The Christian peasants of Syria and Egypt had no religious or political allegiance to the Greek-speaking upper classes. The Aramaean-speaking peasants were closer to the Arabs in blood and language than to their Hellenized overlords, who retreated, with their remaining armies, into the Anatolian highlands. The Copts of Egypt had long been persecuted by the Melkites. They saw no point in making common cause with their persecutors against the Arabs, especially since the latter made no attempt, initially, to convert them to Islam. The loss of Ctesiphon deprived the Sassanids of the political and religious centre from which they might have continued resistance, while the occupation of the well-irrigated and cultivated Iraqi plain deprived them of the revenues with which to finance a counter-offensive. Unlike Syria and Egypt, which were mere provinces of the Byzantine Empire, Mesopotamia was central to the Iranian polity. So, whereas the Graeco-Romans would remain a thorn in the flesh of Islam for eight more centuries, the ancient lands of the Sassanids became the base for much of its later expansion.

But this is to look far ahead. During the reign of 'Umar and his successors, the Islamic polity had still to be consolidated. The conquest of Persia, Syria and Egypt had been accomplished by what was still in effect a loose coalition of Arab tribes under Quraishi leadership. 'Umar's problem, like that of his predecessor Abu Bakr and Muhammad himself, was to prevent this coalition from collapsing into a welter of competing tribal interests which would rapidly tear the Islamic polity to shreds. He achieved his task in two ways: by encouraging the expansion of the empire through the continuing *jihad* or holy war; and by systematic indoctrination of his beduin soldiers, aimed at replacing tribal allegiances with loyalty to the new theocracy based on obedience to God and the commandments of His Prophet.

Muhammad and Abu Bakr had realized that the only way to prevent the Medinese polity from collapse was to maintain its outward momentum. The fragile tribal alliances upon which it depended would survive so long as the prospect of fresh gains continued to attract beduin support. But such a policy, pursued in isolation, must ultimately prove self-defeating. Having made themselves rich with plunder and masters of the settled regions of the fertile crescent, the nomads would want to enjoy their new-found luxuries. Like previous invaders of Egypt, Mesopotamia and Palestine, they would end by becoming a new land-owning elite living off the peasants. In due course their descendants would become assimilated into the more advanced cultures of the region, losing their distinctive identities in the process.

'Umar's way of avoiding this danger was to discourage assimilation. Except in Damascus, the regional Byzantine capital in Syria, the Arab soldiers were kept in military compounds outside the main cities of the conquered territories. The distinctive Arab cities of Fustat, near Egyptian Babylon, and Basra and Kufa in Iraq were founded for this purpose. No attempt was made at first to convert members of the confessional faiths – the Christians, Jews and Zoroastrians – in the occupied territories. On the precedent of Muhammad's treatment of the Jews of Khaibar, they were obliged to pay a special poll-tax – the *jizya*; otherwise they were treated as protected communities in the same manner as the clients (*mawali*) of ruling beduin tribes. The Muslims were thus less likely to face organized opposition from among the conquered peoples, some of whom had in any case welcomed them as liberators.

Most important of all, the Arabs were prevented from settling the conquered lands, which must discourage further military activity. Moveable booty, such as herds and valuables, was divided up among the tribesmen as in Muhammad's time, with a fifth reserved by the caliph for the poor and needy and for military purposes. But the caliph also kept all the land revenues, to be redistributed as part of a central fund in accordance with a register (*diwan*) of the Muslims and their dependents. Seniority in Islam counted for more than military muscle: in effect, the *diwan* enabled the military men to continue campaigning for the faith – and the moveable booty – secure in the knowledge that the state would look after their dependents.

Beduin loyalty to Islam was not, however, to be secured by purely financial measures. The Prophet's religious prestige as the bearer of divine revelation had been instrumental in securing beduin allegiance to him; that this was definitely the case is proved by the fact that, even before his death, several imitators or 'false prophets' appeared on the scene, seeking to supersede older tribal allegiances in a similar manner. The doctrine that Muhammad was the last or 'seal' of the Prophets, only broadly hinted at in the Quran, may well have been fixed during 'Umar's reign, with the aim of finally 'nailing' the false prophets as frauds. In the absence of the Prophet himself, there remained the Quran and the common discipline of prayer. In each of the garrison towns a mosque was built (usually a square enclosure with pillars at one end, a plan derived from the Prophet's home in Medina). Quranic reciters were sent as missionaries to instruct the faithful in prayer and hammer home God's messages to the troops. The Muslim family law, which tended to be laxly observed in the Prophet's time, was tightened up, with a ban imposed on short-contract marriages and tougher penalties for adultery and fornication.

'Umar died in 644, aged 52, murdered by a Persian captive. A great, bearded giant of a man, he inspired fear rather than love. His sternness became proverbial, but he was also respected for his integrity, being as harsh with himself as with others. As he lay dying, he appointed a committee of six – all of them Quraishis – to choose his successor. The leading candidates were 'Uthman ibn 'Affan of the Umayyad clan, husband of the Prophet's daughters Ruqaiya and Umm Kulthum; and 'Ali, the Prophet's first cousin from his own Hashimi clan and husband of his daughter Fatima. 'Uthman was chosen, possibly because it was thought he would continue 'Umar's policies. 'Ali, who had been raised in the Prophet's household and had been closer to him than any other male relative, may already have voiced some opposition to these policies, which he was not convinced accorded with the Quran or the Prophet's own actions. The election of 'Uthman the Umayyad may well have finally confirmed his suspicions that the Quraishis, despite their formal piety, were becoming too worldly and 'selling out' Islam's universal spiritual message. The Umayyads, under their leader Abu Sufyan, had been the most inveterate of Muhammad's enemies and had only embraced Islam opportunistically when there seemed no other way of promoting their clan interests: why should they now be cornering the best jobs for themselves? Although 'Uthman, an early convert and Companion of the Prophet, was personally devout and above suspicion, he may well have been considered by 'Ali and his supporters too weak to oppose the ambitions of his relatives, led by his exceptionally able young secretary, Marwan.

In fact, with the accession of 'Uthman, the Islamic state was about to face its first major internal crisis, resulting in the sectarian divisions that persist to this day. These will be examined in more detail in a later chapter. Here it need only be said that the seeds of conflict such as occur in all ideological movements were present, and that considerations of interest and religious principle were inextricably bound together. 'Uthman faced opposition from two quarters. First there were the soldiers, especially in Egypt, who felt that the stipend system was depriving them of their just deserts as conquerors, and that too many of the most lucrative posts in the empire were going to Umayyads. Second, there were the wealthy Meccans, whose displeasure 'Uthman incurred for similar reasons. Unlike 'Umar, 'Uthman had been unable to prevent the richer Meccan families from settling in the provinces, especially the Iraq, and conducting business ventures there, to the annoyance of the local Arabs. But he had taken a stand to prevent them from appropriating large tracts of state land in the Sawad, the irrigated region, by forcing them to transfer their agricultural holdings to the oases of the Hejaz.

These discontents reached their climax in 656, when a group of Arab soldiers, believing themselves to have been double-crossed in their dealings with the caliph, broke into 'Uthman's house and murdered him. In so doing they unleashed the five-year civil war known as the first *fitna*. The mutineers and most of the Medinese acclaimed 'Ali caliph, as 'First among the Muslims'. But 'Aisha, supported by Zubair and Talha, two of the Prophet's closest companions, called upon 'Ali first to punish 'Uthman's murderers, who had now come out in open support for him. 'Ali withdrew to Kufa, where most of his supporters were ranged, 'Aisha and her followers to Basra. The two armies met near Basra, where 'Ali proved victorious in a battle watched by 'Aisha from the palanquin mounted on the back of a camel (hence its name, the Battle of the Camel). Zubair and Talha were killed, but 'Aisha was sent back to Medina with full honours due to a Prophet's widow.

This, however, proved to be only the beginning of 'Ali's troubles as caliph. Mu'awiya, son of Abu Sufyan (now deceased) and after 'Uthman's death leader of the Umayyads, refused to recognize him. Instead Mu'awiya demanded that 'Uthman's murderers should be handed over to him for punishment, so that vengeance might be done according to the right granted by the Quran to a murder victim's next of kin.[16] 'Ali marched towards Damascus to enforce Mu'awiya's obedience, and was met by Mu'awiya's army near Siffin, on the Euphrates. After several months of inconclusive skirmishing, the two sides eventually joined battle. Victory seemed to be going to 'Ali's men when the Syrians, on the advice of 'Amr ibn al 'As, fixed sheets from the Quran on their lances and called for arbitration. The Iraqis were so convinced of the justice of their case that they allowed a neutral party, Abu Musa al Ash'ari, to act as their arbiter. Mu'awiya, on the other hand, used the services of his supporter 'Amr, ruler of Egypt. The arbiters were supposed to decide whether 'Uthman had been unjustly murdered (which would vindicate Mu'awiya's demand for vengeance), or whether he had, through his unjust policies and reprehensible innovations, brought just retribution upon himself (in which case his murderers were really only executioners of God's will). After several months of discussion the verdict evidently went against 'Ali, who repudiated it as being contrary to the Quran and the practice (Sunna) of the Prophet.

The negotiations therefore remained deadlocked, though by now they had acquired the aim of deciding who should be caliph. Mu'awiya was proclaimed by his supporters, but not confirmed by either of the arbitrators. He continued to play for time, with the connivance of 'Amr. The dispute was now acquiring a character familiar to students of twentieth-century Arab politics: Egypt was on one side, Iraq on the other and Syria between them, locked in a struggle for the leadership of the Arabs. In the end Mu'awiya's patience was rewarded. Dissension within his own camp was the cause of 'Ali's downfall. In 661 he was stabbed to death in the mosque at Kufa by a Khariji, one of a group of erstwhile supporters who had turned against his leadership.

The death of 'Ali brought to an end the Medinese era of Islam, or what has become known as the patriarchal caliphate. Among Muslims it is known as the era of the 'Rightly Guided' caliphs. Non-Muslims may find it astonishing that a period of continuous conquest and almost unremitting violence and civil war should have acquired the after-glow of a golden age. Of the four 'Rightly guided' successors to Muhammad, only one of them, Abu Bakr, died in his bed. Three were assassinated, two of them by fellow-Muslims. On the historical plane, only 'Umar exhibited outstanding qualities of leadership. Abu Bakr's caliphate was too short to make a lasting impact; 'Uthman, according to his opponents, weakly allowed himself to favour his Umayyad kinsmen, most of whom were late-comers to Islam. 'Ali, for all his well-attested saintliness, lacked one of the essential qualities of a leader, which is to carry one's supporters. Whereas his rival, Mu'awiya, knew well how to gain and retain the loyalty of his Syrian troops, 'Ali alienated his own followers by vacillating between a policy of appeasement (towards Mu'awiya) and harsh brutality (towards the Kharijis).

The historic religions all involve the idealization – or 'spiritualization' of events which were originally rooted in the politics of a particular period. The consciousness of the group, like that of the individual, achieves its identity by focusing on certain characters and events which retrospectively acquire an archetypal significance. Just as the child will at a certain stage in its development idealize its parents, being incapable of seeing them as ordinary mortals with an average endowment of virtues and defects, so the founders of charismatic movements acquire a supra-historical aura which raises them above the plane of normal humanity. The immortality conferred upon such figures – the 'giants' of history – may well be a function of the mythopoeic mind; but their potency as archetypes, as bearers of cultural norms and symbols around which individuals or groups can acquire a distinctive image of themselves, cannot be underestimated. The Christians, obsessed with the cruelty of a world which for so long failed to heed the message of the Jewish liberator, focused their consciousness upon the image of his tortured body and convinced themselves that suffering is the price of victory. The Muslims, as heirs to a triumphant period of conquest, could look back to the leaders of this period and find in them the landmarks which gave them their bearings in the new cultural and geographical territory they had won for themselves.

But there was also a historic basis to the seemingly idealized picture of the 'Rightly Guided' caliphs. The four patriarchal caliphs were all men who had been close to the Prophet, who had been in daily contact with him and had assimilated something of his remarkable personality. For this reason they were seen by their contemporaries as bearers of a special authority or charisma which distinguished them from the younger men who would now inherit Muslim power. The conflict between two such men of proven virtue and steadfastness as 'Uthman and 'Ali, and their kinsmen Mu'awiya, Yazid and Husain, is not reducible to petty ambition and weakness, however heroic or black their characters may have appeared to their followers or detractors in later generations. The conflicts they fought out, and in some cases paid for with their lives, were conflicts inherent in all ideological movements. They were the conflicts of idealism versus pragmatism, of the universal claims of truth against the practical needs of politics. In this respect they were not dissimilar from the conflicts which developed after the French Revolution, or after the Bolshevik seizure of power in Russia. Could the revolution be launched over the whole world, or should it first be consolidated within the confines of a single country? Could the new solidarity of the Umma, based on the common observance of the Quran and the Prophet's Sunna, be the ideological base for a new Islamic order, or would that order first have to establish itself on the basis of Quraishi – and specifically Umayyad – power? As in the case of socialism in Russia, Islamic history found no conclusive answer to these questions, which represent the boundaries of its dialectic.

The Prophet of Islam created a new dynamic order out of the fissiparous bickerings of the Arabian tribes. The order was founded primarily on obedience to the commands of God, as revealed through the mouth of His Prophet. God the Creator, who made the world and manifested himself in the natural order, also had a blueprint for the human community which Muhammad, like the previous prophets, was entrusted to communicate to mankind. Belief in the truth of the Prophet's revelations was antecedent to the results it engendered in the world: the Islamic conquests were the *result* of the new religious faith, 'a remarkable testament to the power of human action mobilized by ideological commitment'.[17]

If the plan was divine, its execution was part of human history. If the blueprint was perfect, the material required to make it real and durable was human and therefore flawed. If the Islamic ideal was universal, and therefore consonant with the natural order of divine creation, Muslim society was subject, like all other human societies, to the conditioning of a particular time and circumstance. The problem of finding a balance between the ideal and the real, the perfection of Islam and the human and material facts of life, became the stuff of Islamic history from the Prophet's time down to the present.

Islam is the least 'other-worldly' of the great religious systems, the one which, above all others, seeks to realize its aims in this world. Though the Day of Judgement is perceived as the ultimate moral reckoning by which the worth of individual action is measured, the good society is generally seen as the necessary precondition to salvation. Since there is no church or form of sacerdotal mediation through which men and women may attain salvation regardless of political circumstance, they must in the last endeavour attempt to realize the ideal of pristine Islam – the Medinese utopia – in order to guarantee their survival in the hereafter. Thus the armed prophet of Medina would remain the perfect exemplar for Muslims of all ages, his career a model of moral and political action that would be consciously imitated by those seeking to create a juster social order in this world.

Time and again throughout Islamic history, pious men would follow the stages of the Prophet's life, withdrawing first from the world to develop their spirituality, then making the *hijra* with a devoted band of disciples to a distant place before launching the *jihad* that would reclaim the backsliding pagans for the true Islam. The pattern was a cyclic one, involving the perennial conflict between the city and the countryside, the townspeople and the pastoralists. In analysing the interaction of the religious and material factors governing this process, the great Arab philosopher of history Ibn Khaldun (1332–1406) developed a theory about state formation in North Africa which is still relevant to the study of most Middle East societies. In the arid zones, where rainfall is sparse, pastoralism must remain the predominant form of agriculture. Pastoralists, unlike peasants, are usually organized along tribal lines and are relatively independent of central government. They cannot be taxed or brought under the control of feudal lords who will appropriate a part of their produce. For the tribes, survival depends on maintaining what Ibn Khaldun called 'asabiya, group cohesion. When the tribes decide to unite, their superior cohesion, mobility and fighting skills put the city, the seat of government, at their mercy, for Muslim city life lacks 'asabiya. The reason for the city's lack of 'asabiya will be explained in Chapter 4, but it is due, at least in part, to the uncompromising individualism of the Shari'a law, which recognizes no corporative groups outside the family. When the tribesmen conquer the city, they usually end by founding a dynasty there, which lasts for three or four generations until, corrupted by luxury and the loss of 'asabiya, they are replaced by a new dynasty from the pastoralist fringes, repeating the cycle.

Ibn Khaldun's theory applied, in its classic formulation, to the North African milieu he knew and understood best. But it can be modified to suit the conditions of the more sophisticated societies of Egypt and the Ottoman Empire, where the pattern was institutionalized. In Egypt the Mamluks, who ruled from the thirteenth to the eighteenth centuries, maintained themselves against the disintegration of 'asabiya by constantly replenishing their stock with new warriors, bought as boys from Central Asia, whom they trained up in their own households. Similarly, the Ottoman Sultans maintained a form of, as it were, artificial 'asabiya by recruiting from the Christian Balkan provinces janissaries, whom they systematically trained up for war and administration.

In the classic tradition, as we shall see in the following chapters, the banner of militant Islam, purged of heretical accretions and restored to its pristine purity, would be the rallying point around which tribal forces would coalesce and, fired by religious zeal, descend upon the cities. Here they would often find allies in the 'ulama, guardians of the legal and scholarly traditions, who would ensure the orthodoxy of the newcomers, or at least guarantee that the urban population would be insulated against heretical excesses introduced by the newcomers. Thus the Muhammadan paradigm mediated the conflict between the city and countryside, converting the marauding pastoralists of the 'lands of insolence' beyond government control into the guardians of the orthodox legal tradition: in Ernest Gellner's metaphor, the 'wolves' became 'sheepdogs'. This pattern of Khaldunian 'musical chairs' applied, with regional variations, in most of the central Islamic lands, from Morocco to Chinese Turkestan, until the present century, when motorized transport and air-power enabled central governments, backed by the European powers, to assert themselves effectively and more or less permanently over the marginal regions that had once been the breeding-ground of pastoral revolutionaries. The process is not yet quite complete: there are parts of Kurdish-speaking Iraq, and most of Afghanistan outside the cities, that are not yet subject to central government.

Nor has the factor of *'asabiya* ceased to be important. In the absence of corporative institutions, kinship remains the principal form of social solidarity. In the Middle East and many other Muslim lands tribal and family *'asabiya* have retained their importance as political factors into the age of the computer and the jet aircraft, and in many cases are actively reinforced by these modern inventions. At the same time Islam, paradoxically perhaps, militates against all such sectional loyalties. The Prophet himself is related to have said, in a *hadith* (tradition) recorded by Abu Dawud: 'He is not of us who proclaims the cause of *'asabiya*; and he is not of us who fights in the cause of *'asabiya*; and he is not of us who dies in the cause of *'asabiya*.'[18] When asked to explain the meaning of *'asabiya*, he is said to have replied: 'It means helping your own people in an unjust cause.' Muhammad's career, as well as the social and ideological programme represented by the 'five pillars', was specially designed to break down the barriers of *'asabiya* between rival tribes, replacing it with the deeper and more universal loyalty to the Islamic Umma. Just as Islam was aimed at eroding tribalism, it encouraged the movement of pastoralists into permanent settlements or cities. It was an urban religion conceived in a pastoral milieu, one whose aim was to maintain the supremacy of the former over the latter. It was thus a two-edged sword, upholding the existing political order when this seemed to accord with the commands of God and his Prophet; undermining it, or sanctioning its replacement, when it appeared to deviate too much from the 'boundaries' set by God (*huddud Allah*).

3 ❧ The Quranic World-view

Few things are more indicative of the cultural barriers between Europe and the Arab world than the sounds which emerge from the radio. In Europe the heavy, stressed rhythms of western rock music, punctuated by chat from fast-talking disc jockeys, create contrasting patterns which flash at the ear like so many multi-coloured neon signs. The aural world of Arab radio seems to operate within a much narrower range of frequencies. The complex rhythms and quarter-tones of eastern music are considerably more subtle than the strident impulses which hypnotize western listeners, while the language has a richness of tone and density of texture that seems to combine the warmth of a Bukhara carpet with the silken delicacy of Damascus brocade.

If Arabic is the key to this culture, the Quran is the key to Arabic. The language, if not invented, was specially developed for its transmission. The art of writing was rudimentary until the necessity for accurate versions of the Quran produced a dramatic evolution. According to Muslim tradition, the Prophet's utterances were first written down on whatever materials came to hand, such as shoulder-blades of camels, palm leaves, pieces of wood or parchment. These were later collected into *suras*, or chapters, under the supervision of the Prophet. No 'final' version of the text existed during his lifetime, for so long as he continued to receive revelations, the recension of God's Word was not complete. Nevertheless the order in which it is found is considered to be an aspect of the revelation, so it is assumed he was mainly responsible for its present form, under divine influence.

Many western scholars accept the Muslim version, though with several modifications. The final collection is supposed to have been made during the caliphate of 'Uthman, based on a text collated by the Prophet's principal secretary, Zaid ibn Thabit, and passed for safe-keeping to his widow, Hafsa, 'Uthman's daughter. Because of the manner in which rival versions of the same passages were being used as propaganda in the quarrels that had broken out inside the Muslim community, 'Uthman is supposed to have ordered an authorized version to be collected and copied, and all other variant texts destroyed. All present editions of the Quran (in which there are some slight variations, none of them important) are said to be based upon this so-called ''Uthmanic recension'. Some Western scholars have, however, radically questioned the Muslim account, using methods adapted from biblical textual analysis. They argue that the Quran as we know it was assembled at a much later date out of a fragmentary oral tradition deriving from the Arabian Prophet, but which also included a large quantity of exegetical or explanatory matter developed in the course of polemical disputes with Jews and Christians after the Arab conquest. This revisionist theory of the Quran has radical consequences for the early history of Islam, for it would suggest that the religious institutions emerged at least two centuries after Muhammad's time, to consolidate ideologically, as it were, the Arab conquest. It would mean that the Arabs, anxious to avoid becoming absorbed by the more advanced religions and cultures of the peoples they conquered, cast about for a religion that would help them to maintain their identity. In so doing they looked back to the figure of the Arabian Prophet, and attributed to him the reaffirmation of an ancient Mosaic code of law for the Arabs.

The revisionist theory has several attractions. It fits in with the available palaeographic evidence, which places the development of Arabic script much later than the Muslim sources. It provides an explanation of certain archaeological problems, such as the fact that the *qiblas* of certain early mosques in Iraq face Jerusalem rather than Mecca. It would account for the absence of any references in Jewish sources to Medina as a place where the Torah was studied; and it would account for the repetitious and inconsequential character of the Quran which so exasperated Thomas Carlyle as well as countless others who have struggled through translations in various European languages: 'I must say, it is as toilsome reading as I ever undertook. A wearisome confused jumble, crude, incondite; endless iterations, longwindedness, entanglement . . . insupportable stupidity, in short! Nothing but a sense of duty could carry any European through the Koran!'[1]

Such words would smack of sacrilege, not just to the devout Muslim, but to almost any Arab Christian, for whom the Quran, whatever religious truth it contains, is the perfection of language. Basically, the historiographical controversy about the Quran's origins, regardless of its scientific merits, reflects the same culture-gap which makes most Europeans dislike the sounds emitted by Arab radio, because their ears, and minds, are ill-tuned to them. An assault upon the Quran's authenticity is an assault upon an identity moulded by these very repetitions and subtle inflexions.

In a special sense, the Arabs are a people moulded by their scripture. The Hebrew and Christian texts were translated into Greek and Latin, and from them diffused into other languages and cultures. European ideologies and political movements no doubt owe much to biblical inspiration. The Mosaic vision of a land promised by God may, consciously or otherwise, have influenced the utopian dreams of protestant settlers and communists, as well as Zionists. But in all such cases many other cultural and political strands have been present. In the West, after the Latin Church had lost its liturgical monopoly, such cultural and ultimately political pluralism was encouraged by the translation of the Bible into different European tongues. Translation, which contributed much to the formation of national identities in the West, was made religiously possible by the pluralistic origins of the Bible itself, which consists of most of the Hebrew scriptures plus an originally oral Aramaic tradition transcribed into Greek. For Christians the Word of God was manifested in Christ's person, not in the language in which he revealed God's speech. Thus in the earliest Christian centuries, national and regional squabbles took the form of conflicts about the nature of this Person. The doctrine that the Quran was the eternal and unalterable Word of God, revealed in Arabic (as the Quran itself states on several occasions), prevented any such diffusion of the Muslim scripture into the surrounding cultural landscape: the very intransigence with which the Arabs defended the integrity of their text was decisive in maintaining a common Arab identity, which would otherwise have disintegrated, like that of other nomadic conquerors both before and after Islam, into a multiplicity of new national groupings, such as occurred after Charlemagne in western Europe.

But what of the construction and style of the Quran, which so many Europeans have found dull, repetitious and incoherent? The most obvious difficulty for those brought up on the chronological sequence of biblical narrative, as well as narrative forms such as the epic, is the complete absence of sequentiality. The subject matter, including stories of the earlier prophets, punishment stories about those who failed to heed them, psalm-like lyric passages celebrating the manifestation of God's glory in nature, and the Leviticus-like legal prescriptions, are mostly jumbled up and diffused throughout the text. For instance, the Sura of Light contains one of the most celebrated passages in all mystical literature,* but the same *sura,* a few verses earlier, lays down details for the punishment of adulterers (100 lashes) and slanderers (80 lashes), and urges women not to 'swing their legs [in walking] so as to draw attention to their hidden charms'. This deliberate mixing of the sublime and the mundane, which Westerners might see as evidence of a 'consistent lack of logical structure', has in the didactic and liturgical context a powerful function. For, despite the proliferation of manuscripts of the Quran, and its extensive use in the highly developed art-form of calligraphic embellishment, it is primarily a series of texts designed for oral transmission.

No one who has visited Cairo or any other great Arab Muslim city could fail to notice the position the Quran still occupies in the oral culture of the more traditionally minded sectors of society. Public recitations of the Quran are an important part of such social events as weddings, circumcisions, funerals, wakes and visits to the tombs of dead relatives on feast-days. At Cairo wakes, which are held on the evening of burial and successive Thursdays, male friends and relatives are to be found gathered in brightly lit marquees decorated with arabesques of red and white appliqué work. In the richer, more westernized, parts of the city, they will be seated on gilt salon chairs, of the kind used at concerts or fashion shows. The *muqri,* or professional Quran reciter, may be seated cross-legged on the ground, or loudspeakers may be linked to a microphone in a nearby mosque. Some of the *muqris* become extremely popular – and wealthy. Those who cannot afford to hire a live *muqri* are often to be seen playing their offerings on cassette radios.

Popular piety is still very much alive in Egypt and other Arab countries whose poverty has prevented them from succumbing to the blandishments of consumer capitalism. Taxi-drivers of the traditional kind, who would not dream of overcharging their Muslim passengers, will have the name of Allah on electric-coloured stickers on the facia board, or em-

---

* 'God is the Light of the heavens and the earth. The parable of His light is, as it were, that of a niche containing a lamp: the lamp is [enclosed] in glass, the glass [shining] like a radiant star: [A lamp lit from] a blessed tree – an olive tree that is neither of the east nor of the west – the oil whereof [is so bright that it] would well-nigh give light [of itself] even though fire had not touched it: light upon light!'[2]

broidered on pennants which festoon the interior like the tassles of a lampshade. The meandering nasal tones of the *muqri* will often be playing on the cassette machine, if the driver is especially pious. Cairo taxi-drivers include some of the most devout – as well as the most foul-mouthed – people in the world.

The esteem in which Arabs hold the Quran is not just the result of a religious dogma: it is due to the fact that many people find in its sonorous, rhyming prose an aesthetic pleasure of the kind Westerners usually discover in fine music or painting. Its dense elliptical style is a rich fund of aphorisms, its riddles and allegories the source of countless legends. Although there is a discernible variation in style between the short ecstatic passages from the earliest Meccan period and the much longer *suras* of the Medinese period, the seemingly chaotic organization of the material ensures that each of the parts in some way represents the whole. Good Muslims, especially those groomed for religious leadership, are required to memorize the whole of the Quran at a very early age. Since it consists of some 120,000 words divided into 114 *suras* and 6,000 verses (*ayas*), this is a considerable feat which, in the nature of things, many people fail to master. Nevertheless, almost any one of the *suras* will contain, in a more or less condensed form, the message of the whole. This is especially true of the chronologically later *suras* placed near the beginning, in which most of the legislation is to be found. An only partially memorized Quran will, therefore, contain as much as a conscientious but uneducated Muslim will find it necessary to know.

The illogical organization of the text in fact renders it more accessible, and this is central to the Quran's didactic purpose. The more inaccessible the scripture, the greater the distinction between clergy and laity. While Sunni Islam certainly developed a rabbinical class of *'ulama* with a superior knowledge of the text and its interpretation, the fact that a substantial part of it was known to everyone in society militated against the emergence of a spiritual elite comparable to the Catholic or Orthodox priesthood.

Nevertheless, the need for such a class of interpreters was apparent from an early stage. Many passages are obscure, and cannot be understood without reference to the substantial body of exegetical literature, derived from the oral *hadith*-traditions which came to be selected and written down around the third century of Islam. There are many allusions to events in the Prophet's career which can only be explained from these sources. Thus the punishment stories, composed from

Arabian folklore and biblical materials, mostly date from the late Meccan and early Medinese periods, and are clearly intended as threats and warnings to the pagan Quraishis. The Medinese *suras* contain many references to such events as the division of the spoils after Badr, the cowardice of the 'hypocrites' at Uhud, the punishment of the Banu Nadir, Muhammad's marriages, and other events mentioned in the previous chapter.

The allusiveness of the Quran's style is, however, not confined to the circumstances of revelation. It is, in fact, integral to its didactic method, which could be described as a series of 'one-way dialogues' between God and the Prophet and between Muhammad and his auditors. The effect is not unlike listening to a person speaking on the telephone: one only hears half the conversation. The inaudible part of the discourse, Muhammad's unspoken questions, the arguments of his critics, and so forth, have to be reconstructed out of the exegetical literature, which draws on the vast body of *hadith*-tradition.

This exegetical literature became, in due course, a source of law: for only by detailed study of the so-called 'occasions' of revelation could the general prescriptions and prohibitions contained in the Quran be given the force of law. This was especially necessary in the case of apparently contradictory statements, such as the prohibition on wine. Thus *sura* 16:67 clearly allows the drinking of wine:

> And [we grant you nourishment] from the fruit of date-palms and vines: from it you derive intoxicants as well as wholesome sustenance . . .

However, this is evidently contradicted by 2:219:

> They will ask thee about intoxicants and games of chance. Say: 'In both are great evil and some uses for men. But the sin in them is greater than their usefulness . . .'*

An even stronger prohibition occurs in 5:90–91:

> O you who have attained to faith! Intoxicants, and games of chance, and idolatrous practices, and the divining of the future are but a loathsome evil of Satan's doing: shun it then, so that you might attain a happy state! By means of intoxicants and games of

* The translation of this Quranic quotation differs from that of Muhammad Asad.

chance Satan seeks only to sow enmity and hatred among you, and to turn you away from the remembrance of God and from prayer. Will you not, then, desist?

Without a chronology of revelation derived from the *hadith* literature, it would be impossible to determine whether wine was a possible benefit, an evil to be tolerated, or one to be prohibited absolutely. Although there was some disagreement about the order of some of the verses, the consensus was that 5:90, representing the strongest prohibition, was revealed after 2:219, and therefore overrules it; while 16:67 dates from the Meccan period, when Muhammad still allowed wine-drinking among his followers. One of the famous Quran commentators, Fakhr al Din al Razi, commenting on this passage, cites one of his predecessors:

Al Qaffal said that the wisdom of issuing the prohibition in these stages lies in the following: God knew that the people had been accustomed to drinking wine and drawing from it its many uses. Thus he also knew that it would be unbearable for them if he had prohibited them all at once [from the use of wine] and thus unquestionably [for this reason] he made use of these stages and kindness in the prohibition . . .[3]

More abstruse legal points occur in commentaries on 2:172, where the flesh of swine is prohibited. Are the pig's bristles, used for sewing leather, included in the ban? This was a subject on which authorities disagreed. There was also disagreement concerning the meat of the hippopotamus, known to the Arabs as *khinzir al ma*, 'water-swine'. Argument depended on whether the hippo's presumed 'swinishness' overruled its character as a water-creature, allowed under 5:96: 'Lawful to you is all water-game, and what the sea brings forth . . .'[4]

In order to deal with a host of similar problems, the exegetes developed a doctrine of abrogation, based on 2:106: 'Any verse/message [*aya*] which We annul or consign to oblivion We replace with a better or similar one . . .' According to the great Persian grammarian and exegete, Abu al Qasim al Zamakhshari (d. 1144), the verse was revealed in response to a challenge from the unbelievers, who had said: 'Look at Muhammad, now he commands his companions to do something, and then forbids it to them and commands the opposite. He says one thing today and retracts it tomorrow!' Zamakhshari continues:

> To abrogate a verse means that God removes it by putting another
> in its place . . . Every verse is made to vanish whenever the
> well-being [of the community] requires that it be eliminated –
> either on the basis of the wording or [by] virtue of what is right, or
> on the basis of both these reasons together, either with or without
> a substitute.[5]

Zamakhshari belonged to the rationalistic school of theologians
(Mu'tazilis) who believed that the Quran, having been 'created' in time,
could be interpreted with considerable allowances made for time-bound
changes due to historical and social conditions. The Mu'tazilis were
eventually defeated after attempting unsuccessfully to impose their
doctrines by force during the caliphate of Al Mamun (813–33), but the
doctrine of abrogation survived in a more restricted form. Some modern
authorities, including Muhammad Asad, have rejected it absolutely. The
word 'aya', according to Asad, means in this context a 'message' rather
than a Quranic verse, and therefore refers to the abrogation, by the
whole Quran, of the earlier Hebrew and Christian scriptures.

The activities of the exegetes were very far from being confined to legal
problems. Only about 600 of the Quran's 6,000 verses deal with legislative matters. Stories of the earlier prophets and the punishments meted
out to those who failed to heed them, ecstatic descriptions of God's
power in nature and the eschatological passages about paradise, hell and
the Day of Judgement occupy much of the rest. Sometimes the language
is explicit and self-explanatory, at other times it is highly allusive and
allegorical. The Quran itself is eloquent on this point:

> He it is who has bestowed upon thee from on high this divine writ,
> containing messages [ayas] that are clear in and by themselves, and
> those are the essence of the divine writ [umm al kitab], as well as
> those that are allegorical.[6]

In his commentary on this passage Zamakhshari writes: 'If the [meaning
of the] entire Quran [were clearly] determined men would come to
depend on it since it would be so easily accessible, and would turn away
from what they lack – research and meditation through reflection and
inference.'[7]

The memorizing and study of the Quran, which occupied such a large
part of the traditional Muslim education, has always been regarded as
the most meritorious of all religious activities. Assimilated and internal-

ized through constant repetition, the sacred book became part of the Muslim's very being, the filter through which he received the world and its mental images. Just as Islamic philanthropy and the requirements of law gave rise to the splendid monuments of Islamic architecture – mosques, schools, hospitals, convents, public drinking-fountains and other pious foundations – Quranic piety created out of the divine text literary artefacts comparable in many ways to the plastic images created out of medieval Christian piety. Thus Zamakhshari's embellishments to 19:16–22, where the annunciation and birth of Jesus are described, convey a typical medieval literalism. Here is the original text, slightly shortened, taken from Asad's translation:

> And . . . Lo! [Mary] withdrew from her family to an eastern place, and kept herself in seclusion from them, whereupon We sent to her Our angel of revelation, who appeared to her in the shape of a well-made human being. She exclaimed: 'Verily! I seek refuge from thee with the Most Gracious! [Approach me not] if thou art conscious of Him. [The angel] answered: 'I am but a messenger of thy Sustainer [who says] "I shall bestow on thee the gift of a son endowed with purity." Said she: 'How can I have a son when no man has ever touched me? – for never have I been a loose woman!' [The angel] answered: 'Thus it is: [but] thy Sustainer says: "This is easy for Me; and thou shalt have a son, so that We might make him a symbol unto mankind and an act of grace for Us."' And it was a thing decreed, and in time she conceived him and then she withdrew with him to a far-off place.[8]

Zamakhshari's embellishments to this passage are too long to give in full. But here is a condensed version:

> Some say that Mary settled in an eastern place when she wanted to purify herself from menstruation, and that she concealed herself behind a wall, or perhaps something else that would keep her out of view. The place where she usually stayed was the mosque. As soon as she had her period, she went to the home of her maternal aunt; then, when she was again in the state of purity, she returned to the mosque. Now when she was at the place at which she customarily purified herself, the angel came to her as a young, smooth-faced man with pure countenance, curly hair, and a well-built body, without exhibiting a single blemish in his human

appearance . . . He presented himself to her in the form of a man in order that she might have confidence in what he was to say and not flee from him. Had he appeared to her in the form of an angel, she would have fled from him and would not have been able to hear what he had to say. If Mary now sought refuge with God from this charming, towering, and handsome figure, then this shows that she was modest and pious. Through the appearance of the angel in this manner, Mary had undergone a test and her modesty was made certain . . .

According to Ibn 'Abbas [the Prophet's uncle and founder of the exegetical tradition] Mary found comfort in the words of the angel, and thus the latter approached near to her and breathed under her shift so that the breath reached into her womb and she became pregnant. Some say that the pregnancy lasted for six months . . . Others say that it lasted eight months and that beside Jesus no child capable of living ever came into the world after [only] eight months. Still others say that it lasted three hours. Some maintain that Mary was pregnant with Jesus for [only] one hour, that he was formed in one hour, and that she brought him into the world in one hour at sunset. According to Ibn 'Abbas the pregnancy lasted for [only] one hour. [Also] Mary is said to have brought Jesus into the world as soon as she became pregnant with him.

Some maintain that she became pregnant with him at the age of thirteen. It is also said that this occurred when she was ten years old, after she had had her period for two months previously. [Moreover] some say that every [newborn] infant cries and that Jesus is the only one who did not do this.[9]

Like the Quran itself, which is constructed out of the same body of Arabian, biblical and talmudic folklore, the *tafsirs* (commentaries) incorporated a wide range of popular culture which made it accessible to the masses, and hence intelligible across a broad spectrum of cultural assumptions. In this respect the Quranic commentators fulfilled the function which Christianity reserved for religious painting. The Sunni Muslim ban on representational art drove the imaginative evocation of biblical texts (which forms the material of western painting till after the Renaissance) into the realm of the footnote. As with Christian art, such exegetical expression could acquire an inter-regional character impossible for secular literature. Since the Quran was the 'speech of God' and Arabic was the language through which he chose to communicate his final messages to mankind, to translate it into other languages was tantamount to blasphemy. Non-Arab Muslims could only approach the Quran through Arabic: in this manner the scripture continued to exercise its cultural hegemony, ensuring that Arabic would remain the dominant language of intra-Muslim communication long after Arabic speakers had ceased to be a numerical majority in the Islamic world.

There is a linguistic as well as a religious truth in the dogma that the Quran cannot be translated. (Even today, official Muslim translations always carry the Arabic text and usually refer to themselves as 'interpretations.') Arabic, more than most other languages, eludes translation, at least into European tongues. According to the travel writer Jonathan Raban:

> To live in Arabic is to live in a labyrinth of false turns and double meanings. No sentence means quite what it says. Every word is potentially a talisman, conjuring the ghosts of the entire family of words from which it comes. The devious complexity of Arabic grammar is legendary. It is a language which is perfectly constructed for saying nothing with enormous eloquence; a language of pure manners in which there are hardly any literal meanings at all and in which the symbolic gesture is everything . . . Even to peer through a chink in the wall of the language is enough to glimpse the depth and darkness of that forest of ambiguity. No wonder the Koran is so notoriously untranslatable.[10]

In thus graphically describing his efforts to cope with the language, Raban omits, however, to make a crucial point. Arabic is a language built around verbs. Substantives and adjectives are almost always verbal derivatives, usually participles or verbal nouns. A clerk is a writer, a book is a writ. Aeroplanes and birds are things that fly. European languages, with their multiple origins, are much more rooted in substances: most nouns in English are things-in-themselves, not parts of verbs, which are *processes*. It is precisely because Arabic refrains from classifying words into discrete particles, but keeps them instead in a logical and balanced relationship with a central concept – the verbal root – that it becomes an eminently suitable language for religious expression.

Religious language, by definition, attempts to express something which defies expression and to evoke a perception of something which lies beyond the realm of human comprehension. In Arabic the meanings of many words depend absolutely on context: hence the word *ghaib* ('unseen') can apply to a reality outside human sense-perception, or to the private parts of a woman – 'that which is [i.e., ought to be] concealed'. In many instances the words cannot be fixed in their contexts without the activities of the exegetes, whose task it thus is to supply them with concrete meanings. Without such exegetical activity a word can range across a whole spectrum of meaning, whose relationship with other spectra is determined by concepts lying at the centre of each verbal cluster. The exegete may try to concretize the meaning of a word by extracting it from a particular point on the spectrum, ignoring its surroundings. But whatever concrete meaning it may temporarily acquire, it will continue to evoke meanings across the whole spectrum. Arabic, the supreme linguistic achievement of a highly developed oral culture, eludes concretization. It is motion distinct from stasis, energy rather than matter. This very dynamism gives the Quran a complexity of meaning, combined with a vigour of expression, which absolutely defies translation, because the multiple meanings tend to vanish as soon as the translator tries to fix them semantically into a foreign language.

The best way to grasp the Quranic message historically and to try to measure its impact on Muhammad's contemporaries, as well as on subsequent generations of Muslims, is to make a comparison between the Quranic and pre-Islamic use of certain terms and concepts. This has been done in two brilliant studies by the Japanese philologist Toshihiko Izutsu, who examines a number of key terms, both diachronically (i.e., in their historic evolution) and in relation to the semantic fields they establish, in order to elucidate the character of the new outlook, or *Weltanschauung*, evoked by them. He points out that none of the key terms around which the Quranic message revolves – Allah, Islam, *iman* ('belief'), *kafir* ('infidel') was new to Muhammad's auditors: obviously they would not have understood his meaning if they had been. What was revolutionary, from the linguistic point of view, was the entirely new conceptual network, or *gestalt*, into which these were ordered: '. . . it was chiefly . . . this transposition of concepts, and the fundamental displacement and rearrangement of moral and religious values which ensued from it, that so radically revolutionized the Arab conception of the world and human existence.'[11]

The name Allah is a simple contraction of 'Al Ilah' – 'the God'. The Quran itself (39:4) provides evidence that the word was used by the pagans to describe a supreme deity. As an abstract term it was common to all pre-Islamic tribes: each must have referred to its own deity as 'the god'. A more universal application would occur naturally when the tribes were gathered together in the *haram* area around the Ka'ba. Where tribal deities might be represented by separate symbols, the underlying abstract concept of 'the-god' must have transcended such particularism, retaining its singularity; 'the-god' becomes 'The God'. Belief in such a single God presiding over all other tribal deities is indicated by the references to Allah as 'Lord [*rabb*] of the Ka'ba ('Lord of the House') in both the Quran and Jahili poetry. It is probable that the presiding deity of the Jahili Arabs was assimilated to Jewish and Christian monotheistic ideas. Thus the Christian poet Aid ibn Zaid of Hira refers in one ode to 'the Lord of Mecca and the Cross'. Added to this we find the 'Abrahamic' conception of God attested by the *hanifs*. The poet Umayya ibn Abi Salt, one of Muhammad's bitterest enemies, was an uncompromising monotheist whose poems contain such phrases as 'He is the God of the whole world', 'the Creator of Everything', 'the Absolute Sovereign on Earth, the Omnipotent', and so forth.

The Quran does not accuse the pagans of denying the existence of such a deity: rather it accuses them of inconstancy and ingratitude:

> . . . if you ask them [i.e., the pagan Arabs], 'Who is it that has created the heavens and the earth and made the sun and moon subservient [to His laws]?', they will surely answer 'Allah!'*[12]

In many passages (e.g., 31:31; 29:65) we are told that people, especially seafarers in danger, will cry to Allah for help, only to return to pagan practices when safely ashore. Their polytheistic practices are identified as *KuFR*† ('disbelief'), a word whose original connotations include 'ingratitude'. *SHiRK* – ascribing partners to the divinity – is both ungrateful and illogical because, as the Quran never ceases to point out, these lesser divinities are powerless, mere figments of the imagination.

---

* The translation of this Quranic quotation differs from that of Muhammad Asad.

† For readers not familiar with the structure of Arabic, I have written the root consonants of certain words in capital letters in order to demonstrate their etymological relationships.

Only Allah has the power to create, to destroy, to save people's lives or in any other way to control the fate of human beings.

This latter point is the real theological departure of the Quran, and the one which we know excited intense opposition. Allah claims an absolute and uncompromising exclusiveness. The attribution of any magical or supernatural power to lesser deities amounts to fraud, since these are nothing but 'empty names' invented by the Arabs without any warranty from God (53:23). The sin of *shirk* is an intellectual as well as a moral one: in the Quran the word is related to *zann* ('conjecture'), as contrasted unfavourably with *'ilm* ('knowledge') (53:28–9; 10:37). All *'ilm* proceeds from Allah and leads back to him:

> O verily unto God belongs whoever is in the heavens and whoever is on earth: hence, what is it that they follow, those who invoke beside God [SHuRaKa] beings to whom they ascribe a share of His divinity? They follow but conjectures [zann] and themselves do nothing but guess.[13]

The Quran's insistence on God's uniqueness challenges Christianity as well as paganism: the *sura* just quoted pours scorn on the idea that God could sire a son. Addressing the Christians it says:

> No evidence whatever have you for this [assertion]! Would you ascribe unto God something which you cannot know? Say: 'Verily they who attribute their own lying inventions to God will never attain to a happy state . . .'[14]

As is suggested by the inclusion of the definite article in his name, the God of the Quran is rather more abstract than that of the Old and New Testaments. Fatherhood is explicitly rejected, a matter of considerable significance in a society which set such store by kinship and paternity. The pronoun *hua* ('he') is a grammatical necessity, not an indicator of sex. In the Quran Allah often addresses Muhammad in the first person, both singular and plural, while he orders his auditors to address him in the second person singular: 'They will answer: "Limitless art Thou in Thy glory." It was inconceivable for us to take for us anyone but Thyself'.[15] It is the overwhelming presence of this deity, unique and unknowable, which makes itself felt in every verse of the Quran. Allah is suprapersonal rather than abstractly impersonal. The fact that he addresses the Prophet, or is addressed, employing all three grammatical pronouns, adds to the sense of a complex and pervasive presence completely saturating the text. As Izutsu comments: 'God in the Koranic *Weltan-schauung* does not subsist in His glorious self-sufficing solitude and stand aloof from mankind as does the God of Greek philosophy, but deeply involves himself in human affairs.'[16]

This god, both abstract and pervasive, transcendent and immanent, describes himself in the Quran using a number of adjectival epithets, such as 'the Just', 'the Wise', 'the All-Powerful', 'the All-Seeing'. The most frequently employed are the etymologically related pair *al RaHMan al RaHiM* (usually translated as 'the Merciful', 'the Compassionate'), which appear in the invocatory formula preceding all but one of the Quran's 114 *suras*. (This invocation or *basmallah* is used by Arabs and many other Muslims before eating, embarking on a journey, making love and a host of other daily activities.) A pagan deity possessing the same root, *RHM*, was worshipped in South Arabia. The word has female connotations of nurturing or protection: *RaHiM*, as a noun, means 'womb'. Thus the attributes most generally applied to God are intended to generate the comforting idea of a friendly, all-pervasive presence at work, as it were, behind the scenes of the visible world, a beneficent force or energy permeating the matter of creation, yet utterly distinct from it. Allah is the womb of all created things, the matrix of the universe in which humans find their being.

A very different aspect of Allah, almost as pervasive, is contained in the phrase *Rabb al 'Alamin* – 'Master of the Worlds' (or universe). The word *RaBB* has connotations of leadership or ownership, both masculine and feudal. (It is commonly used, for example, for 'head of the family'.) It is usually translated into English as 'Lord', which gives it biblical and feudal overtones. Muhammad Asad renders it 'Sustainer', since, he says, it not only 'comprises the idea of having a just claim to something, and consequently to authority over it', but also that of 'rearing, sustaining and fostering'.[17]

The 'worlds' or domain over which this all-pervasive 'Sustainer' presides are divided into the 'Unseen' (*al ghaib*) and visible (*al shahada*) spheres. Only the latter is accessible to man, though he has knowledge of the existence of the former, derived from revelation:

> Say: O Allah! Thou originator of the heavens and the earth! Thou who knowest the Unseen [*al ghaib*] and the visible [*al shahada*]!*[18]

* The translation of this Quranic quotation differs from that of Muhammad Asad.

Allah, as the Quran repeatedly and categorically declares, 'encompasses everything in knowledge'. Man's knowledge, by contrast, can only ever be partial. Even the Prophet, a mere human, only possesses such knowledge as Allah has chosen to reveal to him:

> People will ask thee about the [Last] Hour. Say: 'Knowledge ['ilm] thereof rests with God alone; yet for all thou knowest the [Last] Hour may well be near.[19]

God's revelations, leading to knowledge of the unseen, are conveyed to human beings by means of signs (ayas) or miracles. The ayas fall into two categories: first, there are the evidences of the natural world (shahada), which can be known directly. Second, there is the 'miracle' of the Quran itself which provides, as it were, an exegetical commentary on the shahada, as well as hints about its ultimate relationship with the ghaib. Of these two categories, the ayas of the natural world are the most continuously celebrated.

All religions, and indeed most philosophies, address themselves to the ultimate questions concerning the origins and destiny of the human species, its relation to the natural world and to the cosmic order. The Quran, true to the Semitic tradition, locates man's origin, as well as all the phenomena of the observable universe, firmly in the will or command (amr) of a Divine Creator who both stands apart from and participates in his creation. Allah is the creator and sustainer of everything: the angels and jinns who comprise part of the 'unseen' world, as well as such observable realities as the sun, moon and stars, day and night and the earth with its mountains and rivers, its oceans and continents, its trees, fruits, grains and herbs, its variety of animals 'such as crawl on their bellies; and such as walk on two legs, and such as walk on four'.[20] At its broadest and most universal, the Quran is a 'grand hymn in honour of Divine Creation', one that is saturated with the idea of creation and a 'feeling of profound admiration for it'.[21] The observable facts of this universe – those facts, that is, that man can perceive and apprehend, are not so much things-in-themselves as evidence of this unseen creative force: no more nor less than the 'signs' by which Allah reveals himself. Man cannot perceive the deity directly, or acquire knowledge thereof except from behind a veil (hijab). Even Moses, who of all the biblical prophets mentioned in the Quran came closest to the Divine Presence, is not permitted to look God in the face.

The miraculous quality of creation, as the Quran points to it, must really be self-evident to all who look about them. Passages extolling the creation often end with the rhetorical exhortations: 'Will you not then use your reason!', 'Will you not then remember!'[22] These expressions imply that the pagans must already be aware of the truth in their hearts, even if they are not yet prepared to admit to it. A similar rhetoric is used to persuade the pagans to recognize the divine origin of the Quran itself: the unbelievers are challenged to 'produce another *sura*' (or 'ten *suras*') of comparable merit, or otherwise remain 'conscious of the fire whose fuel is human beings and stones, which awaits all who deny the truth'.[23]

In contrast to the *ayas* of the natural world, which are plain for all to see, the *ayas* of the Quran are of a special kind. The revelation (*wahy*) is treated as 'something extraordinary, something mysterious, the secrets of which cannot be disclosed to the ordinary human mind'.[24] This revelation which has been 'sent down from on high' is God's speech, delivered in Arabic for transmission by an Arabian prophet. The speech itself is evidently conceived of as separate from the words or expressions which make it up. God's messages have previously been delivered to, among other peoples, the Jews and the Christians, who are accused of having wilfully distorted or neglected them.[25]

The relation between 'God's speech' and the actual words of the Quran is a complex question which has been implicated in the relations between Arab and non-Arab peoples from the ninth century down to the present time. In the early 'Abbasid period there arose a controversy among the scholars as to whether or not the Quran had been 'created'.* For a period, victory in the dispute went to the Mu'tazilis, or 'rationalists', who believed in the 'created' Quran, until, following a populist reaction led by Ahmad ibn Hanbal, the opposite doctrine became the orthodoxy, remaining so among Sunni Muslims until the present century. The issue is perhaps best understood as the Islamic equivalent of the controversy about the nature of Christ's divinity that erupted at the Council of Chalcedon (451). The Quran, as 'God's revelation' to mankind, is as central to Islam as Christ is to Christianity. Just as it became important for Christians, during the formative period of their theology, to define as precisely as possible the exact nature of the incarnation, and to build a consensus of opinion around it, so for the Muslims the exact nature of 'God's Speech' became a burning and passionate issue.

* See pp. 198–9.

That the Quran is in the Arab tongue is a fact to which the divine text itself refers on several occasions:

> Behold We have sent this down as a discourse in Arabic [literally, 'an Arabic Quran') that you may understand.[26]

> If We had made it a discourse in some non-Arabic tongue they would surely have said, 'Why are not its messages made intelligible? Is it non-Arabic and Arab [i.e., a non-Arabic revelation given to an Arabian prophet]?'[27]

The revelation had to be made in pure Arabic in order to be comprehensible. The question arises, could it have been made in any other tongue? The Quran itself recounts the stories of other prophets sent to other peoples, not all of them Arabic speakers:

> And never have We sent forth any apostle otherwise than with his people's tongue so that he might make [the message] intelligible.*[28]

The Jews and Christians, among those to whom God's messages have been sent, are accused of 'corrupting' the texts of the original revelations made to them. Leaving aside the question of religious truth, this doctrine is logically necessary if actual differences between Jewish, Christian and Muslim doctrine are to be harmonized with the claim that Islam represents the final truth, as the Quran and the Prophet constantly insist.

Does this mean, then, that the messages delivered to the Israelites by Moses, or to the Christians by Christ, as well as to numerous other peoples in their respective languages, are all identical? The testimony, to say the least, is ambiguous. On the one hand we have the assertion, already mentioned, that Jews and Christians have 'corrupted' their scriptures, while their refusal (especially on the part of the Jews) to acknowledge Muhammad as God's Messenger relegates them to the category of unbelievers. On the other hand we have the following passage in the fifth *sura*, said to be one of the last to be revealed during the Farewell Pilgrimage:

> And unto thee [O Prophet] have We vouchsafed this divine writ [kitab], setting forth the truth, confirming the truth of whatever

* The translation of this Quranic quotation differs from that of Muhammad Asad.

there still remains of earlier revelations [*kitab*] and determining what is true therein. Judge, then, between the followers of earlier revelation in accordance with what God has bestowed from on high, and do not follow their errant views, forsaking the truth that has come unto thee.

Unto every one of you We have appointed a [different] law and way of life [*shir'atan wa minhajan*]. And if God had so willed He could surely have made you all one single community: but [He willed it otherwise] in order to test you by means of what He has vouchsafed unto you. Vie, then, with one another in doing good works! Unto God you all must return; and then He will make you understand all that on which you were wont to differ.[29]

This is the clearest of many statements implicitly commanding tolerance towards the Jews and Christians, as other 'people of the Book', and, by extension, towards Zoroastrians, Hindus, Buddhists and adherents of other scriptural religions. The term *shir'a* is a cognate of *shari'a*, literally, 'the way to a watering place', as used in the Quran to denote the system of divinely revealed law. *Minhaj* has a similar meaning, approximating to 'open road'. This clear recognition of a plurality of religious faiths accounts, no doubt, in part for the relative tolerance accorded to other religious communities (or *millets*), with some exceptions, under Islamic governments. At the same time it raises a difficulty about which parts of the scriptures (usually referred to as *al kitab*, 'book' or 'writ', and sometimes as *umm al kitab*, 'the mother of scriptures') are true and which are false. Is the *kitab* coextensive with the Quran, a kind of divine Ur-text, from which the Quran, like other recognized scriptures (including the Torah of the Jews and the Christian Evangel) derives? A 'created' Quran, as a divine artifact, would place the Arabic scripture on the same ontological level as the 'uncorrupted' versions of the divine messages delivered to other peoples. In short, there is a distinction between 'God's speech' or 'thought' pre-existing in the *umm al kitab*, and the actual message as conveyed, in his proper tongue, by the Arabian Prophet. This, broadly speaking, seems to have been the attitude of the Mu'tazilis.

For the advocates of the 'uncreated Quran', by contrast, the 'medium was the message' (to borrow Marshall McCluhan's famous phrase). The Divine Writ was not an artefact of God, one of many created to suit different times and circumstances, but rather a manifestation of the divine in speech, in the distinctive and unique tongue of the Arabs.

Although there is no absolute correlation between theological notions and national groupings in Islamic history, it seems far from coincidental that it was an 'Abbasid caliph, Al Mamun, who tried to impose the doctrine of the 'created' Quran, for the early 'Abbasids, unlike their Umayyad predecessors, sought to integrate the non-Arab Persians into the Empire. Their opponents, not necessarily all of them Arabs, consisted of people who had come to regard Arabic as a *lingua sacra*. As will be shown in later chapters, the Hanbali doctrine which laid particular stress on literalistic or non-allegorical interpretation of the scriptures became a natural rallying point for Arabs who found their linguistic and cultural hegemony diminishing in a multi-national Islamic society dominated numerically by Turks, Persians, Berbers and other non-Arab peoples.

Both groups could, however, agree that the Quran, like the evidences of the natural world it celebrates, is a 'sign' from Allah, a manifestation of his creative power in the medium of language. As with the postulated existence of the supreme deity to which it testifies, we should not suppose that the Quran's claim to a supernatural origin would in itself have inspired or shocked Muhammad's auditors, who were familiar with the inspired rhymes of the poets and the shamanistic utterances of the *kahins* or soothsayers. What was novel was the Quran's claim, consistent with its doctrine that Allah is the only source of supernatural power, that Muhammad's *dicta* came from Allah rather than from some jinn or other spirit.

The English word 'poet' derives from the Greek work for 'maker'; the Arabic equivalent, *sha'ir*, means 'one who has cognizance of' (the unseen world). The contrasting origins of these words say much about the differing Greek and Semitic world-views. For the ancient Arabs, both poets and *kahins* were people with magical powers, presumed to derive from a special relationship with or possession by a jinn, or 'familiar friend' (*khalil*). The poet Al A'sha al Akbar describes this relationship thus:

> Between us we are two intimate sincere friends: a jinn and a human being who is naturally fit for him. If he only speaks [i.e., if he inspires me] then I will no longer be incapable of saying anything I would say. He suffices me so long as he is neither a tongue-tied one nor an awkward stupid fellow.[30]

The jinn's inspiration is conceived as 'coming down' to the poet; the word normally used derives from the root *NaZaLa*. The fourth form of this verb (aNZaLna – 'We sent down') is consistently used by Allah in the Quran to describe his transmission of the divine writ to the Prophet. There is, in fact, an exact parallelism between the changes Muhammad instituted in the Hajj ceremonies and the transposition of pagan concepts of inspiration in the Quran. Just as, after the Farewell Pilgrimage, the rites associated with the local deities of Mecca, Mina, Muzdalifa and 'Arafat are subsumed into the new 'cult' of Allah, rather than abolished altogether, so the familiar jinns of the Jahili poets and soothsayers give way to the notion of the Prophet's direct 'possession' by God, or rather, to be more precise, by the being, later identified as the archangel Gabriel, sent by him.

As with the message, so with the style in which it was delivered. All scholars, Muslims and non-Muslims alike, are agreed that the style of the Quran undergoes some development, if only because the content of the Medinese *suras* addresses itself to many mundane matters, such as questions of law and inheritance, arising out of the needs of the community. In the earliest *suras*, however, Muhammad's utterances closely resemble the oathing formulas sometimes adopted by the *kahins*, where natural phenomena (or their spirits) are invoked to confirm an oath or statement. One such oath, made by the *kahin* Satih to the King of Yemen, is preserved in Ibn Ishaq's Life of the Prophet:

By the evening twilight	*wa-shafaq*
By the darkness	*wa'l ghashaq*
By the dawn	*wa'l falaq*
When it breaks bright	*idha tasaq*
Verily what I have told you	*inna ma anba'tuka*
is truth.[31]	*bi'l lahaq*

This formula is uttered in *saj'*, the metreless rhyming style of the Quran's early *suras*, several of which superficially resemble it. The following is a literal rendering of 79:1–5:

By the rising ones sinkingly	*wa-nazia't ghariqan*
By the lively ones actively	*wa-nashitat nashatan*
By the floating ones sublimely	*fa sabihat sabhan*
And the racing ones taking	
precedence	*wa sabiqat sabqan*
And thus the managers commanding	*fa'l mudaribat amran*

The above passage is evidently addressed to auditors familiar with the *saj'* style, which it echoes. A feature of this style, and of the Quranic style departing from it, is its condensed ellipticism – a characteristic, according to Muhammad Asad, of Arabian beduin speech. It is, so he says,

> . . . the language of people whose mental images, flowing without effort from association to association, succeed one another in rapid progression and often vault elliptically over intermediate – as it were 'self-understood' – sequences of thought towards the idea which they aim to achieve or express.

It is impossible, he concludes, to understand the Quran's method and inner purport without being able to reproduce, to some extent, this characteristic of associative thought within oneself.[32]

The *saj'* style of the Quran presupposed a familiarity with the manners and outlook of beduin society – so much so that without it passages such as the one quoted above are virtually incomprehensible. Processes, not things, are described: the missing substantives can only be inferred by projecting oneself back into the beduin environment. Without such imaginative projection, A. J. Arberry's translation (although justifiably acclaimed as the most elegant in modern English) seems utterly meaningless:

> By those that pluck out vehemently
> And those that draw out violently
> By those that swim serenely
> And those that outstrip suddenly
> By those that direct an affair[33]

The medieval exegetes, influenced, no doubt, by many Persian and Babylonian ideas, assumed that the reference here is to angels, whose activities concern the souls of the dying. This is the sense of Dr Yusuf Ali's translation (first published in 1934), officially approved by the Islamic Foundation in Britain:

> By the [angels]
> Who tear out
> [The souls of the wicked]
> With violence
> By those who gently
> Draw out [the souls
> Of the blessed]
> And by those who glide
> Along [on errands of mercy]

> Then press forward
> As in a race
> Then arrange to do
> [The commands of their Lord][34]

Muhammad Asad follows the earliest commentators, including Hasan al Basri, who considered that the passage refers to celestial bodies. His rendering is not only free from supernatural assumptions about angels, but is also convincingly appropriate to a desert setting, where night skies are unusually brilliant:

> Consider those [stars] that rise only to set
> and move [in their orbits] with steady motion
> and float [through space] with floating serene
> and yet overtake [one another] with swift overtaking:
> and thus they fulfil the [Creator's] behest!

This single example of three different translations demonstrates the problems of interpretation raised by the Quran's elliptical style, which is far from being confined to the earliest *suras*. Asad's translation, the most convincing of those cited, also shows how a formula of conjuration is elevated into a hymn to the miraculous power of the Creator. Free from the chronology which places the act of creation at the beginning of the Bible, this theme runs consistently throughout the Quran, reaffirming the notion of creation as a continuous process, rather than a single act initiated by the Creator.

This vision of a creative energy constantly at work is at the core of the Quranic doctrine: by insisting that its auditors observe the phenomena of the natural world, not as things-in-themselves but as 'signs' or symbols (*ayas*) of God's benevolence or power, the Muslim scripture forces them to look beyond the realm of appearances (*al shahada*) to an unseen world (*al ghaib*) whose ultimate reality is unknowable. Toshihiko Izutsu has pointed out the similarity, in this respect, between the Quranic *Weltanschauung* and the existentialist philosophy of Karl Jaspers. For Jaspers, the whole universe is a vast cryptogram, a *Chifferschrift* or book of symbols. Reality can never be grasped empirically, but must forever recede towards a horizon of inexhaustible appearances. Jasper's term for God is '*das Umgriefende*', 'the Encompassing', consciousness of which can only be acquired by those who move beyond the stage of commonplace everyday reason (*Verstand*) into what he calls *Existenz*, a state of higher philosophical awareness or existential becoming. Izutsu points out that this state exactly corresponds to the state of 'God-consciousness' urged upon believers in the Quran: the truly symbolic nature of Allah's *ayas* can only be perceived by those prepared to exercise their intellects.

Like everything else in the Quran, this attitude towards the symbolic and transient character of reality is not something that proceeds *ex nihilo* from the Prophet's utterances. It is rooted in the outlook of the Jahili poets who never ceased to proclaim – and to lament – the transitoriness of mortal existence. 'Thou seest a man ever yearn and pine for length of life,' concludes an ode by 'Abid ibn al Abras which looks back nostalgically upon the pleasures of wine and love, 'but what is long life's sum but a burden of grief and pain.'[35] In the Quran the same assumption of mortal transitoriness is maintained, but the Jahili mood of pessimism is transposed into a major, life-affirming key: the illusory character of worldly existence is proof of ultimate immortality:

> Know [O men] that the life of this world is but a play and a passing delight, and a beautiful show, and [the cause of] your boastful vying with one another and [of your] greed for more and more riches and children. Its parable is that of life-giving rain: the herbage which it causes to grow delights the tillers of the soil [*kafirs*]: but then it withers and thou canst see it turn yellow; and in the end it crumbles into dust. But [the abiding truth of man's condition will become fully apparent] in the life to come, [either] suffering severe or God's forgiveness and his goodly acceptance: for the life of this world is nothing but an enjoyment of self-delusion.[36]

The same image, of rain reviving the desiccated land, is invoked to justify the doctrine of resurrection – the doctrine, which, as we know, the Jahili Arabs had the greatest difficulty in accepting:

> . . . for among His signs is this: thou seest the earth lying desolate – and lo! when We send down water upon it, it stirs and swells [with life]! Verily, He who brings to life can surely give life to the dead . . . for behold He has the power to do anything![37]

Philosophically this argument in favour of resurrection is similar to Pascal's: what is more remarkable, the fact that a living being should appear at all, or that a once living being should be reborn? An atheism

which takes as given the existence of life, accepting creation and procreation but rejecting re-creation is not necessarily logically consistent:

Allah is both the creator of the universe and its ruler. The laws
instituted by him govern the motion of the stars and the planets, the sun
and the moon, the natural processes of animal and vegetable worlds. In
this essentially harmonious and beneficial world, all created things,
except human beings, submit to their Creator. James Dickie, an English
Muslim convert, has expressed this aspect of the Quranic vision suc-
cinctly, if somewhat arrestingly, by stating that 'all animals and insects
are already Muslims'.[38] Humans alone have a propensity to violate
God's laws because, unlike the animals, they have consciousness and
therefore freedom of choice. This freedom, though contained within the
wider field of Allah's omnipotence and omniscience, is implied in the
doctrine of the Day of Judgement, when all men and women will be
answerable for their actions.

Man's position in the cosmic system created by Allah is unique. On the
one hand he is an earthly being created out of 'dust' and given dominion
over the earth and its creatures as God's 'vice-regent' (khalifa). At the
same time he ranks higher in the hierarchy of creatures than the angels
and jinns, though the latter are purely spiritual beings. In the Quranic
version of the Fall, Satan or Iblis is punished for refusing God's command to prostrate himself before the newly created Adam.

The devil tempts Adam, not Eve, to eat of the forbidden tree, with the
false promise that it will lead to eternal life 'and to a kingdom that will
never decay'. We are not told, as in Genesis, that the forbidden fruit
comes from the 'Tree of knowledge of Good and Evil', merely that the
fruit is forbidden – 'an allegory', according to Asad, 'of the limits which
the Creator has set to mankind's desire and actions'.[39] This act of
disobedience is, however, not dwelt upon. After eating the fruit Adam
and Eve discover their nakedness – to find in sexual activity a pleasurable
compensation for their banishment. In the biblical version the couple's
expulsion from paradise is accompanied by a strong sense of disgrace,
particularly for the woman:

> Unto the woman He said, I will greatly multiply thy sorrow and
> thy conception; in sorrow shalt thou bring forth children; and thy
> desire shall be to thy husband, and he shall rule over thee. And
> unto Adam He said: Because thou hast hearkened to the voice of

> thy wife and hast eaten of the tree . . . cursed is the ground for thy sake; in sorrow shalt thou eat of it all the days of thy life.[40]

In the Quran, by contrast, Adam is forgiven immediately: 'Thereafter [however] his Sustainer elected him [for His guidance] and accepted his repentance, and bestowed His guidance upon him . . .'[41] Adam becomes the first of the prophets, God's vice-regent (khalifa) upon earth. His place of exile, far from being accursed as in the Old Testament, is to become man's 'dwelling place' and a 'source of profit' to him: 'Yea, indeed [O men] We have given you a [bountiful] place on earth, and appointed thereon a means of livelihood for you.'[42]

In effect, man's act of disobedience is understood not as the cause of 'original sin', but as the unavoidable consequence of his humanity. In the words of Muhammad Iqbal, the foremost modern writer on Islam, his 'first act of disobedience was also his first act of free choice', a consequence of his 'rise from a primitive state of instinctive appetite to the conscious possession of a free self capable of doubt and disobedience'.[43]

Allah is omniscient and omnipotent; man is endowed with free will and freedom of choice. This paradox, which cannot be reconciled intellectually, establishes the boundaries of Islam's theological dialectic. In the eighth and ninth centuries the rationalistic Mu'tazilis were so concerned with defending the primacy of free will that they were prepared to limit God's omnipotence: by being subject to the principle of 'adl (justice), Allah, like the Muslim ruler, is obliged to reward the good and punish the evil. The reaction which led to the overthrow of the Mu'tazilis restored God's omnipotence without resolving the problem of free will. The faithful were merely urged to accept the Quranic portrait of God's power as it is, 'without asking how' (bi la kaif). Eventually an uneasy synthesis of the two positions emerged with the teaching of Ash'ari (d. 935) and his followers, according to which man does not possess free will in the strictest sense, but does have the capacity to acquire, through an act of acceptance, the actions that God has already created for him.

The Arabic word for 'man', or rather 'human being', of which Adam, of course, is seen as the archetype, is INSan, from the root ANiSa, meaning 'to be companionable, agreeable or genial' – a concept which recognizes the essentially sociable nature of the human animal. The proper posture of man towards Allah is one of fear – or, to be more precise, self-protection. Though his works are to be marvelled at, celebrated and enjoyed, the God of the Quran is too awe-inspiring and comprehensive to inspire the emotion of love. This idea of religious fear is rooted in Jahili concepts which, like so much else, are transformed and given an entirely new content within the vastly expanded Quranic world-view: 'And give thou the glad tidings [of God's acceptance] unto all who are humble – all whose hearts tremble with awe whenever God is mentioned . . .'[44] The juxtaposition of two key concepts, *KaRiM* and *TaQwa*, in the Quran and Jahili poetry provides a useful insight into this process: 'Verily the noblest among you [*aKRaMakum*] in the sight of God is the one who is most fearful [*aTQakum*].'*[45] The root *KRM* and its cognates denoted nobility of lineage as outwardly expressed in the lavish hospitality and spending with which tribal chieftains felt it necessary to maintain their prestige. Such prestige spending was, until recently, still a feature of beduin or near-beduin society. (In the 1920s, before oil was discovered in Saudi Arabia, the late King 'Abd al 'Aziz, then one of the world's most impoverished rulers, would regularly provide food for all-comers, numbering perhaps two or three hundred people.) The word *TaQwa* – 'fear', as used by the Jahili poets – referred to the instinctive reflexes with which animals protect themselves. Applied to humans, it could mean protection of oneself against social criticism. Thus the poet 'Amr ibn al Ahtam announces: 'Every man of noble [*KaRiM*] nature guards himself [*inTaQi*] against blame with hospitality.'[46] For the Jahili Arab, the *taqwa* is directed against his fellow men. A similar combination of words in the Quran reorientates it towards God. Later, in the post-Quranic framework of an all-Muslim society, *taqwa* acquires the secondary meaning of piety, or spiritual self-protection. Muhammad Asad further spiritualizes the term and its cognates by the rendering 'God-consciousness' or some similar expression.

There are many comparable shifts from the Jahili to the Quranic and post-Quranic (i.e., formally Islamic) use of certain words. The case of *taqwa* is, however, especially significant because it indicates a change from 'animal self-protection', via 'protection against social disapproval', to piety or 'self-protection' *vis-à-vis* God in a manner closely reflecting the changes in Arabian society during Muhammad's career. In the anarchic conditions of the Jahiliya, the tribal group protected itself against attacks (whether unprovoked or vengeance-seeking) from other tribes. In the absence of centralized state authority, justice was administered laterally,

---

* The translation of this Quranic quotation differs from that of Muhammad Asad.

as vengeance. In the Quran God assumes the duty of administering justice 'vertically', while the new Umma or 'super-tribe' is expected to act as a unit in exacting retribution for the attacks of outsiders.

In the new Quranic world-view, people protect themselves against God's wrath by humbling themselves before their Creator and undertaking the duties and responsibilities of Muslims. *Islam* in its original meaning is the primary act of self-surrender: an act of existential choice whereby a person places his or her destiny in the hands of Allah and submits to Allah's 'governance' as revealed through the commands of the Prophet. It is a voluntary act, as implied by the use of the fourth, reflexive form of the verb *SaLiMa*, 'to be safe, unharmed, secure or intact'. One cannot undertake *Islam* on behalf of another person – which is why, in the fullest sense, compulsory conversions are forbidden.[47] In the pre-Islamic context the word *islam* meant 'giving over' or 'giving up' something particularly precious; transposed in the Quran, such an act of surrender embraces any autonomy on behalf of the self or ego. In the primary sense a Muslim (from the active participle, 'one who surrenders himself') is a person who has made this voluntary act of self-surrender or existential commitment to God and his Prophet. The subjective correlative of *Islam* in this primal sense is *IMaN* or faith: just as the Muslim is one who has surrendered his whole being to God, the *mUMiN* is one who is characterized by an unwavering faith in him. Generally the two words are interchangeable; however, where 'Muslim' acquires the secondary meaning of one who is formally or outwardly a member of the Islamic community, but not necessarily a believer in terms of inner conviction, *iman* and *mumin* acquire the added force of committed belief/believer.[48]

The negative values of the Quranic world-view revolve round two key words: *KuFR* ('disbelief') and *JaHL* ('ignorance'). In its original pre-Quranic usage the verb *KaFaRa* meant 'he (or it) covered' something. Thus, in a passage (57:20) cited on p. 124, the word *KaFiR* (literally, 'one who covers') is applied to tillers of the soil – i.e., those who cover the seeds with earth. In the usual Quranic context, however, the term *KaFiR* and its cognates are applied to those who cover or conceal something in the moral sense – i.e., those who knowingly deny the truth as revealed to them through Allah's messages. In the first instance this means *ingratitude* for the *ayas* as revealed in the natural order. In this sense its antonym is the verb *SHaKaRa* – 'to be thankful'. Thus Moses, relating Allah's promise to the Israelites, says:

If you are grateful [*SHaKaRtum*] I will surely give you more, but if you are thankless [*KaFaRtum*] verily my chastisement shall be terrible.*[49]

From mere ingratitude the word acquires the meaning of 'disbelief', in the sense of a refusal to accept or recognize the truths as revealed in the Quran. The most common usage of the term are *KuFR* ('disbelief'), *KaFiR* ('one who denies the truth'), and the more forceful *alladhina KaFaRu* ('those who [wilfully] deny the truth'). In the broader Quranic context, *KuFR* and *KaFiR* are the exact antonyms of *'iman* and *mu'min*. Ultimately, in the post-Quranic context where Islam is the prevailing ideology, the word *KaFiR* is generally applied to unbelievers, including Jews, Christians and pagans. However, it never quite loses its interior meaning of moral ingratitude leading to infidelity. Thus the breakaway Khariji sectarians, like the modern Muslim Brotherhood, redefined themselves as the true Muslims in relation to *kafirs* in the rest of the community. They considered all outside their own group to be 'grave sinners' destined for hell who could justifiably be despatched on their way there. At the intellectual level, the religious scholars, threatened with the challenge to their social power by unauthorized interpreters of scripture, designated as *kafirs* those who deviated from the rigid and arcane rules invented by them. Thus Tirmidhi, one of the six universally recognized Sunni canonists, preserves an (obviously spurious) *hadith* of the Prophet:

> One who interprets the Quran according to his personal opinion, that is, not according to knowledge ['*ilm* – i.e., the recognized methodology] has proved himself by that very fact to be a *kafir*.[50]

The root cause and basis of *KuFR* is the state of *JaHL*. The term Jahiliya is used universally (as in this book) to describe the 'period of ignorance' before the coming of Islam: as such it stands in direct opposition to *'ILM*, knowledge. However, its primary meaning, both in the Quran and in pre-Islamic poetry, is somewhat different. As Ignaz Goldziher pointed out, *JaHL* was originally opposed to *HiLM*, a term denoting something like 'the moral reasonableness of the civilized man'. *JaHL* is the typical behaviour of someone who is arrogant, quick-tempered, hot-blooded and impetuous, someone who easily surrenders himself to the control of violent passions. The pre-Islamic poet 'Amr ibn Ahmar al Bahili (who later embraced Islam) compares the state of *jahl* to the bubbling of a pot:

* The translation of this Quranic quotation differs from that of Muhammad Asad.

> Many the large black ones [i.e., cooking-pots] which our maid-servants cajole: once their belly [i.e., contents] becomes *JaHL* [i.e., boils up] it will never become *HaLiM* [i.e., calm down].[51]

In the Quran the term is employed in the passage where Joseph resists the sexual advances of Potiphar's wife and her women friends:

> 'O my Lord,' cried he, 'I would sooner be cast into prison than do what these women urge me to do: for unless Thou turn away their guile from me, I might yield to the attraction [I feel for them] and so become one of the *jahil*.'*[52]

Since Joseph is one who has been granted judgement and knowledge (*HuKM* and *'ILM*), in this context the opposite of *jahili* behaviour is indicated by his mastery over his own amorous inclinations, due to his understanding of right moral conduct. (Other factors apart, his yielding to the demands of his host's wife would have entailed a gross violation of the laws of hospitality.) Like other Quranic terms rooted in the material and social conditions of Arabia, the word *JaHaLa* acquires its more far-reaching an universal connotations from being employed in a number of different contexts throughout the scripture. The inability to achieve mastery over one's passions, habitually repeated, distorts the judgement. The habitual *jahil* is thus a man incapable of forming a judicious opinion, a person who thinks in a shallow, superficial and rash manner. Because of his incapacity to see the truth of God's signs, the *jahil*, like the *kafir*, frequently oversteps the boundaries of behaviour established by God.

So far, the concepts we have tried to elucidate – *iman* and *kufr*, *Islam* (in the original existential sense) and *jahl* – though terms rooted semantically in the reality of pre-Islamic Arabia, are capable of universal application. They belong to the category of what one might call Islam's 'universal' message, in so far as their evolution from particular, even morally neutral terms, takes them into the field of universal ethical values. If Muhammad had confined himself to articulating this aspect of the message, Islam would probably have developed, like protestant Christianity, in the direction of a purely ethical religion, capable of a wide variety of different applications according to the circumstances of time and place. This is, of course, far from being the case. The Quran, whatever its origins, arises out of the career of Muhammad the Law-

---

* The translation of this Quranic quotation differs from that of Muhammad Asad.

giver. The general ethical principles it endorses are given a positive legal content. Obedience to God and his Prophet demands the observance of certain rituals and rules of social behaviour, as already outlined in the previous chapter. These rules, though only sketched out in the Quran, were elaborated by the scholar-lawyers of the first two or three Islamic centuries to become the basis of the Shari'a law described in the following chapter.

Like most of the terms already examined, the ethical system founded in the Quran also has its roots in the moral and social environment of a desert tribal society. The nearest equivalent to the English word 'good' is *al ma'ruf* – literally, 'the known'. Its antithesis is *al munkar*, 'the unknown'. The most celebrated verse employing these two terms is addressed to the Muslim community as a whole:

> You are indeed the best community that has ever been brought forth for [the good] of mankind: you enjoin the doing of what is right [*al ma'ruf*] and forbid the doing of what is wrong [*al munkar*] and you believe in God.[53]

These two concepts, which the Quran integrates into the new Islamic system of ethics, clearly derive from the moral order of a tribal society where the 'known' or familiar way of doing things is socially approved, while the unknown or unfamiliar is disapproved of because it falls outside the framework of established custom.[54]

Several other key terms, all of them reflecting the desert environment, serve to reinforce this essentially conservative social morality. God is the guide (*hadi* – a term originally applied to the professional guides in the desert); his commands indicate the straight (*mustaqim, rashid*) path (*shari'a, sabil, tariqa, sunna, sirat*, etc.). Those who stray (*dalla, qasata, nahaba*) end by losing their way. In the desert, of course, safety lies in following the well-tried paths of one's ancestors. In post-Quranic usage the *ma'ruf* applies to the structure of *fiqh* (jurisprudence) derived from the Quran and the Prophet's Sunna. Unlike Christian ethical concepts, which in many respects represent a radical departure from traditional Jewish morality, the Islamic ethical system continues to represent itself as observance of the *true* paths of ancestral morality, as contrasted with the 'corruption' or 'straying' of contemporary society. For this reason, among others, Islamic reformers throughout history have invariably been advocates of a *return* to the Sunna of the Prophet and the first generation of Muslims (*salaf*).

Allah, being omnipotent and omniscient, is the ultimate cause of both man's good and his evil actions.

> Whomsoever God wills he lets go astray [*inDaLLihu*]; and whom-
> soever He wills He sets him on a straight path [*SiRaTin*
> *mustaqimin*].*[55]

Those who are good and follow the path are destined for paradise; those who are evil are destined for hell.

The idea of man's responsibility for his actions is a necessary consequence of the doctrine of free will, however much the latter may be modified by a sense of the unfathomable immensity of God's purpose. The examples of punishment in the Quran imply that groups as well as individuals are answerable for their errors. Three types of punishment are indicated for those who wilfully disbelieve in God's laws, or persist in their disobedience. The historical punishment stories are related of peoples who failed to heed the warnings of earlier prophets. Thus the people of 'Ad rejected their messenger Hud and were destroyed by a great wind which blew for seven days and seven nights and wiped out everything except their buildings. The people of Thamud (mentioned by Ptolemy, Pliny and other classical writers) were destroyed by an earthquake, or 'shout', as were the peoples of Madyan who failed to heed their messenger Shu'aib. The people of Tubba and Saba (biblical Sheba) in South Arabia are similarly punished for their unbelief, in the latter case by a flood which resulted apparently from the bursting of the Ma'rib dam.

In addition to these stories, evidently drawn from Arabian tradition, the Quran has several versions of biblical narratives, including the fate of Noah's people, destroyed by the flood, and of Sodom and Gomorrah, all of whose inhabitants except for Lot and his daughters are wiped out for their homosexuality. (The Quran omits the incestuous sequel to the biblical account of Lot's deliverance, in which the patriarch's daughters, anxious to preserve his line, manage to make themselves pregnant by him without his knowledge.[56] Muslim exegetes cite the story as an example of the 'corruption' of the scriptures by the Hebrews.[57]) The people of Pharaoh are referred to as having been punished for their arrogance in rejecting the prophet Moses, though their destruction while

---

* The translation of this Quranic quotation differs from that of Muhammad Asad.

crossing the Red Sea (7:136f.) is recounted in much less detail than in the Old Testament.[58]

The ethical doctrine expounded in the punishment stories is problematic. On the one hand there is the clear statement, repeated several times,[59] that 'no one shall be made to bear another's burden'. This is to say that no one shall suffer for another's guilt (as in the Christian doctrine of atonement, in which Christ suffers, and redeems, the sins of mankind) and no one shall be punished unjustly.

However, it is clear from the punishment stories that the just punishments are meted out to groups as well as individuals: whole societies are destroyed for their failure to heed the warnings of the prophets sent to them – and it is made clear that punishment is always preceded by a warning:

> We would never chastise [any community for the wrong they may do] ere We have sent an apostle [to them]. But when [this has been done and] it is Our will to destroy a community, we convey our last warning to those of its people who have lost themselves entirely in the pursuit of pleasures and [if] they [continue to act] sinfully, the sentence [of doom] passed on to the community takes effect, and we break it to smithereens.[60]

Most of the punishment stories occur in the late Meccan or early Medinese periods, and reflect the Prophet's struggles with the pagan Quraish and the Jews who rejected him as the peoples referred to in the stories rejected those earlier messengers. Clearly they were intended as direct warnings to Muhammad's audiences, and the catastrophes alluded to were almost certainly well known to them. Understood more generally, however, they reflect a communalistic morality, appropriate to a tribal society. As in the Old Testament versions of the destruction of the Temple and the Babylonian exile, political disasters are explained as just punishment for the failure of a whole society to observe the law:

> And we made this known to the Children of Israel through revelation: Twice, indeed, will you spread corruption on earth and will indeed become grossly overbearing! Hence when the prediction of the first of these two [periods of iniquity] came true, We sent against you some of Our bondsmen of terrible prowess in war, and they wrought havoc throughout the land: and so the prediction was fulfilled.[61]

A punishment such as this – military defeat by more powerful neigh-bours – can be understood, quite rationalistically, as a consequence of social or political failure. In Muhammad Asad's phrase it is 'a metonym for the natural law of cause and effect to which, in the long run, the life of man – and particularly the corporate life of nations and communities – is subject'.[62]

It becomes impossible, however, to reconcile the rationalistic idea of punishment as a consequence of human error, and therefore consistent with divine justice, with the natural catastrophes, such as floods and earthquakes, occurring in many of the punishment stories already referred to. One cannot accept rationally the notion that the innocent victims of such disasters are being punished for their sins, unless one also accepts the notion that all men are at all times irredeemably sinful and that an arbitrary and whimsical deity simply chooses to inflict punishments on some of them wherever and whenever he likes. Natural disasters (such as recent earthquakes in Algeria and Yemen, which some of the local *mullahs* were reported as having blamed on the sinfulness of their community) may be subject, like political disasters, to rationally discernible laws of cause and effect. The problem in most religions is how to accommodate the seemingly arbitrary and undeserved sufferings of people within a morally coherent universe presided over by a bene-ficent deity. A personal god who concerns himself with the fate of human beings, as distinct from an abstract deity concerned only with maintaining the cosmic order, must confront the natural human demand for justice. Within the human realm itself reason can explain, and perhaps even remedy, injustice: thus, economic and political theories, for example, will seek to analyse the material causes of poverty or deprivation and try to provide solutions. Within the larger universe, however, whether this is seen as conforming to the laws of 'God' or of 'Nature', reason may be powerless to find causal explanations which are psychologically satisfying to human beings: tectonic plate theory may explain the physical reason for earthquakes without specifying why some people perish in them and others escape.

Ultimately, in Islam, as in Christianity, the gap between the need for a morally coherent and rationally ordered universe and the observable fact that innocence often suffers can only be filled by faith. Faith is an attitude of trust not only that the universe is beneficent in itself, but that the individual has a central part in its ordering and will not be abandoned by his creator. The Quran, like the New Testament, insists that ultimately the demands of faith must supersede those of reason: hence the ethically dubious proposition that the victims of natural disasters are somehow deserving of their fate. At the same time it preaches an essentially rationalist morality: those who disobey God's laws are 'sinning against themselves'[63] and will suffer accordingly: 'Whatever good happens to thee is from God; and whatever evil befalls thee is from thyself.'[64]

Only faith, not reason, can reconcile the ethical contradictions. The Quran, like Christianity, cannot accept that God can be other than good: 'verily, God does not wrong [anyone] by as much as an atom's weight.'[65] Virtue will be rewarded, innocent suffering compensated for in the life to come. In the meantime the victims of injustice must console themselves with the thought that, in the unfathomable depths of God's purposes, not everything man regards as misfortune is really, in its final effects, evil:

> . . . it may well be that you hate a thing the while it is good for you,
> and it may well be that you love a thing the while it is bad for you:
> and God knows, whereas you do not know.[66]

In Islam, as in Christianity, the ultimate reconciliation of faith with reason, morality with history, has to be deferred till the Day of Judgement. The eschatology is not just a consequence of a natural human reluctance to face the finality of death; it is the only context in which the conflicting claims of observable reality and the desire for moral coherence can be fitted together. Muhammad's vision of the Last Hour, a cosmic cataclysm which is simultaneously a moment of judgement, generates some of the most remarkable descriptive passages in the Quran, especially in the earlier Meccan *suras*:

> When the sun is shrouded in darkness,
> and when the stars lose their light,
> and when the mountains are made to vanish,
> and when she-camels big with young, about to give birth, are left
>   untended,
> and when all beasts are gathered together,
> and when the seas boil over,
> and when all human beings are coupled [with their deeds],
> and when the girl-child that was buried alive is made to ask
> for what crime she had been slain,
> and when the scrolls [of men's deeds] are unfolded,
> and when heaven is laid bare,

and when the blazing fire [of hell] is kindled bright,
and when paradise is brought into view;
[on that Day] every human being will come to know what he has
    prepared for himself.[67]

The eschatological vision of a Grand Reckoning at the end of time fills in the gaps in the ethical doctrines. The idea, which can be traced back to Pharaonic and Babylonian notions, is the essential prerequisite for a belief in the divine law: if God is the original legislator, he must also be Judge at the Final Court of Appeal. The imagery of judgement is frequently commercial, reflecting the mercantile milieu of Muhammad's Mecca:

And as for him whose record shall be placed in his right hand [i.e., whose life has been righteous] he will in time be called to account with an easy accounting and will [be able to] turn joyfully to those of his own kind. But as for him whose record shall be given to him behind his back [i.e., because it is so horrible that he will not wish to look at it] he will in time pray for utter destruction, but he will enter the blazing flame.[68]

The horrors of hell, though graphically painted, are not given the more extended treatment reserved for the joys of heaven:

Verily for all who sin against themselves [by rejecting Our truth] we have readied a fire whose billowing folds will encompass them from all sides; and if they beg for water, they will be given water [hot] like molten lead which will scald their faces: how dreadful a drink, and how evil a place to rest![69]

But as for those who have persevered in evil . . . [They will find themselves] in the midst of scorching winds and burning despair and the shadows of black smoke – shadows neither cooling nor soothing.[70]

Heaven, by contrast, is depicted as a place of palpable luxuries and sensuous joys for the righteous:

. . . theirs shall be gardens of perpetual bliss – gardens through which waters flow – wherein they will be adorned with bracelets of gold and will wear green garments of silk and brocade [and] wherein upon couches they will recline: how excellent a recompense and how goodly a place to rest![71]

The joys of paradise find their most graphic description in the earlier *suras*. They were often condemned by medieval Christian writers for their more or less explicit eroticism.

> They will be seated on gold-encrusted thrones of happiness, reclining upon them, facing one another [in love]. Immortal youths will wait upon them with goblets and ewers and cups filled with water from unsullied springs by which their minds will not be clouded and which will not make them drunk; and with fruit of any kind that they may choose, and with the flesh of any fowl that they may desire. And [with them will be their] companions [*hur*] pure, most beautiful of eye like unto pearls [still] hidden in their shells . . . [and they will find themselves] amidst fruit-laden lote-trees and acacias flower-clad and shade extended and waters gushing and fruit-abounding, never-failing and never out of reach. And [with them will be their] spouses, raised high, for behold, we shall have brought them into being in a life renewed, having resurrected them as virgins full of love, well-matched with those who have attained to righteousness . . .[72]

Some Muslim commentators were at pains to point out that these descriptions were purely allegorical. Bukhari, Muslim and others record a *hadith* in which the Prophet is said to have stated of paradise:

> God says: 'I have readied for My righteous servants what no eye has ever seen, and what no ear has ever heard, and no heart of man has ever conceived.[73]

Dr Yusuf Ali, a translator of the Quran recommended by the UK Islamic Foundation, insists that the companions (who have a feminine gender in the Arabic) are purely spiritual beings:

> . . . lest grosser ideas of sex should intrude (he writes in his commentary) it is made clear that these companions for heavenly society will be of special creation – of virginal purity, grace and beauty, inspiring and inspired by love, with the question of time and age eliminated.[74]

Some of the medieval Muslim exegetes, however, were in no doubt that the pleasures of paradise were meant to be enjoyed literally rather than allegorically. One of the best-known accounts, that of Shaikh Jalal al Din al Suyuti, contains a detailed description of paradise (using the

Quran as point of departure) which became immensely popular from the thirteenth century. As well as being a place of abundant rivers and trees of precious stones, of ever-ready horses caparisoned with jewel-studded bridles, it is a place where human beings may enjoy all the carnal pleasures without any attendant inconveniences:

> The food of paradise is everlasting. When the Elect have eaten or drunk something, they will perspire just a little with sweat as fresh and perfumed as musk. The dwellers in paradise have no anuses: these were made for defecating, and in paradise there is no defecation.[75]

The houris, or female companions, come in a variety of colours, including white, green, yellow and red. Their bodies are made of saffron, musk, amber and camphor, and their hair is of raw silk. Each one of the Elect may have 70 houris in addition to his earthly wives and any other woman he finds attractive. All become more beautiful each day. A man's virility becomes vastly increased. The couples make love as on earth, but each moment of pleasure lasts twenty-four years. Paradise, however, is not just a place of sensuous delights in Suyuti's vision. Its joys will culminate in the ultimate spiritual experience: the vision of God, when the faces of the Elect will 'be bright with happiness looking up to their Sustainer', while the faces of the damned will be 'overcast with despair, knowing that a crushing calamity is about to befall them'.[76] For Suyuti, the 'Beatific Vision' of Allah, seated on a hyacinth throne 'a thousand years high', surrounded by the prophets and the rest of the elect arranged in order of virtue, is the final goal of paradise and hence the end of life itself:

> The Elect then gaze upon the Face of the Everlasting One, resplendent in all His glory. They see him, unveiled, without mediators. As the light of Truth shines upon their faces, they remain transfixed for three hundred years before the Face of Truth, Glory be to His Name, God the One, the Incomparable.[77]

The Muslim vision of paradise – in contrast to the occidental Christian version – represents a steady progression through the senses towards the ultimate ecstasy of the Beatific Vision. Whatever its meaning in religious terms, paradise represents culturally the vision of the Ultimate which society places before itself and before those individuals whom it seeks to persuade to abide by its norms. In the West a celibate Christian

Church, infected from early on with Manichaean dualism, taught that the flesh and its joys were essentially evil and that paradise must therefore be a place of purely 'spiritual' pleasures. Just as the political dualism apportioning separate allegiances to God and Caesar upheld the eventual separation of church and state, so the mind–body dualism of Helleno-Christianity forced Western consciousness to divide the world into separate categories of spirit and matter. A world thus 'disenchanted' was not only de-sacralized and made secular; it ceased to have any terms in which its own significance could be communicated. Without the sense of an ultimate reality capable of conferring meaning on human existence, ordinary living, with its ecstasies and sorrows, its pleasures and inconveniences, becomes a kind of drudgery in which people are required needlessly and pointlessly to consume their energies.

For all the obvious difficulties it contains as a system of ethics – and therefore as a source of divine law binding human behaviour – the Quranic message militates powerfully against the division of the world into profane and spiritual spheres. The orgiastic vision of paradise may seem naive to a sophisticated modern sensibility, though no less so than the pictures created by European artists. But it is of a piece with the whole of the Quranic vision and its fundamental life-affirming message. It is an integrated vision of ordinary living in which the transcendent is made manifest in every aspect of daily experience. 'Herein is a Message for those who think,' it proclaims incessantly, pointing to the stars, the sky, the trees, the birds and the animals, as well as to the ordinary activities of men and women. The same concern with concrete experience extends to the descriptions of the end of the world, which never so lose touch with sense perception as to become the source of empty theologizing.

In conclusion, it should be emphasized that the positive legal content of the Quran only accounts for a relatively small proportion – about ten per cent – of its overall message. This central message demands an existential commitment to the cause of human freedom, by liberating human consciousness from a fetishistic attachment to limiting objectives. Tribal particularism is replaced by Islamic universalism, the perception of objects as things-in-themselves gives way to a recognition of the contingent character of all existing things. The whole universe is seen as a hugely complex allegory or metaphor of the divinity. Two aspects above all stand out. First, that all dimensions of existence are part of a totality, that every individual object of perception is really a symbol of a much more comprehensive, unifying reality called the divine. Second, that the totality of this reality can never be fully understood by human beings, because of inherent limitations in the structure of their intelligence. There is a portion of totality – the category of *al ghaib* – whose existence has to be taken on trust.

The continuing relevance of the Quran, like that of other great religious works of antiquity, is that it seeks to provide a cosmic context in which to locate humanity and its activities. It places it in a universe that is both beneficent and purposeful, and yet unfathomable. Addressed as it is to Arabic speakers, the Quran also lays down some simple rules – or, rather, guidelines – about the conduct of social and personal life. These rules are specific to geography and period and are addressed to a particular audience whose social and cultural norms are taken as given. The rules of marriage and diet incorporate existing customs: they become increasingly inappropriate the further one is removed from the Arab world, both socially and geographically. The essential message embodied within the rules is the simple one that, since man is a social animal, he needs to accept the social and cultural norms of the society in which he finds himself, since social life depends on them. Unfortunately, the undue emphasis on these rules (which have come to acquire a symbolic meaning for Muslims, especially in non-Arab lands, who are uncertain of their identities) has created a misleading impression of Islam as a religion of Pharisaic legalism backed by harsh 'medieval' punishments. This emphasis detracts from the main body of the Quranic message, which contains far broader, indeed universal, implications.

The universal message contained in the Quran, and in the example of the Prophet's life to which it is inseparably linked historically and literarily, has a certain timeless relevance. It is, essentially, that man is not the Lord of the Universe, that he cannot do as he lists regardless of the moral laws that inhere in its very structure – laws which, though he may continue to discover them for himself, are known in their entirety only to the Creator. There are limits to human knowledge, just as there are limits to the permissible range of human behaviour. How these limits can be defined in practical terms is something that different societies and different generations must necessarily decide for themselves. For Muslims – and for non-Muslims who take the trouble to investigate its meanings – the Quran contains the guidelines to such limits: but it cannot define them absolutely, nor does it seek to do so.

4 ✾ Law and Disorder

Between Cairo's Citadel and the leafy suburb of Ma'adi, much patronized by Egypt's foreign community, there is a fine thirteenth-century
mosque and tomb belonging to the Imam al Shafi'i, the most influential
of the early lawyers of Islam and founder of one of the four *madhhabs* or
legal schools. The mosque and its tomb stand out from the labyrinthine
streets of the Southern Cemetery, known as the City of the Dead, an area
which is in fact a good deal livelier than its name suggests. The fine stone
tombs in which the Cairenes traditionally bury their dead are really
houses built from the same Muqattam limestone as the pyramids,
according to the standard Arab pattern consisting of a simple courtyard
flanked by rooms and an open loggia. The deceased are buried either in
vaults beneath the courtyard, the steps of which are usually covered,
except when needed to admit a new occupant, or beneath stone cenotaphs with pillars standing fore and aft, like masts of a ship. In the past
the rooms were occupied by the *bawwabs* or doorkeepers employed by
the wealthier families to protect the tombs and such valuables as the
silver and plate brought out on special occasions – the night after
Ramadan, the Prophet's Birthday or the anniversary of someone's
death. Despite Islam's discouragement of mortuary cults, many ancient
pharaonic practices have survived in Egypt, a fact which is hardly to be
marvelled at considering that the pharaonic religion lasted at least three
times longer than Islam's fourteen centuries.

Nowadays many of the tombs have been abandoned by their owners
and taken over by squatters, who find them considerably more attractive
to live in than the crumbling tenements of 'Abbasiya or Bulaq. Many
have equipped themselves – legally or otherwise – with electric light and
running water, and it is not unusual to see the flicker of a TV set among
the chickens, the bare-legged children and the paraffin stoves that perch
on the cenotaphs. The main thoroughfare of this necropolis has

developed a lining of cafés, food-stalls and other small shops, most of them of a standard which suggests that the tomb-squatters are far from being the least privileged members of Cairo's teeming social antheap.

At almost any time after sundown, when the people are going about their business, the street leading to the Imam's tomb comes alive with animals and humans, mopeds and handcarts – that special combination of medievalism and modernity that gives the traditional parts of Muslim cities their characteristic flavour. During the second week of Sha'ban, the eighth month of the Muslim calendar, the hubbub reaches its zenith. This is the time when the people celebrate the Imam's *maulid* or anniversary festival. The mosque is festooned with fairy-lights, and antique swings and roundabouts are hauled into the streets to occupy the children. Sufi dervishes congregate near the tomb to perform a *dhikr*, or ritual dance, by the tomb of the saint. A female beduin singer, face tattooed, sings suggestive love songs in praise of the Almighty, whose name – ALLAH – is emblazoned in green neon lighting on the wall of the mosque, bathing the whole carnival in a ghoulish glow. Holy, gaudy, erotic and mystical, the Imam's *maulid*, like other Cairene festivals, promiscuously mingles the sacred and profane in a manner which puritans usually find deeply disturbing.

It is proof of Islam's vigour and catholicity that the saint in whose honour this festival is held is by no means a hero of folklore, renowned for some improbable miracle. The Imam al Shafi'i was the greatest scholar and systematizer of early Islam, the man who, more than any single figure after Muhammad and 'Umar, left his personal mark on its history. In Christian terms, it would be as if the holy razzmatazz were being held in honour of St Augustine or St Jerome. Even at the most popular level, Islam is still a legalistic faith in which saints are expected to dispense justice as well as miracles.

The Imam al Shafi'i is a case in point. His mausoleum was built by Salah al Din's (Saladin's) brother Afdal in 1211, after Egypt had finally been won back to the Sunni fold following the fall of the Shi'ite Fatimids. Saladin's dynasty, the Ayyubids, sought to revive the Imam's memory as the true architect of Sunnism, the mainstream tendency based on observance of the Prophet's Sunna or practice. Their efforts were entirely successful: the Shi'ite tendency, with its 'personality cult' of leaders claiming descent from the Prophet's family, was virtually eliminated, despite almost two centuries of government by the Fatimid caliphs. The Imam is now the object of a popular cult among peasants who address letters to him seeking redress from injustices unremedied by Egypt's lumbering and corrupt judicial system.

The letters to the Imam are placed inside the iron grille surrounding his cenotaph. In 1965 a selection of them was published by a criminologist, Sayyid al Awais, and they make fascinating reading. Many of the writers seek cures for their sickness or vengeance for injuries, real or imagined: 'I demand that my neighbour 'Abbas be paralysed to the ground, so that he may know that people other than himself have someone to defend them.' (The plaintiff had had his face slapped and his beard pulled by the aforesaid 'Abbas – in public, during the Holy Month of Ramadan.) Other letters contain requests for employment:

> I am the breadwinner of a large family but cannot provide the bread for lack of an income. I wrote – O Imam, my master – to the manager of the government factory explaining my situation, but he did not bother about me. So I hope that you will take an interest in my case and see that I obtain a job in one of the government factories so that I may live and guarantee the bread of my children. I have no one to go to but you. So help me for the sake of the grandfather of the believers, our master Muhammad, and for the sake of the Quran![1]

Some of the letters are actually written in the form of legal submissions to the Court of the Bataniya, a kind of celestial Supreme Court presided over by the Imam, Sayyida Zainab and Sayyid Husain (the Prophet's granddaughter and grandson, much venerated in Egypt) and Sayyid Ahmad Badawi (a popular Sufi saint).

> Our shaikh attacked and threatened to beat and insult me, in spite of his being the Crown of Islam in our village, whom I respect and venerate . . . And Na'ima Hafiz took my cotton crop in 1952, but denied that she took it . . . I have already submitted a complaint to our master, Husain, and to our virtuous Lady, Umm Hashim al Sayyida Zainab (may God be satisfied with them). And they accepted my petition and saw to it that the value of my cotton was recorded in the public prosecutor's investigation. But till now the case is still held up in the advisor's office, and has yet to come before the court . . .[2]

It is not inappropriate that the Imam al Shafi'i, though the leading intellectual of early Islam, should be revered as a popular saint by the

Egyptian *fallahin*. More than any other figure of his time, he restored a form of unity to an Islamic state undergoing a process of disintegration. He did not succeed in achieving a consolidation at the political level: nor was this his aim. The geopolitical tensions inherent in the vast new territories conquered by the Arabs made an Islamic state with centralized political control an impossible dream. But he founded something which, in the end, would prove much more durable than the Arab imperium. This was the science of *fiqh* (literally, 'understanding') or religious jurisprudence, by which a whole range of customs and practices, derived from the Prophet's teachings, Arabian customs and the customs of the newly conquered peoples, could be merged into a single system of law governing the daily life of the Muslims. It is really from Shafi'i's systematization of *shari'a*, developed according to principles first devised by him, that modern Muslims, both Shi'ite and Sunni, derive their common identity and sense of being-in-the-world.

The development of *fiqh* occurred over a period of two centuries against the background of the expansion and threatened disintegration of the Islamic empire. The political conflicts during this, the formative period of an Islamic religious and political culture destined to last for a millennium or more, became the basis of the sectarian divisions to be examined in the next chapter. Here it will be necessary only to sketch in, as briefly as possible, the historical background.

After the first wave of conquest the Arabs became a new ruling class which deliberately avoided integrating itself with the conquered peoples. The soldiers were kept in garrison towns and subject to the rule of *qadis* or judges appointed by the caliph or his governors. The rest of the population, whether Jewish, Christian or Zoroastrian, were accorded protection upon payment of the *jizya*, a poll tax first instituted by the Prophet after the conquest of Khaibar. Conversion to Islam, if not actively discouraged, was scarcely encouraged: the economic privileges of the Arabs depended on the subject peoples retaining their status as *dhimmi* or client communities. Those foreigners who did convert were generally treated as second-class citizens. Many tried to get even with the Arabian aristocrats by discarding their Greek or Persian names and adopting the names of famous Arab families, buttressing their claims with forged pedigrees. That this was above all an Arab, rather than a Muslim, conquest is best demonstrated by the fact that the Christian Arab tribes which had joined in the conquest were not taxed with the conquered *dhimmi* Christians. Nor was it anomalous that the greatest poet of the Umayyad period, Akhtal (c.640–710), panegyrist of the caliph 'Abd al Malik, was himself a Christian.

The social distinction between Arab and non-Arab, however, became much harder to maintain once a significant number of the latter had converted. Despite the lack of coercion, the financial advantages of becoming a Muslim – quite apart from any religious attractions it may have had for people seeking more enlightened forms of piety – were obvious enough. Conversions among the poorer elements of the subject peoples were facilitated both by the egalitarian character of the Quranic message and the 'levelling' effects of conquest, which greatly reduced the power of the great land-owning Christian and Zoroastrian families. Landless peasants who drifted to the cities in search of work no doubt discovered that there were considerable advantages in becoming Muslims, even though converts were at first given the definitely inferior status as *mawalis*, or clients, of the Arabian tribes. Membership of the Umma ceased to be the badge of a new ruling class: instead it became something of an alliance between the rulers and the least privileged sections of the conquered peoples. A not dissimilar situation occurred after the Muslim conquest of India, when the Moghul rulers succeeded in 'liberating' and converting members of the lowest Hindu castes.

As a result of these conversions and of the growing economic links between the different communities, it became impossible to maintain the dualism of 'Umar's time, with one law for the Muslims and another, autonomously administered, for the subject communities. The customs of the Arabs, based on tribal habits and a few simple rules laid down in the Quran, were beginning to mingle, and sometimes to conflict, with the laws of the majority in the new territories.

Geopolitical tensions were also developing. Under the Umayyad caliphs, Damascus was the capital of a flourishing empire, much of which was administered by the Christian clerical class inherited by the Arabs from their Byzantine predecessors. But increasingly the economic weight of the empire came to be in Iraq and the distant highlands of Khurasan, territories belonging to the former Sassanid empire. Under Walid I (705–715) the Arabs continued to expand, westwards to Spain and eastwards into Transoxania and Sind. But the attempt in 717 by Walid's successor, Sulaiman, to take Constantinople failed, and the Arabs were thrown back behind the Taurus mountains, which still remain their northern frontier.

While Christian Anatolia remained unconquered, the economic – and hence the political – centre of gravity shifted eastwards towards the former Sassanid lands. The powerful Umayyad governor of Iraq, Hajjaj (d. 714) did much to increase that province's prosperity by extending the irrigation works. At the same time he antagonized the Arab garrisons by his ruthless centralizing policies which rode roughshod over older habits of tribal autonomy.

During the third and fourth decades of the eighth century, social and economic tensions began to develop which seriously threatened the unity of the empire. A Syrian-based administration with centralizing tendencies created strong resentments among the garrisons in Iraq and Khurasan. At the same time the new class of non-Arab converts was becoming increasingly resentful of the privileges still enjoyed by the Arabs. The strongest centres of dissent tended to be in Basra and Kufa, one a port of growing importance and both of them garrison towns. It was partly for this reason that, in Kufa especially, factions loyal to the Prophet's family against the 'usurping' Umayyads began to attract support.

The opposition movement was not without an intellectual leadership capable of expressing itself in religio-legal terms. The Umayyad caliphs had from the first found their critics among men and women who accused them of abandoning the pious simplicities of Medina for the new-found luxuries of empire. The movement was compounded of many elements. A traditional Arab element, consonant with the polarities of beduin life – plunder and starvation – expressed itself in terms of an austere puritanism which somehow complemented the excesses of the new, fabulously wealthy, caliphal order. (The same polarities may be observed in modern Saudi Arabia.) A distinctively political element crystallized into support for the extreme Kharijis – who tried to secede from the corrupt Islamic community and recreate the Medinese ideal of a community of saints. A similar trend existed among the people – many of them *mawalis* – who would later be dubbed the Shi'a, or partisans of 'Ali and his house. At a superior cultural level there existed small but influential groups of pious men who spent much of their time in the mosques, reciting the Quran and no doubt asking themselves how, in the vastly expanded world in which they now found themselves, its messages could be properly applied.

A debate, involving moral and philosophical arguments about the right to rebel against unjust rulers, was already in progress when a series of revolts culminated in the downfall of the Umayyad dynasty in 750.

The new rulers, who took power with the key support of the garrison tribes in Khurasan, enjoyed the backing of the moderate Shi'ite elements and most of the pious intellectuals. Though not of 'Alid descent, they were descended from the Prophet's uncle 'Abbas, and were therefore closer to his line than the Umayyads. The 'Abbasids built a new capital for themselves at Baghdad, hard by Ctesiphon, the Sassanid seat of government. From here they ruled an empire which, though it rapidly lost most of its western territories in the Mediterranean, had a solid agrarian base in Mesopotamia and was free to develop extensive trading contacts across the newly unified Indian Ocean. The 'Abbasid caliphs became fabulously wealthy: their golden age has been aptly summarized, for both Muslims and Westerners, in the reign of Harun al Rashid (786–809).

The coming of the 'Abbasids failed to heal the political divisions that were developing between supporters of 'Ali's line and the rest of the Muslim community. Though allowing Shi'ite expectations of a *mahdi* or messiah to work in their favour, once in power the 'Abbasids turned against their former Shi'ite supporters, initiating the long history of persecution and martyrdom that came to characterize the sect. The more moderate intellectuals, however, including the Qadaris and their successors the Mu'tazilis, rallied to the support of the new regime, under whose auspices they laid the foundations of the first truly universal Islamic order.

Intellectuals do not necessarily create history; but at certain times they design institutions through which historical change is effected, which gives them an influence as great as that of rulers or their generals. The formative period of Islamic history was really the first two centuries of the 'Abbasid era. The model of the Medinese polity, elaborated and adjusted to suit contemporary circumstances, was its inspiration. Its architects were the scholar-jurists (*'ulama*) of the eighth and ninth centuries, the most outstanding of whom was Shafi'i.

The task facing the pious *'ulama* at this time was a formidable one. Under the Umayyads they had become increasingly restive, both about the regime's injustices and about the arbitrary manner in which it took over non-Islamic laws and administrative practices from its Byzantine and Persian predecessors. The 'Abbasid revolution provided the *'ulama*, for the first time, with an opportunity to put their criticisms into practice: they must find Islamic solutions to the problems the Umayyads had often solved by recourse to Graeco-Roman precedents. In view of the vastly expanding Muslim community that was coming into being, the task was an urgent one. Since the time of the late Umayyads, the caliphs had been actively encouraging conversions to Islam. After the 'Abbasid revolution, which enjoyed the support of the *mawali*, the stream of conversions became a flood. With peasants flocking to the cities, converting and bringing Islam back into the countryside, the demand for Islamic solutions had a populist character.

The Medinese polity offered little more than a few general guidelines. It had been above all a community with an 'ideal' orientation: Muhammad's aim had been to build a society basing itself on the godly life, and by and large his community had responded. It had been a relatively small community, consisting of about 30,000 persons, most of whom would have been known to each other. Moreover, it had been a culturally homogeneous community, in which common Arab custom had been modified by group allegiance to Muhammad and observance of the relatively few, simple Quranic rules.

Clearly it would have been impossible to have recreated such conditions in the vastly expanded social context of the 'Abbasid empire. The rules governing life in the Medinese community had already been overlaid in many cases by the practices of the Umayyads. This was hardly surprising in view of the amount of time – more than a century – that had elapsed since the death of the Prophet. The Quran itself, as we have seen, contained relatively little legislative material. Only 600 verses out of more than 6,000 deal with legal obligations, and the majority of these are actually concerned with religious matters such as prayer, fasting or pilgrimage. Only 80 or so verses deal with legal topics in the strict sense of the term and the majority of these are about women, marriage and the laws of inheritance. As we have seen, during his lifetime the Prophet had been not only the Quran's transmitter but the ruler of an Islamic state whose authority grew with the progress of his military campaigns. On legal questions, the Prophet himself must have provided detailed guidance. Thus he is said to have clarified ambiguities in the law of inheritance by giving heirs under Quranic law precedence over relatives entitled to legacies under the older Arab customary law. In general the Prophet's practice or Sunna, in both legal and religious matters, became normative within the community.

Despite the political conflicts in which they became involved, the earliest caliphs inherited something of the Prophet's charismatic power and freedom to legislate. Thus 'Umar appears to have had no scruples about instituting the penalty of stoning for adulterers in place of the milder Quranic punishment of flogging, or increasing the penalty for wine-drinking from 40 to 80 lashes. During the latter years of Umayyad rule, however, the caliph's discretionary power became increasingly unacceptable in the eyes of the pious opposition. The authority of the Prophet was invoked to counter the authority of the caliphs. The intensive study of the Quran itself produced a demand for data about the Prophet's life, for only by establishing the 'occasion' of revelation – the historic context in which a particular verse or group of verses 'came down' – could its meaning be fully elucidated. One school of tradition-ists, tracing itself from 'Abdullah ibn 'Abbas, son of the Prophet's uncle, tried to give the context of as many of the occasions of revelation as possible in order to clarify the meaning of the divine messages. Other scholars collected narratives about Muhammad's campaigns and his life, based on well-authenticated accounts drawn from oral materials.

In the generations when the actual memory of the Prophet was alive, the law had developed in a more or less *ad hoc* manner around the decisions of individual authorities, such as Malik ibn Anas (d. 796), a lawyer and collector of traditions in Medina. Malik's school could claim, with some justification, to represent a 'living tradition' or *sunna* going back to the Prophet's time. At the same time a certain flexibility had been introduced in interpreting the Quranic rules. The opinion (*rai*) or prefer-ences (*istihsan*) of the jurists were allowed to influence legal doctrines, as was the principle of analogy (*qiyas*) in dealing with new situations unmentioned in the Quran or the Sunna.

During the latter Umayyad period, however, the pious opposition began to adopt an increasingly doctrinaire attitude, rejecting judge-ments based on anything other than the Prophet's own Sunna. Legal practices that had grown up more or less organically in Medina or Kufa were no longer regarded as acceptable by the pious; nor were *hadiths* attributable to the Prophet's Companions – the 30,000-odd members of the original Medinese community whose statements the earliest lawyers had virtually placed on a par with those of the Prophet himself.

The origins of *hadiths* attributed to the Prophet himself are still the subject of dispute, and some ill-feeling, between Muslims and non-Muslim scholars. The vast majority of Muslims believe that these *hadiths*, which are contained in six canonical collections, genuinely represent the sayings and deeds of the Prophet as preserved in oral tradition and written down in the ninth century. There is no doubt that the *hadith*-collectors, the best-known being Muhammad ibn Isma'il al Bukhari (810–870) and Muslim ibn al Hajjaj (d. 875), travelled vast distances to seek out reliable individuals and devoted prodigious amounts of energy to the attempt to distinguish true from false transmitters of the Prophet's alleged sayings and deeds. According to the system they developed, each tradition was equipped with an *isnad*, or chain of authorities, tracing it back to the prophet, rather in the manner that dealers provide rare art objects with provenances tracing them back to their original owners. A doubtless exaggerated story records that Bukhari himself examined 600,000 *hadiths*, 200,000 of which he actually memorized before committing a mere 2,700 of them, which he regarded as unimpeachable, to paper. Another story is told which demonstrates his extreme punctiliousness in rejecting transmitters considered even remotely unreliable. Having traced a particular *hadith* to a pious Iraqi scholar, he eventually, after much travelling, found the source in question, who confirmed the *hadith*, providing it with an impeccable *isnad*. Afterwards the scholar invited Bukhari to inspect a new colt of which he was especially proud. In order to attract the animal the scholar gathered up the folds of his gown as though he were carrying corn in his lap. The colt duly approached him in the expectation of food. Bukhari ruefully rejected the *hadith* which he had heard from the lips of the scholar: a man who would so deceive an animal could not be regarded as a reliable source of the Prophet's Sunna.

The scholars developed an elaborate technical vocabulary defining the degrees of reliability in the chains of transmitters. Their criticisms were, however, confined to the *isnads*: the content of the *hadiths* themselves was never subject to critical examination. Since the pioneering work of the Hungarian Arabist Ignaz Goldziher during the nineteenth century, most western scholars have questioned the authenticity of even the best-attested *hadiths* on the grounds that many are anachronistic in content, contradict each other or are at variance with the spirit or letter of the Quran. Joseph Schacht, following Goldziher, argued that many of the traditions in the classical collections must have been invented shortly before their inclusion, because they were not employed at an earlier date in the course of legal discussions when 'reference to [them] would have been imperative'.[3] Every legal tradition attributed to the Prophet, until the contrary was proved, must be taken not as an authentic expression valid for his time, but as the 'fictitious expression of a legal doctrine formulated at a later date'. Schacht insisted that positive proof of authenticity was lacking in every single *hadith* he examined.

Schacht's conclusions have not been accepted by the leading Muslim authorities, although some liberal scholars, such as Professor Fazlur Rahman, have been prepared to accept the validity of his method. However, the conclusion that follows from his work is not necessarily that all so-called 'sound' traditions are legal fictions, but rather that we are unlikely ever to be able to distinguish between the true and the spurious with absolute finality. The process of winnowing 'true' from 'false' traditions, which had been completed by the early tenth century, was not really an exercise in scholarship, though in a predominantly oral culture the technique of *isnad* criticism was probably the best available method of testing the data: it was primarily an exercise in cultural formation. The scholars who collected and sifted through the hundreds of thousands of *hadiths* extant during the eighth and ninth centuries were really determining what should be included within the new 'Islamized' culture and what should be rejected. In the supremely capable hands of Muhammad ibn Idris al Shafi'i, this process was far from being either arbitrary or irrational.

Shafi'i was born in Syria towards the end of the eighth century. After growing up as an impoverished orphan in Mecca, he studied with Malik ibn Anas in Medina before going to Egypt, where he finally settled after taking part in an unsuccessful Shi'ite rebellion against the caliph Harun al Rashid. In Cairo he undertook a systematic revision and harmonization of the existing Muslim law, which, beset by the rising tide of traditions on one side and the increasing divergences between the legal schools on the other, was becoming ever more confused. Shafi'i's main concession to the traditionists was to insist on the primacy of the Prophet's Sunna over the *sunna* of the Companions, their successors or the 'living' traditions of the Kufan and Medinese schools. He employed a formidable argument against those who tried to oppose the traditionists by upholding the supremacy of the Quran over all other sources of law: 'The Quran does not contradict the *hadiths*, but the *hadiths* explain the Quran.'

In effect, the Quran cannot stand alone as a source of law: Shafi'i demonstrated 'by an incisive critique of its language (in which he brought out all the diverse ways in which it called for interpretation) that the Book presupposed Muhammad not only as its deliverer, but as its interpreter'.[4] It followed that it was not the Quran alone, but the Quran plus the Prophet's Sunna, as recorded in *hadiths*, that must guide the Muslims. In Shafi'i's hands the word *sunna* acquired the specific meaning it has today, when the mainstream followers of Islam are known as *ahl al sunna* – 'People of the Sunna' (Sunnis or Sunnites). In its original pre-Islamic meaning, *sunna* had been applied to ancestral custom: the word has associations with a beaten path in the desert, advancing age, sharpened teeth and well-honed implements. Employed by the legists of the so-called ancient schools, it means the living 'practical' tradition, assumed to be based on the general practice and authority of the Prophet and his companions. By Shafi'i's time a considerable divergence had developed between the 'living' *sunna*, or practical tradition, which varied from one geographical region to another, and the rising tide of *hadiths* attributed to the Prophet. From contemporary writings it is clear that defenders of the living *sunna* regarded the latter as an unacceptable innovation.

The confused arguments surrounding the question eventually crystallized into a debate between two groups: the 'rationalists' (*ahl al kalam*), who defended the supremacy of the Quran, and the 'traditionists' (*ahl al hadith*), for whom the Prophet's example was supreme, even as against the specific injunctions of the Quran. During the early years of the 'Abbasid caliphate, the rationalists won the day: part of their case was that many so-called *hadiths* contained anthropomorphisms which were theologically unacceptable. In this they were certainly closer than their opponents to the Quranic doctrine of God. The problem, however, was that the remote and abstract deity of the Quran was bound to be less attractive to popular piety than the more accessible figure of the Prophet, repository of every local proverb and hero of countless anecdotes. Shafi'i's essential achievement was to accommodate these diverging attitudes within a single system which took on board the popular figure of the Prophet while actually maintaining the orthodoxy of the rationalists. By insisting on rigorous *isnad*-criticism before any *hadith* could be accepted, Shafi'i and his successors among the *hadith*-collectors ensured that newly minted *hadiths* would be rejected.

The system of which Shafi'i was the chief designer matures into the Shari'a, or Divine Law of Islam. The word *shari'a*, like *sunna*, has essentially conservative associations. In non-religious terms, it means the road or way to a watering-place, the well-trodden path which must always be followed. For the beduin, safety lay in following the paths of one's ancestors. Innovation – *bid'a* – was hazardous: *bid'a* would acquire pejorative connotations – equivalent almost to heresy – in the religious vocabulary.

The Shari'a or holy law is both Islam's greatest achievement and its most signal failure. As a system of divine law it theoretically governs every aspect of the Muslim's life, from the movements of prayer down to the manner of defecation, exercising an influence over individual behaviour unparalleled in other systems. Until modern times the shared identity of Muslims from Morocco to China was based not just on a common faith but on common cultural patterns reinforced by common behavioural conditioning. This is not to say that Muslim social life was everywhere uniform: inevitably the effects of Islamization tend to diminish according to a population's cultural or geographic distance from the West Asian epicentre. Berber tribesmen, Egyptian *fallahin*, Pathan warriors and Javanese smallholders, all of them in various ways adopted the Islamic patterning to suit a way of life and a view of the world that had been moulded by previous cultural, religious and social institutions. But the Islamic model proved flexible enough to suit most of the peoples of Asia and Africa who were conquered by Muslims or who came into contact with them through trade or migration. Only in the centres of vigorous high culture, such as India, China and Europe, were the legal, social and military obstacles sufficient to prevent the process of Islamization from eventually gaining control.

However, a price had to be paid for the success of the Shari'a as a normative system; this lay in its failure to measure up to the political and religious aspirations of the first generations of Muslims. Politically, the Islamic state was in continuous disarray, almost from the death of its founder. No sooner had it established itself than it began to fragment, ideologically at first and subsequently into warring political factions. The very success of the Shari'a in producing a distinctly 'Islamic' way of life was accompanied by a failure in the area of public, constitutional and criminal law, not to mention human rights in general and an aspect of them which lay close to the heart of the Prophet, the emancipation of women.

The flaws in the system lay less in Shafi'i's original design than in its application. At the level of private behaviour, the elaboration of the Muhammadan model, whether based on the historic actuality of the Prophet or on a fictionalized adaptation of 'Abbasid norms, was highly effective. Using impeccably logical analytic methods, Shafi'i developed a self-consistent legal method, known as *usul al fiqh*, 'roots of understanding'. Since the law of God had been revealed once and for all time in the Quran and the Sunna, *fiqh* meant the knowledge of something already assumed to exist – the inquiry into how the divine law works out in practical terms – rather than the development of a body of jurisprudence based on case law and human legislation. The foundations of *fiqh*, established by Shafi'i, were based on four roots (*usul*): the Quran, the Prophet's Sunna, the consensus of the community (*ijma'*) any analogical reasoning (*qiyas*). In theory the Quran ranked supreme in the hierarchy of legal roots. In practice, since the divine text required interpretation by reference to *hadith*, the Sunna ranked equally with the Quran and in some cases was superior to it. For Shafi'i the Quran and the Sunna were the final unquestionable authority in matters of law: 'What is based on the Quran,' he wrote in his classic treatise, the Risala, 'and on the unanimously recognized Sunna, is true both outwardly and inwardly [*fi al zahir wa al batin*].'[5]

One consequence of this dual sovereignty of God's Word and the Prophet's example was the eventual elevation of Muhammad to a status barely subordinate – in the popular imagination – to that of Allah himself. The Prophet's statements and actions being necessary for the interpretation of the divine text, it followed that the Prophet himself must have been operating continuously under divine inspiration. Certain of his statements came to be regarded as 'sacred' *hadiths*: though not included in the Quran, they were represented as having been revealed by Allah (though not, as in the Quran, in 'Allah's Words'). A logical consequence of the development of *hadith* and its sanctification in the Shari'a was the doctrine of Muhammad's 'sinlessness': whatever decisions or pronouncements had been authoritative during his lifetime became *infallible* after his death. Hardly surprisingly, Europeans who came into contact with Muslims saw them as 'Muhammadans' whose veneration of their prophet was no less exaggerated than that which they themselves accorded to Christ.

The remaining roots of the religious law, *ijma'* (consensus) and *qiyas* (analogical reasoning), though theoretically subordinate to the Quran and the Sunna were structurally part of the system. *Ijma'* as a principle was enshrined in a *hadith* according to which the Prophet is said to have declared: 'Never will God make my community agree upon a wrong course.'[6] Shafi'i's opponents, the *ahl al kalam* and the legists of the ancient schools, had upheld the principle of scholarly *ijma'* to defend their positions. By a dexterous piece of legerdemain, Shafi'i substituted for the *ijma'* of the religious intellectuals the *ijma'* of the people, who demanded that the traditions of the Prophet, and no other, should be, with the Quran, the source of law. *Ijma'* determined that only those *hadiths* with 'impeccable' *isnads* should be part of the Sunna Shafi'i identified as 'unanimously recognized'. In later generations the *ijma'* of the people was once again replaced by the *ijma'* of the religious scholars or *'ulama*. The principle of *ijma'* did not imply democracy in any modern application of the term. But it did introduce a certain social and intellectual flexibility into the system. The doctrine made it impossible for pious fanatics among the religious leadership to make prohibitions which the generality of people found uncongenial.

Two examples in the field of drugs – coffee and hashish – illustrate the impact of *ijma'* on community practice. Neither was known in Arabia in the Prophet's time. When the use of both became popular from around the thirteenth century, the more puritanically minded *'ulama* sought to prohibit them by analogy with the Quranic ban on wine, which, they argued, extended to all intoxicating substances. The use of coffee, however, could be justified as an anti-soporific helpful to nocturnal devotions. The *ijma'* in its favour was overwhelming and both rulers and *'ulama* were powerless to ban it. The supporters of hashish or Indian hemp, introduced by Sufis from India at about the same period as coffee, publicized their case in witty verses condemning as *ultra vires* those *'ulama* seeking to ban the drug:

> Hashish contains a hidden secret
> Too subtle for human minds to grasp
> They have declared it forbidden
> Without any justification based on reason or *hadith*
> Declaring forbidden what is not forbidden is forbidden.[7]

The victory of *ijma'* against attempts to ban coffee-drinking was total. *Ijma'* in favour of hashish was almost as successful, and it is still widely used among the traditional classes in Egypt, Morocco and other Muslim countries.

Qiyas, the technique of systematic analogical reasoning, was the method by which the legal experts sought to incorporate new situations within the system of divine law while maintaining the primacy of the Quran and the Sunna. *Qiyas* allowed a role for individual opinion on the part of the judges, although, as can be seen from the foregoing, it was generally subject to the dictates of *ijma'*, expressed as the consensus of the *'ulama* or as the consensus of the community in opposition to the rulers and the *'ulama*. If *ijma'* represented in general a conservative social force, this was but a reflection of the wider Muslim social order, in which the heads of families, rather than representatives of the state, were the repositories of social power. The supreme achievement of Shafi'i's system was the establishment of a structure ensuring a maximum degree of cultural homogeneity in which each individual could be held personally responsible for his actions.

Shafi'i's system never attained complete uniformity. Generally speaking his successors stuck to the ground rules laid down by him, while adhering to some of the principles of the 'ancient schools' he superseded. Variations, on matters of detail rather than questions of principle, crystallized into four distinctive *madhhabs* or legal schools which disputed among themselves over the method and rules of *fiqh*. The schools were named after the most prominent figures associated with them. The Medinese school was named after Malik ibn Anas, Shafi'i's teacher. The Kufans adopted the name of their most prominent early legist, Abu Hanifa (699–767), a well-to-do merchant of Iranian descent. Shafi'i's pupils, established in Egypt, founded a school which they named after him. The fourth of the Sunni *madhhabs* to have survived into modern times is associated with one of the prominent early traditionists, Ahmad ibn Hanbal (d. 855) who is said to have collected more than 80,000 *hadiths*.

Despite the differences between the three principal schools (the Hanbalis became active as a source of legal authority only after the Wahhabi reform movement began in the eighteenth century), they were generally agreed in accepting the system of roots developed by Shafi'i. For that reason his role as the greatest systematizer of early Islamic law makes him more than just the 'founder' of one of the four *madhhabs*. Viewed retrospectively, his historic achievement was to forestall the development of independent regional legal systems based on Medina or Kufa; though the Malkis and Hanafis kept some of the distinctive traditions of their respective schools, they were obliged, after Shafi'i, to accommodate them within an overall framework rooted in the Quran and the Sunna. This supreme intellectual achievement makes Shafi'i one of the great unifiers of Islam.

The Malikis remained the most conservative of the four *madhhabs* and continued to follow the consensus of Medina, which could be justified in

Shafi'i's terms because it was the place where the Prophet himself had governed. Thus in questions of marriage they reflected the customs of the northern Arabs: marriages could only be contracted by the parents or guardians of marriage partners, but divorce for the husband was relatively easy. The Hanafi marriage rules by contrast reflected the more complex urban society of Iraq, with the social positions of both husband and wife taken into account in drawing up the marriage contract; for this purpose a detailed hierarchy of the professions was recognized. Generally speaking, the Malikis had a more moralistic view of the law, in which the intentions – good or bad – of a person's actions were taken account of in determining their permissibility. The Hanafis had a more formalistic approach, emphasizing the external conduct of the actor and endorsing the use of legal stratagems (*hiyal*) to get around particular prohibitions – such as the ban on lending at interest. In line with the Kufan tradition, the Hanafi school allowed a greater role for individual reasoning and judicial opinion. The Shafi'is, who followed their master in trying to reconcile the extremes of traditionalism and reasoning, occupied a position midway between the Malikis and the Hanafis.

Apart from his achievement in accommodating the schools of law within a comprehensive system, Shafi'i may be said to have contributed to the unity of Islam in a territorial sense. The Hanafi school became the official doctrine of the 'Abbasid caliphate; for a period, followers of the other *madhhabs* were banned from preaching in the mosques or giving judgements. Without this accommodation of the different schools within a single framework, it is difficult to see how, after the collapse of the caliphal state, the divine law could have avoided falling into the kind of politico-religious fragmentation which produced the wars of religion in Europe. As it was, the political disunity of Islam developed within the context of an underlying legal and religious unity which ignored territorial divisions and in which the use of violence was generally limited to military elites and radical sectarian groups. The pluralism of the Shari'a was sanctioned by a well-attested *hadith*: 'The differences of opinion among the learned within my community are [a sign of] God's Grace.'[8]

The distinctive character of Islam, as compared with that of Christianity, lies less in the fusion of religion and politics (which also occurred in the West) than in the fact that the division between the religious and the secular occurs at a different point, between the legal and political realms. Whereas Christianity inherited a body of secular law developed under the pagan Romans, Islam developed a system of religious law more or less independently of the political sphere. The failure of the caliphal state to realize the Islamic vision of a politically unified Umma extending throughout the known world had the effect of placing politics *outside* the purview of religion. Muslim rulers needed no formal authority, sanctified by religion, comparable to the impressive titles conferred by the papacy upon Christian kings and princes. Once the royal bodyguards and over-powerful regional governors (sultans) who inherited the caliphal power had come into their own, whether they were formally recognized by the caliphs or not was largely irrelevant, since the caliphs had ceased to have any power. All they required was the consent of the *'ulama*, and in Sunni communities this was usually forthcoming. At the same time the *'ulama*, though appointed as judges by the rulers, were often extremely reluctant to compromise the purity of the divine law by serving the establishment. Far from being integrated (as many Muslims claim), the political and religious institutions remained distinct. Had they been fused as in Europe up until the French Revolution, the anarchic division of the Arab empire into unstable territorial segments controlled by rival war-lords would have had much more devastating consequences. As it was, the religious pluralism allowed in the system of *fiqh* prevented the full mobilization of religious forces in the service of political or sectarian conflicts. Society existed more or less independently of the state, a feature which is still evident in the Muslim world today.

The system of *fiqh*, which is the real offspring of the Divine Law, is the most enduring legacy of the Prophet's career and of the creative generation of Sunni *'ulama* which ended with the death of Ibn Hanbal in 855. The legal consensus linking the flexibility of the Hanafis with the traditionalism of the Hanbalis was broad but delicate. It was not subject to any controlling body with authority to decide upon changes of course: it was maintained entirely by the *'ulama* themselves, who coalesced around the four *madhhabs* which established the boundaries of the religious law. Radical innovations in legal or ritual matters would naturally threaten this consensus, and it was no doubt for this reason that after the tenth century there gradually developed the doctrine, sanctioned, of course, by the *ijma'* of the scholars, that the gates of *ijtihad* (creative interpretation of the law) had been closed. Henceforth legal decisions would be arrived at according to the principle of *taqlid* ('imitation'), based on the judgements of the four legal schools. New attempts at *ijtihad* came to be condemned as *bid'a* – innovation. Only among the Shi'a, whose imams

were regarded as all-powerful in matters of religion, were the doors of
ijtihad to remain open.

Nowhere, perhaps, is the Sunni consensus given a more impressive
concrete demonstration than in one of the finest of all Islamic buildings,
the great *madrasa* (college) of Sultan Hasan in Cairo, completed in 1363.
After the destruction of Baghdad by the Mongols in 1258, Cairo became
the unchallenged capital of the Muslim world, a city of about half a
million people and the largest in the Old World. The Mamluk rulers, a
self-selecting military elite of Turcomans from the Volga region, sought
to live down their lowly origins by excelling in works of piety, building
and liberally endowing the religious colleges, Quranic schools and
hospitals adjoining their tombs. If Chartres cathedral is an emblem of the
medieval Christian vision of a hierarchical society pointing ever upward
towards heaven, Sultan Hasan is an architectural expression of the
Islamic vision in its maturity. Its centre is a vast paved courtyard flanked
on each side by four great vaulted enclosures, or *liwans*, one for each of
the four *madhhabs*. The skilful juxtaposition of voids and solids makes of
the sky a ceiling stretching out into infinity, seemingly containing the
uncontainable, a brilliant feat of architectural manipulation which
creates out of interior space the soaring effect achieved by the exterior
of the Gothic cathedral. Here, under the covered *liwans*, the aspiring
'ulama would congregate around their respective teachers to study the
Quran and the *hadiths* and to memorize the complicated and exacting
rules of *fiqh*, before setting off to all parts of the Muslim world.

Outside the radical Shi'ite groups, the message of Islam was rarely
spread by conscious missionary activity. Rather, it extended itself autonomously along the trade routes by means of the conversion of tribal
chieftains who sought social or political advantages in joining the Umma
and becoming part of its advanced culture and civilization. Because the
fiqh operated at a popular cultural level, no central administration was
required to mastermind the process. In the more distant reaches of Africa
and Asia, wandering merchants or marabouts would attract groups of
followers, not least because they enjoyed the cultural prestige conferred
by membership of a wider cosmopolitan world. In sub-Saharan Africa,
for example, conversion was often a gradual process, in which the local
animistic religions were first Islamized and then replaced altogether.
Converts usually began by accepting the simple emblems of Muslim
culture, such as amulets or costumes which enhanced their prestige

locally, before adopting the ritual of prayer and recognizing the categories of the permitted (halal) and the forbidden (haram) which eventually replaced the local taboos.

In the areas where Muslim culture had taken root, increasing adherence to the rules of fiqh gradually squeezed out non-Muslim cultural
traditions. Similarly, knowledge of the Quran and the law tended to
filter down gradually. Education has always been a pious duty for
Muslims, and any merchant or wandering scholar might open a kuttab
(Quranic School) provided he was reasonably competent in the law,
having perhaps read the Quran and studied fiqh in one of the cities. The
spreading of the fiqh was thus a process which often lasted for generations. In many parts of the world today, including parts of tropical
Africa and South East Asia, the process is still far from complete: Islamic
worship, law and practice coexist with other religio-cultural forms, of
animist or Hindu–Buddhist origin. Religious intolerance of shirk (idolatry) is a characteristic of most resurgence movements in Islam. In the
outer fringes of the Muslim world such movements represent less a
restoration of religious purity than the completion of Islamization.

Although the four schools of fiqh coexisted in the great metropolitan
cities such as Cairo, in practice they did become normative in specific
geographical areas. As the official madhhab of the 'Abbasid caliphate, the
Hanafi system took root in western Asia, whence it spread, after the
conversion of the Mongols, to the Indian subcontinent. Maliki law,
though indigenous to Medina, spread westwards into north and Central
Africa. Shafi'i law, indigenous to Egypt, also became prominent in
Southern Arabia, whence it spread along the monsoon route to East
Africa and South East Asia.

The diversity of doctrines within the Shari'a was often compared by
Muslim writers to the holes of a fishing net. The metaphor is apt, for the
fiqh is less a system of law, with a developed apparatus of procedure and
enforcement, than a process of socialization and acculturation which
progressively transforms human societies in a more or less autonomous
manner. To change the metaphor only slightly, the Shari'a may also be
compared to the interlaced patterns characteristic of Islamic design
which can be extended indefinitely, like wallpaper patterns. In time the
process of Islamization takes root, imposing a degree of cultural
homogeneity. Observance of the divine law becomes a social factor
functioning more or less independently of the state.

Outside the Arabian Peninsula, where the Shari'a was more or less suited to social conditions, the system of *fiqh* remained limited to matters of ritual, family and personal conduct. The jurists could not extend *de jure* recognition to the hereditary caliphate established by the Umayyads and later by the 'Abbasids, although they came to recognize their power *de facto* as the preferable alternative to anarchy. At the same time the caliphs took over and adapted much of the criminal, commercial and constitutional law of their Byzantine and Sassanid predecessors. The Shari'a thus remained an only partly realized ideal. The caliphs had little difficulty in restricting its competence to matters of private or community behaviour. The *qadis* (Shari'a judges) had no power to enforce legal decisions on the rulers. The rulers, while formally committed to upholding the Shari'a, were rarely prepared to submit to the decisions of the *qadis*, whom they themselves had appointed, if such decisions, in public, commercial or criminal matters, went against their interests. In due course the legal scholars (*'ulama*) themselves became increasingly reluctant to serve as *qadis*, thereby compromising the divine character of the revealed law. The rulers established their own *mazalim* (complaints) courts, which sometimes overturned the judgements of the *qadis*, underlining the fact that in the real world it was the rulers, rather than the divine law, which enjoyed supreme judicial authority. Much of the *fiqh* therefore remained theoretical – developing out of scholarly discussions about hypothetical situations rather than out of cases arising from the courts. Criminal law, for example, remained largely confined to the offences specifically mentioned in the Quran (the so-called *hadd* offences), including *zina* (illicit sex) and slanderous allegations thereof, armed robbery, theft, wine-drinking and apostasy; it did not exist in the technical sense of a comprehensive scheme of offences against the public order. Even homicide, though regulated in meticulous detail, was treated as a private, not as a public, offence.[9]

It is, of course, a moot point whether the Shari'a's failure to accommodate the broader aspects of criminal, commercial and constitutional law was the result of Allah's omniscience or of the typical inadequacy of a purely human institution. The devout Muhammad Asad states:

> . . . the limited scope of the explicit ordinances contained in the Quran and the Sunna was not due to an oversight on the part of the Law-Giver but, on the contrary, was meant to provide a most essential, deliberate safeguard against legal and social rigidity: in short, it is reasonable to assume that the Law-Giver never in-

tended the Shari'a to cover in detail all conceivable exigencies of life. He intended no more and no less than to stake out, as it were, the legal boundaries within which the community ought to develop, leaving the enormous multitude of 'possible' legal situations to be decided from case to case in accordance with the requirements of time and changing social conditions.[10]

According to this essentially reformist view, the Shari'a – based exclusively on the Quran and the Sunna – is divine, while the structure of *fiqh* deriving from it is a purely human construction. In this sense the Shari'a always remains an essentially abstract ideal which can inform, but not govern, the activities of Muslim courts: 'Floating above Muslim society as a disembodied soul, freed from the currents and vicissitudes of time, it represents the eternally valid ideal towards which society must aspire.'[11]

If the vision was to maintain itss iegrity, however, a price had to be paid, and that price was the growing divergence between the Shari'a ideal and the real world. In its formative period the *fiqh* represented a kind of transmission belt between the visionary engine and the wheels of human society. During its later decadence, which reached its nadir around the seventeenth and eighteenth centuries, the structure of *fiqh* had become congealed; or, to pursue the original metaphor further, the gears of the Shari'a had seized up, preventing forward motion. The movements of Islamic resurgence which developed in the course of confrontation with the European powers in the nineteenth century invariably involved attempts to reform or even abolish the *fiqh*, to liberate Muslim society by restoring the primacy of the Quran and the Sunna and to purge the Shari'a of its numerous irrelevances and accretions. If the tree was to survive or grow stronger, it must first be pruned of its overweight branches.

Space does not allow more than a brief glance at the actual content of *fiqh*. In the voluminous books compiled by the *faqihs* (specialists in *fiqh*) lists of human actions were compiled and graded according to a scale of moral valuation. There were six main categories according to which almost every activity from prayer to defecation was classified:

1. Obligatory acts (*fard*), omission of which constituted a sin.
2. Forbidden acts (*haram*), commission of which constituted a sin.
3. Allowed acts (*mubah*), commission or omission of which did not make someone a sinner. These *mubah* acts were subdivided into the following:

(i) Recommended acts (*mandub*), where there is merit in doing them but no sin in omission.

(ii) Undesirable acts (*makruh*), where there is merit is abstaining from them but no sin in commission.

(iii) Unspecified acts (*mutlaq*), neither meritorious nor sinful, whether committed or omitted.[12]

In practice, for reasons already mentioned, the *fiqh* became most closely involved in the area of religious and family law – a position it still occupies in many Muslim countries. On questions of ritual there were differences of detail between the four *madhhabs*, for example over the positions of prayer, none of which carried much significance. The requirements of ritual ablution preceding prayer, however, carried a significance extending far beyond the ritual itself: they became part of a recurring cycle of pollution and purification extending to the most mundane functions of everyday life. A North African psychiatrist writes:

> Muslim education is a drill which pays permanent attention to the functioning of vegetative life. Drinking, eating, urinating, farting, defecating, copulating, vomiting, bleeding, shaving, cutting one's nails . . . all of them become the object of detailed prescriptions . . .[13]

The sensible and rational Quranic demand that people should wash regularly before prayer with water, and if water were unavailable with sand, became converted, in the hands of the *faqihs*, into a fetishistic and neurotic obsession with bodily functions. The normal products of the human body, such as urine, semen, menstrual fluid and excrement, became the subjects of rules so elaborate that, if observed to the letter, the Muslim must constantly pursue states of purity impossible to obtain. The point of departure for such detailed rules is a climate, a life-style and a civilization in which the categories of purity and impurity impart an ethical view of physiological existence. Right and wrong are as involved in the trivia of vegetative life as in the macrocosmic context of man's relation with God and the universe. The universalism in the Quranic message shades imperceptibly into the particularities of Muslim social life. Ultimately the fetishistic attachment to the details of ritual purity not only obscures that universalism, but implicitly rejects it. The cycle of pollution and purification becomes divorced from its ethical origins. Thus, a typical *fiqh* manual determines that the fast of Ramadan (when sexual abstinence is obligatory during daylight hours) is not broken technically in an unnatural act with a young boy unless there is actual ejaculation – despite the fact that according to the Shari'a all homosexual acts are sinful. Similarly the ritual ablutions required after legitimate sexual intercourse in marriage may be dispensed with after unnatural acts with animals, corpses or 'such children as are not normally susceptible to penetration'.[14]

Many of the *fiqh*'s absurdities resulted from the attempt to delimit and precisely codify purely hypothetical situations: the medieval jurists were dealing with what had become a theoretical system of law rather than one based on the development of actual cases in the courts. In matters of ritual, an undue concern for the correctness of the detail invariably ends by obscuring the original purpose. Cleanliness is a sound principle in itself and whenever enforced by religious observance confers undoubted benefits. The universal Muslim custom of touching food only with the right hand because ablutions are conducted with the left no doubt helped to keep a society lacking soap and disinfectants in a reasonable state of health. Unfortunately there are occasions when good rituals have the opposite results from those intended. In the villages of the Egyptian Delta the custom of washing the anus after defecation provides the optimal conditions for breeding the country's great curse, bilharzia, which must pass directly from the human body into water in order to complete its life-cycle.

Outside matters of ritual, the area in which the Shari'a has been most consistently applied has been in marriage and family law. Here again, however, the Quranic spirit gradually succumbed to the suffocating and restrictive practices sanctioned by the *fiqh*. The centuries following the coming of Islam saw a progressive deterioration in the status and education of Muslim women.

During the Prophet's time the women of Arabia had enjoyed a relatively high social status within the prevailing patriarchal system, and the Quranic legislation endeavoured to improve it by granting them rights of inheritance which, though unequal to those of men, did at least assure them economic rights as individuals (rights for which European women had to wait until the nineteenth century). In particular, the *mahr* or bride-price was changed from a payment made to the bride's father to a sum of money or goods given to the woman herself, to be retained by her in the event of her husband's divorcing her. In the religious and social life of early Islam, so far as we know, women prayed along with their menfolk and certainly took an active part in the affairs of the community. We know for a fact that 'Aisha actively campaigned against 'Ali during the 'First Fitna'; her high standing among the earliest Muslim scholars is evident from the large number of *hadiths* traced back to her.

The Quran itself is addressed equally to both sexes. There is a story, recorded in the *hadith* literature, that several of the women in the first Islamic community were ardent feminists. One of them, Nusaiba, who actually took part in Muhammad's battles, asked the Prophet why, in the Quranic utterances, Allah always addressed himself to men rather than women. According to the story God himself recognized the justice of her complaint, and henceforth the revelations were addressed to the faithful of both sexes. (The Quranic locutions are usually *'muslimin wa muslimat'* and *'muminin wa muminat'*). Despite this, there is undoubted inequality in some of the specific Quranic legislation. Apart from sharing the prejudice, common also to Judaism, that menstruating women are 'impure' or 'polluted', Allah appears to discriminate against them by apportioning to them only half the inheritance of their brothers and by stipulating that, in cases where a male witness to a business transaction is unavailable, two female witnesses may be substituted.[15] It has been argued, of course, that in a society in which men are obliged to shoulder much greater economic burdens than women, the fact that boys inherit twice as much property as their sisters is not inequitable: the women will keep their property while the men will be obliged to spend theirs on maintaining them.[16] If the Quran is seen as the unalterable, eternally valid Word of God, however, the inescapable conclusion must be that the economic dominance of men in society cannot be altered, because it is sanctioned by divine decree. The doctrine, fundamental to Islam, that the Quran is holy writ must prove an obstacle to feminist aspirations. A similar argument arises in the case of witnesses. Muhammad Asad, following Muhammad Abduh, argues that this stipulation 'does not imply any reflection on woman's moral or intellectual capabilities: it is obviously due to the fact that, as a rule, women are less familiar with business procedures than men and, therefore, more liable to commit mistakes in this respect'. While this may have been true for all times up to the present, it can only be regarded as being valid for the future if women continue to be prevented, by men, from familiarizing themselves with business procedures. Again, divine writ appears to insist that women's subordinate economic status is an unalterable fact of existence, rather than the result of time-bound circumstance.

A possibly more important result of these divinely decreed inequalities was that they could be invoked to sanction misogynous attitudes among the faithful generally. Thus Bukhari records a *hadith* which explicitly justifies the denigration of women by reference to the Quran:

> He [i.e., the Prophet] went out on the day of the victims and Bairam [i.e., the 'Id al Adha) to the place of prayer, and passing some women he said: 'O company of women, give alms, for I have seen that many of you will be inhabitants of hell.' 'Why?' said they. Replied he: 'Because you curse much and deny the kindness of husbands. I have not seen – despite your deficiency in intelligence and religion – any sharper than you in captivating the mind of the resolute.' They said: 'What is the defect in our religion and intelligence?' He answered: 'Is not the witness of a woman equal to half the witness of a man? This is the defect in her intelligence. And when she is ceremonially impure, [i.e., menstruating] she neither prays nor fasts. This is the defect in her religion.'[17]

Many comparable *hadiths* would be invoked to justify absolute masculine domination.

The misogynism in Islam may perhaps be partly attributed to the absence of outlets for celibacy. Ascetical tendencies are usually strong among the pious: the whole history of western religions illustrates an intimate connection between religious enthusiasm and sexual repression. In Islam, however, celibacy was explicitly discouraged both by the Prophet's own example and by the famous *hadith*, 'There is no monasticism in Islam – the monasticism (*rahbaniya*) of my community is the *jihad*.' A celibate clergy to whom women are forbidden sexually may legitimately relate to them as individuals, including them within the religious life of the community. Partly, no doubt, in response to the needs of its female members, the Roman Catholic Church allowed the cult of a female archetype, the Virgin Mother, to develop freely during the Middle Ages. Female religious orders were also encouraged. Although at the popular level Sayyida Zainab and certain female Sufi saints were thought to have powers of intercession, official Islam allowed no female cults, nor can it be said to have encouraged a specifically feminine approach to the deity. After the Arab conquest of western Asia and North Africa women were to be progressively excluded from the religious and public areas of social life. By Edward Lane's time (in the early nineteenth century) they were forbidden to pray along with the men in the mosques, because 'the Muslims are of the opinion that the presence of females inspires a very different kind of devotion from that which is requisite in a place dedicated to the worship of God.'[18] Few women, even of the upper class, could read or write, and, though they were urged to do their praying at home, very few of them, according to Lane, bothered to do so.[19]

Social practice combined with the reactionary judgements of the *faqihs* to traduce the Quranic vision of sexual bipolarity. The Quranic legislation generally involves an improvement on pre-Islamic custom in the status and rights of women, even though a degree of inequality was sanctioned (for example, in the laws of inheritance). Unfortunately, because they were presented dogmatically and ahistorically as part of an eternal order decreed by God, they could be and were invoked to justify the belief that women were basically inferior to men, spiritually and intellectually. Nevertheless the Quranic vision of sex and procreation as the greatest of Allah's miracles did not altogether disappear from the Muslim world-view. Numerous *hadiths* testify to a positively modern attitude towards sex. The contrast with Christian attitudes is striking. The Christian position on marriage was authoritatively laid down by St Paul: 'It is a good thing for a man not to touch a woman; but since sex is always a danger, let each man have his own wife and each woman her own husband.' Celibacy is superior, but if marriage (which is no sin) is embarked on, there must be absolute equality between the sexes:

> The husband must give his wife what she has the right to expect, and so too must the wife to the husband. The wife has no rights over her own body; it is the husband who has them. In the same way the husband has no rights over his body; the wife has them. Do not refuse each other except by mutual consent, and then only for an agreed time . . .[20]

Islam places far more emphasis on the value of marriage and sexuality, but, unlike St Paul, fails to stress the equality of marriage partners:

> And [you ought to] marry the single from among you as well as such of your male and female slaves as are fit [for marriage]. If they [whom you intend to marry] are poor, [let this not deter you;] God will grant them sufficiency out of His bounty . . .[21]

'Marriage is the half of religion,' states a popular *hadith*, and the Prophet certainly bore out this maxim in his own behaviour. A *hadith* in Bukhari's collection urges the faithful: 'Copulate and procreate! I shall gain glory from your numbers on the Day of Judgement!'[22]

Frustration on the part of either sex is seen as a potential threat to the social order. According to another well-known *hadith*, if a man sees a woman he fancies, he should go at once and make love to his wife. The attitude stresses women's sexuality at the expense of their individuality, and clearly reduces them to the status of sex-objects:

> The Prophet saw a woman. He hurried to his house and had intercourse with his wife Zainab, then left the house and said: 'When the woman comes towards you, it is Satan who is approaching you. When one of you sees a woman and is attracted to her, he should hurry to his wife. With her it would be the same as with the other one.'[23]

Commenting on this *hadith*, the traditionist Muslim states that, in comparing her to Satan, the Prophet was referring to the 'irresistible attraction to women God instilled into man's soul', as well as to 'the pleasure man experiences when he looks at the woman and the pleasure he experiences in anything related to her. She resembles Satan in his irresistible power over the individual.'[24]

Several western writers have contrasted Islam's active view of female sexuality with the assumptions of female passivity in the western tradition, up to and including Freud. The Imam Ghazali, the most influential of Islam's medieval theologians, made it clear that a man must satisfy his wife (or wives) in order to prevent the frustration of women from becoming a threat to the social order:

> The virtue of the woman is a man's duty. And the man should increase or decrease sexual intercourse with the woman according to her needs so as to secure her virtue.[25]

In his chapter on marriage, Ghazali cited a *hadith* emphasizing the need for skill in love-making:

> The Prophet said: 'No one among you should throw himself on his wife like an animal. Before making love there should be a messenger between you and her.' People asked him: 'What sort of messenger?' The Prophet answered: 'Kisses and words.'[26]

A woman, of course, is similarly obliged to satisfy her husband. According to other *hadiths* in Bukhari's collection, a wife who refuses her husband is cursed by the angels till she returns to his bed. A woman must never refuse her husband, even on the saddle of a camel.[27]

Whereas the sexual ideal in Christianity involves a progressive sublimation of the instincts, that in Islam (and Judaism, which it more closely resembles) is a symbol of cosmic harmony:

> When a man looks upon his wife [goes another *hadith*] and she upon him, God looks mercifully upon them; when they join hands together their sins disappear in the interstices of their fingers. When he makes love to her the angels encircle the earth. Voluptuousness and desire are as beautiful as the mountains. When the wife becomes pregnant, her reward is fasting, prayer and jihad.[28]

However, the Shari'a ideal of love, based on the complementarity of the sexes, contrasts strongly with the reality of human society. Sexual bipolarity is strongly affirmed in the vision; the divine power of sex is a force so dangerous that if allowed to escape from the proper channels it will bring about social chaos. In theory the marriage rules are simple and flexible. In practice, because marriage is an economic institution involving family interests, sexual expression is dampened by economics, and it is mainly women who pay the price.

The erosion of the rights granted to women begins with the early schools of law. For example, the Maliki rule that marriage contracts must be signed by parents or guardians contradicts the Quran's individualistic spirit. Other rules are given restrictive interpretations. For instance, the Quran stipulates that the woman's *'idda* period before being allowed to re-marry after divorce should be three menstrual periods.[29] If she is not menstruating or is irregular in her periods, the interval is three calendar months. Malik, however, insisted that non-menstruating or irregular women should have to wait for twelve months before re-marrying. The Quranic right of divorce by declaration (*talaq*) was similarly abused in favour of men. The Quran demands that the woman should be fully supported by her husband during the *'idda* in accordance with her normal standard of living[30] – a right which Malik reduces to mere subsistence. Most of the early jurists were agreed that the three pronouncements on the part of the husband which made the divorce irrevocable should be evenly spaced over the waiting period, to allow time for reconciliation. The Quran hints at this in 65:1: '[For though] thou knowest it not, after that [first breach] God may well cause something new to come about.' Yet the Sunni *faqihs*, though officially disapproving of it as an 'innovation' (*bid'a*), came to recognize as legal a form of *talaq* in which the three pronouncements were made simultaneously and irrevocably, allowing the husband to re-marry during the *'idda*. Thus the *'idda*, intended to ensure paternity and allow for reconciliation, became a device whereby men could circumvent the rule restricting the number of wives to four and indulge in multiple polygyny. A man could have four wives legitimately, as well as several others on the *'idda* at one time. This device was much used in Somalia after the abolition of slavery and concubinage.[31] The triple *talaq* also produced some paradoxical results, for, since it was irrevocable, the husband who changed his mind could not take his wife back until she herself had been married to, and divorced from, another man. In Lane's time it was not unusual for a wealthy and irrascible husband to pay a pauper ('generally a very ugly person and one who is blind') or to purchase a slave (often a pre-adolescent boy) to become his wife's husband for one day. In the case of a slave, he would be 'presented' to the wife, which would automatically annul the marriage, since marriage between a woman and her own slave was illegal.[32]

Similar economic and legalistic restrictions were applied to the *khul'*, the Muslim woman's right of divorce at her own behest. According to several traditions the wife of one of the Prophet's Companions came to him and demanded a divorce from her husband on the ground that, despite his irreproachable character and behaviour, she 'disliked him as she would dislike falling into unbelief after having accepted Islam'. The Prophet allowed the divorce, but stipulated that she should return to her husband the garden he had given her as a dower.[33] The early authorities agreed that when a woman initiated a divorce she must, as the contract-breaking party, return the dower to her husband. This right of *khul'* was, however, widely abused. Payment of the dowry was often made in two instalments, the second and larger part being paid only in the event of the man's divorcing his wife. Under this rule, a divorcing wife might be obliged to 'return' property which she had never, in fact, received, since the wife was not allowed to employ the *khul'* unilaterally, but had to abide by the normal provisions of the marriage contract. In the case of a wealthy wife, the husband could make it extremely expensive for her to purchase her freedom. A poor wife would have no chance of acquiring the unpaid part of the dower.

Beyond the Arab world the Islamic marriage rules had to be accommodated to a variety of social structures moulded by economics, custom and other non-religious elements. Thus in western Asia and North Africa, where the position of women had been traditionally weak, the *fiqh* effectively consolidated their inferior social status. The customary laws of the Berbers, still applied in parts of Morocco and western Algeria, and those of certain Yemeni tribes, continue to deny females the right of inheritance altogether. In parts of West Africa and South East Asia, on the other hand, Islamization produced almost opposite effects. In Northern Nigeria, the practice of *khul'* was assimilated to the customary rule which allowed a women to divorce her husband on returning the bride wealth.[34] Among the Yoruba of Western Nigeria, on the other hand, as in the matriarchal societies of Sumatra and Java, the Shari'a applies exclusively to religious duties, while marriage and inheritance are governed by customary laws. Even where Muslim laws appear to sanction certain institutions, such as polygyny, this can have very different social consequences in countries with different traditions: thus, whereas in Arab countries additional wives and their children would demand to be housed in separate establishments, in Indonesia the second wife of a mainly absent husband might end by becoming an unpaid servant to the first.

Another device by which female property rights were eroded lay in the institution of family *waqfs*. Basically, a *waqf* is a pious endowment such as a mosque, school or public drinking fountain. An adaptation of the Byzantine *pia causa*, it embodied the principle of tribal ownership of property. *Waqfs* were originally institutions for the poor and needy. Endowed by wealthy rulers or merchants, they were at the core of the medieval system of public welfare which exceeded anything outside the Muslim world before the twentieth century. In theory, the property held by a *waqf* had been 'given to God' and was therefore inalienable. The income from it belonged to the poor. However, wealthy families were able to use the *waqf* system to avoid parcelling up property in accordance with the inheritance laws stipulated in the Shari'a. Both agricultural and urban property could be made into *waqfs*, the income from which was to be enjoyed indefinitely by the family until it reverted, in an ever-receding theoretical future, to God and the poor. Such *waqfs*, furthermore, could in fact change hands between families according to a device known as the 'sale of the air' – in effect, assignment of the tenancy of 'God's property'. One of the principal results of the 'waqfization' of property which was very widespread in the Muslim world till the twentieth century was the effective disinheritance of a family's female members. Under the laws governing family *waqfs*, only the males were permitted to pass on their share of the usufruct to their own children. A female's interest in the income terminated with her death. In addition, the founders of a *waqf* had the right (which of course they would not have under the Shari'a laws of inheritance) to exclude their female children from enjoying the fruits of a family *waqf* altogether.[35]

The veiling of women, a custom which came to characterize urban Muslim society, was also the result of a seemingly distorted interpretation of the divine text which came to be used, systematically and deliberately, to deprive Muslim women of freedom of movement. The Quran itself merely enjoins women – like men – to dress and behave with decorum:

> Tell the believing women to lower their gaze and to be mindful of their chastity, and not to display their charms [in public] beyond what may [decently] be apparent thereof; hence, let them draw their head-coverings over their bosoms. And let them not display [more of] their charms to any but their husbands, or their fathers [and other, listed, male relatives]; and let them not swing their legs [in walking] so as to draw attention to their hidden charms.[36]

There is no mention of the veil (*hijab*) in this. The earliest scholars, notably Qiffal, regarded the phrase 'beyond what may . . . be apparent' as meaning 'that which a human being may openly show in accordance with prevailing custom'. According to Muhammad Asad, 'the deliberate vagueness of this phrase is meant to allow for all the time-bound changes that are necessary for man's moral and social growth'.[37]

After the conquest of the Persian and Byzantine lands, the Muslims came under the influence of people with very different social customs to themselves. The veil had been worn by women of the upper and urban middle classes as a mark of rank, to emphasize their seclusion not from men but from the lower orders generally. Paradoxically, the social mingling of classes, at prayer and in the market place, encouraged by Islam, helped to popularize the custom of veiling among the urban classes generally. The Quranic verses enjoining modesty were interpreted by way of *hadiths* to justify the segregation of women – a social feature which was to become one of the traditional hallmarks of the Islamic way of life. Even the verse enjoining that the Prophet's wives should be addressed 'as from behind a screen [*hijab*]'[38] as a special mark of respect due to them as the Mothers of the Believers was used, somewhat impudently, to sanction the custom of veiling ordinary women.

The custom of marriage between first cousins, still widely practised in the Arab Muslim world today, was another device by which improvement in the status of women, as envisaged by the Quran, was circumvented in practice. Because the Quran allows first cousins to marry, the endogamous Arab family was able to keep property under its control by actually forcing them to do so. Matrimonial alliances within the same family group became a further method of ensuring male predominance.[39] In the Arab world especially, marriage became not the source of sexual and spiritual fulfilment envisaged in the Quran, but a burdensome duty for men and a domestic prison for women. The ideal of sexual harmony was replaced by the reality of sexual anomie – for the Quranic vision, unlike the Christian, kept the prospect of sexual fulfilment at the forefront of the imagination. Among the wealthier classes, men could find relief in concubinage (which, though not formally allowed by the Shari'a, was inseparable from the institution of slavery), or by disporting themselves with professional dancing girls – often members of whole beduin tribes given over to prostitution. Married women – if Edward Lane is to be believed – spent their lives engaged in 'intrigues', which must have been mostly imaginary since they were too closely guarded to have real ones. Lane wrote of the Cairene women:

> It is believed that they possess a degree of cunning in the management of their intrigues which the most prudent and careful husband cannot guard against, and consequently that their plots are seldom frustrated, however great may be the apparent risk of the undertakings in which they engage.[40]

The *hiyal*, or tricks, by which the *faqihs* managed to find their way round certain inconvenient Shari'a provisions were not confined to questions of family law and inheritance. As Maxime Rodinson has demonstrated, the prohibition of *riba* (lending at interest) was widely evaded by such devices as the double contract of sale or the artificial purchase of merchandise concealing an interest-bearing loan. However, it would be wrong to conclude from this or similar studies that the Shari'a had no impact on the economic life of Muslim societies. Laws, even when observed in the breach, can still impede the growth of institutions which their absence might allow to develop. The prohibition of *riba* may have been widely evaded in an *ad hoc* kind of way; but the sum of exceptions does not amount to a system.

This raises a question that has been the subject of lively debate among scholars and specialists. Was 'Islam' an obstacle to capitalist development? Marxist writers, including Rodinson and Bryan Turner, are inclined to argue that whatever impeded the emergence of capitalism in the Muslim world cannot be attributed to religious factors. Rodinson, after reviewing the Prophet's very positive attitude towards trade, points out that in general the *fiqh* 'condemned practices that might disturb the free play of supply and demand'.[41] On the basis of what he admits is rather slender evidence, Rodinson suggests that by the beginning of the period of European intervention, wage labour was already being widely employed as part of a process of petty commodity production – an early stage, according to classical Marxist theory, in the development of capitalist production. Commensurate with this, and with the related process of early capital accumulation, was the development of a 'bourgeois class' – also in line with classical Marxism. However, as Rodinson points out, unlike its European counterpart, 'this bourgeoisie, conscious as it was of itself, of its strength and value, never achieved political power as a class, even though many of its individual members succeeded in occupying the highest appointments in the state'.[42]

Unfortunately, Rodinson, who is as erudite as he is persuasive, does not satisfactorily explain why the Muslim bourgeoisie failed to achieve political power as a class, thereby inaugurating a capitalist revolution along the lines achieved in eighteenth-century Europe. He contents himself with an essentially negative formulation:

> If the bourgeoisie did not maintain and develop the strength it possessed in the first centuries AH; if the states dominated by a hierarchy of nobles and soldiers prevented it from exercising sufficient weight in relation to political power; if the town did not succeed in acquiring sufficient domination over the countryside; if manufacturing capital did not develop on the same scale as in Europe or Japan; if primitive accumulation of capital never attained the European level – all this was due to factors quite other than the Muslim religion.[43]

Among the non-religious factors, he suggests the availability of cheap labour from the countryside which gave little incentive to technical innovation, the Eastern tradition of a strong state depending on public works, and the unpredictable waves of invaders from central Asia.

In his study, Rodinson briefly examines, and rejects, Max Weber's thesis that European capitalism developed, out of the formalistic legal thinking in the tradition of Roman law, a collective mentality marked by a 'superior degree of rationality'. Rodinson argues that Weber was mixing cause with effect – his examples of 'rationality' being the result, and not the cause, of capitalist development. He points out, quite correctly, that 'the Quran accords a much larger place to reason than do the sacred books of Judaism and Christianity'.[44] Bryan Turner, in a study devoted to Weber's rather disparate writings on Islam, does rather more justice to the great sociologist, stating:

> Weber shows that rational, formal law, autonomous cities, an independent burgher class and political stability were totally absent in Islam . . . Industrialization was not impeded by Islam as the religion of individuals . . . but by the religiously determined structure of the Islamic *states*, their officialdom and their jurisprudence.[45]

However, by a subtle analysis which attempts to demonstrate that the views of Marx and Weber are not in fundamental conflict, Turner concludes that it was socio-political rather than religious factors which prevented the autonomous development of capitalism in the Muslim world. He quotes with approval a statement by Sami Zubaida: 'It was not the attitudes and ideologies inherent in Islam which inhibited the development of a capitalist economy, but the political position of the merchant classes *vis-à-vis* the dominant military–bureaucratic classes in Islamic society.'[46]

Space will not allow a proper account of Turner's analysis, which is substantially based on the same historic premises as Rodinson's – namely that the Muslim merchants did not develop autonomous organizations comparable to the powerful European city guilds which classical Marxists regard as a prerequisite of capitalist development. However, in denying the presence of a positive religious factor in this situation, both writers seem to have overlooked the *negative* impact of the Shari'a law in preventing the growth of such autonomous organizations. Moreover, this is not simply a historic debate about the origins of capitalism inside or outside the Muslim world. It concerns some fundamental differences in social and political behaviour which still account for many divisions and misunderstandings between Muslims and Westerners. Many of these differences may be reduced to a single proposition: namely that the individualism and moralism inherent in the Shari'a world-view – however much abused or misapplied in practice – were in fact decisive influences in preventing not only the development of urban autonomy, but that of all corporate institutions, as well as the group loyalties commanded by them. Such institutions and group loyalties lie at the heart of western capitalism, and were fundamental to the development of the occidental socialist states as well.

Few things are more pregnant with culture shock for the western visitor than a first encounter with a traditional Muslim city such as Cairo. Instead of orderly boulevards flanked by pavements and rows of buildings, public or private, such as are to be found in any European city from Madrid to Kiev, one is confronted with a twisted labyrinth of lanes and dark alleys, low houses stretching into the distance between closed courtyards with high walls.[47] In the past, before Muslim cities became swamped by immigrants from the countryside, the bustle of the bazaar areas, with their specialized sections of merchandise (cottons, silks, carpets, spices, metal goods and jewellery – the latter located centrally for maximum security), contrasted with the silence of the residential areas, often dingy dead-ends with nothing to indicate their function beyond the *mashrabiya* lattice-work windows that project above street-level like the sterns of so many men o' war. The quiet spaciousness and dignity of the traditional houses, with their paved courtyards, trickling fountains and pleasant gardens – designed, according to Lane, to ensure the seclusion of females, but also perfectly adapted to the climate – indicate above all the primacy of family life among middle- and upper-class urban Muslims. The higgledy-piggledy confusion of the streets outside, inaccessible to wheeled traffic, where pack-animals and humans fight for space, was not the result of bad planning on the part of the Arab conquerors. They were an unintended consequence of a fact of Muslim life: the continuous encroachment on public space by private interests. Thevenot, a Frenchman who visited Cairo in the mid-seventeenth century, was quick to notice the point:

> There is not a single fine street in Cairo, but a mass of little ones turning hither and thither, which clearly demonstrates that all the

houses were built without design, each person choosing all those places which pleased him to build on, without considering whether he stop up a street or no.[48]

This encroachment of the public domain was not confined to the affluent merchants or *'ulama* who could afford to build houses. An examination of many small workshops or coffee-houses lining the streets would reveal that they had been placed in front of the original buildings – and in the case of the coffee-houses (of which there were more than 1,000 in Lane's Cairo) half the lattice-work structure would be out in the road. The customary right to use public places for private purposes is still a feature of many Muslim cities where the authorities have abandoned attempts at draconian European-style policing. In modern Cairo, many of the streets of the splendid nineteenth-century 'European' city, built by the Khedive Isma'il to impress the royalty of Europe, have reverted to type and are now littered with open-air workshops for making furniture or repairing motor vehicles.

The key to the seemingly anarchic or 'irrational' growth of the Muslim city is in a singular fact of the Shari'a law: the absence of the Roman-law concept of 'legal personality'. In Europe the public right is an abstraction which can be upheld by defending it in law as a 'legal person'. Litigation between the public and private interest can therefore – for civil purposes – take the form of an adjudication between two parties. In criminal law one party is always the state, which brings a case against a suspected criminal as though it too were a legal party on a par with the accused. This principle applies not only to the state but to companies and corporations, groups of individuals endowed for the purposes of the law with legal personalities.

The absence of juridical personality in the Muslim law may not have been an oversight: it is certainly consistent with the uncompromising individualism of the Shari'a. Many aspects of Roman–Byzantine law and administration were taken over by the Arabs, including those concerned with municipal organization. The *muhtasib*, for example, a powerful official charged with ensuring equality of measures and other fair dealings, and who eventually accumulated considerable power to enforce public order generally, was the direct successor of the Byzantine official known as the *agronamos* (market overseer). But in the public sphere the Shari'a seems to have taken no steps to define the interests of the community *vis-à-vis* those of the individual. The principle was taken so far that

> . . . stealing from the public treasury was not held subject to the
> *hadd* punishment for theft, because the illegal act was not commit-
> ted against a juristic agent independent of the thief who was, along
> with every other Muslim, considered part-owner of the *mal Allah*,
> and thus part-owner of what he had stolen.[49]

This absence of a juridical definition of the public sphere had far-
reaching consequences. Islamic law did not recognize cities as such, nor
did it admit corporate bodies.[50] Whereas in late medieval Europe the
cities came to be administered by powerful corporations representing
the merchant classes, the Muslim city remained in certain respects a
collection of villages in which the group interests of families predomi-
nated over class interest. This may have been the 'original sin' of the
Muslim bourgeoisie in the Marxist sense: they failed to develop consciousness of themselves as a class, and therefore never acted as one. It
therefore seems quite wrong to assume, as do many Marxist writers, that
this failure 'must not be misinterpreted or attributed to Islam'.[51]

Legal institutions are not just expressions of social realities, though
they may originate as such. In the course of time, by ascribing a certain
status in law to individuals or groups, they can mould the identity of
individuals, persuading them to act in conformity with certain specific
and clearly defined expectations. Class consciousness in most European
societies was rooted not just in the economic environment, but in the
status ascribed to certain social groups – the aristocracy, the clergy, the
city guildsmen, the artisans, as well as the various categories of agriculturalist from yeoman farmers down to free peasants, villeins and serfs.
All this took place under a legal order adapted and developed from the
Roman law during the late medieval period. In Islamdom, though
parallel categories undoubtedly existed in terms of their social and
economic functions, the Shari'a denied them formal recognition in public
law. The doctrinaire assumption that each individual is answerable for
his actions only to God, implicit in the Shari'a and elaborated through the
'science' of *fiqh*, strongly militated against any public recognition of
group interests other than those based on kinship. Thus the individual
depended for support on the only social structure which enjoyed unqualified divine – and hence legal – recognition: the family. To this day,
in much of the Muslim world, the interests of kinship usually predominate over those of office, profession, class or state. What is denounced as
'corruption' (whether this consists in accepting bribes, taking private

commissions on government contracts or 'stealing from the public treasury') may often be described in less moralistic terms as a simple matter of putting one's family first.

A further consequence of the Shari'a involves the somewhat ambiguous relationship that has always existed – and persists – between Islam and the state. Theoretically the ruler's legitimacy (outside the Shi'ite tradition) depended on his willingness to 'enjoin the good and forbid the evil' in accordance with the Divine Law. In practice Muslim rulers proved unwilling to submit themselves to the Shari'a when it affected their personal interests, and Muslim *qadis* were powerless to enforce judgements against high or powerful state officials. Thus, while in the realm of personal or family matters the Shari'a could be implemented on the basis of doctrines elaborated by the *faqihs*, in matters concerning the relation between the ruler and his subjects, land transactions, and even substantial areas of criminal law, power of decision remained with the rulers, who governed by decree or settled disputes through their own *mazalim* (complaints) courts. Thus state institutions grew up parallel to Islamic ones, leading to a *de facto* separation of the religious and secular spheres which contradicted the theoretical unity of *din wa dunya* (religion and world). However, such a state and its institutions involved at best a qualified recognition on the part of the *'ulama*: it was a necessity to be tolerated rather than a positive, earthly expression of the divine ideal. In time, however, the *'ulama* generally became upholders of the status quo, lending their weight to support established authority. Thus the famous Hanbali jurist Ibn Taimiya (d. 1328) would argue:

> God has imposed the duty of enjoining the good and forbidding the evil, and that is possible only with the authority of a chief. Similarly, all the other duties which He has ordered, like the *jihad*, [the administration of] justice, pilgrimage, public prayer, festivals, brotherly help, the application of punishments and so forth can only be observed by means of the power and authority of the leader. It is thus that people say 'the Sultan is the Shadow of God on earth' and 'Sixty years with an unjust imam is better than one night of anarchy'.[52]

Nevertheless, accepting the necessity of government was not the same as according divine–legal recognition to the ruler in the realm of public law; and whereas in occidental polities the divinely appointed sovereignty of the monarch would eventually be appropriated by 'the people', acting through representative institutions, the Muslim state retained its essentially arbitrary character, *de facto* successor to a divinely instituted polity, but not a corporative entity embodied in the person of a monarch or a formalized assembly representing the 'estates' of his realm. The absence of legally recognized institutions, either at state level or at that of much smaller units, largely accounts for the 'informal' style which still governs Muslim politics, and the manner in which biological ties of kinship still remain politically decisive. Even where kinship did not always function directly, as with the *futuwa* guilds or Sufi brotherhoods, kinship became paradigmatic of social organization: lacking formal recognition in law, such groups were bound solely by moral ties comparable to the group loyalties operating within families.[53]

5 �֍ Sects and Solidarity

The divisions of Islam, in contrast to those of Christianity, have their origins in politics rather than dogma. This is not to say that dogmatic and theological questions do not form part of these divisions. However, the questions over which they first crystallized were political to the extent that they were primarily concerned with leadership of the community. Having a religious ideology built on the social foundations of tribalism, the Muslims expressed their aspirations first in the terms of group loyalty, and only afterwards in terms of the doctrinal and theological accretions surrounding these loyalties.

The factor of 'asabiya, or group solidarity, thus had a religious as well as a political dimension. During the formative period of Islam, up until about the tenth century A D, the allegiances involved in the early struggles for power in the Muslim community acquired an archetypal significance. For posterity, history became overlaid with meta-history, so much so that the actual events were less important than the accretions of myth and sentiment surrounding them. There is nothing unique to Islam in this process: all the historical religions contain a similar core of fact surrounded by the cloud of meta-history. What distinguishes meta-history from history is significance as distinct from factuality. If religion can be defined as a set of symbolic forms which relate man to the ultimate conditions of his existence, then a historic religion is one which creates out of certain events a structure of meaning which transcends the immediacy of circumstance and makes them permanently symbolic of the human predicament.

From the first, opposition to the prevailing currents in Islam centred on the person of 'Ali, the Prophet's cousin and husband of his daughter Fatima. Later Shi'ite doctrine maintained that the Prophet explicitly designated him as his successor (at a place called Ghadir Khumm, on their return from the Farewell Pilgrimage). Sunni writers dispute this, saying that the Prophet merely urged his followers to hold 'Ali in high esteem. Although after the Prophet's death some of the Ansar may have favoured the succession of 'Ali, no significant party at the time appears to have backed his claims against Abu Bakr. His comparative youth (he was between 33 and 36) was probably against him in a society in which leadership was usually exercised by older men. However, 'Ali is said to have held himself aloof after Abu Bakr's election, and to have refused to make his homage to the caliph. Fatima is said to have had claims on lands held by her father which Abu Bakr rejected on the ground that 'Prophets have no heirs'.

Nevertheless, in the course of the first three caliphates a number of factors contributed to make 'Ali a leading focus of opposition. Foremost among them was his own uncompromising character. According to several sources, he was a balding, broad, stocky man, with a hairy body and a long beard which became white as he grew older. Having an unrivalled knowledge of the Quran, he was so meticulous in matters of prayer and ritual that many of his contemporaries attributed the burnished surface of his rather prominent forehead – which they likened to the knee-joint of a camel – to the frequency of his prostrations. During the caliphates of Abu Bakr and 'Umar, he evidently kept himself apart, implicitly criticizing their policies by failing to endorse them. He seems to have been an uncompromising, somewhat naive idealist. We are told that he unsuccessfully urged 'Umar to distribute the entire revenues resulting from the conquest, without holding back anything for the public treasury. More significant for future developments was his behaviour in the electoral council, or Shura, convened by the dying 'Umar to choose his successor. According to several traditions, 'Ali was offered the caliphate by his peers, on condition that he would rule according to the Quran and the Sunna, and that he would accept the precedents established by his two predecessors. 'Ali absolutely refused to accept the second condition, presumably because he disapproved of some of Abu Bakr's and 'Umar's acts. 'Uthman was then offered the caliphate on the same terms and accepted.

Under the caliphate of 'Uthman the seeds of dissent germinated. 'Ali attracted to himself dissident elements, including some soldiers who had lost out in the distribution of lands and pious Quran reciters who resented the way in which 'Uthman allowed his Umayyad clansmen to acquire the most important administrative posts. One outspoken critic of 'Uthman's regime was Abu Dharr al Ghifari, a personality often invoked by left-wing movements in Islam. When 'Uthman sent Abu Dharr into exile, 'Ali insisted on publicly escorting him out of Medina, despite an explicit prohibition from the caliph. When mutinous soldiers from Egypt, joined by rebel contingents from Kufa and Basra, besieged the caliph in his house, 'Ali tried to mediate on their behalf. Although he refused to place himself at their head, his attitude was not entirely discouraging and he may even have agreed with their demands for the caliph's abdication. However, he was unable to prevent the situation getting out of hand and the caliph was murdered.

Although 'Ali denounced the murder as an act of *jahiliya*, his failure to produce the culprits made him unacceptable as caliph to that section of the Umma (including the Syrian troops and 'Uthman's Umayyad clansmen) who remained loyal to the dead caliph's nephew. Moreover, though overwhelmingly supported in Medina as the only leader capable of restoring order, he was soon faced by dissent on both flanks. Two leading Companions, Talha and Zubair, renounced their allegiance to him and, supported by 'Aisha, threatened to cut him off from his Iraqi supporters. Soon after defeating them at the Battle of the Camel (in which Talha and Zubair were killed) 'Ali found himself confronting the Syrian Governor Mu'awiya's army at Siffin. His eventual decision to seek a compromise with Mu'awiya promoted a rebellion of his more militant supporters, mainly from the tribe of Tamim, which included a large number of Quran reciters. During the armistice following the agreement at Siffin, a group of several hundred of these so-called 'seceders' (Kharijis – literally, 'those who went out') left 'Ali's camp at Kufa and established themselves on the bank of the Nahrawan canal near the site of what is now Baghdad. Although 'Ali inflicted a severe defeat on them in July 658, enough of them survived to continue the secessionist movement and one of them, Ibn Muljam, avenged his comrades by assassinating 'Ali three years later, in 661.

The Kharijis were the first of the radical sects to alienate themselves from the mainstream of Islam during its formative era. As with most other sects, their position involved a mixture of political and religious attitudes. Politically, their rejection of both 'Uthman and 'Ali as caliphs drove them to the position that any good Muslim could be the leader of the community, even a former slave, so long as he enjoyed the Umma's whole-hearted confidence. Consciously replicating Muhammad's original movement, Khariji groups made their *hijra* to camps in the desert, whence they made war on the rest of the Muslims, whom they regarded

as infidels. In law they observed the Quran and the Sunna with puritanical strictness, considering as an apostate anyone guilty of serious
crime. Like other militant groups which came after them, including the
Nizari Isma'ilis ('Assassins'), the followers of the Sudanese Mahdi in the
nineteenth century, and the Takfir wa'l Hijra group recently active in
Egypt, they endeavoured to actualize the Quranic eschatology in their
own activity. They were the People of Paradise. All other Muslims,
including the 'grave sinners' among them, were the People of Hell,
whom they themselves, as instruments of God's justice, were obliged to
punish. Today, in surviving Khariji communities, known sinners are still
punished by the ultimate religious sanction – denial of the rite of burial.

The Kharijis were extremely puritanical in sexual matters. One of their
sects even went so far as to suppress from the Quran as unworthy of
God's word the story of the attempted seduction of Joseph (12:23–35), in
which a very positive attitude towards human sexuality is displayed. As
a major Islamic movement, however, they suffered from a fatal weakness: they never succeeded in developing their group solidarity beyond
the primitive tribal stage, making it impossible for them to take control of
the metropolitan centres. In Iraq they enjoyed for a time the support of
the rural peasantry, who resented the exactions of their Arab conquerors. But they never had much support from the garrisons of the
cities, and were eventually destroyed by the armies of the caliphs. Despite these defeats as a major movement, however, Khariji doctrines continued to inspire revolts among oppressed or marginal groups throughout Islamic history. In the ninth century a group of black slaves imported
from East Africa to work the saltpetre mines of Lower Iraq revolted
and enslaved their masters. Their leader, 'Ali ibn Muhammad, adopted
Khariji doctrines to justify killing and those who refused to join the rebellion. At one stage in the revolt, which lasted thirteen years, the rebels
decapitated all their prisoners and threw the heads into a canal, which
floated them down to Basra where relatives were able to identify them.

Though the Azraqis and other sects were suppressed, a modified form
of Kharijism survived among the followers of 'Abdullah ibn Ibad. Realizing that a majority of the Muslims would never support them, Ibn Ibad
taught a version of the Khariji doctrine which enabled them to compromise, at least temporarily, with the realities of 'infidel' rule. The absolute
polarization of the world between the People of Paradise and the People
of Hell was replaced by a kind of purgatory – the 'Sphere of Prudent
Fear'. The Imam of the People of Paradise was replaced, for the nonce, by

a temporary 'Imam for Defence'. The draconian laws which equated such offences as wine-drinking and fornication with apostasy were modified – these matters would be dealt with on the Day of Judgement.

The Ibadis created a flourishing state among the Berbers of Western Algeria. Its capital, Tahert, attracted Khariji settlers from many other parts of the Muslim world. The chronicler Ibn Saghir, who was not a member of the sect, drew an idyllic picture of this Muslim Geneva:

> There was not a foreigner who stopped in the city but settled among them and built in their midst, attracted by the plenty there, the equitable conduct of the Imam, his just behaviour towards those under his charge, and the security enjoyed by all in person and property.[1]

Tahert was destroyed by the Fatimid caliphs in the tenth century. Another Khariji revolt, led by the scholar and preacher Abu Yazid, lasted nearly forty years, and almost destroyed Fatimid power in the Maghreb, before the rebels were defeated in a bloody battle at Mahdiya in 946. Though Abu Yazid escaped, he died from his wounds the following year, and his body was brought in triumph to the caliph. 'His corpse', wrote Ibn Khaldun, 'was flayed and the skin was stuffed with straw and placed in a cage as a plaything for two apes which had been trained for this task.'[2]

The Ibadis were virtually wiped out in the Maghreb, and all that survive are a few communities in the Mzab area and on the island of Jarba. At the opposite end of the Arab world, however, they fared a great deal better. In Oman, Ibadism is still the official creed; while as recently as the 1950s an Ibadi Imam, Ghalib ibn 'Ali, held sway in the traditional stronghold of Nazwa in the Jabal Akhdar. Before his overthrow by the Sultan with the help of British forces in 1954, he played (with some help from the Saudis) the classic role of an Ibadi leader: guardian of Khariji puritanism against the corrupting foreign influences represented by the Sultan and his British allies. Although a small minority in today's Muslim world, the Khariji attitude of treating Muslim sinners as infidels closely resembles that of modern fundamentalist groups, such as the Muslim Brotherhood.

In their first secessionist movement, as in their later revolts and actions, the Kharijis had created a tradition, founded on the Prophet's career, of seeking to realize the Islamic vision through deliberate political action. The activism of the Kharijis expressed itself in classic Khaldunian form – in the social cohesion or 'asabiya of the tribe with its elected chief. The vision has been described by W. Montgomery Watt as that of the 'charismatic community'. It was clearly ill-suited to the needs of metropolitan societies such as Egypt and Mesopotamia, where tribalism interacted with the more diversified patterns of urban life. A tribal society, with its powerful sense of group cohesion and hostility to innovation might successfully transform itself into a small city-state such as Tahert or even Nazwa; but it could hardly expect to evolve into an urban culture without a radical transformation of its natural allegiances. In a more complex society, based on a higher degree of specialization and the division of labour, the 'asabiya of the 'charismatic community' was inadequate: the group needed something more durable around which to coalesce.

The centralized polities of Egypt and Mesopotamia also contained the relics of much more ancient cultural traditions which Islam might transform or modify, but could never eliminate. These traditions combined urban populism with a history of divine kingship, both of which were capable of finding expression in Islamic terms. The populist elements re-emerged in the association of normal, 'civilized' social behaviour with the figure of the Arabian Prophet. Elaborated and systematized by the legists, it crystallized into the classical system of *fiqh* examined in the last chapter.

But however popular the figure of the Prophet and universal the norms associated with his utterances, this was hardly an adequate pole for urban group loyalties to revolve around. The very success of the *fiqh* as a normative social system left a vacuum in the consciousness of the masses once the universal system of Islam had become triumphant. Private pietism might find expression in the meticulous observance of ritual, but it did not stimulate the public enthusiasm capable of commanding group loyalties. In most areas of Islamic society the vacuum was largely filled by personal devotion to figures of outstanding piety endowed with charismatic prestige. In the formative period these figures were, *par excellence*, members of the *ahl al bait*, the Prophet's household – in particular, the tragic figures of 'Ali and his son Husain, the Prophet's martyred grandson. It would be a mistake to suppose that this devotion was peculiar to Shi'ism. However, it was in Shi'ism that it took on its characteristic sectarian form.

*

Every day is 'Ashura and
Every place is Karbala

For the Shi'a, literally 'partisans' of 'Ali who make up some 12 per cent of the Muslim community, the tragic débâcle of the House of 'Ali has become a major religious festival. Karbala rivals Mecca as a place of pilgrimage. The Day of 'Ashura (the tenth of the month of Muharram, when Husain was killed) is comparable to Yom Kippur or Good Friday in the Jewish and Christian calendars. In the traditional 'Ashura celebrations, processions of flagellants would pass through the streets, flailing the skins off their backs to expiate by their own agonies the sufferings of the Imam Husain and his small band of companions. These funeral processions are not dissimilar from the Good Friday celebrations in many Latin countries where the crucifix is paraded through the streets, followed by an effigy of the Virgin draped in black and accompanied by a brass band with a specially dirgeful timbre. Whether experienced religiously as vicarious suffering, or aesthetically as tragedy, such occasions have a cathartic function. They penetrate the human psyche and its emotional structure, activating and renewing them in the same way that physical exercise activates and renews the body.

In Iran, where Shi'ism is the national cult, the death of Husain is regularly celebrated in *ta'ziya* passion plays and at weekly religious gatherings of families and neighbourhood groups, where professional narrators, known as *rawzeh-khans*, make lingering word-pictures out of every poignant detail of the Karbala tragedy. The long hot trek across the desert by the holy family and its little band of followers; the cruelty of Ibn Ziyad, the Umayyad commander, who cut them off from their only source of water; the final act of martyrdom by the Imam, as he donned his grandfather's sacred mantle, perfumed himself and mounted his white horse, carrying his youngest child: all this is recounted solemnly and ritualistically, like the passion of Christ in the liturgy.

> With his six-month-old son 'Ali Asghar in his arms, the Imam cried out to the enemy that as this innocent babe had defiled none, at least he should be spared and a little water given to him to allay his thirst. But the reply was an arrow shot at the child's neck which pinned it to his father's arm. After returning the cruelly murdered child to its sorrowing mother's arms (who then sang a mournful mother's lament over her dead child) the Imam returned to pay the last of the sacrifice with his own blood. Arrow after arrow followed

piercing his body into a sieve until, when the aged Imam fell from
his horse his body did not touch the ground but was held off the
ground by the arrows that were sticking out of his body. Shamr
[one of the Umayyad soldiers] who has earned everlasting shame
for himself, after deriding the fallen hero, cut off his head.
Ruqaiya, Husain's young daughter, weeps over the death of her
father whose head is then brought into her presence whereupon
she falls upon it moaning and sobbing until she, too, dies of
sorrow, prostrate over the severed head.[3]

At each of these details, noted the observer who recorded this *rauza*,

. . . the audience bursts into loud, unrestraining sobbing,
moaning and slapping of the forehead and beating of chests. The
words . . . are carefully chosen by the narrator to maximize the
sentiments and emotions associated with filial and parental love
which are strongly felt by each of the participants.[4]

The event of Karbala, that unhappy episode in Islam's long and sometimes bloody history, is thus elevated into an archetype of human
suffering, a suffering made tolerable by its incorporation into a wider,
and ultimately beneficial, cosmic order.

If Sunni Islam, with its Pharisaic attention to the detailed observance
of law and ritual projects, like orthodox Judaism, a continuous awareness of the sacrality of everyday living, in which eating, defecating,
washing and a host of other routine actions are conducted within a
framework of divine law linking the individual with the cosmic order,
Shi'ism like Roman Catholicism places its distinctive emphasis on the
experience of suffering and the problem of evil. Suffering and death are
the most difficult issues with which ordinary people, and societies, have
to come to terms. Why do people suffer? Why is there evil in the world?
Why do the unjust seem to prosper, while the righteous or the weak so
often go to the wall? Many sociologists have seen in religious beliefs and
customs attempts to resolve these problems symbolically, by means of
culturally constituted defence mechanisms. As Clifford Geertz writes:

As a religious problem, the problem of suffering is, paradoxically,
not how to avoid suffering but how to suffer, how to make physical
pain, personal loss, worldly defeat or the helpless contemplation
of others' agony something bearable, supportable – something, as
we say, sufferable. The problem of suffering passes easily into the

problem of evil, for if suffering is severe enough it usually, though not always, seems morally undeserved as well. [Both problems] raise the uncomfortable suspicion that the world, and perhaps man's life in the world, has no genuine order at all . . . And the religious response to this suspicion is in each case the same: the formulation, by means of symbols, of an image of such genuine order of the world which will account for, and even celebrate, the perceived ambiguities, puzzles and paradoxes in human experience.[5]

Shi'a Islam and Christianity, in contrast to Sunni Islam and Judaism, draw upon the historic experience of defeat and martyrdom, elaborating symbolic defences against the realities of suffering. Both movements were born out of failure and frustration. What little is really known about the historic origins of Christianity suggests that it was a Jewish messianic movement related to, though distinct from, the national movement of the Zealots. The failure of Christ's movement, which ended ignominiously in the leader's execution by the Romans, confronted his followers with the choice of either accepting defeat, which would have entailed disintegration of the movement and the betrayal of its founder, or of overcoming defeat by sublimation. The second course was adopted by Christ's disciples, who put it about that Christ was not really dead but would shortly return as Messiah. This gave the movement an added impetus and urgency: preparation for the Second Coming which most early Christians believed to be imminent.

Like the early Christians, the followers of Husain refused to 'face the facts' after the defeat of their leader at Karbala. An even closer parallel with Christianity is suggested by the Shi'ite historians who emphasize the voluntary nature of Husain's sacrifice. Instead of trying to raise military support in the Hejaz, the Prophet's grandson made his way towards Kufa with a tiny band of fifty companions. On the way his sympathizers warned him that the situation was desperate. 'The hearts of the Iraqis were for him but their swords were for the Umayyads.' If he proceeded to Kufa he and his party would certainly be butchered. Husain persisted in his plan, despite these friendly protests, deliberately seeking the martyrdom that he knew must revitalize the cause of the Prophet's House. His decision proved fully justified. In later generations the whole Muslim community – and not just the Shi'ite sectarian militants – would look back with horror at the enormity of Karbala, where the Prophet's surviving grandson, leader of the *ahl al bait* (literally, 'people of the house'), was massacred along with his pathetic band of followers by Muslim forces of the corrupt and cynical Umayyad caliph, Yazid ibn Mu'awiya.

In early Islam, as in early Christianity, history and meta-history constantly interact. The actual events of history, mythologized and writ large in the popular imagination of a mainly non-literate society, become the source of a new consciousness leading to distinctive social and political affiliations. One can discern in the results a new form of *'asabiya* in which the sense of tribal community, lost in the transition from pastoral to urban society, is regained – albeit in a sublimated form – by means of membership of a religious subculture. During the medieval period the organizations which filled the gap between the individual Muslim, isolated in his aloneness before the awesome Quranic deity, were the Sufi *tariqas*, whose functioning will be investigated in the next chapter. However, during Islam's formative centuries the same function was performed by groups owing allegiance to the *ahl al bait* and its numerous representatives.

We know that many of 'Ali's earliest supporters were *qaris* – Quran reciters – who were renowned for their piety. Though some of them deserted to the Kharijis because of what they regarded as his weak political leadership, many remained under the Umayyad dictatorship, forming a kind of opposition group critical of its worldly policies. After 'Ali's death and the events of Karbala these pious elements tended to become increasingly attached to the cause of the *ahl al bait*. In due course they became adherents of various members of the Prophet's family – 'Abbasids, Zaidis, Ja'faris, Ismai'lis, Fatimids or Nizaris – not so much because there existed an unbroken continuity between the 'founders' and the later generations of followers who came to make up these communities, but rather because all of them represented a religio-political outlook which sought legitimacy by associating itself with one of these august figures.

The first response to the death of Husain was an action, partially religious in character, which helped shape the future direction of Shi'ite religiosity. About 3,000 of the Kufans, led by several prominent *qaris*, sought to avenge him by attacking Ibn Ziyad, the Umayyad governor responsible for the massacre. Rejecting support from the rebel caliph, who at that time controlled much territory in northern and central Arabia, they first visited the grave of Husain, where they gave them-selves up to wild expressions of grief, before proceeding to attack an

Umayyad force of at least three times their number. A proclamation of these so-called Tawwabin, or Penitents, has survived, which makes it clear that they would restore the caliphate to the Prophet's family or die in the attempt, thereby atoning for the death of his grandson, caused by their desertion. Not surprisingly, the Tawwabin were cut to pieces by the forces of Ibn Ziyad and very few survived. However, a more militant group led by Mukhtar al Thaqafi espoused the claims of Muhammad ibn al Hanafiya, a son of 'Ali by 'the Hanafi woman' and therefore no descendant of Muhammad. It was in Mukhtar's propaganda that another characteristically Shi'ite theme (but one that is also present in other sections of the Islamic community) first appeared: the idea of a promised *mahdi* (literally, 'the expected one') or messiah who would bring peace and justice to a world torn by strife and oppression.

The idea of the *mahdi* has variously been ascribed to Persian, Jewish and Christian influences, as well as to an independent development in the Arab–Muslim tradition. Probably mahdism assimilated all these influences from the new cosmopolitan society of the Arab empire. Divine kingship had existed among the southern Arabs and Persians before the coming of Islam. In the crisis following Muhammad's death some of the Ansar (whose ancestors migrated from southern Arabia) may have resisted paying homage to Abu Bakr, preferring 'Ali because they believed that Muhammad's prophethood somehow inhered in members of his family. The mixed Arab–Persian population of Kufa, centre of Mukhtar's rebellion, included several Christian–Arab tribes, while the southern Arabs outnumbered the northerners by a ratio of three to two. The Iraqi city was evidently fertile soil for ideas of charismatic leadership. The Persian element included former captives converted to Islam, peasants and other migrants, traders and craftsmen who felt themselves the victims of social and ethnic discrimination. The Persian tradition itself included the 'ancient Indo-Aryan idea of a chosen, God-begotten family transmitting the Glory of God from generation to generation and eventually producing a *saoshyant* or messiah'.[6]

Nevertheless, in contrast to the Tawwabin, Mukhtar's movement was primarily one of political and social protest. This much is apparent from the fact that Husain's surviving son, 'Ali Zain al 'Abidin (the soubriquet means 'ornament of the pious'), who refused to back Mukhtar's movement, was replaced by Muhammad ibn al Hanafiya, who evidently permitted Mukhtar to use his name in the course of a revolt that was suppressed in 687. The activists wanted a candidate who would be prepared to make an open bid for the caliphate, even if he were not a direct descendant of the Prophet.

The more moderate followers of 'Ali and Husain pursued the quietist line of Zain al 'Abidin, accepting the *de facto* rule of the Umayyads without according it *de jure* recognition. 'Ali Zain al 'Abidin contributed to the specifically religious tradition of Shi'ism. Before his death in 712 or 713 he is said to have nominated his eldest son, Muhammad al Baqir, as his successor and heir to his spiritual heritage. The more activist Shi'ites, however, transferred their allegiance to his son Abu Hashim. Others, who may have been influenced by the fact that neither Ibn al Hanafiya nor Abu Hashim was of the Prophet's line, gave their support to Muhammad al Baqir's younger half-brother Zaid, who also wished to pursue an activist policy aimed at overthrowing the Umayyad caliphate and restoring the Prophet's heritage. Thus, early in the eighth century there were at least three groups of 'Alid loyalists: two of them representing the activist approach of Mukhtar and a 'legitimist' group following the quietist and spiritualizing attitude of Zain al 'Abidin.

The first of these groups to make a serious attempt at political action were the followers of Zaid ibn 'Ali. While Muhammad al Baqir and his son and heir by designation, Ja'far al Sadiq, continued to reside peacefully in Medina, eliciting much respect from the pious for their scholarship and devotion to religious duties, but showing little inclination towards rebellion, Zaid insisted that the caliph–imam's duty lay in 'establishing the good and prohibiting the evil', if necessary by force. In so doing he managed to win over some of Baqir's supporters, as well as erstwhile followers of Ibn al Hanafiya and Abu Hashim. His programme also drew support from the Mu'tazili group of theologians active in Kufa and Basra. As advocates of the doctrine of *qadar*, or free will, it was logical that they should espouse the cause of political action. Zaid, however, also alienated the more militant Shi'ite activists by the concessions he was prepared to make in order to win maximum support for his movement: this involved accepting Abu Bakr and 'Umar (but not the reviled 'Uthman) as legitimate caliphs, despite their 'inferiority' to 'Ali.

Although Zaid's revolt in 740 was a failure, he himself being killed along with many of his followers, his son Yahya continued the struggle in Khurasan, where he won some support from troops loyal to 'Ali, before meeting the same fate as his father in 743. Moreover the movement survived in two remote and widely separated mountainous areas. By the late ninth century a Zaidi state had been established in Tabaristan, south of the Caspian, and another based on Sa'da in the mountains of Yemen. The Zaidi doctrine of the Imamate, developed by their leading theorist Qasim al Rassi (d. 860) lay somewhere between the Shi'ite and Khariji positions. The true Imam must be a descendant (like Zaid) of 'Ali and Fatima; he must combine mastery of religious knowledge ('*ilm*) with the political acumen necessary to sustain the rebellion against the authorities. He need not, however, be the son of an Imam, nor need there be an Imam at all if no suitably qualified candidate emerged. Like Kharijism, Zaidism represented an attempt at reconstructing the early Muslim polity on the basis of a very personal relationship and sense of responsibility between the Caliph and his community. Like Kharijism, it was unsuited to a large-scale international society demanding more complex forms of socio-political organization; like Kharijism, it proved highly resilient and durable in mountainous regions remote from the centres of power. The Imamate of Yemen survived, virtually untouched by foreign influences, until well into this century under a succession of remarkably competent – if sometimes severe – rulers. Although a weak and incompetent Imam proved unable to hold his country together following the death of his father in 1963, the 'royalist' tribesmen emerged the real victors of a seven-year civil war in which the 'republican' side was supported by considerable numbers of Egyptian troops, armaments and aircraft. A revived Imamate, under a 'suitably qualified candidate', though unlikely, does not seem to be beyond the bounds of possibility in the future.

Shi'ite activism proved rather more successful at the second attempt. A series of revolts, beginning in Khurasan but backed overwhelmingly by the pious intellectuals of the major cities, finally brought down the Umayyad caliphate in 750. It was led by Abu Muslim, a former slave of Ibrahim, Imam of the Hashimis, who inherited the 'Alid movement of Mukhtar and Ibn al Hanafiya. Ibrahim claimed descent from 'Abbas, the Prophet's uncle and a late-comer to Islam. But he had an additional claim to the support of 'Alid loyalists, having acquired the Imamate by designation from Abu Hashim, which allowed him to benefit from the pro-'Alid organization set up by Mukhtar. Many Shi'ite supporters would no doubt have been unhappy about this arrangement had they known about it. Not only were these 'Abbasids (as they came to be known) not descended from the prophet, they were not even descendants of 'Ali, who by now had acquired his own special claims to loyalty.

The 'Abbasids could claim, however, that in terms of patrilineal descent (which was all that counted in Muslim society) they stood in the same relation to the Prophet's family as did 'Ali himself. Moreover, in his propaganda Abu Muslim carefully concealed the fact that the rebellion was being undertaken on behalf of the 'Abbasids, announcing only that the Umayyads would be replaced by a member of the *ahl al bait*. Thus the 'Abbasids succeeded in gaining Shi'ite support that might otherwise have been denied to them.

In the event, the Umayyads got wind of these developments and had the Imam Ibrahim imprisoned and murdered. According to some accounts, the local leader of the movement in Iraq, Abu Salama, did not feel duty bound to Ibrahim's designated successor, his younger brother Abu al 'Abbas, and offered the caliphate instead to Ja'far al Sadiq, whose claims, of course, were far superior. Ja'far is said to have refused. If true, the story suggests that Ja'far and his supporters were by now irrevocably set upon the course that would eventually separate them from the Muslim community religiously as well as politically. By refusing the challenge of political power, Ja'far was effectively echoing Christ's statement: 'My Kingdom is not of this world.' It could be argued, of course, that he was merely acting out of caution; but such an attitude would hardly have been worthy of Husain's great-grandson. At all events, after Abu Muslim's movement was successful, political power passed to the family of 'Abbas, who held it for more than a century and, in the purely titular form of the caliphate, for very much longer, until the Mongol irruption of 1258.

After their triumph the 'Abbasids – like many revolutionary victors after them – turned on their erstwhile supporters, especially the extremists among them. Generally, the change of government was welcomed by the pious elements. The fact that the new rulers were not from the inner circle of the Prophet's family was less important than the fact that they agreed to rule more strictly in accordance with the Quran and with the Muhammadan norms that were in the process of being developed (as described in the previous chapter). However, like all successful rulers they found it necessary, upon acquiring power, to exchange revolutionary fervour for broad consensus. This they achieved by conceding the principal demands of the former 'pious opposition': equality of opportunity for Arabs and *mawali*; appointment of judges from among the *'ulama*; and, in general, government in accordance with the Quran and the Sunna. At the same time, they were bound to disappoint the activist elements among the Shi'a, whose eschatological hopes had seen in the coming of the 'Abbasids the dawn of a universal age of equality, righteousness and justice. The quietist or 'spiritualizing' elements around the Imam Ja'far al Sadiq were probably left more or less unmolested – although Shi'ite tradition suggests that the Imam and all his successors in the 'Twelver' line (see pp. 203–6), barring the last, were poisoned by the 'Abbasid caliphs. Ja'far's version of the Imamate and of the expected coming of the *mahdi* does not seem, for the time being, to have disturbed the new emerging social order.

Mahdist ideas had, however, by now become widely disseminated. The demand for universal justice invariably accompanies the collapse of an unpopular government. Popular movements, as many 'moderate' revolutionaries have found to their cost, rarely stop short at demanding a change of rulers. In a religious society the utopian demands of the oppressed tend to be couched in eschatological language. The day of reckoning promised in scripture is deemed to be nigh, when sin will be punished and virtue rewarded. At times of social unrest and economic stress, it is the rich and powerful who are usually thought to be sinful, the poor and oppressed virtuous or at least innocent. Biblical eschatology animated such radical movements as the Anabaptists of Munster and the English Levellers. In the Quran the socio-political possibilities of the Last Day are even more apparent than those contained in the Book of Revelation, for it is clear in many passages that the Quraishi rulers will be among the damned. The Umayyads were literally as well as metaphorically kin of the merchant aristocrats who resisted God's message. To save their own skins they had embraced Islam at the last possible moment, and had then proceeded to take over the movement, corrupting it from within, distorting or ignoring its universal message.

In a society in which lines of kinship were all-important, it was natural that mahdist claims should be made on behalf of leaders close to the Prophet's inner family (even though, in many traditions, the expected messiah was identified with the second coming of Jesus). It was from this group, from within the Quraish, that God had chosen His Messenger, with such spectacular results. As pretenders in the line of Muhammad ibn al Hanafiya, the 'Abbasids to some extent benefited from these eschatological expectations. By contrast, the failure of Zaid's revolt may partly be attributed to the fact that he refused to allow mahdist claims to be made on his behalf. The 'Abbasid caliphs encouraged these expectations by giving themselves grandiloquent titles: Al Saffah ('the Blood-shedder': 750–754); his brother Al Mansur ('the Victorious': 754–775); and, most appropriately, Al Mahdi (775–785), father of Al Rashid ('the Righteous': 786–809). Al Mahdi, whose full name was Muhammad ibn 'Abdullah was given his title by his father at a time when a well-known *hadith* was in circulation:

> Even if there remains for the world but one single day, God will extend it until He sends a man from the people of my house [*ahl al bait*], whose name will be the same as mine, and the name of his father will be that of my father. He will fill the earth with equity and justice, just as it is now filled with tyranny and oppression.[7]

Within a generation or so the 'Abbasids had developed the caliphate along absolutist lines, incorporating many of the Sassanid traditions. The imperial style, with the caliph as 'God's Shadow upon Earth', was reinforced by the decision to build a new capital at Baghdad, near the former Sassanid capital at Ctesiphon. At the height of their glory, during the reign of Rashid, the 'Abbasids controlled territory comprising most of Western Asia, all Arabia (except for Oman) and the lands south of the Mediterranean. The only fully independent Muslim states were in the Berber Maghreb and in Spain, where an Umayyad prince who escaped the general massacre of his family founded an independent kingdom. Trade flourished and expanded. Ocean-going dhows carried by the monsoons sailed to China in the east, where the emperor granted Muslim merchants special privileges; trading colonies were founded on the East African coast as far south as Mozambique. The unification of the Indian Ocean brought immense prosperity to the empire. The caliphs appropriated much of this wealth in taxes, only to redistribute it again in a somewhat arbitrary manner in which politics mixed with piety and prestige.

The 'Abbasid government combined the traditions of Persian absolutism with some distinctively Islamic features. The remoteness of the caliphs, dramatized by an elaborate court ceremonial drawn directly from Sassanid models, emphasized their elevation above the factional disputes of ordinary men and women. As God's vice-regents upon earth they elicited an adoration which scandalized the pious, savouring as it did of *shirk*, the 'association' of lesser beings with the divinity. The caliph was supported by a dependent bureaucracy which, though aristocratic in origin, disposed of no power of its own. The famous Barmakid family, formerly Buddhist priests at Balkh, near the Oxus, discovered this to their cost when Rashid, jealous of the enormous power they had acquired as state secretaries to successive caliphs, literally destroyed them overnight: one was beheaded, his father and brother died soon afterwards in prison.

At the popular level, however, Islamic egalitarianism contributed to the breakdown of social and ethnic barriers. In an expanding economy extending over a vast area of the globe, the 'Abbasid empire offered an unprecedented range of social and geographical mobility. Moreover this mobility was achieved from a relatively small though sound agricultural base in the Sawad by maximizing the possibilities of trade. It was a society in which birth counted for less than wealth and in which almost any man endowed with sufficient talents 'could make a fortune or reach the highest positions with little regard for his birth'.[8] As an ever-growing proportion of the subject peoples converted, Islam became free from its associations as the religion of the conquering Arabs. New converts became plain Muslims on a par with other believers. They were no longer, as in Umayyad times, required to become the 'clients' of Arab tribes. The Arabic language now became the *lingua franca* of a vast new international society. 'Islam became a badge, not of a ruling class, but of a cosmopolitan, urban-oriented mass'[9] transcending ethnic and social boundaries.

Historically the 'Abbasid caliphate, though short-lived, was no mean achievement. However, it inevitably failed to satisfy the aspirations of the pious and the revolutionary militants who had sought in the overthrow of the Umayyads a chance to restore the Islamic purity of the Medinese community (which by now was coming to acquire the glow of retrospective perfection). Disillusionment had set in quickly. A Shi'ite revolt in the Hejaz in 762, backing the mahdist claims of Muhammad al Nafs al Zakiya ('the Pure Soul'), great-grandson of the martyred Husain's elder brother Hasan, won the support of, among many others, the great jurists Malik and Abu Hanifa. After suppressing the revolt the caliph Mansur had Malik flogged, while Abu Hanifa ended his days in prison. Further Shi'ite revolts, always supported in the Hejaz and its Holy Cities, occurred in 786 (when one of the rebel leaders, Idris ibn 'Abdullah, escaped to the Maghreb, where he founded a kingdom based on Fez), and in 814–15. Most of the *'ulama*, however, expressed their attachment to the *ahl al bait* less politically. If intellectual activity supplies a psychological substitute for action, then perhaps the development of a rational jurisprudence based on Muhammadan tradition provided an avenue for the pious less dangerous than politics. The outcome of this development was, however, a growing 'culture gap' between the intellectual circles around the court and the popular movement led by the traditionists, the *ahl al hadith*.

The philosophical and intellectual controversies of early Islam originated in the discussions of the pious intellectuals during the Umayyad era. Their point of departure was essentially political: Umayyad supporters argued that their rule, whatever injustices it entailed, had been decreed by God. The opposition countered by insisting that man, not God, is responsible for evil actions. Out of this discussion arose the more general question of determinism versus free will. Is the sinner predestined to sin, because God is omnipotent? Or is he responsible for his own evil acts, which to some extent limits God's power, since He is bound to punish them? Since advocates of both positions enlisted the Quran in their support, the dispute became involved in the argument, referred to in Chapter 3 (see pp. 117–20), about the status of the divine text. The advocates of predestination argued that the Quran was the 'uncreated' speech of God because it refers to certain specific events which God in His omnipotence and omniscience must have willed and known about. The advocates of free will replied that the Quran clearly insists on human responsibility, as implied in the doctrine of the Day of Judgement; the Quran is thus God's speech, 'created' under certain circumstances – a view which implied that God could have created a different Quran should the circumstances have been different.

The advocates of the 'created' Quran emphasized the references to an 'Arabic' Quran which occur in the divine text; they accused their opponents of a form of *shirk* or bi-theism in allowing that an eternal being – the Quran – coexisted with God. The controversy ranged around the interpretation of the Quran as well as its status. An 'uncreated' Quran, being, as it were, an aspect of the Godhead, was absolutely unchangeable. The decrees of a 'created' Quran, on the other hand, were evidently subject to time and place, and might possibly be overruled by a divinely inspired Imam or caliph. The advocates of free will and 'createdness', who eventually came to be known as the Mu'tazilis, emphasized the uncompromising character of God's unity (*tawhid*). Their conception of the deity, not uninfluenced by neo-Platonist ideas, was more remote and abstract than that of the *ahl al hadith*. They believed that anthropomorphic expressions such as 'God's hand' or 'face' must be understood allegorically, and developed a style of defining God by negation: 'He is not a body, not a form, not flesh nor blood, not an individual, not substance nor attribute . . . etc.'[10] Similarly, the expression 'God's speech', referring to the Quran, must be understood figuratively, since speech, a human function, belongs to the category of 'things created'. Their opponents replied by insisting that, since the anthropomorphisms are mentioned in the Quran, they must be understood literally. Eventually the advocates of the 'uncreated' Quran won the day, but not without a struggle.

During the reign of the 'Abbasid caliph Mamun (813–833), the Mu'tazili intellectuals in court favour were allowed to establish a kind of inquisition, known as the *mihna*, before which the leaders of the *ahl al hadith* were obliged to proclaim their adherence to the doctrine of the 'created' Quran. Many of them refused to do so, including the redoubtable Ahmad ibn Hanbal, despite torture, imprisonment and threats of death. In 849 the policy was abandoned as a failure, and the government stabilized its position towards the *'ulama*, most of whom supported the *ahl al hadith*, by conceding them supremacy in matters of doctrine. The dogma that 'the Quran is the speech of God, uncreated' became a shibboleth of Sunni orthodoxy, and Mu'tazili theology was confined to the ranks of the Shi'a until resurrected by Sunni reformers in the last century.

Socially, the victory of the doctrine of the 'uncreated' Quran served to strengthen the role of the *'ulama* as the interpreters of the divine word, making them guardians of the *ijma'* of the community in the face of the absolutism of the rulers. This, of course, gave them considerable social and political power. Theoretically, the Quran was available to everyone. In practice it could only be read and understood by those with a sound knowledge of classical Arabic and access to the works of *tafsir*, or scholarly exegesis. Such scholars, who were drawn from all social classes, effectively counter-balanced the influence of the bureaucrats and secretaries (*katibs* and *wazirs*) who clustered round the dynastic courts. This influence was often of a conservative nature, making it difficult for the rulers to introduce changes. But it had the positive effect of counteracting the growing inequality and social stratification which always occur when a ruling elite has a monopoly of education.

The polity which resulted from the compromise between the caliphs and the *'ulama* has been called a 'divine nomocracy' rather than a 'theocracy', for it consisted in a society based on the rule of laws transmitted by God, rather than a state governed by someone claiming to be His earthly representative.

Culturally, the theological victory of the 'ulama gave support to the iconophobic tendencies common to Judaism and some eastern churches. Whereas the Umayyads had employed Byzantine artists to embellish their mosques, palaces and hunting lodges with delightful representations of birds, plants and animals, Islamic art in the mainstream Sunni culture was to develop in a wholly abstract direction. Calligraphy alone was permitted to give revelation a visible form. No images of created things were to be allowed to seduce the mind away from the contemplative absorption of the divine word, that powerful solvent of all mental fixations. With its exuberant variety of styles, its contrasting modes of geometrical rigour and melodious rhythm, Arabic calligraphy became a flamboyant elaboration of the text on the visual plane which complemented the music of its recitative upon the ear.

The theological underpinning of Sunni Islam was completed by Abu al Hasan al Ash'ari (873–935) who occupies a moderate position comparable to that of Shafi'i in law. Following the *ahl al hadith*, Ash'ari held to the doctrine of the 'uncreated' Quran and did his utmost to defend God's omnipotence. Originally a Mu'tazili, he converted to the traditionists after having several dreams during the month of Ramadan, during which the Prophet Muhammad appeared to him and urged him to support 'what was related from himself' – i.e., the *hadith*. Ash'ari promptly abandoned the Mu'tazili camp and went to the other extreme, joining the Hanbalis. However, in a subsequent dream the Prophet appeared once more and, looking somewhat displeased, said to Ash'ari: 'I did not tell you to give up rational arguments, but to support the true *hadiths*!'[11]

Thus inspired, Ash'ari developed a theological position which gave philosophical support to the Quran and the Sunna on the basis of rational arguments. Free will, in Ash'ari's system, was reduced to the bare minimum compatible with personal responsibility on the Day of Judgement. God's omnipotence was illustrated in the famous story of the Three Brothers. The First Brother had a high position in paradise, having lived long and done many good works. The Second Brother had died as a child, and found himself in limbo, on the edge of paradise. The Third Brother, a wicked man, had been consigned to hell. In Ash'ari's story, the Second Brother complained to God that by being made to die early he had been deprived of the opportunity to earn himself a place in paradise by good works. To this God replied that He had forseen that, had the Second Brother been allowed to grow up, he would have become a sinner, thereby ending up even worse off. On hearing this the Third Brother cried out angrily from hell, asking God why He had not cut him off early, before he had committed the sins which brought him there. To this, of course, there was no answer.

Ash'ari's point was similar to Alexander Pope's 'Presume not God to scan!' God's omnipotence and his omnibenevolence cannot be reconciled within the bounds of ordinary logic. By the same argument, the Quran, God's revelation, cannot be subjected to rational explanations. The anthropomorphisms and the eschatology must be taken as they stand, not metaphorically, 'without specifying how'(*bi la kaif*) God, as Creator, may ultimately be responsible for evil in this world, but this detracts neither from His goodness nor from the responsibility of men for their actions. The Ash'aris rationalized God's omnipotence within an atomistic theory of creation, according to which the world was made up of discrete points in space and time whose only connection was the Will of God which created them anew at every moment. Such a world of course implied the possibility of miracles. For, although natural laws were no different from 'God's custom', there was nothing to prevent the Creator from breaching them at will. Accounts of prophetic miracles in the Quran could thus be taken literally, while attention was focused on their purpose within the overall context of the divine message.

The Ash'ari system was 'philosophically anti-philosophical', rather in the manner that Shafi'i's jurisprudence was rationalistically anti-rational. Both thinkers erected formidable intellectual defences in order to uphold the Sunni consensus in favour of the primacy of revelation – the unique and unrepeatable irruption of the divine into human history represented by the Quran and the Prophet's Sunna. The Mu'tazilis and their philosopher successors had fought for the primacy of reason, in the belief that a God who was good could not be other than rational. Though they produced such outstanding thinkers as Farabi, Ibn Sina (Avicenna) and Ibn Rushd (Averroës), the rationalists were never able to acquire a substantial following among the urban *'ulama* – though they were patronized and inspired by the more elitist Shi'ite leaders. For the 'Abbasid caliphs, and thence for the great majority of the rulers who succeeded them, Quranic literalism and *taqlid* (imitation of the established authorities in matters of doctrine and law) were an intellectual price that had to be paid for the continuing loyalty of the urban populations. Freedom in ideas and social equality are not always found to be compatible.

The systematic philosophers like Farabi and Ibn Sina tried hard to limit the cleavage between philosophy and dogma by pursuing their speculations within the framework of *tawhid* (divine unity). However, the attempt to synthesize the remote and abstract God of the philosophers with the all-pervasive and omnipresent deity of the Quran was never successful in the sense of becoming socially acceptable. The philosophers tried to maintain the principle of Quranic infallibility by arguing that it contained one message, to be understood literally, for the masses and another for the philosophical elite who were entitled, by virtue of superior intelligence, to interpret scripture allegorically. Such elitism, however, went against the populist grain of urban Sunni Islam and the systems of the philosophers were confined mainly to the sectarian Shi'a groups, or re-emerged, heavily disguised, as the products of gnosis in the writings of the Higher Sufis.

There was, however, an alternative to the swamping of rational exegesis by populist sentiment masquerading as the defence of revelation against the attacks of reason. This was the path, chosen by the Shi'a, of enlightened spiritual leadership. Unlike the *ahl al sunna*, the Shi'a found in the doctrine of the Imamate a device which enabled them to erect a quasi-sacerdotal structure within the framework of Islam. The Shi'ite *'ulama* were not endowed with any formal sacerdotal authority: there are no sacraments in Islam and nothing comparable to the medieval Catholic doctrine that certain rituals are automatically efficacious, even when performed by wicked and corrupt priests. Nevertheless the Shi'ite idea of *nass* (designation) contains a notion of spiritual succession broadly comparable to the Apostolic succession in the Catholic priesthood. This in turn permits a flexibility in the interpretation of scripture on the part of the Imams or their representatives, who are assumed to be in possession of the understanding necessary to reveal the innermost truths contained in them.

The idea of *nass* was closely associated with another aspect of Shi'ism, namely that the Quran contains esoteric meanings that can only be properly interpreted by the Imams of the *ahl al bait*. The divine text itself states:

> He it is who has bestowed upon thee from on high this divine writ, containing messages that are clear in and by themselves – and

these are the essences of the divine writ – as well as others that are allegorical . . .[12]

For the Shi'a, the esoteric interpretation of the Quran (*tawil*) opened the way for a spiritual elite capable of exercising considerable social power. A modern Shi'ite text explains:

> . . . *tawil* or hermenuetic interpretation of the Holy Quran is not concerned simply with the demonstration of words. Rather it is concerned with certain truths and realities that transcend the comprehension of the common run of men; yet it is from these truths and realities that the principles of doctrine and the practical injunctions of the Quran issue forth.
>
> The whole of the Quran possesses the sense of *tawil*, of esoteric meaning, which cannot be comprehended directly through human thought alone. Only the Prophets and the pure among the Saints of God who are free from the dross of human imperfection can contemplate these meanings while living on the present plane of existence. On the Day of Resurrection the *tawil* of the Quran will be revealed to everyone.[13]

In the earliest period of the Shi'a only the 'sinless' Imams of the *ahl al bait* could provide authoritative interpretation of the scriptures. Even today, Shi'ites of the Twelver (Imami) tradition only accept as authoritative clarifications of the Quran which come from the Prophet himself or members of his family.

The spiritual and intellectual elitism of the Shi'a is projected back on to the authority of the Imams of the *ahl al bait*, all of whom (apart from 'Ali and Husain) are said to have been poisoned at the behest of the Umayyad or 'Abbasid caliphs. Whatever the truth of these traditions, they illustrate and to some extent serve to justify the deep ambivalence existing in Shi'ite Islam towards the exercise of political power.

The sanctity of the Imams of the Shi'a, together with their spiritual authority, increased with their distance from political power. The main body of the Twelver Shi'a came, in effect, to recognize that exercising political power could only undermine their spiritual authority. They found the solution to the resulting dilemma by announcing that the last of their living Imams, Muhammad al Muntazar, had finally 'disappeared' in 940, to reappear at the end of the world as the promised *mahdi*, to 'fill the earth with equity and justice as it was filled with oppression and tyranny'. This doctrine of *ghaiba* (occultation) enabled moderate Shi'ites to come to terms with the *de facto* political authority of the 'Abbasids without according them *de jure* recognition. The solution was not radically different from that of the Sunni *'ulama*, who likewise chose *de facto* acceptance of the monarchy as the preferable alternative to anarchy. The difference for the Shi'a, however, was that their *'ulama* came to exercise authority on behalf of the Imam *in absentia* – a fact which, combined with the greater emphasis placed upon the esoteric meanings of the scriptures, endowed them with proportionally greater intellectual and spiritual authority.

The effect of the moderate Shi'ite 'Twelver' compromise became apparent within a decade or so of the last Imam's 'disappearance'. By the mid tenth century the 'Abbasid caliphs' temporal power had effectively disintegrated. Where Shi'ite movements failed to gain outright control, provincial governors became autonomous and founded hereditary dynasties, or local tribesmen seized power, giving the caliph only nominal allegiance. In 945 a Shi'ite dynasty, the Buyids, actually established itself in Baghdad. However, the leader, who called himself 'Amir al Umara' ('Commander-in-Chief'), acknowledged the theoretical supremacy of the 'Abbasid caliph and made no sustained effort to force the *'ulama* to adopt Shi'ite theological attitudes or to acknowledge the authority of the 'Hidden Imam' or his representatives. It was to be another five centuries before Twelver Shi'ism established itself as the official doctrine of the Iranian state.

Despite its early compromises with the temporal power Shi'ite Islam has continued to exercise its potential for revolutionary mobilization – or, to be more accurate, to provide the ideological underpinning for revolutionary movements – for more than a millennium, from the early tenth century to the present day. Time and again, the millenarian doctrines associated with the *mahdi* have proved an effective means of mobilizing popular discontent: a pretender who claimed descent from the *ahl al bait* and proclaimed himself the promised messiah was automatically assured the support of a sizeable section of the community. Not surprisingly, Shi'ism in its radical versions has had a natural attraction for tribal and other solidarity groups seeking to replace the political power.

Prior to the establishment of Iranian national Shi'ism in the sixteenth century the most successful movement of this kind was that which led to the founding of the Fatimid dynasty in North Africa. Like other more radical Shi'ite groups, the Fatimids were Isma'ilis, followers of Isma'il ibn Ja'far, elder son of the Sixth Imam, who predeceased his father. The Isma'ilis believe that before Isma'il's death Ja'far had already chosen him as his successor by *nass* (explicit designation), and that prior to his own death Isma'il in turn so designated his own son Muhammad. Isma'ilis are sometimes known as 'Seveners', since, according to them, Isma'il ought to have been the Seventh Imam. The 'Twelvers', or Imamis, as the mainstream body of the Shi'a are called, deny this, claiming that Ja'far passed over Isma'il for the succession because he committed the sin of drinking wine. The Seventh Imam of the Twelvers is Ja'far's second son, Musa al Kazim, who died of poisoning on the orders of Harun al Rashid in 799.

In the differences between Twelvers and Seveners much more is involved, however, than a mere dispute about the succession. The early Isma'ilis belonged to the extreme 'batinist' persuasion, which placed the most emphasis on the esoteric (*batini*) meanings of the Quran. Their intellectual temperament was elitist and conspiratorial. Aware of the dangers to which they were exposed, they practised *taqiya* or dissimulation, protecting themselves against accusations of disbelief and preserving from the prying eyes of the ignorant the secret knowledge they believed themselves to possess.

There is no exact Islamic equivalent of the notion of heresy. The term implies the existence of an orthodoxy ('right teaching') from which it has deviated. Since knowledge (*'ilm*) of Islam all comes from the same source – i.e., God and His Messenger, as transmitted in the Quran and *hadiths* – it is theoretically accessible to every member of the community. Differences of opinion therefore focus on the interpretation of texts rather than on their content. (Much of the *hadith* literature attributed by the Shi'ites to their Imams contains the same material as the official Sunni collections, which is one reason why Shi'ism differs more from Sunnism in theory than in practice.) The nearest equivalent in Islam to the idea conveyed by orthodoxy is *ijma'* (consensus), either of the community as a whole or of the *'ulama*. Interpretations of the recognized texts may deviate from the accepted patterns in two ways: by capriciousness or arbitrariness, as conveyed by the term *ahwa* (caprices); or by exaggeration (*ghulu*). Both terms were used freely by the *'ulama* to castigate their opponents. *Ghulu* referred in particular to the development of religious ideas and a vision of the destiny of the Islamic community which, in the eyes of the majority, seemed to over-emphasize a certain doctrine or tendency to the point where the whole structure of belief informed by the Sunni consensus was called into question. In general the Imami Shi'ites fell short of *ghulu* exaggeration – though during the nineteenth century they produced extremist offshoots which eventually led to the formation of a completely new religion (Bahaism).

The doctrine of the Hidden Imam conveniently disposed of the problem of the Imamate, with its potential for creating political and religious factionalism. However, there would always be those for whom the *de facto* acceptance of existing political authority and an unjust social order would seem to represent a fundamental betrayal of Islam's activist message. The Prophet had transmitted God's Word, around which he had built the first Islamic community. His actions as a statesman and leader had also been inspired, or even controlled, by God. It was but a small step from this to seeing in his person an immanence or manifestation of the deity: a step which the Christians had taken with their belief in incarnation. Those who identified themselves with the dissenting tradition associated with the *ahl al bait* naturally saw this immanence as descending, by *nass* designation, down the line of the Imams. Indeed the extremists (*ghulas*) among them made the First Imam, 'Ali, the equal, if not the superior, of the Prophet.

The elevation of 'Ali to almost god-like status occurred in gradual stages. The first consisted in placing rather more emphasis upon the *batini* (esoteric) than the *zahiri* (exoteric) interpretation of the Quran. Although the Prophet was assumed to have the special *'ilm* or secret knowledge necessary to understand the secret meanings of the scripture, the fact that as an archetypal figure he featured so largely in Sunni tradition encouraged the exaggerators among the batinists to place more emphasis upon the Imamate of 'Ali and his successors: this was the second stage. The third stage – only achieved by such extremist communities as the 'Alawis (Nusairis) and Druzes of Syria, the 'Ali Ilahis of Iran and the Nizari (Agha Khanid) Isma'ilis or Khojas of India, entailed the elevation of 'Ali and the Imams to a position not far below the deity – a belief regarded with horror by all the Sunnis and most other Shi'ites. However, because these *ghula* beliefs involve a flexibility of scriptural interpretation denied to the *ahl al zahir* and the Sunni consensus, they allow for the accommodation of antinomian, revolutionary, rationalist and syncretist tendencies. The Imams or their representatives – following the example of the 'Abbasids – found it possible to activate eschatological expectations by declaring themselves to be the long-awaited *mahdi*. In at least one case they took this a stage further by taking it upon themselves to abrogate the Shari'a, announcing that, spiritually speaking, the Day of Judgement had come. Intellectually they freed themselves from the confines of received knowledge (integral to the doctrine of revelation) to indulge in free-range speculative thinking in philosophy and metaphysics. Thus in spite of their religious isolation, they exercised a considerable influence on Islamic intellectual culture. At the more popular level, they permitted the accommodation within a broad Islamic framework of some of the earlier religious traditions of West Asia and the Indian Subcontinent: in particular the pre-Hellenistic and Hellenistic cults of ancient Syria (among the 'Alawis and Druzes), the gnostic traditions of the Zoroastrians in Iran, and the Hindu–Avatar traditions of Iran and northern India.

Extreme or antinomian religious positions can often be related to socio-economic factors, although the traditions to which they give rise may eventually acquire an autonomous existence. Ideas – whether or not these are expressed religiously – are sometimes like time-bombs waiting to be activated at the right moment. As an influence on medieval Islam, batinism had a somewhat similar function to that of Marxism today, rationalizing revolts and occasionally guiding the actions of the leaders of popular movements and the founders of radical new dynasties. Because such movements occurred within a society in which pastoralism exercised a major influence and the principal social structure was the family based on patrilineal kinship, they were usually described in terms of allegiance to allegedly ancestral figures from the *ahl al bait* and the Imams descended from them, rather than in terms of a particular set of ideas or the individuals propagating them. Thus schisms, intellectual rivalries or ideological differences were usually presented as disputes about the succession. In this way the group allegiances characteristic of the early Arabian Islam came to inform the much wider urban-based Islamic political culture. In the Christian and post-Christian West we find Arians, Nestorians, Donatists, Manichaeans, Lutherans, Calvinists, and so on down to the Marxists, Leninists and Trotskyists of our own day, all of them adherents of movements labelled with the names of their founders. In contrast, most of the groups formed in the earliest period of Islam (roughly up to the tenth century), including 'Alawis, Fatimids, Isma'ilis, Musta'lis, Taiyibis, Nizaris and so forth, all of whom claimed allegiance to members of the *ahl al bait*, are defined, as in most segmentary tribal formations, at a point of bifurcation in a supposedly common family tree.

The central tradition among the *ghulas* or *batinis* is the Isma'ili one. Most of the splinter-groups associated with it, including the Qarmatis (long defunct), the Druzes, the Nizaris (Khojas or Aga Khanids) and the Musta'lis (Bohoras) share a common heritage of religious and theosophical ideas which set them apart from the mainstream of Islam. Some of these ideas would later emerge in the teachings of the Sufi masters and so find their way back into the central tradition. The central concept, as in the Quran itself, is that of *tawhid*, the Divine Unity. The *batini* thinkers took the Mu'tazili rejection of any kind of anthropomorphism or 'Association' (*shirk*) to its logical conclusion:

> Allah, in His majestic unity, stands totally above and aloof from the chains of cosmic and spiritual entities . . . No attributes derived from sense experience can be attributed to Allah, no efforts of the human imagination, however fertile and far-reaching, can grasp His unique nature; and no analogy, comparison or resemblance can be drawn between Him and His creatures. Indeed, Allah is asserted to be beyond even the categories of being and non-being, of existence and non-existence.[14]

The cosmos comes into being through the Universal Intellect (*'aql al kull*), representing a final principle of logic, order and reason. This in turn engenders a principle of animation known as the *nafs al kull* (universal self/soul), which, by informing a combination of elements (the earth, air, fire and water of traditional medieval science), formed the mineral, vegetable and animal orders of the physical world. A contrary motion proceeds back through this hierarchy of compound beings to the *aql al kull*. The return to the ultimate source of being which the Sufis sought by the mystics' path was, for the Isma'ilis, primarily intellectual. They saw themselves as a hierarchy of worshippers seeking rational truth on ever higher levels, a hierarchy culminating in the Imam, or, rather, his ancestor 'Ali, representing the *nafs al kull*, the principle of universal animation which set the whole community in motion.

This system, typically rationalistic and hierarchical, embodied many Ptolemaic and neoplatonic ideas; in due course it managed to accommodate many Zoroastrian and Vedantic influences as well. While accepting revelation as the core of its epistemology – for the Isma'ilis knowledge was acquired spiritually, by means of gnosis – it was also supra-rational:

the cosmos had a miraculous coherence and order, proceeding as it did from the Universal Intellect. Being essentially speculative and anti-dogmatic, the system proved, like theosophical Sufism, with which it later became intermixed, less hostile to scientific inquiry than the scrip-turalist mainstream of Sunni Islam. In its own time the *batini* tradition particularly encouraged mathematics as an instrument for freeing the mind from bodily images and attachments, and complex numerological patterns were elaborated around the One. Unlike most modern science, however, it did not proceed from an ontological or metaphysical vacuum: scientific inquiry was a kind of meditation on nature, a fleshing out with facts of underlying assumptions accepted as part of revelation. In such a world-view scientific inquiry becomes a form of *tafsir*, or exegesis, an interpretation or discovery of truths already given.

Modern Muslim writers, such as Sayyid Ahmed Khan and Muham-mad Iqbal, who sought to harmonize religious truth with modern scientific discovery, found much to inspire them in the writings of the Ikhwan al Safa ('Brothers of Purity'), a group of Isma'ili-influenced speculative thinkers writing at Basra in the early tenth century. The early Isma'ilis also exerted considerable influence on the development of Muslim philosophy. Ibn Sina's father was a convert to Isma'ilism. Another Isma'ili convert, Nasir al Din al Tusi (d. 1274), proposed a new model of planetary motion which Copernicus may have learned of through Byzantine and Greek sources. Tusi himself established an astronomical observatory at Maragha which became the model of the earliest European observatories of Tycho Brahe and Kepler.

The *batini* systems contained some ingenious routes for linking their cosmology with human history. Drawing on Pythagorean, Babylonian and Chaldean traditions, they became fascinated with number anal-ogies, mystic numerals and letters, which they incorporated into a complicated hiero-history of prophetic emanations. Each age had a prophet who was accompanied by an *'asas*, or 'silent one', who under-stood the inner meanings of revelation. (Moses had Aaron, Jesus had Peter, Muhammad had 'Ali, and so forth.) It is not difficult to see how, if the *batini* meaning of the Quran were stressed above the *zahiri*, 'Ali would supplant Muhammad in the minds of the believers.

Sectarian offshoots of the Shi'a, including the Nusairis ('Alawis) of Syria and the Druze community (now divided between Syria, Israel and Lebanon), produced their own distinctive versions of these hierarchies. The Nusairis developed a trinitarian doctrine of emanation, in the persons of Muhammad, 'Ali and Salman al Farisi. (The latter, a Persian freedman and Companion of the Prophet, featured very largely in Shi'ite tradition, partly, no doubt, because he was the first Muslim with whom the *mawali* could identify). A previous manifestation of the divine, according to the Nusairis, occurred in the persons of Socrates, Plato and Aristotle.

Central to the extreme Shi'a doctrines, is the role of the Imam, usually traced through the line of Isma'il ibn Ja'far. (Not always, however: some of the Nusairis trace their religious lineage back to 'Ali Naqi, the Tenth Imam of the Shi'a.) Although the Nusairis, like the Twelvers, regard their Imam as having gone into concealment, two of the most successful Isma'ili movements benefited from the presence of a living Imam able to command powerful group loyalties and to activate them for political and social aims. One of them led to the founding of the Fatimid dynasty which ruled Egypt for nearly two centuries. The other has survived into our own time, in the remarkable community headed by the Aga Khan.

The cult of the sacred person is, in one form or another, as central to Shi'ism as it is to Christianity. Whereas Sunni egalitarianism called upon all men to accept a minimum number of injunctions and symbols derived from the unique and unrepeatable event of the Quranic revelation and the Life of the Prophet, Shi'ism graded men into a hierarchy in accordance with the stage they had reached in the pursuit of spiritual knowledge. In a medieval social system contained within the material limits of a modest agricultural surplus, such a hierarchy represented an ideological complement to the existing social order. Whereas the Sunni ideal of social equality remained largely unrealized, Shi'ite elitism proved, time and again, a potent instrument for effecting social and political change.

The Imam was the microcosm, the perfect man in whom the divine intelligence was manifested. The idea of a hypostatic union between the human and the divine need not necessarily be attributed to Christian influences. It finds expression in much more ancient cultures throughout the world. In the Islamic heartland it formed part of the tradition of Egypt, South Arabia and Persia. As Hodgson has pointed out:

> The infallible Imam as such was not so hard for any Medieval to conceive of. Given an approach to knowledge as a finite quantity of foreordained facts – rather than a process of inquiry within experi-

ence – it could seem not impossible that some person, by inheritance or by nature, should possess all of these facts.[15]

The Imamate could be activated either directly by a claimant from the *ahl al bait*, or indirectly through someone claiming to be his deputy. In either event the source of its political power lay in the network of *da'is* or missionaries acting on his behalf.

The *da'is* were highly trained in the esoteric sciences. Like the Jesuits of the Counter-Reformation, they were taught to sound out their targets carefully before declaring themselves. They rarely indulged in polemics or openly engaged their opponents. Indeed, there is a close parallel between the various *da'i* networks and the esoteric doctrines preached by them. They adopted the practice of *taqiya*, concealment of one's true beliefs, to protect themselves from persecution. In consequence they deemed it prudent to preach not frankly but allusively, according to a kind of 'code'. Such a practice was bound to reinforce the elitist idea that the 'truth' was only known to the innermost members of the movement – i.e., those *da'is* who were closest to the Hidden Imam. Those extreme Shi'ite sects which eventually crystallized into closed communities, such as the 'Alawis and Druzes, developed elaborate rites of initiation to protect these 'secret' truths, endowing them with a mystique which made outsiders suppose that they were too dangerous for general consumption. Opponents of these movements naturally imagined the worst of them. Accusations of paganism and sexual promiscuity were made against Qarmatis, Nusairis and Druzes. More significant was the extent to which the habit of coded communication affected the development of their actual doctrines, and this helps to explain how, paradoxically, the more esoteric traditions espoused by them proved more compatible with intellectual modernization. As Hodgson remarks with his usual penetration, it was natural for them to suppose that

. . . even the Author of the Universe Himself will adopt an allusive way of speaking on subtle matters, both in revealed books and in the very laws of nature. Now if one is thus persuaded that God may speak in cipher, as it were, it is not absurd to seek for the traces of such a cipher; and if a code is suggested which gives consistent results whenever applied in God's works, there will be a high presumption that it is the right one. This is what the Isma'ilis thought they had in their *tawil*, their system of interpretation which they applied so freely, both to sacred books and to all nature.[16]

The first Isma'ili movement to make a major impact upon Muslim society was started by Hamdan Qarmat in the latter part of the ninth century. He seems to have begun his mission (da'wa) in Kufa during the 860s as part of a wider movement against the 'Abbasid caliphate conducted in the name of Muhammad ibn Isma'il. In the tenth century the Qarmatis founded a dynastic state based on Bahrein which achieved notoriety in 969 when its leader occupied Mecca and carried off the Black Stone. The Qarmatis are said to have practised a form of communism, in which all personal property, including animals, jewellery and furniture, was pooled. It was even claimed that women were held in common. However, most of these reports came from their enemies and need to be treated cautiously. The famous Persian writer Nasir i Khusraw was highly impressed by the high level of justice, internal order and social welfare he found in the Bahreini state, although public prayers and fasting had been abolished. The Qarmati state in Bahrein survived until 1077, when it was overrun by beduin tribesmen.

The most far-reaching dynasty created by the Isma'ilis was that of the Fatimids (so-called because they legitimized themselves by claiming descent from 'Ali and Fatima), who established themselves in North Africa in 909 and conquered Egypt sixty years later. North of Fustat, near the site of ancient Memphis, they built themselves a fine new capital of gardens and palaces which they named Al Qahira (Cairo), 'the Victorious One'. At its height, Fatimid power extended from the Atlas mountains to Sind. They ruled in Ifriqiya (Tunisia), Egypt, Syria, the Hejaz, Yemen and Oman at a time when, under its Buyid overlords, the 'Abbasid caliphate was confined to Mesopotamia and the Iranian plateau.

The original base for Fatimid power had been in Qairawan, in what is now Tunisia, where an Isma'ili da'i, Ubaidallah, proclaimed himself mahdi in 909, gaining the support of the Kutama Berbers of western Algeria. Although his claims were rejected by da'is loyal to Hamdan Qarmat in Syria and Khurasan, after the Conquest of Egypt in 969, during the reign of the fourth Fatimid ruler, Al Mu'izz, most of the da'is in Persia, Sind, Syria and Yemen came round to recognition of the new caliphate. Although the Isma'ili venture was to end in failure – they never succeeded in uniting the whole of Islam under a new Fatimid caliphate – they governed successfully as Imam–Caliphs for more than a century before succumbing like their 'Abbasid rivals to the domination of their troops. Their political influence extended a network of *da'is* operating everywhere except Spain and the central 'Abbasid territories. For a time they were recognized in the holy cities of Mecca and Medina, which greatly enhanced their prestige, since it gave them control of the Hajj. For one glorious year (1058) Fatimid rule was even proclaimed in Baghdad, when a dissident Turkish general decided to recognize the Cairo caliph. But they never persuaded the Shi'ite Buyids to recognize them as legitimate descendants of 'Ali. Soon afterwards the remaining 'Abbasid lands and most of Syria were overrun by the Seljuk Turks, who remained staunchly Sunni and chose to preserve the formal office of the Baghdad caliphate.

By developing Cairo as an entrepôt between the Mediterranean and the Indian Ocean, building up their sea power and controlling much of the trade between Europe and the Indies, the Fatimids made the Egyptian capital a great centre of culture and learning. They founded Al Azhar (reputedly named after Fatima al Zahra) as a training centre for their *da'is*. Said to be the world's oldest university, it is still the leading institution of religious learning in the Muslim world, though long since, of course, a bastion of Sunnism. The elegant keel-form arches surmounting the delicate colonnades of Al Azhar's central courtyard are still a reminder of the excellent architectural taste of the Fatimid era.

The decline of the Fatimids began when strife broke out among their Sudanese and Turkish troops, and ended with the Crusader attacks and the rising Seljuk power in the East. In 1171 Salah al Din al Ayyubi (known to the west as 'Saladin'), a Kurdish general who had risen in the service of the Seljuks, took power in Syria and Egypt after reconquering Jerusalem from the Franks, and restored the Sunni consensus as the most generally accepted doctrine in the Middle East.

The Isma'ili attempt to win the whole of Dar al Islam for their Imams resulted, eventually, in failure. But it leaves a legacy in three religious sects which have survived into the present – the Druzes, the Bohoras and the Khojas.

The Druzes are far removed from the mainstream of Islam, having carried their belief in the divine Imamate to the point where they may be said to constitute a separate religion. The cult originated during the reign of the third Fatimid caliph, Hakim (996–1021), who, as an Isma'ili Imam, held a position in his community corresponding to the cosmic intellect (*'aql al fa'l*). In person, however, he proved a highly eccentric and at times extremely cruel autocrat. As he became increasingly unpopular there was considerable public disorder, especially when he ordered anathemas pronounced in all the mosques against the first three caliphs.

A small group of the Caliph's entourage, however, saw in his very eccentricities a manifestation of the divine. Encouraged by two preachers, Darazi, a Turk, and Hamza, a Persian, these religious intellectuals began to propagate the doctrine that Hakim was not merely the Imam, but was an actual personification of the *'aql al kull*, the highest cosmic intellect – in other words, God Himself. After Darazi's death and Hakim's subsequent disappearance under circumstances that suggest he may have been murdered, though no corpse was ever found, Hamza proclaimed that Hakim, as the One and Unique embodiment of the highest cosmic principle, had gone into concealment, with a view to testing his followers. Hamza himself then proceeded to disappear, announcing that he was the Imam who would return as *mahdi* with Hakim at the end of the world. During his concealment Hamza continued to communicate with the faithful through a deputy, Baha al Din al Muktana.

Little is known about the early followers of the Hakim cult, though they must have included many antinomian elements awaiting the abolition of the old religion, both *batini* and *zahiri* versions. The cult soon disappeared in Egypt, but in Syria it eventually supplied the ideology of a peasant revolt – no doubt because of its antinomian character. The followers of Hamza and Darazi (after whom the Druzes are named) gained control of some mountain areas, where they are said to have torn down the mosques and established their own distinctive system of law, having got rid of the previous landlords. Later the writings of Muktana and Hamza, and some attributed to Hakim himself, were compiled into a scripture known as the *Rasail al Hikma* ('Epistles of Wisdom'). Over the centuries the Druzes developed into a closed community. Their doctrines, which are still supposed to be secret, acquired their final form in the fifteenth century.

The principal commandments are clearly designed to reinforce group cohesion. The faithful must always speak the truth among themselves, but lying to 'unbelievers' is permitted. They must always defend one another, if necessary by force of arms. They must renounce all other religions, including the Islamic law, although *taqiya* (outward conformity to avoid persecution) is, as with other Shi'ites, permitted. Druzes do not observe Ramadan or the Hajj, but *taqiya* allowed them to adopt a modified version of the Hanafi *fiqh*, official *madhhab* of the Ottoman Empire. They practise endogamy, insisting on equal treatment for men and women in marriage, and, with rare exceptions, refuse converts.

In a simplified version of the Isma'ili hierarchy, which distinguishes between the enlightened leadership around the Imam and the masses for whom the truth is dangerous, the Druzes are divided into two ranks, the *'aqils* ('sages') and *jahils* ('ignorant ones'). The *'aqils*, who may include women, are initiated into the inner secrets of the faith after passing a series of rigorous spiritual tests. They are required to live sober, devout lives, supported by the toil of their hands. They must avoid stimulants and participation in raids or feuding. The more respected among them become *shaikhs*, presiding over weddings, funerals and other religious functions. The *jahils* are allowed more personal licence than the *'aqils*, but it is assumed that they will be denied spiritual growth. They may, however, have the chance of initiation in a future life, for, like Hindus and some Greek gnostics, the Druzes believe in the transmigration of souls. The *jahils* believe that there is a finite number of souls in the community, and that a dead person's spirit enters the next child to be born. While such popular beliefs clearly reinforce Druze *'asabiya*, the *'aqils* appear to have a much more sophisticated and developed theology, including emanationist ideas derived from neoplatonism and Vedantic sources, and some of the pantheistic doctrines common to Ibn al 'Arabi and other Sufi writers.

Like other religious minorities who sought refuge in the Lebanese Mountain, the Druzes acquired feudal overlords who, in return for the protection they offered, were encouraged to adopt the religion of their clients. The most outstanding were the Ma'ni family, who under the Amir Fakhr ul Din II (1590–1635) controlled the whole of Mount Lebanon, the Shouf and the Hawran region, as well as much of northern Galilee. Although in the eighteenth century power passed to the Shihabs, a Sunni family claiming Quraishi descent, some of whose leaders converted to Maronite Christianity, the Druzes continued to provide the Lebanese amir's military underpinning. Since the eighteenth century the leading Druze overlords have been the Arslans and the Jumblatts, a family of Kurdish origin.

The decline of Druze hegemony in Lebanon began with the immigration of Maronite Christian peasants from the north to work for Druze overlords in the Shouf area. Though welcomed at first as cheap labour, the Maronites increased at the expense of the Druzes, many of whom emigrated to the Hawran region further south. (This area, adjoining the Golan Heights, is now somewhat confusingly called Jabal Druze, 'Druze Mountain', a name originally given to the Shouf.) Though there was factionalism and sometimes bloody strife between the great Druze and Maronite families, there is virtually no record of sectarian rivalry until the mid nineteenth century. Foreigners generally found the two sects indistinguishable, though Volney, travelling in the final decade of the eighteenth century, remarked on the greater tolerance shown by the Druzes. The first sectarian troubles occurred late in the 1830s after the Druzes had inflicted a severe defeat on the armies of Muhammad 'Ali, Egyptian conqueror of Syria. The Amir Bashir Shihab II, by now an Egyptian puppet, was ordered by the Egyptian commander, Ibrahim Pasha, to mobilize several hundred Christians against the 'treacherous and infidel Druze sect'.

After Ottoman rule had been restored, with British help, in 1840–41, the Druzes decided to make it impossible for the Shihabs to continue as regional autarchs. The Lebanese Mountain was divided into two administrative districts, north and south, under Christian and Druze deputies answerable to the Turkish governor of Sidon. The dividing line was the Beirut–Damascus road, still the front line between the mainly Christian north and the Druze/Muslim-dominated south. The new system, an unmitigated disaster, institutionalized sectarianism, adding to the mutual antagonism of both communities. Feelings were further inflamed by the machinations of the French on the side of the Maronites and of the British and Turks on the side of the Druzes. In 1860 the country collapsed into a bloody civil war, sparked by a Maronite peasant revolt in the north. Unlike the Maronite priests, who sided with the peasants, the Druze 'aqils made common cause with their feudal overlords: the whole Druze tradition of communal solidarity, reinforced by religious teaching, combined to outweigh class antagonism. Convinced that the Maronites were planning to exterminate them, the Druzes attacked a number of Christian strongholds, killing some 11,000 in the space of four weeks. The trouble spread to Damascus, where a pogrom resulted in more than 5,000 Christian deaths.

A new Christian governorate, imposed by the Powers, kept the peace in Lebanon until after the First World War. Sectarianism had by now, however, already taken root. Whereas the Druzes and some, mostly

Orthodox, Christians were content to promote a relatively modest version of nationalism which sought to guarantee Lebanese autonomy within the predominantly Arab-Muslim context of the region, a vociferous and influential section of the Maronites became wholehearted francophiles, regarding their society as an outpost of Western civilization. In 1958 they persuaded the Americans to suppress a Muslim-leftist revolt inspired by Gamal Abdul Nasser and led by the Druze Kamal Jumblatt. In the 1970s, faced with an alliance between Palestinian guerrillas, Druzes and Muslim elements, the Maronites turned increasingly to Israel for support.

In the summer of 1982 the Israelis invaded Lebanon in order to destroy all Palestinian strongholds and to ensure the election to the presidency of a hard-line Maronite, Bashir Gemayel, with whom they planned to make a a treaty. Although the Palestinians were rounded up in the south and forced to leave Beirut, the plan misfired, as Israel came under increasing domestic and international pressure to pull back its troops. The Maronites were forced to withdraw from areas they had hoped to gain permanently with the help of their Israeli allies. The Israelis, however, had been reluctant to disarm the Druze militias, since they were threatened with mutiny from Druzes serving in their own armed forces. The following year the Lebanese Druzes, now allied with the Syrians, consolidated their position in the Shouf, despite the presence of US troops actively supporting the Lebanese Maronite government. In the fragmented turmoil of Lebanese politics, Druze solidarity had again proved effective. Although one of Lebanon's smaller minorities, numbering about 160,000 people, or 7 per cent of the population, their warlike traditions and social cohesion had made it possible for them to challenge, successfully, the greatest power on earth.

Perhaps the most remarkable and celebrated relic of Isma'ilism is the Khoja community of India, best known through the person of its Imam, the Aga Khan, who claims descent from Nizar, a Fatimid pretender who died in prison having been deposed. Like other Isma'ili splinter-groups, including the Musta'lis who survive in India's Bohora community, the Nizari da'is abandoned the Fatimid caliphate in its declining years and established an autonomous da'wa enabling them to survive, and eventually prosper, as a community. The Nizari Isma'ilis, whose adherents now live in India, Pakistan, Syria, Britain, East Africa and Canada, have become a wealthy religious sect. Their Imam, Aga Khan IV, controls a vast business empire which includes more than seventy industrial enterprises in Asia and Africa, newspapers in East Africa, hotels, supermarkets and stud farms in Europe, not to mention untold investments in international companies. Curiously enough, this eminently respectable trading community was once a byword for political terrorism, and gave the world a term – assassination – which described its principal tactic.

The 'Assassins' attacked the Seljuk armies from their strongholds in Iran and Syria. They specialized in killing the commanders, since this usually caused the Seljuk formations, bound by personal loyalties, to disband. Although their famous last stronghold at Alamut was overrun by the Mongols in the 1250s, the Nizaris survived as an underground movement in Iran and Syria and prospered in Gujerat, where the *da'is* had made a number of converts from among the lowest Hindu castes. The basis of the sect's modern revival was a decision by the Bombay High Court in 1866 to award the tithes of this now wealthy Indian merchant community to the Nizari Imam, Aga Khan I, who had recently arrived from Persia after quarrelling with the Shah. The Aga Khan and his successors used the wealth so acquired not only to amass enormous personal fortunes but to win for the community a 'place in the sun' of the British Empire. The Aga Khan's spiritual authority has enabled him to impose religious and legal obligations on his followers which have allowed them to adjust to modern conditions without loss of religious faith – something which Sunni Islam, with its legalistic and literalistic traditions, has found much harder to achieve. The Isma'ilis have become the world's most prosperous Islamic community outside the oil regions; it is a community, moreover, whose prosperity has been achieved as a result of its own efforts under a succession of astute and capable 'living Imams'.

Another Shi'ite faction which has survived and gained some prominence – as well as notoriety – in recent times is the Nusairi community based on Latakia in Syria. The Nusairis (generally known as 'Alawis) trace their *isnads* back to Ibn Nusair, a notable of Basra who proclaimed himself *bab* ('gate') to the Tenth Imam of the Shi'a, 'Ali Naqi, in 859. During the tenth century his movement gained a following in northern Syria among people thought by some scholars to be of Phoenician descent. The movement also seems to have been influenced by Qarmati ideas circulating in the same area during this period. Like the Druzes, whom they resemble theologically, the 'Alawis are an initiatory sect who keep their secrets closely guarded. Little was known about them until

1863 when one Sulaiman Effendi of Adana converted to Christianity and published one of their texts.

According to 'Alawi belief, manifestations of God occur cyclically in three persons. In the Muslim era this trinity consisted of 'Ali, Muhammad and Salman al Farisi; previous manifestations included Aristotle, Plato and Socrates. There is an elaborate cosmology relating these manifestations to the planets. Like the Druzes, the 'Alawis believe in the transmigration of souls and think that each human soul will one day return to its primordial state as a star. 'Alawi doctrine evidently contains many traces of pre-Islamic beliefs, including Christianity, neoplatonic Judaism and ancient Syro-Phoenician Sabaism.

Within the community the process of initiation, which is only applied to men, encourages a strong sense of loyalty to the religion. Those who betray its secrets are condemned to eternal damnation. Externally the group cohesion of the 'Alawis has been reinforced by persecution. Although they took part in several revolts against French colonialism during the period of the Mandate, the French decided to recruit them, along with other minorities, into the armed forces. Their policy, a classic one of 'divide and rule', also accorded with the old Khaldunian precept of turning the 'wolves' of outlying areas into 'sheepdogs'. A hardy peasant people with a long tradition of self-protection, the 'Alawis proved excellent soldiers, able and willing to counter the growing weight of Sunni-based nationalism in the cities.

Under the aegis of the Ba'ath party a number of Alawi families have acquired a predominant position in the Syrian armed forces, including the President Hafez el Asad, who came to power in 1970, and his brother Rifaat, commander of the 'Special Forces'. Alawi dominance, allied to other social, political and economic factors, led to a state of virtual civil war in Syria between 1979 and 1982, culminating in the abortive Muslim Brotherhood rebellion in Hama, suppressed at an estimated cost of 10,000 lives.

The most dramatic manifestation of Shi'ite radicalism in modern times occurred within the main body of the Twelvers or Imamis, when the fall of the Pahlavi monarchy in 1979 and its replacement by the militantly 'Islamic' government headed by Ayatollah Khomeini created an upheaval in international relations as drastic as any since the Second World War. The full implications of the Iranian revolution have yet to emerge. The main lines of development were, however, laid down from the sixteenth century.

About ten per cent of all Muslims are Shi'ites of the Imami (Twelver) faith. Most of them are concentrated in Iran and its peripheral territories – Pakistan and Afghanistan to the east, Soviet Turkmenistan and Azerbaijan to the north, Turkey, Iraq, Bahrain and the Saudi province of Hasa to the west. There is also a semi-autonomous Shi'ite community in the strife-torn region of southern Lebanon. The distribution of Shi'ites around the Iranian highlands and in areas, such as Bahrain, once subject to Persian rule is not accidental. Since the sixteenth century Shi'ism has been the religious ideology of the regimes holding power in Iran and such territories as the fortunes of war brought into its orbit.

From the beginning there were elements in the Shi'ite faith which made it particularly appealing to the Persians. The dispossession of 'Ali and his clan from their rightful inheritance by the worldly Umayyads was a cause with which non-Arabs could readily identify. Many of the Persian *mawali* supported the 'Abbasid revolution, which, before it developed into a new, expanded Arab caliphate, represented the claims of Islamic universalism against the tribal *'asabiya* of the Umayyads, whose behaviour so often resembled that of their Quraishi ancestors. The doctrine of the Imamate was well suited to the needs of non-Arabs without direct access to the Quran through oral or written media. Whereas any illiterate beduin could both hear and memorize passages from the divine text, Persian speakers needed to have it transmitted to them through mediators who, in due course, were represented as acting on behalf of the Hidden Imam. Moreover Imamism was able to act as an Islamic bearer of Persian national and cultural values. Whereas Byzantium survived the Muslim conquest for eight centuries, remaining a beacon of hope for defeated Eastern Christianity, Sassanid Persia had been destroyed completely. The Churches survived as protected communities, but Zoroastrianism, though granted scriptural status, all but disappeared. As an 'opposition' movement within Islam, Shi'ism supplied an ideological alternative to a Sunnism which, with its overwhelming emphasis on an Arabic text, represented the official ideology of the conquerors. The Shi'ites could look on their rules as usurpers without rejecting the broader religious and cultural framework of Islam.

There were also historic figures who symbolized the link between Shi'ism and Persian national identity. As has already been suggested, Salman al Farisi, the Persian freedman who allegedly instructed the Muslims in digging the *khandaq* ditch which saved Medina from the

Quraishi cavalry, loomed large in the *batini* tradition partly, one suspects, because of his national origin and his unusual standing as one of the earliest non-Arab Companions. (For similar reasons the Abyssinian Bilal has latterly become a cult-figure among some American Black Muslims.) The Fourth Imam, Zain al 'Abidin, also known as Sajjad, was the son of the martyred Husain by the daughter of Yazdigird, last of the Sassanid kings. Thus most of the Imams of the Shi'a had the Persian blood royal running through their veins. Among other things, the messianic expectation of a *mahdi* from this line conveyed the hope of a deliverance of Persia from the Arab conquest (rather as the Jewish messiah was expected to come from the Royal House of David).

There were intellectual factors as well. The potential for rationalization contained in the *batini* tradition seems to have had a particular appeal for thinkers of Persian ancestry. Ibn Sina (Avicenna) was the son of a convert to Isma'ilism, and though he broke with the *batinis* he absorbed much of their method and overall approach. The spiritualizing aspect of Shi'ism, contrasting with the public and formal religiosity of the Arabs, also found some *rapport* with Persian tradition. Like Augustinian Christianity, Shi'ism was profoundly influenced by the Manichaean dichotomy between the material and the spiritual, a dualism entrenched in the distinction between *batini* and *zahiri* interpretations of the Quran. Imami Shi'ism thus eventually became a suitable bearer of Persian cultural values and assumptions within the framework of Islam. The eventual 'Shi'ization' of Iran, however, was not accomplished without compulsion.

The Safavid dynasty which ruled in Iran from 1501–1722 was the first in Islamic history to make Shi'ism a state ideology. Previously Shi'ite rulers, including the Buyids and Fatimids, had been content to claim a Shi'ite legitimacy for their power, leaving most of their subjects to practise Sunnism. The network of *da'is* emanating from Egypt during the height of Fatimid power seems to have been more concerned with extending Islam in far-reaching territories or attacking their 'Abbasid enemies than with consolidating Isma'ilism in Egypt; this was one reason why Saladin encountered practically no opposition when he assumed full power in Cairo.

The Safavids were originally Sunni Azeris from the highlands of Azerbaijan in north-west Persia. Their eponymous ancestor, Shaikh Safi al Din Ishaq (d. 1334), had become leader of a local Sufi order, extending his authority among the semi-nomadic Turcoman tribesmen who eventually became the elite corps of the Safavid forces. The movement does not appear to have acquired a Shi'ite character for at least a century. It eventually did so probably in order to distinguish itself from the rising Ottoman power in the west and to enlist the support of Shi'ite elements, not only in Iran, but in Syria and Anatolia as well. The founder of the dynasty, Shah Isma'il I, who seized power in Tabriz in 1501 and extended his sway over what is now Iran during the next decade or so, claimed descent from the Seventh Imam of the Twelvers, Musa al Kazim, according to a forged genealogy. Shi'ism was proclaimed the state religion, the Shah exercising his authority directly on behalf of the Hidden Imam. The Turcoman tribesmen who upheld Isma'il's power wore special red turbans containing twelve folds commemorating the twelve Imams. Known disparagingly to the Ottomans as Qizilbashis ('Redheads'), they were fanatically devoted to their leader, whom they may even have thought of as God.

Without a Shi'ite ideology to distinguish its rulers from the Ottomans, Persia might well have become absorbed by its more powerful Sunni neighbour. The Safavids imported Shi'ite 'ulama to provide the ideological underpinning for their government. Many of them may have been Isma'ili da'is from Syria or Bahrain, who were willing to change their allegiance in order to promote the essentials of the batini faith. The Safavid rulers also appointed commissar-type officials known as sadrs, whose duty it was to ensure the allegiance of the 'ulama. Resistance was met with force. The new Shi'ite 'ulama, backed by the power of the state, were in a strong position to enforce religious conformity. In due course ideological uniformity cemented territorial unity. The modern Iranian nation came into being.

The crucial developments affecting modern Iranian Shi'ism occurred in the period of turmoil following the decline of the Savafids during the eighteenth century. Having come to power, like the 'Abbasids and Fatimids, by exploiting messianic expectations, they found they could consolidate it most effectively by exercising it on behalf of the Hidden Imam. The eschatological hopes, actualized during the revolution, were, as usual, deferred indefinitely once power had been achieved. However, after the Savafids had begun to show the classic symptoms of Khaldunian decline (their zenith had been reached during the reign of 'Abbas the Great from 1587–1629), the Shi'ite 'ulama began to exercise an increasingly independent authority. The long interregnum (1722–79) that followed the end of the dynasty witnessed a vigorous debate between two groups of *'ulama* – the *usulis* and the *akhbaris* – which replicated in many respects the much earlier debates between the *ahl al kalam* and the *ahl al hadith* under the 'Abbasids.

The *akhbaris* argued that, in the absence of the Imam, it was not permissible for an *'alim* (scholar) to exercise *ijtihad* (individual interpretation) or reason in determining the law. Instead he must rely exclusively on the traditions (*akhbar*, 'reports' – another term for *hadith*) which the Shi'a derived from the Quran, the Prophet and the Twelve Imams. The *usulis* (from *usul*, 'roots' or 'origins') held that since their authority came from the Hidden Imam, they had the right, even the duty, to exercise individual *ijtihad* on his behalf. There were theological as well as political dimensions to the debate. The *usulis* inherited the rationalism of the Mu'tazilis, which is also prominent in Isma'ili tradition. Man has free will. God's justice is both rational and comprehensible: he is obliged to reward good and punish evil. In other words God Himself is subject to a version of natural law. It follows that knowledge of the divine purpose must be accessible, not only to the Hidden Imam, but to virtuous men using the faculty of reason – i.e., *ijtihad*.

The debate continued into the nineteenth century, with victory eventually going to the *usulis*. They won partly because Iran's rulers never regained the spiritual authority lost to the *'ulama* during the period of Safavid decline. The Qajar Shahs, who held power from 1785 to 1924, never succeeded in establishing a centrally controlled bureaucratic state comparable to the Ottoman Empire after the administrative reforms (*tanzimat*) or to Muhammad 'Ali's Egypt. *Usuli* doctrines conferred more spiritual authority, and hence more social power, upon the *mujtahids* than the doctrines of the *akhbaris*.

After their victory the *usulis* were free to develop the characteristic institutions of modern Iranian Shi'ism. Foremost among them was the special position of the *'ulama*. For the *ijma'* of the community, always latent in Sunnism, though usually exercised by the *'ulama*, they substituted the exclusive *ijma'* of the *mujtahids*. The latter, while not organized into a 'Church' on the Catholic model, nevertheless constitute a hierarchy with exclusive access to religious knowledge. Ordinary believers, including the ruler, are supposed to place themselves under the guidance of a *mujtahid* of their own choice, known as a *marja' i taqlid*. The senior *mujtahids*, known as Ayatollahs (from *aya*, 'sign' [of God]), elect their own *marja' i taqlid*, who, in effect, exercises supreme religious authority. Many of the Ayatollahs (including the revolutionary leader

leader Khomeini) belong to the hereditary class of Sayyids, who claim descent from the Prophet.

The *mujtahids* receive a rigorous training in the religious sciences, including the school of *fiqh* traced back to the Imam Ja'far al Sadiq. Ja'fari *fiqh* reached its full development in the nineteenth century and was eventually accepted by most of the Sunni *'ulama* as a fifth *madhhab* on a par with the Hanbali, Hanafi, Maliki and Shafi'i schools of *fiqh*. Even though the sources of Ja'fari *fiqh* are different, deriving from the teachings of the Imams as well as those of the Prophet, its overall content is generally similar to that of the Sunni *madhhabs*. The best-known Imami Shi'ite legal institution is the *mut'a*, or temporary marriage contract, made for a fixed term of years, months or even days. After the termination of the contract, the woman only has to observe half the *'idda* period of a normal marriage. Even this, however, can be avoided if the couple immediately makes a second contract which remains unconsummated. The custom seems to have existed in Arabia during the time of the Prophet. The fact that it was prohibited by the caliph 'Umar, who is not recognized by the Twelvers, probably accounts for its adoption by them.

Western and some Muslim critics of *mut'a* regard it as a form of legalized prostitution. The fact that a proportion of the *mahr* or dowry paid by the man to the woman is returnable if she terminates the contract prematurely, as is her right, has been used to justify the claim that the woman 'hires' herself to the man for purely sexual purposes. Undoubtedly the institution has been abused in this way. In the past, travellers in strange cities would be met by professional brokers who, for a fee, would arrange a temporary marriage for the period of their sojourn. The institution's defenders, however, maintain that the Prophet and the Imams allowed it because it provides a morally acceptable and socially regulated alternative to adultery, thereby serving to uphold permanent marriage and family values. These arguments are, of course, not unlike those put forward by the advocates of legalized prostitution in the West. They do not, however, dispose of the problem of sexual inequality: a man may contract as many temporary marriages as he likes (in addition to up to four permanent ones), whereas a woman is only permitted a single sexual partner at one time. Advocates of *mut'a*, as of regular polygamous unions, argue that this differential flows from inherent biological and psychological differences between men and women, something which few Westerners would find acceptable. A more persuasive defence of *mut'a* has been put forward recently by the

Iranian Ayatollah Morteza Mutahari, who sees in it an appropriate form of union for young people not yet psychologically or economically prepared for permanent marriage. An exclusively Twelver institution, *mut'a* is not permitted by the Isma'ilis or any other Shi'ite sect.[17]

Apart from *mut'a*, there are a few ritual practices distinguishing Imami Shi'ism from mainstream Sunni Islam. Although, like the Sunnis, the Shi'a regard the Hajj as one of the 'pillars' of the faith, they are accustomed to making supplementary pilgrimages to the tombs of the Imams – especially those of Husain in Karbala, Fatima in Qum and the Eighth Imam, 'Ali Rida, at Mashad. In the past, Friday congregational prayers featured much less prominently in Shi'a than in Sunni practice. There was even learned discussion as to whether, in the absence of the Imam, it was necessary or appropriate to hold Friday prayers at all. The use of mosques as rallying points during the Iranian revolution, particularly at Friday prayers, which have been massively attended, is one of many indications of how the revolution has activated latent eschatological expectations. Though Khomeini never made any formal statement to the effect that he was the Hidden Imam, his tumultuous reception on his return from exile, and the fact that since he took over the leadership of the state he has been known to all his supporters as 'the Imam', point to the same conclusion.

Whatever its contributory causes, whether social, economic or political, the outcome of the Iranian revolution has been a direct consequence of the position occupied by the religious leadership in Iran since the eighteenth century. The *mujtahids* were not just a spiritual elite. They disposed of a degree of social, economic and political power which made them a growing force in the land. They had the right to collect and distribute the two religious taxes, the *khums* (a 'fifth', or 20 per cent) on all trading profits, and the *zakat*, normally a wealth tax assessed annually at 2½ per cent. In a decentralized polity the collection and distribution of these taxes made the *mujtahids* the only welfare agency. In addition to acting as tax collectors (which, of course, provided opportunities for illicit self-enrichment), the *mujtahids* and the *mullahs* controlled by them were entitled to a 10 per cent commission on the *waqf* properties they administered – which provided them with a legitimate source of independent wealth. Another institution which added considerably to their social power was *bast* – the right of sanctuary in mosques and other holy places – which included the homes of the *mujtahids*. Two of the Qajar rulers, Muhammad Shah (1834–48) and Nasr al Din Shah (1858), tried to abolish *bast*, but were defeated by the organized resistance of the *mujtahids*.

In addition to the protection it afforded the Shah's political enemies, *bast* symbolized an important strand in Twelver Shi'ism: the illegitimacy of the state. *Bast* was justified theologically as a refuge from illegal tyranny with the only legitimate authority – the territory under the direct control of the Hidden Imam's representatives. The institution of *bast*, and *mujtahid* independence generally, were strengthened by the fact that after the loss of Iraq in the seventeenth century the principal Shi'ite shrines of Najaf and Karbala in Iraq were situated in Ottoman territory. Nineteenth-century travellers recorded how Karbala actually afforded a sanctuary to thieves preying on Shi'ite pilgrims. But this situation also enhanced the political independence of the *'ulama*, since the Sunni Ottoman rulers were not averse to an institution which could be used to embarrass their Persian neighbours. As Nikki Keddie has observed, the location of the religious leadership beyond the borders of the state, together with the selection of a senior *mujtahid* as the *marja' i taqlid* for all the others, created in nineteenth-century Iran a form of church–state dichotomy similar to that which prevailed in medieval Christian Europe. The religious organization asserted, and was often able to support, claims superior to those of the merely secular government.

The independence of the Shi'ite *'ulama* in nineteenth-century Iran expressed itself in two ways: against the state itself and against the increasing pressure of European influence in the form of Russian and British imperialism. The two elements came together in the famous tobacco agitation of 1891–2, when Nasr al Din Shah was forced to revoke a concession granting a British subject a monopoly over the production and sale of tobacco. This highly successful clerical intervention into the affairs of state was not simply one in a long chain of incidents in which the *mujtahids* used their power to veto government decisions. It also represented the beginnings of the continuous political involvement of the clergy which culminated in the Constitutionalist Movement of 1906 and which – after the interruption of seven decades – was to erupt once more in a clergy-led revolution against the Qajars' Pahlavi successors. But this is to look too far ahead. By 1900 the strands of Twelver sectarianism had already become entangled with those of the modernist movement. Before this can be assessed, a further tradition of classical Islam must be examined, that of the Sufi saints and the religious orders spawned by them.

6 ✤ Spiritual Renewal

If one could sum up in a phrase the essential difference between the two great western monotheisms, one might say that whereas Christianity is primarily the religion of love, Islam is above all the religion of justice. This does not, of course, mean that Christians are necessarily better at loving than Muslims, or that Muslim society lends itself more successfully to the realization of justice. A pessimistic view of religion would suggest exactly the opposite. The Christian imperative, 'to love one's neighbour as oneself', is far too universal to be given practical application, except at a purely individual level. The admonition to 'love one's enemy' takes little account of the social and political circumstances in which the majority of people find themselves. A very few Christians have found it possible to follow the conclusion of Christ's teaching to the point where they become pacifists. The cruellest and most destructive wars in human history have been waged against each other by nominally Christian states.

Similarly, most Muslim states are ruled by bloody and repressive dictatorships which, far from satisfying the imperative of social justice exemplified by the Prophet's career, seem to be incapable of granting even the most basic human rights to their citizens. Official murder, arbitrary imprisonment and extra-legal government in all its forms can be found in Muslim states from Morocco to Malaysia. The very promise of justice conveyed in the Quranic message seems to militate against its realization: by raising expectations of such a political character, Islam presents its rulers with an impossible challenge. Like Marxist governments, which they resemble in this respect, Muslim rulers find it necessary to pre-empt ideologically inspired attacks upon themselves by appropriating the vocabulary and rhetoric of their potential opponents. 'Islamic' justice, like 'Christian' love, acquires a hollow ring.

Nevertheless, despite this perversion, or rather inversion, of their respective ideals as they are applied or misapplied, in practice, the two watchwords, love and justice, can usefully act as signposts to a wide range of differences between the two religions in terms both of their acknowledged practices and dogmas and of the unconscious prejudices of their adherents. Love is the warmest and most deep-rooted of human emotions. Its intensity is felt in proportion to the paucity of its objects. One loves a parent, a child or a sexual partner more strongly or deeply than a multitude. As the cement of most family and sexual unions, love is essentially exclusive. In order to universalize this emotion, to utilize it in the service of religion, the Christians have had to humanize the deity, investing it with the character of a love-object. 'Jesus loves you,' proclaim the slogans. The relationship is personalized and, like all true love, must be reciprocated. Gentle Jesus, a model of young manhood, inspires an intensely personal kind of love. Alone and naked on the cross, he excites a pity not unmixed with eroticism. However, love of the human person in Jesus is but a stage on the road to the love and awareness of a God 'who so loved the world' that he sent his only son to die in it. The personal and intimate nature of Christian love ensures that the divine is conceptualized in essentially human terms. We cannot love what we cannot understand: the corollary of Christian love is a deity who resists all attempts at de-anthropomorphization.

In contrast, the God of the Quran is approached with awe and veneration rather than love.

> Know, then, that God is sublimely exalted, the Ultimate Sovereign, the Ultimate Truth: there is no deity save Him the Sustainer, in bountiful almightiness enthroned![1]

God is described in this passage and elsewhere as 'Malik al haqq' – 'King of Truth and Justice'. The word *al haqq*, according to Asad, 'signifies "the Truth" in the absolute, intrinsic sense, eternally and immutably existing beyond the ephemeral, changing phenomena of His creation'. The same word is used, significantly, in connection with the prohibition on killing:

> Do not take any human being's life – [the life] which God has declared to be sacred – otherwise than in the pursuit of justice [*ila bi'l haqq*].[2]

Justice and truth, as well as mercy, are thus seen as essential attributes of God. 'God's decrees' are the natural laws instituted by him. Those who disobey them 'sin against themselves': God himself remains unaffected by their foolishness.

> Whoever does what is just and right, does so for his own good; and whoever does evil, does so to his own hurt: and never does God do the least wrong to His creatures.[3]

The proper approach for a Muslim is to submit to the decrees of God, as represented by the laws of nature and the rules laid down in the Quran and the Prophet's Sunna:

> O you who have attained to faith! Pay heed unto God and pay heed unto the Apostle and to those from among you who have been entrusted with authority.[4]

As if to underline the identity of the Muslim's submission (*islam*) to God with the working of the natural order, the Quran combines the cosmic imagery of shadows with the prostrations of prayer:

> And before God prostrate themselves, willingly or unwillingly, all [things and beings] that are in the heavens and on earth, as do the shadows in the mornings and the evenings.[5]

God's 'reward' for the essentially rational and self-interested submission to his decrees by mankind is the altruistic gain of human social harmony:

> Say [O Prophet]: 'No reward do I ask of you for this [message] other than [that you should] love your fellow-men.'[6]

Love, it would seem, belongs to the human sphere. The all-embracing cosmic deity conveyed in the Quran cannot be apprehended closely enough to elicit the warmth of love in the average human. Yet from the first there were Muslims whose psychic or spiritual needs were unsatisfied by mere obedience to the deity and the dutiful observance of his commandments. They sought a closer and more intimate relationship by means of ascetic practices, arduous spiritual exercises and complicated liturgies. They came to be known as Sufis, after the woollen garments (*suf* = wool) allegedly worn by the earliest exemplars of this movement, as well as by the followers of Jesus whom they particularly admired. Through the work of its saints, its theosophers and, eventually, by means of its organized lodges of lay adherents, the Sufi movement brought an inner spirituality into an Islam which otherwise tended to crystallize into a religion concerned mainly with the outward forms of legal observance and the pursuit of political power. The contemplation of the 'god within' revitalized Islam, replenishing its psychic reserves and fructifying its structures, both legal and intellectual, with a new injection of energy.

The 'God within' is well attested in the Quran:

> Now verily it is We who have created man and We know that his innermost self whispers within him: for We are closer to him than his neck-vein.[7]

In addition to the general experience of Muhammad's revelation, mystical by definition, the Quran alludes to two particular visionary experiences: the visitation of an angel who appeared 'two bow-lengths away, or even nearer,[8] and the celebrated Night Journey (Al Isra, title of the 17th *sura*) in which the Prophet was 'transported' to Jerusalem. Early Muslim opinion was divided as to whether the Prophet travelled physically or only in spirit. 'Aisha, one of the most important sources of *hadith* reports, maintained emphatically that 'he was transported only in his spirit, while his body did not leave its place'.[9] The mystics of Islam have always rejected the naive view that the Isra was a miraculous occurrence.

Direct experience of the numinous tends to call into question the absolute validity of the visible and material world. The mystic perceives epistemologically what the ascetic feels morally: for this reason the two are usually combined in one person. For the Muslim ascetic, the Quran is also a point of departure:

> Know [O men] that the life of this world is but a play and a passing delight, and a beautiful show, and [the cause of] your boastful vying with one another, and [of your] greed for more and more riches and children.[10]

Piety and asceticism are intimately bound up with a rejection of the world's 'vanities'. As Louis Massignon, the greatest modern authority on Sufism, put it:

> The mystic call is as a rule the result of an inner rebellion of the conscience against social injustices, not only those of others but primarily and particularly against one's own faults: with a desire intensified by inner purification to find God at any price.[11]

Psychologically, the intensity of personal faith, understood in terms of a sense of proximity to God, sustains the mystic–ascetic in his or her decision to withdraw from the world of outward deceptions. The mystic's 'rebellion' is a quietist one, but contains within itself the potential for political action. The sense of proximity to God does not necessarily lead to withdrawal. In certain personalities, and under certain conditions, it becomes converted to revolutionary activism, as we shall see later in this chapter. The transition was exemplified by the Prophet himself in the *hijra* from Mecca to Medina. Sufis would often interpret the *hijra* individualistically, as a personal 'migration' from evil. Among the Kharijis, and among the later reformist movements such as the Almohads, the Wahhabis and the Muslim Brothers, the *hijra* retained its two-sided character of personal purification and prelude to a crusade aimed at reforming the whole community. Sometimes this transformation from quietism to activism was stimulated by foreign, particularly European, encroachments on *dar al Islam*. However, this was not necessarily the case: the transition from a spiritual to an active *jihad* is intrinsic to Islam, as will be shown in the cases of the Berber, West African and Indian reform movements described at the end of this chapter.

In view of the intimate connection between ascetic withdrawal and pious activism, it is not surprising to find that figures associated with opposition movements within Islam figure largely in the Sufi hagiographies. Most of the Sufi orders traced their chains of mystic teachers back to 'Ali whom the Shi'ites, of course, also regarded as a repository of esoteric knowledge. The Sufi master Abu al Qasim Junaid (d. 910) regarded 'Ali as a 'natural mystic' who, however, had been too preoccupied with worldly affairs to develop the higher gnostic disciplines. Other figures from whom they claim spiritual descent include Abu Dharr al Ghifari and Hasan al Basri, both of whom are associated with the pious opposition to the Umayyads.

A letter from Hasan al Basri, who died in 728, has been recorded which contains most of the attitudes later associated with Sufism:

> Beware of this world with all wariness; for it is like a snake – smooth to the touch, but its venom is deadly. Turn away from whatsoever delights thee in it . . . put off from thee its cares, for that thou hast seen its sudden chances, and knowest for sure that thou shalt be parted from it; endure firmly its hardships, for the ease that shall presently be thine . . . Hard is the life of man if he be prudent, dangerous if comfortable, being wary ever of catastrophe, certain of his ultimate fate.[12]

The prophets, according to Hasan, had been sent by God as a warning to men against the dangers and snares of the world:

> For this world has neither worth nor weight with God; so slight it is, it weighs not with God so much as a pebble or a single clod of earth; as I am told, God has created nothing more hateful to Him than this world, and from the day He created it He has not looked upon it, so much He hates it. It was offered to our Prophet with all its keys and treasures, and that would not have lessened him in God's sight by so much as the wing of a gnat, but he refused to accept it . . .[13]

Among the earliest Sufi adepts was Rabi'a al 'Adawiya, the famous freedwoman of Basra. In her rejection of marriage, she sought the ultimate mystic's path of union with God:

> The contract of marriage is for those who have a phenomenal existence. But in my case there is no such existence, for I have ceased to exist and have passed out of self. I exist in God and am altogether His. I live in the shadow of His command. The marriage contract must be asked from Him, not from me.[14]

Rabi'a sought to approach God with a love that was wholly altruistic, and absolutely free from the self-interest of Quranic morality. Taking a flaming torch in one hand and a jar of water in the other, she dramatized her disinterest, proclaiming:

> I am going to light fire in Paradise and to pour water on to Hell, so that both veils may be taken away from those who journey towards God, and their purpose may be sure and they may look towards their Sustainer without any object of hope or motive of fear. What if the hope of Paradise and the fear of Hell did not exist? No one would worship his Sustainer or obey Him.[15]

Explaining her own attempts to love God purely for his own sake, she exclaimed: 'I should be a wretched hireling if I served God from fear.' Her verses on the two kinds of love, the pure and the interested, are much quoted:

> I have loved Thee with two loves, a selfish love and a love that is
> worthy [of Thee]
> As for the love which is selfish, I occupy myself therein with
> remembrance of Thee to the exclusion of all others,

As for that which is worthy of Thee, therein Thou raisest the veil
    that I may see Thee
Yet there is no praise in me in this or that
But the praise is to Thee, whether in that or this.[16]

Disinterested love of God, celebration of poverty and a desire to purify
oneself inwardly in order to come closer to the transcendent are the
perennial themes of Sufi writing and practice from the earliest times.
They inject a warmth into Islam which is lacking in the legalistic
observance advocated by the Sunni *'ulama* or in the fanatical loyalty of the
Shi'ites to the tragic memories of their Imams. Even the ascetic practices
of the Sufis have a disinterested quality. In the absence of a doctrine of
original sin, writes Michael Gilsenan, an anthropologist who has made a
study of Sufism,

> . . . salvation is not imperilled by man's inherently sinful nature
> and his endless need for penance and the renewal of intention . . .
> Suffering . . . whether just or unjust, of the individual or of the
> community, is not a dominant mode of purification or redemption
> or a path to salvation; it has no positive soteriological meaning
> crystallized in the symbol of the human–divine crucified saviour or
> the persecuted community in exile . . .[17]

The aim of the ascetic practices of the Sufi masters was not to earn
themselves credits in the next world by mortifying the flesh in this, but
rather to liberate the spirit for improved communication with the divine.
Once this had been achieved, ascetic practices were often relaxed. Many
of the Sufi masters married, thereby becoming founders of saintly
lineages.

The same author has described the rigours to which a modern Sufi
shaikh (born in Cairo in 1867) subjected himself in order to 'refine his
nature'. The practices are essentially the same as those performed by the
earliest Sufi masters:

> For three hundred days in the year he fasted; each night he recited
> twelve thousand times the formula *la ilaha illa Allah* (there is no god
> but God); for six years he repeated as an individual *dhikr* (Sufic
> exercise) the name of Allah thirty thousand times in a night, and
> for two years he abstained from sexual intercourse, avoiding even
> the company of women. Finally, he prayed to the Prophet
> Muhammad, whom he always held in the highest reverence, for

two hours each night. Such a discipline had a severe physical effect
– piles, bleeding and excessive thinness. He himself is quoted as
saying that his parents and friends became increasingly concerned
and others mocked him. At last . . . he came to see that effort of
this kind was not sufficient and that truth might be sought within
the individual soul without following so demanding a bodily
ascetic regime. He then relaxed these practices, but never entirely
gave them up, remaining a *zahid* (ascetic) until he died.[18]

Muslim asceticism doubtless owed something to non-Muslim influences. The Prophet himself may have acquired the habit of nocturnal
vigil and prostrations from Christian hermits; and there is no doubt that
the earlier Sufi masters drew on the mystical traditions of the Eastern
churches. One of the most celebrated of these was Abu Yazid al Bistami
(d. *circa* 875) whose sayings (about 500 of them) have been recorded in
oral tradition. His teacher, called Abu 'Ali al Sindi (possibly an Indian
from Sind), was ignorant of Arabic, and in return for instruction in the
techniques for achieving mystical communion, Abu Yazid taught him
the Quran. While we know little of these techniques, the language
through which Abu Yazid sought to express his mystic experience was
wholly Quranic. In particular, he adapted and developed the stylistic
peculiarity known as *shath* ('roaming' or 'straying'), whereby the pronoun shifts from the third to the first person: like Muhammad in the
Quran, Abu Yazid addressed his auditors as if he were God, implying a
mystical exchange of roles with the Almighty. The conventionally pious
were, unsurprisingly, scandalized by such ecstatic utterances (*shathiyas*)
as 'Glory be to Me!','How great is My Majesty!'. A lengthy report of his
efforts to achieve a state of union with God (*fana*), however, reveals two
themes which would recur in the theosophy of Ibn al 'Arabi: the
annihilation of the subject–object relationship in the supreme mystical
encounter, and the related idea of a return to an undifferentiated state of
identity with the Absolute:

> Then I gazed upon Him with the eye of truth, and said to Him
> 'Who is this?' He said, 'This is neither I nor other than I. There is no
> god but I.' Then He changed me out of my identity into His
> Selfhood, and caused me to pass away from my selfhood through
> His Selfhood, showing me His Selfhood uniquely; and I gazed
> upon Him with His Selfhood . . . Then I gazed upon Him with His

Light, and knew Him through His Knowledge, and communed
with Him with the tongue of His Grace, saying, 'How fares it with
me with Thee?' He said, 'I am thine through thee; there is no god
but Thou.'[19]

Such statements claiming *fana*, or union with God, were far from
acceptable to the pious *'ulama*. Nevertheless, with a few rare exceptions
Sufism did not meet with the religious persecution encountered by other
bàtini extremists, such as the Qarmatians, whose challenge to the *status
quo* had a more overtly political character. From the earliest period men
such as Abu 'Abdullah al Harith al Muhasibi (781–837) and his famous
pupil Junaid sought to combine asceticism and mystic communion with
the divine with strict observance of the Shari'a. In his commentary on the
sayings of Abu Yazid, Junaid developed a somewhat disingenuous way
of explaining away the apparent blasphemies contained in them. If
someone said, 'There is no deity save Me so worship Me', he was
obviously quoting Quran 21:25. In the same way, when Abu Yazid cried,
'Glory be to me!', he was simply reporting God's speech, not referring to
himself.[20]

Junaid, known as the 'paragon of the sober Sufis', laid the foundation
of the systematic theosophy which would later find its supreme expression in the work of Ibn al 'Arabi. According to the doctrine of *tawhid* or
'Oneness' first enunciated by Junaid, everything, including the human
self, pre-existed in God and must eventually return to Him. On the basis
of a somewhat idiosyncratic interpretation of two Quranic verses
(7:166–7), Junaid elaborated the theory that God made a covenant with
mankind at the time when the latter 'did not exist except in so far as it
existed in Him'. By adopting the Way of Sufism (*tasawwuf*) a man would
'die to himself' in order to 'live in God'. This dying is the *fana* or
self-extinction referred to by Abu Yazid. The new 'life in God' is called
baqa (subsistence):

> By passing away from self the mystic does not cease to exist in the
> sense of existence as an individual; rather his individuality, which
> is an inalienable gift from God, is perfected, transmuted and
> eternalized through God and in God.[21]

By recognizing this double dimension to existence, according to which
the adept can live, as it were, simultaneously in a state of union with God
and on an earthly plane, Junaid circumvented the obvious difficulties

created by those, like Abu Yazid, who claimed to be 'part of God' and therefore, logically speaking, above the law.

The victory of 'orthodox' or moderate Sufism over the ecstatic or 'drunken' variety was not achieved without a prolonged struggle. The victors were the moderates from both camps – the Sufi-minded legists and their mystic counterparts, the lawfully minded Sufis. The most celebrated victim of the struggle was Al Husain ibn Mansur (857–922), known as Al Hallaj, or 'the wool-carder'. The life and death of Al Hallaj, martyr, mystic and saint, has been the subject of a massive two-volume study by the French orientalist Louis Massignon, so rather more is therefore known about him than about other equally influential figures.

An Arab speaker from Fars, Al Hallaj first adopted Sufism in Basra, where he became a fervent ascetic. On his first pilgrimage to Mecca he remained immobile for a whole year in the courtyard of the Haram, constantly fasting and maintaining a perpetual silence. On returning to Persia he gave up his formal adherence to Sufism, urging his followers to seek the 'God within' by bringing an inner significance to bear upon ritual acts. ('Proceed seven times round the Ka'ba of your heart,' he said.) His enemies among the *ahl al zahir* accused him, quite wrongly according to Massignon, of wishing to abolish the 'outer' acts themselves.

After further pilgrimages and a lengthy missionary journey to India, beyond the frontiers of *dar al Islam*, he settled in Baghdad, where he proclaimed the doctrine of 'unity of witness' (*wahda al shuhud*), a not uncomplicated theosophy according to which the adept's 'union with God' is to be understood not as a 'unification of substance', but as the result of 'an act of faith and love' in which the Sufi's intention to merge his intelligence, his will and his ego with God is acted upon by divine grace. In announcing that God was witnessing to Himself 'in the heart of his votary', Al Hallaj aroused the suspicions of the *ahl al zahir*, even though he took care, in his dogmatic theology, not to depart from the framework of Sunni orthodoxy. His claim to be 'the truth' (*al haqq*) was taken by his enemies to imply a blasphemous identification with the Almighty. 'If you do not recognize God,' he said, 'at least recognize His signs. I am that sign, I am the creative Truth [*ana al haqq*] because through the Truth I am a truth eternally . . .'[22]

Al Hallaj foresaw, and welcomed, his martyrdom. The parallels with Christ are compelling, and were certainly in his mind as he faced imprisonment, trial and execution on the gibbet. Like Jesus he prayed for his enemies while dying:

> Here are these Thy worshippers who have come together to kill me, out of zeal for Thee, to approach Thee [by offering a sacrifice] . . . Forgive them! If Thou had revealed to them what Thou hast revealed to me, they would not do what they are doing. And if Thou hadst hid from me what Thou hast hid from them I would not have been put through the trials which I am now undergoing. Praise be to Thee for what thou doest! Praise be to Thee for what Thou willest![23]

His last words as he hung on the gibbet, his hands and feet having been cut off, were, 'All that the ecstatic wants is to be alone with the One.' He was exposed on the gibbet for two days before being decapitated. His body was then sprinkled with oil, set on fire and the ashes thrown into the Tigris from the top of a minaret.

The fate of Al Hallaj was exceptional. His real offence, in the eyes of the authorities, was that he proclaimed in public what the 'sober' Sufis experienced privately. Some of his statements had a distinctly Shi'ite tinge, such as his insistence on the 'inner meanings' of ritual acts. The authorities were afraid that his popularity, which was considerable, would encourage antinomian attitudes among ordinary people, inspiring them to question the formal religiosity of the caliphs and the *zahiri 'ulama* who upheld their authority. 'Sober' Sufis such as Junaid, who had been friendly with Al Hallaj, criticized his outspokenness without questioning the validity of his religious experience.

Indeed, Junaid himself was the first architect of the compromise between the ecstatics and the theologians that would culminate with the work of Abu Hamid al Ghazali in the eleventh century. For the time being the 'drunken' Sufis circulated mystic *hadiths*, such as one according to which the Prophet is supposed to have said: 'I have moments of familiarity [with God] when neither cherubim nor Prophet can contain me.' The 'sober' Sufis sought to maintain the supremacy of the Quran and the Sunna and insisted on reversing this dictum by containing Muhammad the mystic within the figure of Muhammad the Prophet. Whereas the mystic consciousness must remain satisfied with the individual experience of 'union' with God, the Prophetic consciousness, as exemplified by Muhammad's career, implied that moral activism must remain dominant. If God had not commanded the Prophet to 'return to society' after his experiences on Mount Hira, *dar al Islam* would never have come into being.

While Junaid was a 'sober' Sufi who sought to contain the mystic's ecstasy within the framework of the Shari'a, Ghazali approached the problem from the opposite direction. An *'alim* (scholar) trained in theology and *fiqh*, he aimed to achieve the revitalization of the Shari'a way by re-injecting into it the altruistic love and pietism of the Sufis. In this he succeeded where the misrepresented and misunderstood Al Hallaj had failed. This was largely because his credentials as a *faqih* and a formal theologian were impeccable.

Born at Tus in Khurasan (Persia) in 1058, Ghazali became a pupil of Juwaini, the foremost theologian of his time. His gifts were such that by the age of 33 he had been appointed professor at the new academy of religious studies at Baghdad, established by Nizam al Mulk, vizier of the Seljuk Sultan Malikshah to defend Sunnism against the spread of Isma'ili propaganda. Despite his intellectual success, Ghazali had a restless, self-questioning temperament, which he describes in his autobiography:

> From my early youth since I attained the age of puberty . . . until the present time when I am over fifty, I have ever recklessly launched out into the midst of these ocean depths, I have ever bravely embarked on this open sea, throwing aside all craven caution; I have poked into every dark recess, I have made an assault on every problem, I have plunged into every abyss, I have scrutinized the creed of every sect, I have tried to lay bare the innermost doctrines of every community. All this I have done that I might distinguish between true and false, between sound tradition and heretical innovation.[24]

The science of theology (*ilm al kalaam*), which was the first to engage his attention, failed to satisfy him: while attaining its own aims, the preservation of orthodoxy and its defence against the deviations of the heretics, it did not serve his purpose, which was the search for truth. Seeking enlightenment elsewhere, he turned to 'philosophy', including the natural sciences, which gave him a powerful insight into the marvels of creation. According to Ghazali, no one who had studied anatomy could fail to wonder at the perfection of human and animal organs, and to recognize in them evidence of the Creator's master hand. However, he found himself unable to go along with the natural scientists: in particular, he rejected their denial of the resurrection and the future life.

He accepted that there was much truth in Aristotle, whom, like Plato and Socrates, he regarded as a 'theist'. Nevertheless, some of the works of the philosophers contradicted the teachings of Islam and must be counted as heresy or unbelief. As for the theoretical sciences, including mathematics and logic, Ghazali concluded that they served neither to prove nor disprove the existence of God. Anyone who thought Islam could be defended by going against mathematical or logical truth was committing a grievous crime against religion.

Ghazali found politics too worldly a discipline to satisfy him. Ethics, as taught by the philosophers, tended to mix truth with falsehood and was clearly unsuited for popular instruction. Like the philosophers, Ghazali believed that the majority of people had to be protected from potentially harmful ideas. He inveighed against the Isma'ilis or *batinis* and their writings, particularly the *Epistles* of the Ikhwan al Safa: 'Just as the poor swimmer must be kept from the slippery banks, so must mankind be kept from reading these books.'[25] His most sustained campaign, however, was aimed at the Muslim neoplatonists, particularly Farabi and Ibn Sina. Having mastered their writings so thoroughly that his study of their method and doctrine in *The Intentions of the Philosophers* led to the belief among Latin scholars that 'Algazel' was himself a neoplatonist, he rounded on them in his celebrated *Tahafut al Falasifa* ('The Collapse [or 'Incoherence'] of the Philosophers'), using philosophical arguments to refute a number of propositions put forward by Aristotle and the Muslim neoplatonists. He condemns them for their emanationist belief in the eternity of the world, for the belief that God is simply an intellect having knowledge only of universals, for their rejection of causal necessity and for their denial of the resurrection of the body. The 'natural' sequence of cause and effect – such as fire burning cotton – was not, as the philosophers had argued, an automatic or necessary conjunction of events, since God is not bound by any order, causal or other, it is merely the effect of God's will, acting directly or indirectly through an angel. God could just as well decide not to let the cotton burn. The miracles mentioned in the Quran (such as Jesus' resurrection of the dead or Moses' transformation of a stick into a serpent) might therefore be understood factually. The resurrection of the body, denied by the philosophers, was similarly possible. The *Tahafut* reaffirmed official Sunni hostility to philosophical rationalism rather in the manner that Ashari had restored traditionalism against the theological rationalism of the Mu'tazilis. Once again, urban populism had found its intellectual champion against the subversive elitism of the rationalists, and had succeeded in arming itself with some of the enemy's weapons.

Philosophically speaking, however, Ghazali's was far from being the last word. The same century saw Ibn Rushd's celebrated rebuttal of Ghazali's *Tahafut* – the *Tahafut al Tahafut* ('The Collapse of "The Collapse"', better known as 'The Incoherence of "The Incoherence"'), in which the Spanish-Arab philosopher tried to restore the balance between scripturalism and philosophy by rehabilitating *tawil*, or allegorical interpretation. Ibn Rushd's method, however, made it necessary for him to resort to an intellectual double standard far more elitist than anything proposed by Ghazali. According to Ibn Rushd, the Quran's 'ambiguous' passages could only be understood by the philosophers; and he attacked Ghazali and other theologians for sowing the seeds of heresy and discord in Islam by unlawfully revealing secrets of interpretation which should be reserved for those who are fit to comprehend them. The fact that Ibn Rushd, Sunni Islam's last great speculative philosopher, was quite content to hold the office of Grand Qadi of Seville shows how far preservation of the Shari'a, symbolizing the Quran's external (*zahiri*) message, had come to outweigh all other dimensions of the Quranic message in the hearts of the faithful.

Ghazali's search for truth, and the difficulty he experienced in finding it, involved him in a severe moral and psychological crisis. He felt himself to be on the brink of a crumbling sandbank, in constant danger of hell-fire. Satan told him that this was merely a 'passing mood' that would soon disappear. But his sense of chronic unease and imminent personal doom refused to leave him. He became incapable of delivering his lectures. God caused his tongue to dry up, he could hardly swallow or eat a single morsel of food. He became so weak that the physicians gave up hope. The trouble arose from the heart, they said, whence it spread to the constitution. Finally, at the age of 37, Ghazali took the plunge. He gave away his wealth and made provision, by means of a *waqf*, for his family. 'Nowhere in the world', he would write, 'have I seen better financial arrangements [than in Iraq] to assist a scholar to provide for his children.'[26]

After a sojourn in Damascus, Ghazali proceeded to Jerusalem. For ten years he lived the life of a Sufi, engaging in ascetic practices, seeking solitude and mystic truth. Ecstasy he experienced only occasionally, though he did not cease to hope for it. 'Things innumerable and unfathomable' were related to him. Like the Sufis, Ghazali came to the conclusion that there were modes of cognition lying beyond the realm of the intellect. The knowledge so acquired could only be communicated by revelation. This realization brought him to believe in the absolute necessity of ritual observance, based on a reaffirmation of the Quran and the Sunna. Ghazali's renewed commitment to the Shari'a found expression in his most influential work, the *Ihya 'ulum al din* ('The Revival of the Religious Sciences'), which he wrote after returning to Baghdad on the caliph's orders. In essence, the *Ihya* is a manual for daily living, one which, as W. Montgomery Watt has pointed out, would not be out of place in a monastic order with a very strict rule. The details of vegetative life – eating, sleeping, ablutions, entering the lavatory – as well as the religious offices, including prayer, fasting and supererogatory exercises, must be conducted in such a way as to maintain a consciousness of God's presence at all times. Sin must constantly be avoided, the various organs protected from all varieties of evil: the ear from heresy, slander or obscenity; the tongue from lies, slanders and the 'backbiting . . . [which] is more serious than thirty adulteries', from wrongly discussing theology and metaphysics, from cursing or scoffing at God's creatures; the stomach from unlawful foods and that 'which hardens the heart, impairs the intellect and weakens the memory'; the private parts from everything unlawful, including harmful thoughts; the hands from beating a Muslim, from receiving unlawful wealth, from harming any creature or from writing what may not be uttered; the feet from going to an unlawful place or from hastening to the court of a wicked ruler; the heart from envy, hypocrisy and pride – sins which, according to Ghazali, 'are the most prominent among the *'ulama* of our time'.[27]

Ghazali's work lays down the rule of an earnest, somewhat joyless religiosity, pregnant with *gravitas* and unleavened by humour. He cites a *hadith* according to which 'the man who speaks a word to make his friends laugh is thereby hurled into the pit of hell for seventy years'. He is far removed from the ecstatic vision of the 'drunken' Sufis, even though he fully acknowledges the value of their religious experience. For all his efforts to discover God by following the mystics' path, Ghazali's vision remains that of the plodding conformist. It is this very quality that explains his immense and abiding influence. The *Ihya* became (and probably still remains) the most-quoted religious text after the Quran and the classical *hadith* collections. Its essential spirit, informed by Ghazali's immense intellectual authority, is that of the Sufi orders which came into being within a generation of his death in 1111. Indeed, study of the *Ihya* was compulsory for members of many orders up to the present century. It was the bedside reading of Hasan al Banna, founder of the Muslim Brotherhood (d. 1949).

Although Ghazali himself never founded a Sufi brotherhood, remaining always an *'alim* rather than a Sufi *shaikh*, his influence, both on the brotherhoods and upon Islam itself, proved to be incalculable. By animating the 'outward' framework of legal observance with the 'inward' quality of mystic experience he helped bridge the gap which must always exist between personal virtue and institutionalized religiosity. Both the *'ulama* and the mystically inclined would look to his works for edification and instruction, and both groups would find in them arguments with which to confront the subversive influence of the philosophers and other intellectual elitists such as the *batinis*. Like Shafi'i, he employed his intellectual gifts to endow the piety of the urban classes with intellectual respectability, reaffirming populist values by reestablishing the primacy of the Quran and the Sunna. In one respect his achievement surpasses that of Shafi'i: whereas the great *faqih* brought uniformity to the structure of the Shari'a law, maintaining its cohesiveness in the face of the developing rivalries between the Hanafis and Malikis, Ghazali's work served to re-integrate the whole legal superstructure with the psychic or spiritual infrastructure, re-injecting into the Quran and the Sunna, and into the edifice of law built upon them, the sanctity of the Prophet's mystic consciousness. For this he has been called the greatest Muslim after Muhammad.

Before consideration of the Sufi brotherhoods and their contribution, in both their original and reformed versions, towards the spread of Islam and its renovation, two individuals should be mentioned who, in different ways, brought the development of mystic consciousness to its furthest conclusion. They are Ibn al 'Arabi (1165–1240), the theosophist, and Jalal al Din Rumi (1207–1273), the poet of the Mawlawi dervishes. Though neither had an influence on mainstream Islam comparable to Ghazali's, both cultivated the individualistic tradition of 'intoxicated' Sufism to the point where their work transcends the boundaries of Islam and emerges into the realm of universal religious consciousness. For this reason they are almost better known, and more highly regarded, outside the Islamic tradition than within it.

Muhyi al Din ibn al 'Arabi, known to his admirers as the 'Shaikh al Akhbar' ('the Greatest Master') was born in Spain, where he spent the first thirty years of his life. His father was a friend of the philosopher Ibn Rushd (Averroës), who was impressed by the depth of Ibn al 'Arabi's religious convictions. His 'conversion' to Sufism occurred when he was quite young, in the course of an illness. The experience so changed his life that he subsequently came to regard his earlier years as a period of *jahiliya*, or ignorance. At the age of about 30 he left Spain, travelling first to Tunis and then on to Cairo and Jerusalem before making the pilgrimage to Mecca. He spent two years in the Holy City, frequently performing the '*umra*, reading and meditating near the Ka'ba, which he regarded as the meeting point of the invisible (*ghaib*) and visible (*shuhud*) worlds. In 1204 he was persuaded by a group of Anatolian pilgrims to settle at Malatya on the Euphrates. Later, at the age of 65, he went to live in Damascus under the protection of the influential Ibn Zaki family.

Ibn al 'Arabi was an immensely prolific writer. In the course of his life he is said to have composed some 846 works. More than 400 works attributed to him have survived, most of which are believed to be genuine. The best known are the massive *Futuhat al Makkiya* ('The Meccan Revelations'), a veritable Sufi encyclopedia built round his visions of the Holy City; the *Fusus al Hikam* (The Essentials of Wisdom), which he claimed the Prophet actually dictated to him in a dream; and the *Turjuman al Ashwaq* ('Interpreter of Desires'), a collection of love poems addressed to the daughter (whom he eventually married) of a Persian resident in Mecca, to which he appended his own commentary.

Ibn al 'Arabi combined mystical insight with vast erudition. Not only was he perfectly familiar with the writings and teachings of Sunni theologians, '*ulama* and philosophers, but he was also widely read in the literature of the Isma'ilis and Mu'tazilis. In some respects his learning imposes an obstacle for scholars, since he never developed a systematic frame of reference, instead borrowing eclectically from the different vocabularies of his authors. In the main, however, he took over the legacy of the Muslim neoplatonists, including Farabi, Ibn Sina and his father's friend Ibn Rushd, and reissued it as the product rather of mystic intuition than of reason. In this respect his position is similar to that of Ghazali, who also placed intuitive revelation (*kashf*) and the knowledge deriving from it (gnosis or *ma'rifa*) above intellectual reasoning. However, whereas Ghazali's mystic meditations led him back to a strict reaffirmation of the Quran and the Sunna, Ibn al 'Arabi's brought him close to the attitude of identity with God for which Al Hallaj was martyred.

Though scarcely more cautious in his statements than Al Hallaj or Bistami (he claimed to be 'the Seal of the Saints', a 'perfect manifestation' of the 'Spirit of Muhammad'), he lived in a more tolerant age and, probably more important, enjoyed the protection of powerful interests.

Ibn al 'Arabi's theosophy embodied many of the assumptions of the Muslim neoplatonists. God is pure being (in philosophical terms, a necessary existent), free from all other attributes. This was a view the Muslim philosophers had developed from their understanding of Aristotle, neoplatonism and the ideas of the Mu'tazilis. (A certain confusion about Aristotle's real ideas resulted from the fact that an Arabic collection of neoplatonist writings, including fragments of Plotinus' *Enneads*, was thought to be a 'Theology' by Aristotle; even Ibn Rushd, whose great commentary on Aristotle re-introduced that philosopher to the West, was ignorant of Greek.) Like Farabi, Ibn Sina and other Muslim neoplatonists, Ibn al 'Arabi rejected the Aristotelian dualism of God and matter, the Unmoved Mover and his creation, adopting instead the emanationist view of reality as a continuum or 'unity of being' (*wahda al wujud*) made up of different grades. He tried to avoid the pantheistic implications of this view by making a distinction between the 'hidden' aspect of the divine, which cannot be known or described, and the aspect of lordship (*rububiya*), through which God enters into a relationship with the world as its creator. The divine, in its uniqueness, manifests itself through a series of *logoi*, or prophetic epiphanies, starting with Adam and culminating with Muhammad. Ultimately, the creation belongs to the same reality as God, having originally existed as a series of archetypes in the divine mind, whose highest manifestation is the Adamic *logos*, or 'perfect man'.

Ibn al 'Arabi conceived of human consciousness as existing along the scale of a similar continuum, characterized by 'light'. Just as the stream of being proceeds by a process of emanation, from the Absolute Indivisible One through the various 'intellects' down to the lowest animate or inanimate creatures, so the light of consciousness flows down the hierarchy of human intelligences. Subject and object merge in the same continuum. Any disjunction between them is illusory, as is the difference between the One and the many, the first and the last, the eternal and the temporal, the necessary and the contingent. Within such a system, in which the observer perceives himself as being part of the observed, the categories of thought and being are indistinguishable. Man (or microcosm) is patterned on to the universe (or macrocosm). The result is a mystical humanism in which man is the 'microcosmic being' through which God contemplates himself, God's *khalifa* (vice-regent) on earth.

Divinity and humanity are thus not two distinctive natures, but rather 'two aspects which find expression at every level of creation', divinity corresponding to the hidden aspect of reality (*al batin*), humanity to the external (*al zahir*). The relation between God and his creation is that of a mirror to the image:

> Try . . . to see the body of the mirror as well as looking at the form that it reflects: thou wilt never see it at the same time . . . God, then, is the mirror in which thou seest thyself as thou art, His mirror in which He contemplates His names.[28]

In Ibn al 'Arabi's system, God is the only Reality: all things pre-exist as ideas in the knowledge of God from which they emanate and to which they must ultimately return. His argument suggestively combines the metaphysical idealism of the neoplatonists with the theology of *tawhid* adopted from the Mu'tazilis. Like previous exponents of Sufi theosophy, Ibn al 'Arabi arrives at a fusion of theology and philosophy by way of mystic illumination: human reason alone, he believed, was far too limited to guide the seeker towards real understanding of the 'unity of being' running throughout creation. Such unity must be felt before it can be grasped intellectually. Ibn al 'Arabi constructed what has been called 'the most imposing monument of mystical speculation ever seen'.[29] If the language through which it was articulated sounds arcane to modern ears, the reality it sought to express seems to conform both with the fundamental world-view of the Quran and with the conviction which underlies much modern scientific research, that there must be a unifying principle in nature.

Jalal al Din Rumi, the greatest mystic poet of Persia and possibly of all Islam, was born into a family of *'ulama* in Khurasan in 1207. At the age of 12, during the Mongol invasion, he and his family settled at Konya in Turkey, then usually known as Rum (Rome) from its Byzantine associations. He was initiated into Sufism by one Burhan al Din, a former pupil of his father's, under whose tutelage he passed up the various rungs in the Sufi ladder of spiritual awareness. On Burhan al Din's death in 1240 Rumi himself became a Sufi *shaikh*. He soon acquired a number of *murids* or foollers, who were attracted by his extraordinary eloquence and personality. In 1244, however, there occurred a strange transformation in the Master* which greatly disconcerted his followers. A wandering holy man – who came to be known as Shams al Din of Tabriz – appeared in Konya, and Rumi, despite his growing reputation as a Sufi *shaikh*, seems to have fallen completely under his spell. For Rumi the dervish represented the 'Complete Being' or 'Perfect Man' (*al insan al kamil*), the true image of the 'Divine Beloved' which he had long been seeking. Ignoring his own disciples, the Master became a pupil once more. The dervish persuaded him to discard his books and devote himself to him. Twice the *murids* and Rumi's family drove the dervish away in order to reclaim their Master. Eventually they murdered him in secret. (His coffin is thought to have been found during recent repairs to the mosque in Konya.) Though the loss of Shams brought Mawlana to the brink of madness, he devoted more and more of his time to declaiming poetry, listening to music and dancing. In 1249 he announced that Shams al Din had reappeared in the person of one his *murids*, a handsome but illiterate goldsmith named Salah al Din, whom Rumi appointed his deputy. Salah al Din died in 1258; his successor as deputy, Husam al Din Hasan, became the inspiration behind Rumi's greatest poem, the *Mathnawi* ('Epic'). On Rumi's own death in 1273 he became head of the order.

Rumi's literary output was staggering. In addition to the *Mathnawi*, which consists of six books of about 25,000 rhyming couplets, he composed some 2,500 mystical odes and at least 1,600 *ruba'is* or *ruba'iyat* (quatrains). Virtually the whole of the *Mathnawi* was dictated to Husam al Din in the decade and a half before Rumi's death. Mawlana recited the verses whenever and wherever they occurred to him – dancing, in the bath, standing, sitting, walking, by day or by night. Husam repeated the verses back to him before making any necessary corrections. Although the structure is apparently formless, with anecdotes, animal fables and materials drawn from the Bible, the Quran and Persian folklore irrationally juxtaposed and sometimes unexpectedly interrupted, there is an underlying thematic coherence. What Ibn al'Arabi ratiocinates through metaphysical speculation, Rumi, the 'drunken' Sufi driven to express his ecstasy in poetry, conveys by shifting images and Aesop-like morality tales. The unity of God, perceived throughout the natural order, is constantly and paradoxically proclaimed in the discursive and fragmentary utterances of the poet. The result is not wholly unlike a re-rendering

---

* *Mawlana*, literally, 'Our Master': hence the name of Rumi's order, the Mawlawiya, usually anglicized in its Turkish form, Mevlevi.

of the Quran itself: indeed the *Mathnawi* has been called both 'the Sufi Quran' and 'the Quran in Persian'.

No doubt the *Mathnawi*'s emotional intensity derives in part from the poet's own vulnerable personality: his longing for love is sublimated into a kind of cosmic yearning. The Love Object, though divine and therefore unknowable, yields a very human kind of love. In the Quran a remote and inaccessible deity addresses man through the mouth of his Prophet. In the *Mathnawi* it is the voice of the human soul, bewailing its earthly exile, which cries out, seeking reunification with its creator. The poem's famous opening lines establish a theme which constantly recurs:

> Listen to the reed, how it tells a tale complaining of separations –
> Saying, 'Ever since I was parted from the reed-bed, my lament
>   hath caused men and women to moan;
> I want a bosom torn by severance, that I may unfold [to such a
>   one] the pain of love-desire.
> Everyone who is left far from his source wishes back the time
>   when he was united with it.'[30]

The divine source from which man comes and to which he yearns to return is often linked to the ocean in Sufi imagery. The individual is a drop of water temporarily detached from the sea, to become part of it again when life is extinguished. The same image is suggested by Sigmund Freud's expression 'oceanic consciousness', a state of mind whose origins, he suggests, derive from the time when the infant has not yet acquired a sense of its own identity or separateness. In Rumi's poem the dyadic relationship refers not just to the individual *vis à vis* the mass, but to the outward or phenomenal forms ('accidens') on the one hand and creative energy ('substance') on the other. In the following passage they are symbolized respectively by the foam at the top of the waves and the sea or ocean itself:

> The grief of the dead is not on account of death; it is because they
>   dwelt upon the phenomenal forms of existence
> And never perceived that all this foam is moved and fed by the sea
> When the sea has cast the foam-flakes on the shore, go to the
>   graveyard and behold them!
> Say to them: 'Where is your swirling onrush now?' and hear them
>   answer mutely, 'Ask this question of the sea, not of us!'
> How should the foam fly without the wave? How should the dust
>   rise to the zenith without the wind?

> Since you have seen the dust, perceive the wind; since you have
> seen the foam, perceive the ocean . . .[31]

Man himself is a vehicle of the divine consciousness, an intelligence which emerges through the ascending hierarchy of created forms:

> First he appeared in the world of inorganic things
> Thence he passed into the vegetable state and lived
> The plant-life many a year, nor called to mind
> What he had been; then he passed from the vegetable state
> To animal existence, once more
> Remembering not the vegetable state,
> Save only when moved towards it in spring,
> The season of sweet herbs,
> Like babies which seek the mother's breast unconsciously;
> Or like the excessive inclination the young Sufi novice
>   feels towards his Sheikh,
> Drawn by [his] Universal Intelligence . . .*[32]

Thus Rumi suggests that the intelligence which manifests itself in humanity is a spiritual dimension which inheres in the very structure of the universe that gave rise to it. As the passage cited above suggests, the idea of spiritual evolution has an important social ramification: the spiritual attraction the young Sufi feels for his master becomes the cement of the Sufi *tariqa*† or brotherhood. For it was this 'divine' intelligence, manifested in saintly charisma and transmitted down the generations, which converted the individual spiritual athleticism of the *shaikhs* into human associations capable of wielding social power and exercising political authority.

It may not be coincidental that the first Sufi order or *tariqa*, the Qadiriya, was founded within a generation of Ghazali's death in 1111. Towards the end of his life he had abandoned teaching for the second time and returned to his native Tus. Here he established a *khanqa* or hermitage, where young disciples were trained in a monastic atmosphere. Ghazali did not, however, become the founder of any Sufi *tariqa*. The credit for being the first of these is usually given to 'Abd al Qadir

---

* The Logos with whom the Perfect Master is identified.

† Literally 'path' or 'way'. In popular usage the word came to signify the organization as well as its theoretical basis (see p. 251).

Jilani (1077–1166), Ghazali's younger contemporary and, like him, of Persian ancestry.

A story is told about the special Sufi quality of 'purity', or disinterestedness, for which Jilani became famous. Like Ghazali, he had been sent off as a very young man to study in Baghdad. Before he set out, his mother had given him all his inheritance in the form of eighty gold coins sewn into his coat. On the way, the caravan in which he was travelling was set upon by bandits. Jilani, who seemed fairly impoverished, was almost ignored. However, as they were about to leave, one of the bandits asked him casually if he had any money – whereupon Jilani, without hesitation, showed him where his coins were hidden. Astonished at such honesty, the bandit took Jilani to the chief of the gang. The young scholar explained to him that if he had begun his search for truth by telling a lie, he could not have expected to get very far. The robber chief was so impressed, we are told, that he abandoned his predatory ways and adopted a life of piety – becoming the first of many converts allegedly made by the saint.

After a time spent studying philosophy and Hanbali law, Jilani became the disciple of the Sufi Shaikh al Dabbas (d. 1131). In 1127 he began preaching publicly, proclaiming his desire to 'close the gates of Hell and open the gates of Paradise for all mankind'. The main thrust of his teaching was an attack on worldliness and a Christ-like emphasis on charity. For many Sufis, including Jilani, Jesus was the symbol of pure human altruism: they revered, and sometimes practised, his injunction to appease aggression by 'turning the other cheek'. Jilani's popularity was such that a *ribat* or monastery was built for him outside the city. Many Jews and Christians are said to have been converted to Islam as a result of his ministry. In later generations many miracles would be attributed to him.

It is unlikely that Jilani intended to 'found' a religious order, apart from training his immediate spiritual disciples. However, after his death his sons carried on his work, and eventually branches of the Qadiriya order were founded from West Africa to South East Asia. Two other important early traditions, which in due course bifurcated into distinct brotherhoods, were the Suhrawardiya and the Rifa'iya. The former was founded by the nephew of a Sufi master, Abu al Najib al Suhrawardi, who had studied with Ahmad al Ghazali, brother of the famous Abu Hamid and a renowned Sufi master. The nephew, 'Umar (d. 1234), was befriended by the caliph Al Nasr, who built a *ribat* for him. In many respects the Suhrawardiya remained an aristocratic order, patronized by the elite. However, towards the end of the fourteenth century it gave rise to a more populist order, the Khalwatiya ('seclusionists'), which became highly influential in the Ottoman Empire when one of its members, the 'Sufi' Bayazid, became Sultan (1481–1511).

The Rifai'iya order was founded by Ahmad ibn Ali al Rifai'i, a holy man who spent all his life at his home in the marshes of Basra, except for one pilgrimage to Mecca. His followers became famous for the spectacular frenzies in which they indulged, during which they would eat live poisonous snakes, enter blazing ovens, ride upon lions or other dangerous animals, or perform comparable feats, including acts of self-mutilation. According to Ibn Battuta, who visited some Rifai'i dervishes in Khurasan, they would 'place iron rings in their hands, necks and ears and even their male members so that they are unable to indulge in sexual intercourse'. The original aim of these exercises, of course, was to signify the victory of the spirit over the flesh and to mark the latter's temporary annihilation in 'Absolute Reality'. By the nineteenth century, however, as Lane suggested, many of these feats had been reduced to mere conjuring and other forms of charlatanry designed to impress the credulous.[33]

The Rifai'iya in due course gave rise to two important Egyptian orders, the Badawiya and the Dasuqiya. Badawi (b. 1199) has become an Egyptian national hero for rousing his followers to fight the Crusader invasion of Louis IX in the thirteenth century. His shrine at Tanta in the Delta is widely venerated and his *maulid* (anniversary) has become one of the most popular festivals in the whole of Egypt. Ibrahim al Dasuqi (d. 1288) was originally admitted into the Suhrawardiya, Rifai'iya and Badawiya (membership of the *tariqas* was rarely, if ever, exclusive), but eventually founded his own independent *tariqa*, the Dasuqiya. Another order which became prominent in Egypt was the Shadhiliya, founded by Abu al Hasan al Shadhili (d. 1258).

As they evolved, the *tariqas* developed into social structures through which an individual master's holiness or charisma was transmitted to posterity. Like other groupings in Islamic society, such as the Futuwa trade-guilds to which they were sometimes linked structurally, they were relatively informal associations. Their popularity in urban society was largely due to 'the almost complete absence of corporate life or institutions'.[34] In the Shari'a vision nothing stood between the individual and the totality of the Umma except the family, to which the individual was tied not only by blood, but by a whole series of legally enforceable duties. In urban society the orders constituted a form of solidarity which made up for the lack of alternative groupings outside the family. Reinforced by initiation ceremonies and group practices such as i'tiraf (public confession), a tariqa conferred a close sense of brotherhood upon its members. In cities it was not uncommon for an individual to belong to several tariqas, though in country districts village organization was often interlocked with membership of one particular tariqa.

The role of the brotherhoods in spreading Islam in the peripheral areas among nomads and peasants, pagans and the adherents of more advanced religious cultures, can hardly be underestimated, and will be considered in the last section of this chapter. In general, however, it can be said that the Sufi tariqas performed a function of mediation between the divine and human worlds such as the Sunni 'ulama, with their uncompromising scripturalism, were prevented from exercising in any formal manner. A faqih, a mufti or a qadi could decide upon questions of law which, as we have seen, theoretically included all spheres of human activity. He was less likely to be disposed, by temperament or training, to provide a model for social behaviour, or inducements to more active forms of devotional activity. The religious duties enjoined by the law were few, simple and austere, being largely confined to prayer and the observance of Ramadan and major festivals such as the 'Id al Fitr. The Sufi tariqas supplied the ground for a much richer and more colourful liturgical growth, based on the supposed devotional practices of the early adepts.

The tariqa itself is, strictly speaking a 'theoretical and sound method of guidance'[35] devised by a Sufi shaikh and transmitted through his followers. The organization through which a tariqa extends itself in Muslim society is properly referred to as a ta'ifa; in non-specialist usage, however, the word tariqa is usually taken to mean both the rule and the order. The brotherhoods themselves, writes Michael Gilsenan,

> . . . became as multi-faceted as the worlds of which they were so integral and representative a part – now military, now pietistic, now devoted to scholarly and theoretical pursuits, now to ecstasies and the intoxication of the senses; now the province of the religious and social elite, now of the illiterate and deprived masses; dedicated to the highest mysteries of the few, and to the exoteric simplicities of the many.[36]

We should be wary, therefore, of making facile generalizations about the social organization or internal functioning of the *tariqas*. Nevertheless a certain structure is common to most, if not all, the pre-modern Islamic brotherhoods. Full membership is usually confined to males (usually as much because of existing social custom as by any formal rubric). The members, known as *murids* (aspirants), *faqirs* or dervishes (mendicants) are bound together by an oath of allegiance (*bay'a*) to their Guide (*shaikh, murshid* or *pir*), who heads a hierarchy of ranks within the order and is connected by a chain (*silsila*) of inherited sanctity (*baraka*) or kinship to the founding Saint. The *silsilas*, modelled on those originally devised to authenticate *hadith* reports, usually extend back, via the founders of the earliest orders, through such early masters as Hasan al Basri, Junaid and Abu Yazid to members of the Prophet's household and ultimately to the Prophet himself. The Sufi *tariqas* thus legitimized religious authority in the same manner as the sectarian groups. The idiom of kinship, so ubiquitous in the social sphere, was extended to the religious, the lines of blood and *baraka* frequently overlapping. The main difference between the sects and the orders was that the latter, in their earliest phase of development, renounced even implicitly political aims (though later the *shaikhs*, like the *'ulama*, would assume an important political role as guardians of Islamic tradition). In fact, they re-channelled much of the spiritual energy formerly animating the sectarian groups: their rise to influence coincided with the overthrow of Shi'ite governments in Baghdad (1055) and Egypt (1171) and their replacement with Sunni regimes by the Seljuks. The *tariqas* took over from the Shi'a the *bay'a* or oath of allegiance originally given to a member of the House of Ali or his representative. The idea of *baraka* being transmitted either genetically or spiritually from master to pupil down the ranks of the orders bears a close similarity to the Shi'ite idea of *nass* (designation).

In their proliferation, which was accelerated in the Central Islamic lands after the Mongol conquest brought many learned refugees into the countryside, the *tariqas* accommodated both 'orthodox' and 'heterodox' attitudes. Safi al Din (d. 1334), progenitor of the Safavid dynasty, began his career as a Sufi *pir* by studying with a *shaikh* of the Suhrawardi order. However, after his descendant Shah Isma'il (d. 1524) had made Shi'ism the Iranian state religion, the Shi'ite *'ulama* became the most avid persecutors of the Sufi orders, partly, no doubt, because they realized that the *pirs* were capable of exercising a similar socio-religious power to themselves. The Bektashi order in Anatolia, though closely associated with the Ottoman state until the abolition of the Janissary Corps in 1826, showed such reverence for the House of 'Ali that they may be regarded as crypto-Shi'ites, many of their adherents being drawn from the so-called Alevi community. At the opposite end of the spectrum one finds the militantly Sunni Naqshbandi order, which includes both Abu Bakr and Ja'far al Sadiq in its *silsila*. The Naqshbandiya has always been closely associated with 'official' Islam, having no separate organization of *zawiyas* or convents and holding its *dhikr* ceremonies in public mosques. In the nineteenth century Naqshbandi *shaikhs* were instrumental in winning recognition of the Ja'fari (Shi'ite) *madhhab* as a school of *fiqh* on a par with the four Sunni schools.

From about the twelfth to the nineteenth centuries Sufism in all its varieties became so widespread and pervasive as to be virtually synonymous with Islam itself. The orders had become both bastions of orthodoxy and refuges of dissent. Saladin, restorer of Jerusalem and arch-suppresser of Shi'ite sectarianism in Egypt, welcomed the Asiatic Sufis there and founded several convents or *zawiyas*. His example was followed by the Mamluk sultans and their amirs: many of the magnificent buildings with which they endowed the city of Cairo were Sufic foundations. By the end of the fifteenth century the orders were well represented at the centre of state power. Hundreds of Sufi dervishes took part in the attack on Constantinople in 1483 which finally delivered the last outpost of Byzantium into the hands of the Ottomans; while in Egypt thirty-two years later the last independent Mamluk sultan, Qansuh al Ghuri, faced the armies of the Ottoman conqueror, Selim the Grim, flanked by dervishes of the Badawi, Qadiri and Rifai'i orders grouped round their *shaikhs* and their banners.

The triumph of the brotherhoods as popular movements was not achieved without strong and continuous opposition from the *'ulama*. From the time of Al Hallaj, official Islam had found the claims of the Sufi masters hard to swallow. At the heart of their objections was the challenge which the Sufi *shaikhs* offered to the spiritual hegemony of the *'ulama*. From the time of Shafi'i onwards, the Sunni doctrine held that revelation had been a 'once-and-for-all-time' occurrence, never to be repeated. Only those well versed in the scriptures were competent to dispense spiritual guidance, which could only consist in interpretations of the divine text or rulings based on the Sunna. Sufi pietism cut across this essentially legalistic and formal version of Islam. The veneration of the *murids* for their *shaikhs* not only challenged the social power of the 'ulama, but questioned the very basis of the Shari'a as representing 'power of the law over life and thought'.[37] The pirs themselves represented a 'natural' religious aristocracy, walis ('friends') of God preselected by the Almighty on account of their spiritual purity. The absolutist claims of the shaikhs obviously called into question the book-learning, often arduously achieved, of the official 'ulama. Most of the leading shaikhs claimed to have received their vocations, or confirmations of them, directly from God or the Prophet in dreams or visions. Like the Prophet himself, they were not thought of as men going out into the world with the aim of founding tariqas: they were believed to be acting under direct divine guidance. The vocational or confirmatory visions are not only found in stories about the foundation of new tariqas; they also appear in accounts of disputes following the death of a shaikh, when one or more of the murids might have a vision confirming one of their number in the succession.

In addition to these visions, and the absolute claims to religious authority sustained by them, there were other challenges with which the official authorities had to contend. Miraculous claims were constantly made on behalf of the saints. They were credited with thaumaturgic powers, and the belief that their baraka retained its potency after death, lingering around their tombs like some beneficent radioactivity, gave rise to the saint cults which flourished mainly in mountainous, rural and desert areas far from the disapproving eyes of the 'ulama. Saint-worship has generally diminished in recent times, having succumbed to the combined onslaught of official Islam and secular governments capable of extending their authority into formerly marginal areas. But it is still possible in most Arab and Muslim countries to find country-folk, especially women, praying at the tomb of some long-forgotten local saint, usually a crumbling edifice containing a sarcophagus draped with fading green banners embroidered with Quranic inscriptions. In their heyday the orders provided an outlet for female devotion denied by official Islam, which tended to uphold the essentially male supremacist values of desert and city. Women were enrolled into the orders as associate members and were even sometimes permitted to preside over groups of female murids. It was customary for them to visit the tombs of saints on Fridays and other holy days while the menfolk attended congregational prayers at the mosques.

As well as being reputedly able to cure physical ailments, the saints tended to create a miraculous ambience around their persons. Virtually anything they did could acquire a miraculous character in the eyes of their followers. Michael Gilsenan collected a number of stories about a modern Cairene saint, Shaikh Salama ibn Hasan Salama (1867–1940), founder ôf the Hamidiya branch of the Shadhili order. They range from supernatural interventions (such as the occasion when the Shaikh eliminated the writing from the ledger of an English clerk who had offended him) down to such mundane but agreeable occurrences as the unexpected discovery of a sum of money or the catching of a fast bus. Other pieces of good fortune attributed to the saint include avoidance of disaster (missing a train which later crashed or a service-taxi which drove into the Nile) and the rescue of a *murid* from the path of an oncoming train. (This incident, occurring after the Shaikh's death, was attributed to his intervention from beyond the grave.) Significantly the Shaikh, despite his lack of formal scholarly training, is said to have effortlessly defeated the *'ulama* on their own territory, answering correctly the subtle doctrinal questions they put to him, or posing to the Shaikh al Islam (as the Rector of Al Azhar University, the chief theological dignitary of Sunni Islam, is known) theological questions to which he could find no answer. As Gilsenan sees it, these 'miracles' (*karamas* – literally, 'acts of divine grace') are part of the wider 'universe of explanation' by means of which the *murids*, many of whom are illiterate and all of whom are poor, come to terms with their world. The Shaikh 'is a means that a mysterious, transcendent, predestinating God is assumed to use in the regulation of all things'.[38] A 'symbolic representation of a total order of things', he becomes, in other words, a personalized channel of communication with the divine: 'Linking men with their concepts of the Divine plan, he restates it and guarantees its mysterious outworkings. From him they can obtain baraka and through him they intercede for assistance in mundane affairs.'[39]

As has already been intimated, the idea of inherited *baraka* suggests itself inevitably in societies (such as those which predominate in the Muslim world) which set considerable store by patrilineal descent. As in Shi'ism, the lines of biological and spiritual inheritance often overlap, but not necessarily so. While mystic power, or *baraka*, may be transmitted through the blood-line, by means of designation, by visionary appointment, or by a combination of all three, it usually suffers some diminution of potency – not least because a portion of it is bound up in the personality of the original founder. However, both the decline in the leadership's real charismatic power and that in the *baraka* associated with the tomb of a departed saint serve, in different ways, to institutionalize the Saint's following. From having been a relatively informal gathering of disciples, brought together and animated by the master's living presence, the *tariqa* develops its own institutional dynamic: one which must sometimes be replenished by occasional injections of authentic 'living' *baraka* from new divinely inspired leaders if the institution is to last.

A notable example of *baraka*-exploitation, corresponding to Max Weber's famous concept of the 'routinization of charisma' is provided by the Kazeruniya order which became the 'Lloyd's' of medieval Islam. Though actually founded in the fourteenth century the *tariqa* associated itself with Abu Ishaq of Kazerun (d. 1035), a saint of southern Iran whose *baraka* was thought specially effective against the dangers of sea-travel in the Indian Ocean. Agents of the brotherhood could be found in many major sea-ports on the monsoon route, including Calicut, Malabar and Chuan-Chow in China. Intending travellers would make a vow promising to pay a certain sum of money to the brotherhood if they reached their destination safely, with a premium for surviving a specially hazardous situation. A promissory note was passed from the agent to the brotherhood, which disposed of an elaborate organization for collecting the exact amount pledged. The funds were employed to finance the brotherhood's wide-ranging charitable activities.

The characteristic institutions of the brotherhoods were the convents or hostels known by various names in different regions: *khanqas* (hospices) mainly in areas of Persian influence; *ribats* (frontier posts) in marginal areas of the Mashriq and Maghreb; *zawiyas* ('corners') mainly in North Africa; *khalwas* ('retreats') in western Asia; *tekkes* (centres) in Turkish-speaking areas. Trimingham has characterized the evolution of these institutions, within the context of the orders as a whole, in three stages. The first he calls the *khanqa* stage, during which the master and his pupils moved around fairly informally from one district to another. There were few regulations; the lodges and convents were relatively unspecialized and undifferentiated. As in the case of Jilani, the master and his pupils were sometimes housed at the expense of a friendly ruler. *Ribats* were originally fortified dwellings built to defend the faithful in predominantly non-Muslim areas. They often became centres of teaching and religious propaganda, and were sometimes built, and endowed, as *waqfs* around the tombs of fallen *mujahids*. The term *ribat* was adopted by Sufi adepts to describe the place where they waged the 'spiritual *jihad*' against worldly passions.

During the *khanqa* stage the *shaikh* was essentially a spiritual guide. Internal discipline was relatively democratic: the brothers sought permission from their companions rather than from the *shaikh* if they wished to be absent. A list of rules dating from the eleventh century urges cleanliness, both private and common devotions, Quranic recitation, theological and devotional exercises (*wird*) and ministering to the needs of the poor. The inmates are discouraged from gossiping or selfishness. The *khanqa* was an association of people prepared to live a common Islamic life, rather than a guidance centre for instilling a distinct Islamic religious discipline. Anyone could be admitted to a *khanqa* provided he could satisfy the *khadim* (steward) that he had studied under a recognized *shaikh*. The *khanqas* were also used as inns for ordinary wayfarers.

Trimingham describes the second phase in the development of Sufi organization as the *tariqa* stage. Occurring mainly during the primacy of the Sunni Seljuks during the thirteenth century, the *tariqa* stage involved the formalization and transmission of distinctive mystical doctrines, rules and methods. For the individual, whereas the *khanqa* stage involved the replication of the primary act of 'Islam' or Self-surrender to God, the *tariqa* stage implied submission to a specific rule, such as the Qadiri, Suhrawardi or Rifai'i, as outlined above. This period saw the development of *silsilas* legitimizing the order by referring it back to a suitably august holy personage (and ultimately, of course, to the Prophet himself). The imposition of a disciplined rule on otherwise wayward religious impulses can be described, using Weberian terms, as the 'routinization of mysticism'. The individualistic experience of the wandering dervish who moves from *pir* to *pir* or *khanqa* to *khanqa* is channelled into larger cooperative organizations. The characteristic Sufi ritual known as the *dhikr* ('remembrance') is developed at this stage, with the aim of inducing a state of collective ecstasy. Dervishes who remained outside the *tariqa* institution were known as *malamatis* and *qalandris*. *Malamatis* rejected all outward show of religiosity, including prayers and the supererogatory exercises (*tarawih*) associated with Ramadan. *Qalandaris* exhibited more extravagantly antinomian attitudes, shaving their heads and placing iron rings in their hands, ears and penises, like the Rifa'iya. Some took their contempt for official Islamic *mores* so far as to invite accusations of immorality and debauchery.

The third and final phase in Trimingham's classification is the *ta'ifa* (organization) stage. This occurred primarily during the fifteenth century, during the founding period of the Ottoman Empire. The *ta'ifa* stage develops more authoritarian patterns. The *murid* must surrender to a person – the *shaikh* of the order – so there is a consequent narrowing in the focus of mysticism. A favourite image of the early Sufis, the adept's 'corpse' being washed by his *shaikh*, is given a formal, institutionalized meaning. The *shaikh* becomes the doctor of souls, the teacher who alone can give correct guidance to the *murid*. He is 'the calm light in the veiling darkness, the shade of the verdant tree in the desert', the 'spiritual father completely possessing the *murid* who will do nothing save by his opinion or guidance in all affairs and will only leave him to obtain his daily bread'.[40] It is at the *ta'ifa* stage that the orders become deeply implicated in the cult of saints.

The *zawiyas*, *tekkes* and *khanqas* associated with the final stage of Sufic development were often built around the tomb of the founding saint. The North African *zawiya*, for example, is usually a complex of buildings, including a small mosque, a Quran school, a large room for *dhikrs* and *hadhras* (religious occasions) and dwellings for the *shaikh* and his family, as well as rooms for affiliates, pilgrims and travellers. Just how prevalent these institutions were throughout the Maghreb may be gathered from the instances of the word Sidi (from Sayyid, as saints are called in North African parlance) in Maghrebi place-names. A few orders practised celibacy but generally this was discouraged. In Turkish *tekkes*, for example, married dervishes had their own dwellings, but were obliged to sleep in the convent once or twice a week. *Murids* usually kept their wives and children in neighbouring villages, only the *shaikh* being entitled to house his family in the *khanqa* or *zawiya*. The latter was often endowed as a *waqf* by the founding saint's family or some of his wealthier followers. Not infrequently, however, they were self-supporting, having their own flocks and areas of cultivation.

The organization of the *tariqas* was hierarchical, and, as they developed, increasingly complex. The hierarchy was built around the concept of ascending gradations of spiritual illumination. Sufis used the word *tauba* (repentance) to indicate their 'conversion' to Sufism, their resolve to abandon the worldly life and devote themselves to the service of God. Two key terms from the early Muslim experience are taken over and given internalized, spiritualized application. The act of joining a *tariqa* is described as making one's *hijra* – that is, forswearing evil ('Mecca') and espousing the good life ('Medina'); while the spiritual struggle against 'the world, the flesh and the devil' is described as *jihad*. The term *mujahada* (a collateral form of *jihad*) is taken, in Sufi terminology, to mean the 'earnest striving after the mystical life'. A *hadith* of the Prophet places this 'striving of self' (*mujahadat al nafs*) above the 'lesser' *jihad* against infidelity.[41] Thereafter (according to an early text dating from the eleventh century), the Sufi progresses through various stations (*maqams*) in his search for God. These range from *khalwa* (withdrawal), through *murakaba* (constant 'God-consciousness'), leading to 'satisfaction' (*rida*) and freedom (*hurriya*) from material considerations, to the final states of gnosis (*ma'rifa*), love (*mahabba*) and a 'yearning' (*shauq*) to be constantly with God.

The Sufi who decided to climb this arduous spiritual ladder had, during the latter phase of the movement, to join one of the recognized *tariqas*. Aspiring Sufis usually served a three-year novitiate. The first was devoted to 'service of the people', the second to 'service of God' and the final year to 'watching over his own heart'. Communal service included doing household chores. Among the Mawlawis the domestic aspect of the novitiate lasted almost three years: 1,001 days of unbroken service were required, the last year being spent in the kitchens. The initial ceremony of initiation was presided over by the chief cook. Khalwatis, on the other hand, were expected to go into retreat from the first, reporting on their visions to the *shaikh*. After completing the novitiate, the aspiring Sufi usually underwent a ceremony of investiture. Initially this included the adoption of the characteristic woollen garb worn by the early ascetics. From about the eleventh century this was gradually replaced by a patched garment known as the *muraqqa'* or *khirqa*. The *khirqa* was the outward sign that the *murid* had made his oath of fealty (*bay'a*) to the *shaikh*. In some Turkish and eastern orders the *khirqa* was supplemented by distinctive trousers, waistbands and headgear. After completing the appropriate initiation rituals, the novice or affiliate (someone merely taking a 'short course' in Sufi studies) was presented with a certificate (*ijaza*) containing his name, that of his *shaikh*, and the *silsila* of his order. In times of Sufi decadence, from about the fourteenth century, *ijazas* were easy to come by. Ibn Battuta, himself no Sufi, collected them as traveller's trophies. In the nineteenth century, when modern forms of transport had greatly increased the number of pilgrims from Africa, and the Far East, the revived orders made Mecca a centre of recruitment, and many pilgrims were to be seen returning from the Hajj sporting tubular cases containing their *ijazas* round their necks.

The *shaikh* who is head of the *ta'ifa* often claims descent from the original founder. By analogy with the political organization of Islam, he is usually known as the Saint's *khalifa* or deputy. Ordinary members are usually divided into regular *murids*, who have dedicated their lives to the order, and lay affiliates. Outsiders usually refer to the former as *faqirs* ('poor ones') in Arabic, or its Persian equivalent, *darwish* ('mendicant') from which the anglicized 'dervish' is derived. The formal offices within an order do not necessarily correspond to the hierarchy of spiritual states outlined above; they are concerned exclusively with the order's 'external relations' with the outside world. Only the *shaikh* himself combines seniority within the organization with assumed spiritual superiority.

The central feature of Sufi ritual is the *dhikr* or remembrance. The Quranic basis for it is found in the verses urging believers to 'remember God with increasing remembrance and extol His limitless glory from morn to evening'.[42] According to a modern Sufi writer, Frithjof Schuon, "the remembrance of God" is at the same time a forgetting of self; conversely the ego is a kind of crystallization of forgetfulness of God.'[43] Repetition of the divine names, an essential part of most *dhikr* ceremonies, is supposed to result in a 'knowledge of God' by way of contemplation. The *dhikr* usually begins and ends with a repetition of the divine name, a type of religious activity also found in the 'Jesus prayers' of Eastern Christianity and in Buddhism. In Islam it is often linked to the *tahlil* formula (*la ilaha ila Allah*: 'There is no deity but God'), which is pronounced rhythmically, accompanied by controlled breathing. The technique seems to have been handed down from the earliest masters: according to a *hadith* of Abu Yazid al Bistami, 'for gnostics, worship is the observance of breaths.' Breath control is an important part of other religious disciplines, including Yoga, and may be employed to induce unusual psychic states by limiting the supply of oxygen to the brain. Controlled ecstasy may also be induced by certain physical movements. Among the orders these range from the gentle turning from right to left with which the Qadiris accompany the *tahlil* formula, a technique attributed to 'Abd al Qadir al Jilani himself, to the spinning of the Mawlawiya or 'Whirling Dervishes', who have performed their famous dance in several European cities. The eleventh-century mystic Ahmad al Ghazali described the significance of these movements:

> The dancing is a reference to the circling of the spirit round the
> cycle of existing things, on account of receiving the effects of the

unveilings and revelations; and this is the state of the gnostic. The whirling is a reference to the spirit's standing with Allah in its inner nature and being, the circling of its look and thought, and its penetrating the ranks of existing things . . .[44]

The dance of the Mawlawiya produces a disciplined ecstasy apparent to anyone who watches it. Rumi's intoxicated energy survives in the dance of his order, but it is harnessed into a brilliantly choreographed display that achieves a delicate balance between symmetrical precision and spontaneous movement. The dance, perfected over seven centuries, has none of the self-conscious theatricality of classical or modern ballet. The viewer is a vicarious participant in the action, not a member of an audience; the dancers seem oblivious to the presence of observers – so much so that the viewer enters to some degree into the interiority of their experience.

All communal *dhikrs*, though differing in form and style, seek to achieve a submergence of the individual into the communal identity and, by means of such temporary loss of ego-consciousness, a sense of the 'unity of the beyond and the within'. Ontologically speaking, the inner state at which the adept arrives may not differ from that achieved by means of yogic exercises: what makes it characteristically Islamic is the liturgical and communal context in which it happens. The sense of human brotherhood and physical solidarity to which Islam gives tangible manifestation in the Hajj and the ritual discipline of congregational prayer remains an essential element in the mystic communion of the *dhikr*. The pressure towards social conformity forces the *murid* to purge his search for a higher consciousness of any antinomian or individualistic elements. Before he can approach God, he must first attend to his fellow beings, subsuming his identity within that of a group which represents, in microcosm, the whole Islamic community.

In its liturgical meaning also the *dhikr* remains a characteristically Muslim activity. The ritual's dominant purpose is the 'saturation' of self in Allah. Gilsenan points out in connection with the Hamidiya Shadhiliya that the names of God employed in their *dhikr* are those which focus above all on his transcendence and power:

No plea is addressed to the Almighty; there is no supplication, no imploring of His grace . . . the concentration is on the Absoluteness of God, His Transcendent, Eternal Being, *not* His attributes such as those of Mercy and Compassion. No action of God is expected, or requested, in the *dhikr*. No material blessings will follow. From this point of view, the *dhikr* is non-instrumental in character.[45]

The *dhikr*'s character is non-contingent, its spirit the disinterested search for the divine in the tradition of Rabi'a al 'Adawiya and Ibn al 'Arabi. This is not to say, however, that such states of 'being' are achieved without a certain amount of psychological manipulation, which can degenerate into 'mystical mechanization'. The constant attacks on popular Sufism mounted by 'official' Islam in modern times owe much to the general disrepute into which it was brought by undisciplined *dhikrs* and the more primitive forms of saint-worship.

REFORM, RENEWAL AND THE SPREAD OF ISLAM

Apart from contributing towards the creation of group identities within the loosely textured societies of the Muslim cities, the most signal historic contribution of the Sufi orders was towards the spread of Islam in the peripheral regions. In this respect the *tariqas* inherited earlier traditions of Isma'ili *da'wa*, evangelizing distant tribes and communities in mountainous and tropical regions. Where the *da'is* had proclaimed the divine government of their Imam, the Sufi dervishes cultivated the veneration of saints. Both movements centred on the cult of personality rather than on the proclamation of scripture. A Sunnism based mainly on the upholding of legal norms enshrined in an Arabic text could hardly be expected to penetrate the cultures of non-Arab illiterates far removed from the cosmopolitan world of the great Islamic cities. Yet, in the long term, official Islam was to benefit from the very practices which orthodoxy condemned. The wilder extravagances of the intoxicated dervishes, which earned such disapproval from grave city gentlemen learned in *fiqh*, took on a different colouring in societies familiar with shamanism or witch-doctors. The easy-going tolerance of wandering marabouts, equipped with prayer-mats and magical formulae borrowed or adapted from scraps of Islamic lore, was well suited to the winning of converts in pagan regions, for, while the symbols of religious power were familiar and hence reassuring, the dervishes nevertheless carried with them the cultural prestige of the greater Muslim society. Islamization was mostly a gradual process, occurring over generations. In contrast to the official *'ulama*, the dervishes were free to bend the rules to suit the customs and habits of different peoples. Only after a period of 'cultural Islamization' had passed were partly converted peoples suitably prepared to take on the full burden of Shari'a conformity. This was particularly the case with pagans in non-Arab regions, where a long process of acculturation was required before they were even in a condition comparable to the *jahiliya* of the pre-Islamic Arabs. The Shari'a accommodated and legitimized many pre-Islamic Arab customs, which made its observance less burdensome to Arabs than to other peoples.

In many parts of the Islamic world, notably Indonesia and West Africa, two of the most populous Muslim regions, Islamization was far from complete when European colonial power intervened in the process, delaying it in some places and accelerating it in others. Whether or not the European presence acted as a catalysing force, the final stage in cultural Islamization took the classic form of a *jihad* against pagan 'backsliding'. The model of a polytheism resulting from the degeneration and fragmentation of an atavistic monotheism served, as in Muhammad's original movement, to legitimize a variety of local campaigns to impose reforms on different societies, bringing them more closely into line with Shari'a norms. In some instances the *tariqas* themselves provided the institutional framework through which reform was enacted. In others the reform of Islam embraced a frontal attack on all varieties of Sufism. Such differences were, however, more apparent than real. All the reform movements sought, in different ways, a 'return' to a purer Islam closer to Shari'a norms. To this extent all of them, whether or not explicitly opposed to certain Sufi practices, come within the scope of the neo-Sufic revival.

The spread of Islam in the peripheral regions occurred almost imperceptibly. Any attempt to describe it is bound to be over-schematic if tedious repetition and detail are to be avoided. Conversion was never the exclusive preserve of the Sufi orders. In trading centres resident Muslim immigrants observed the law and attended the local mosque in a conventional manner owing little or nothing to Sufi organization or practice. Nevertheless, members of the orders with their impressive spiritual lineages were sometimes credited with bringing the 'truth' to these metropolitan outposts of the faith. At the same time there is little doubt that the loose, relatively informal structures of both official and unofficial Islam allowed syncretist tendencies to develop in areas which were either remote from the literary culture of the cities or which came within the orbit of non-Muslim high cultures. The former category applies particularly to the spread of Islam in the Maghreb, Black Africa and Central Asia; the latter to its development in southern Asia and the Far East.

THE MAGHREB AND BLACK AFRICA

The process of islamization can be a highly complex one, involving as it does the gradual adoption of Islamic norms and outlook by people of widely differing cultures. In parts of West Africa the initiative came mainly from above. Muslim traders and marabouts who journeyed south of the Maghreb into what are now Mauritania, Mali and Nigeria, and into the riverine states of Senegal and the Volta, carried with them an aura of cultural prestige that commended them to the rulers of these territories. A king who protected Muslims or even converted to Islam became part of the international community, giving him considerable advantages over non-Muslim rivals. Literacy (in Arabic), the expansion of trade and even the opportunity to dispossess his non-Muslim neighbours by launching a *jihad* against them provided the inducements which made Islam an attractive 'royal cult' for many West African princelings. A successful *jihad* need not necessarily lead to mass conversions: subject peoples might more usefully furnish slaves and booty whilst remaining *kafirs* without any rights. The cultural prestige associated with Islam was often expressed in terms of admiration for its superior magic. A green turban received from the Sharif of Mecca during attendance at the Hajj was a more impressive symbol of authority than any local tribal fetish. In the 'royal' Islam of West Africa, Islamic practices often coexisted with pagan cults. An *'alim* who visited the court of Askiya Dawud (1549–83), ruler of Songhay on the Upper Niger, who had the reputation of a scholar and patron of Islamic learning, was scandalized to find the rituals of divine kingship being observed, and dared to tell the ruler to his face that he must be 'mad, corrupt or possessed'. The Askiya's reply showed how far this nominally Muslim ruler felt compelled to go along with his people's barbarian traditions: 'I am not mad myself,' he told the scholar, 'but I rule over mad, impious and arrogant folk. It is for this reason that I play the madman myself and pretend to be possessed by a demon in order to frighten them and prevent them from harming the Muslims.'[46]

The success of Islam in propagating itself, particularly in its Sufic and maraboutic versions, in regions where a direct assault by conquest was impracticable was largely due to what I. M. Lewis calls 'its truly catholic recognition of the multiplicity of mystical power': '. . . in the voluminous Quranic store-house of angels, jinns and devils, whose number is legion, many of these traditional powers find a hospitable home; and passages from the Quran are cited to justify their existence as real phenomena.'[47] So long as Allah's lofty pre-eminence was not compromised, many local cults could be accommodated within the realm of *al ghaib*, the 'unseen' or 'hidden' world. The supreme deities which exist in many pagan traditions could be assimilated to Allah. Lesser local deities could be Islamicized or explained away as vernacular terms for God's attributes, or as the jinns or spirits of Quranic folklore. Ancestor cults could be accommodated to Islam by tagging local kinship groups on to Sufi *silsilas* or Arab lineages. By such methods the Somali cattle-herders, originally evangelized under Qadiri auspices, acquired Quraishi ancestry. This 'canonization' of ancestors as Sufi saints conferred inherited *baraka* upon the Somali clans, providing them with the prestige of an Arabian spiritual ancestry. Elsewhere, for example in the Central High Atlas, special 'saintly' lineages, traced back to 'Ali and the Prophet through one or other of the many Sufi *silsilas*, provided a kind of theocratic 'constitutional' framework through which a fissiparous tribal society achieved a basic minimum of cooperation. The leaders of saintly families, who usually resided in the vicinity of the tombs of their holy ancestors, would undertake the supervision of tribal elections, arbitrate in intertribal disputes and generally help guarantee the complex seasonal arrangements governing the movement of people between the high mountain pastures and the desert's edge. The function of such saintly families was virtually identical to that of the Quraish, hereditary guardians of the Ka'ba, during the time of the Prophet.

In Islam, syncretism in ritual is much more difficult to justify than syncretism in theology. Whereas every kind of religious belief can be accommodated within the framework of Islamic concepts merely by the adoption of Islamic terminology or symbols, the outward recognition of these symbols in formal religious observance is a matter on which orthodoxy is severe and uncompromising. One may privately think of Allah as Waq or Soko; one cannot, however, perform rituals such as prostration or 'dusting' oneself before the king in accordance with local traditions without inviting accusations of *shirk* – polytheism, or the 'association' of lesser beings with God. In Africa syncretism of belief inevitably spilled over into the corruption of ritual. Rain-making ceremonies were accompanied by Muslim prayers; Sufi *dhikr* came to be held not merely in 'remembrance' of Allah, but also to appease pagan goddesses credited with malevolent powers.[48] Such practices as the *zar* cults (exorcism ceremonies) or the ingestion of *baraka* by physical means (including copulation with a holy man, or drinking his vomit) are part of a pattern of diffusion in the peripheral and marginal regions of the Muslim world, where the absence of the literate class of urban scholars left spiritual power, untempered by learning, in the hands of those who were free to exercise it in any manner they found congenial or appropriate. Wherever conditions allowed, however, they provided the pretext for reformers who sought to purify Islam by bringing local practice more closely into line with Shari'a norms.

Broadly speaking, these reformist movements fall into two categories: the *jihad* and mahdist movements which sought to recreate a purified Islamic society *in toto*, rebuilding, as it were, the Medinese caliphate on new foundations; and the reformed *tariqas*, which sought to regenerate existing polities by bringing the Sufi orders more closely into line with Shari'a norms. One should not, however, make too much of this distinction. All the reform movements represent a common ambition to restore or impose stricter Shari'a practice and ritual in accordance with the models established by the Prophet and the earliest Muslim community. They also represent, in varying degrees, the desire to restore the pristine Islamic state in the face of real or perceived threats of pagan backsliding and non-Muslim rule. The forms taken by such movements varied considerably, occurring as they did in many different social and cultural milieus. But their inspiration was usually scriptural and charismatic.

Generally the *jihad* and mahdist movements led to the founding of new states on Khaldunian lines, based on a combination of religious authority and tribal *'asabiya*. They occurred mainly in peripheral and undeveloped regions, far from the great cities, where pastoralism in one form or another remained the predominant mode of agricultural production. The reformed *tariqas* operated both in arid regions, on the basis of tribal organization, and in more highly centralized agrarian states. The flexibility of *tariqa* organization enabled reformers to seek their objectives by more variable means than the classic sequence of *hijra* followed by *jihad*. Under certain conditions, a reformed *tariqa* might transform itself into a *jihad* movement, creating a state on the basis of *tariqa* organization. But whereas *jihad* and mahdist movements in general were radical, utopian and aggressive, neo-*tariqas* were more inclined to be compromising, pragmatic and defensive.

The model of the *jihad* movement, despite the occasional use of mahdist eschatology, was the secessionism of the early Kharijis, who made a Manichaean division of the world into two camps, the true Muslims, or 'People of Paradise', and the 'People of Hell', comprising everyone else, including pagans, non-Muslims and any Muslims who refused to join their camp. The model of the reformed *tariqas* was initially the piety and asceticism of the early Sufi masters. In each case the Quranic vision, interacting with the real world, was subtly different. The mahdist or *jihad* leader tended to imitate the armed Prophet of Medina, doing battle against God's enemies under divine inspiration. The neo-*tariqa* leader was generally more influenced by the Meccan phase of the Prophet's career, when, in the face of the prevailing infidelity and corruption of the Holy City, he gathered around himself a group of followers committed to reforming themselves by observing a common religious discipline, leaving aside, for the present, the wider question of transforming society.

IBN TUMART AND THE ALMOHAD EMPIRE

An early and far-reaching movement in the *jihad* tradition was the Mahdiya of Ibn Tumart (d. 1130), which overthrew the Almoravid Empire in Spain and the Maghreb and led to the foundation of the most durable and civilized of all the Berber states. Ibn Tumart was born in a settled Berber village in the anti-Atlas, and like many reformers spent a period studying in the East before returning to his homeland. The story that he met Ghazali in Baghdad is probably untrue; in Baghdad, however, he was strongly influenced by the Ash'ari school of theology which, in contrast to the Maliki school prevailing in the Maghreb, allowed the figurative interpretation of the Quran. The Maliki *'ulama* of Spain and the Maghreb had been among the most conspicuous targets for Ghazali's attacks, and it is reported that the Almoravid rulers had, at their behest, ordered all copies of the *Ihya* to be destroyed.

On returning to the Maghreb, Ibn Tumart began preaching the uncompromising unity of the divine (*tawhid*) according to Ash'ari tenets. His followers (like the Druzes and later the Wahhabis) described themselves as Muwahhidin ('unitarians'), from which the Spanish 'Almohad' derives. The Berber preacher took a stern line on sexual segregation, women's dress, the consumption of alcohol, music and dancing: the puritanical austerity of his doctrine is still in evidence in North Africa to this day. The most original project he sponsored was the translation of the Quran into the Berber tongue. His attacks on the life-style of the Almoravid amirs brought him increasing political trouble. Consciously emulating the Muhammadan and Khariji models, he eventually made the *hijra* to his native district in the anti-Atlas, accompanied only by a few followers. Here he made many converts among the local Berber tribes and, having received their *bay'a* (homage) proclaimed himself Mahdi or 'Imam of the Age'. Though he died shortly after his first major (and far from successful) encounter with the Almoravid armies, his successor, 'Abd al Mumin, eventually overthrew them and proclaimed himself caliph, transforming what had been an ideological movement into a dynastic state. Under a survey commissioned by 'Abd al Mumin in 1159, all non-Almohad Muslims were classified as infidels and made liable to forfeit their property. At the height of their empire the Almohads controlled territory stretching from Cyrenaica to the Atlantic and from Mali to Valencia. Three of the greatest philosophers, Ibn Tufail (d. 1185) Ibn Rushd (Averroës) (d. 1198) and the Jew Ibn Maimun (Maimonides) (d. 1204), flourished under their rule. The Ashari doctrines held by Ibn Tumart enabled the Almohad rulers to harmonize the Arab and Berber elements in their culture and to maintain intellectual double standards: strict adherence to the Shari'a for the masses, free intellectual speculation for the enlightened few. The contrast was well illustrated by Ibn Rushd himself, who, in addition to being the most enlightened and rationalistic philosopher produced by medieval Islam, was grand *qadi* charged with administration of the Shari'a.

From about the middle of the thirteenth century the Almohad empire began to suffer the classic symptoms of Khaldunian decline. The moral and psychic energy which had sustained it became diffused once more, leading to a collapse of the empire into a number of competing Berber kingdoms. The disintegration of central power saw a corresponding rise in the influence and authority of the *tariqas* and *zawiyas*. By the time a new imperial power had succeeded in reunifying the Maghreb, the *tariqa* habit and maraboutism had become so ingrained that even the rulers claiming to carry the Prophet's blood in their veins were incapable of governing without the support of one or other of the leading orders.

DAN FODIO AND THE EMPIRE OF SOKOTO

Whereas the Almohad movement sought to revitalize and purify the already Islamicized society of the Maghreb, the *jihad* of Shehu Usumanu

Dan Fodio (in Arabic, 'Uthman ibn Fudiy) (1754–1817) took place in a mixed society of 'court Muslims' and pagans. While representing itself as an attack on the 'corruption' of Islam by the rulers of Hausaland, it also contained a proselytizing dimension, for by attacking the syncretic practices of 'royal' Islam and paganism it brought into the Umma many people without previous attachment to the faith.

The towns of the Sahel, the 'shore' of arid and cultivable land south of the Sahara, had been infiltrated by Muslim settlers and pastoralists from Umayyad times. However, the cities and townships witnessed a growing tension between the class of urban *'ulama* and their rulers who, as already indicated, were prone to mixing formal adherence to Islam with court rituals of pagan origin. The tension between the *'ulama* and their rulers was further complicated by the influx of pastoral peoples from the north, a movement which in the eighteenth century gave rise to a series of *jihads*, the most celebrated and far-reaching of which was Dan Fodio's. Fulani cattle-herders, light-skinned Muslim tribesmen moving southwards from Mali in search of pasture, were the main bearers of this sub-Saharan version of the Khaldunian cycle. In 1725 Ibrahim Musa, a Fulani *'alim*, proclaimed the *jihad* and founded the state of Futa Jallon in the highlands where the Senegal and Gambia rivers have their source. The movement spread to Futa Toro on the coast (modern Guinea), where an independent imamate was formed which lasted till the French conquest.

Dan Fodio was born in 1754 into a family of urban Fulani scholars, in the independent Hausa kingdom of Gobir. He spent much of his early life moving from one town to another, in order to study with different scholars. Influenced by the Berber theologian Muhammad al Maghili, he argued that syncretic practices were more outrageous in the sight of Allah than outright paganism, because, whereas pagans were backward people who knew no better, the 'mixers' (including, of course, the court Muslims) were in a position to corrupt Islam by leading good Muslims astray. The Shehu's attacks were clearly aimed at, among others, the King of Gobir, who responded by forbidding his followers to wear turbans or veils. In the classic Muhammadan manner, in 1804 Dan Fodio made his *hijra* to beyond the borders of the kingdom.

The emigrants began raiding. Other Hausa rulers began to persecute their Muslim subjects. A number of Fulani shaikhs, Qadiri Sufis and *'ulama* from Futa Toro joined the *jihad*; other Fulani, backed by the Tuareg, joined the enemy. By 1807 Dan Fodio had overrun Kano, Zaria and other Hausa city states. In 1808 Alkalawa, capital of Gobir, fell to the *mujahiddin*. The conflict cut across ethnic and kinship ties, local antagonisms and group loyalties. After the fall of Alkalawa Dan Fodio devolved much of his authority to his son, Muhammad Belo, who became first Sultan of Sokoto, the most powerful Muslim emirate in what eventually became the British colony of Nigeria. A descendant of Dan Fodio, Sir Ahmadu Belo, Sardauna of Sokoto, was regional premier of Northern Nigeria until his assassination in the military coup of 1966 which overthrew the Federal Government.

ARABIAN WAHHABISM

The syncretic accretions which *mujaddids* ('renovators') such as Ibn Tumart or Dan Fodio found so objectionable were the inevitable result of the penetration of Islam into non-Arab cultures where local Berber or African custom ran against the current of Islamization. It is not without significance that both leaders drew their inspiration from the 'Abbasid rather than the Medinese caliphate. The period of formative Islam which had most relevance for their situation was that of assimilation and growth in the pluralistic society of the ninth and tenth centuries, rather than the purely Arab Islam of the Prophet's era. Ibn Tumart, while strictly adhering to Shari'a norms based on the Quran and the Sunna, was almost Mu'tazili in his condemnation of literalistic and anthropomorphic interpretations of scripture. This was not simply due to his hostility to the Maliki *faqihs* who held sway in the Maghreb: non-Arabs, however 'fundamentalist' their disposition, can only be expected to accept Islam on terms which recognize that all speech, including the 'divine', has a contingent character – an attitude of mind which lends itself naturally to allegorical interpretation. For this, if for no other reason, it seems wrong to dismiss his theology as being of merely 'minor importance'.[49]

Similarly, Uthman Dan Fodio was 'fundamentalist' only in the most general sense of the term. Regardless of his explicit statements, he sought, not to restore a pristine Islam that had never existed in Africa, but to introduce the metropolitan Islam which represented the highest culture of which he was aware. The legal sources quoted in Fulani literature are mostly late 'Abbasid. With so many pagan practices around which could be condemned as *shirk*, the African had no need to identify this sin in terms of 'innovative' practices.

The culture of the Arabian Peninsula being predominantly Arab, the *jihad* of the Wahhabis had a subtly different character from that proclaimed by the Berber and West African innovators. Whereas the latter sought to employ Islam, as the 'Abbasid caliphs had done, as a way of integrating their societies into the high culture of the Fertile Crescent, the Arabs of Najd had a different, almost opposite objective. For them, Islam affirmed their distinctive identities as Arabs. It was no accident, therefore, that the ideology through which they sought to reaffirm this identity in the face of the cosmopolitan culture of Iraq and the Hejaz was a version of pristine Islam derived from their ideas about the Medinese caliphate, one which laid particular stress on strict adherence to the divine text's linguistic integrity. Culturally speaking, Wahhabism represented a primitive, pre-modern version of Arab nationalism.

Muhammad ibn 'Abd al Wahhab was not particularly original as an *'alim* or theologian. His real importance is that he acted as a channel for the uncompromising Quranic literalism of Ahmad ibn Hanbal and his most famous disciple, Ibn Taimiya, becoming the vehicle by which their emphasis on the unique character of Arabic developed into the basis for an appropriate ideology for a modern Arab state. Although Ahmad ibn Hanbal had been rehabilitated when the official line on the 'created' Quran changed in favour of the traditionists, the Hanbalis always remained something of an opposition group within the wider Muslim culture of the Mashriq. Though eventually recognized as one of the four legal *madhhabs*, they never constituted a school of *fiqh* comparable to the other three: they would be better described as a school of *hadith*ists fundamentally opposed to codifying the Shari'a into a comprehensive system of *fiqh*. For them the Quran and the Sunna were not really the sources of law; rather they were the law itself. Although Ibn Hanbal was capable of the subtlest juridical reasoning, he eschewed any formal rationalization of legal methodology, believing that legal decisions must be arrived at by continually referring back to these sources (as distinct from reference to a body of *fiqh* derived from them). *Ijtihad* – the scholarly effort involved in determining the law – must be constantly exercised. The system was conservative but far from rigid: the plurality of the material allowed for considerable variations, more so than under a codified system of *fiqh*.

Ibn Hanbal's determination to retain the integrity of scripture in all its completeness often gave rise to criticisms of anthropomorphism and extravagant literalism – criticisms that were sometimes exaggerated.

While explicitly opposed to *tawil* (allegorical interpretation) and the negative theology of the Mu'tazilis, he also rejected the extreme anthropomorphism (*tasbih*) of their opponents. In brief, Ibn Hanbal's views were anti-theological, just as he was against legal formalism. He opposed the elaboration of a theological superstructure on the basis of Quranic ideas about God, just as he opposed the systematic development of religious jurisprudence. His uncompromising scripturalism, being unsuited to the metropolitan and pluralistic civilization of the Fertile Crescent, never took root there. Until its re-emergence, via the refinements of Ibn Taimiya, under the banner of Wahhabism, Hanbalism remained in something of an Arab ghetto. However, precisely because it laid such stress upon the non-contingent character of revelation and the language through which it was mediated, Ibn Hanbal's doctrine proved highly congenial to Najdi *'ulama* who needed an ideology which would justify, in Islamic terms, the supremacy of Arabian Islam over the more cosmopolitan and sophisticated versions current in Iraq and the Hejaz.

Taqiy al Din ibn Taimiya (1263–1328) was a Hanbali scholar who spent much of his time in prison. His first incarceration occurred after a quarrel in his native Damascus with a Christian whom he accused of insulting the Prophet's memory. Indicted by his enemies for anthropomorphism, he replied by accusing them of antinomianism and hashish-taking. A brilliant polemicist, he wrote pamphlets attacking both the monism of Ibn al 'Arabi and the spiritualizing *tawil* of Ibn Tumart. He made himself unpopular with the *'ulama* of his day by his condemnation of all forms of legal innovation (*bid'a*), particularly the triple *talaq* (repudiation) by which Sunni husbands could instantly divorce their wives without going through a tedious process of reconciliation, and numerous other *hiyal* ('tricks') by which the *'ulama* violated the spirit, if not the letter, of the Shari'a. Though initiated into the Qadiriya, he was almost as unpopular with many Sufi *shaikhs* for his attacks on tomb-cults and saint-worship. Though his doctrines enjoyed the support of the Bahri Mamluk Sultans in Cairo, Ibn Taimiya encountered continuous opposition in Syria, and he died imprisoned in the Damascus citadel.

In his doctrine Ibn Taimiya refined and developed the Arabism implicit in Ibn Hanbal. Rejecting both *tawil* and *tasbih* (anthropomorphism), he shared Ibn Hanbal's belief that God could only be described as 'He has described Himself in His Book and as the Prophet has described Him in the Sunna' – that is to say, in those scriptures that are completely accessible only to Arabs. In legal matters he preferred the ideas of the 'men of old' (*salaf*) to the doctrines of the founders of the *madhhabs*. *Ijtihad* was a constant imperative: there was no question of its 'gates' having ever been closed. The text of Quran and *hadith* had absolute primacy over *ijma'*, the consensus of the community, although *qiyas* (analogical reasoning) was admissible. Though the chief function of the state was to uphold justice and the law, without which it must dissolve into tyranny, Ibn Taimiya was too much of a realist to seek a political restoration of the universal caliphate. Islam required only obedience to 'God and His Prophet': there was no limit to the number of righteous imams to whom obedience might be owed. He regarded the Umma, realistically enough, as a natural confederation of Muslim states.

Ibn Taimiya's influence in Egypt declined after the Ottoman conquest in 1517 made Hanafi law supreme. The revival of his *'salafi'* ideas in modern times is primarily due to his influence on Muhammad ibn 'Abd al Wahhab, ideologist and co-founder of the original Saudi state. The great Najdi *'alim* was not an exclusive disciple of Ibn Hanbal and Ibn Taimiya: his most important teacher in Medina had in fact been a member of the reformist Naqshbandi order, the Hanafi scholar Muhammad Hayat al Sindi (d. 1751). From the Naqshbandis (see p. 274ff.) he took over the Sufic notion of absolute submission, making God Himself, as it were, the *shaikh* of his *tariqa*. At the same time he strenuously resisted any anthropomorphism implicit in this approach by stressing God's overwhelming wholeness and unity (*tawhid*). Nevertheless he took from Ibn Hanbal and Ibn Taimiya the uncompromising scripturalism whereby legal decisions must be arrived at by directly consulting the Quran and the Sunna, bypassing or eliminating the superstructure of *fiqh*. In theory Wahhabism allowed that anything not explicitly forbidden in the Quran or the Sunna was permissible. In practice, during militant phases of the movement, attacks on ritual innovations such as tomb-worship tended to spill over into attacks on practices not explicitly sanctioned by the Prophet. Ibn Hanbal himself is said to have abstained from eating water-melons because of the lack of any *hadith* on the subject. The original Wahhabis banned music, dancing, poetry, silk, gold, all ornaments and jewellery because of alleged *hadiths* condemning them. Their twentieth-century imitators, among both the Ikhwan and more recent religious opponents of the Saudi monarchy, have attacked tobacco-smoking, the telephone, radio and television as 'innovations' unsanctioned in scripture.

Nevertheless, the flexibility implicit in these doctrines has allowed the Saudi rulers to push through reforms with the minimum of opposition from the 'ulama (whose most influential elements, the Al Shaikh, are descendants of Ibn 'Abd al Wahhab). Telephone, radio and television were introduced – once it had been proved that they could be used to transmit the Word of God. A host of other innovations have followed, including the abolition of slavery (though this is sanctioned in the Quran) and the introduction of female education (something which mysogynistic hadiths could be cited to oppose). In short, Wahhabism has not proved an insuperable obstacle to development in what has become one of the world's most rapidly changing Muslim societies, although, as was seen in the opening chapter of this book, it can still supply the ideological ground for an attack on such innovations as would-be reformers, radical or revolutionaries deem to be corrupt and un-Islamic.

NAQSHBANDI REFORMISM IN ASIA

The reformed tariqas and jihad movements which specifically addressed themselves to the situation created by European colonial conquest in the nineteenth century will be referred to in the following chapter. No account of the heritage of Sufism in pre-colonial times would be remotely adequate, however, without reference to the oldest and longest-established reformist tradition, the Naqshbandiya. This medieval order, which became immensely influential in Central Asia and the Indian Subcontinent, faced many of the dilemmas encountered by reformist movements in the twentieth century. Its responses to the challenge of non-Muslim power as well as to the predicament of Muslims living in a predominantly non-Muslim cultural and religious milieu, ranged from the rejectionist jihad to a spiritualizing doctrine permitting total collaboration with infidels on the political front. The range of the Naqshbandiya's responses from the fifteenth to the nineteenth centuries corresponded more or less accurately to the responses of dar al Islam as a whole when presented with the even more formidable challenge of non-Muslim power in the nineteenth and twentieth.

The Naqshbandi order, which includes 'Ali, Abu Bakr, Salman al Farisi, Ja'far al Sadiq and Abu Yazid al Bistami in its silsilas, derives from the tariqa of Abu Yaqub al Hamadhani (d. 1140), but takes its name from that of a latter shaikh, a Tajik mystic named Baha al Din al Naqshbandi (d. 1389). The early Naqshbandi masters were closely linked with the malamatis (literally, 'blameworthy ones'), who rejected all outward show of religiosity, concentrating upon the inner life while engaged in the affairs of the world. One of the order's most distinctive rituals is the 'silent *dhikr*' (*dhikr khafi*) practised alongside the spoken *dhikr*. Naqshbandis say that 'Ali used to read the Quran out loud, while Abu Bakr did so silently. Two Naqshbandi sayings express the order's outlook: 'The exterior is for the world, the interior for God'; and 'Solitude within society'. Like practical Christians, Naqshbandis believe that piety may better be expressed by social activity than by withdrawal from the world – an attitude which separates religious from political commitments, accounting for the order's success in adapting itself to varied political environments, collaborating with worldly powers when necessary, but resisting them by force where circumstances made this seem desirable.

Since the order reserved the 'interior' or mystical life for God, it remained firmly committed to outward Shari'a observance where this was the norm. 'There is no *tariqa* outside the Shari'a' is another Naqshbandi maxim. Hence it had little difficulty in adapting to existing social or religious patterns. It was above all the order of the *'ulama*. In the Ottoman empire Naqshbandi *shaikhs* often doubled as the imams of public mosques, where the *murids* held their *dhikrs*. Although at the height of its influence in Turkey the order controlled a widespread network of *tekkes* (there were more than 50 in Istanbul during the 1880s), separate *zawiya* organizations were never considered essential. Under adverse conditions, however, Naqshbandis do not even consider it necessary to hold regular meetings between the *shaikh* and his *murids*: once the *bay'a*, or oath of allegiance, has been sworn, an esoteric connection is supposed to have been established which transcends physical separation. The *murid* is given a set of *wirds* or daily recitations to make, if necessary in private. Similarly, in the Naqshbandi *silsilas* there are chronological gaps which were presumably bridged by purely spiritual initiations via dreams or visions – for example, the initiation of Abu Yazid al Bistami (d. 879) by Ja'far al Sadiq (d. 765). The three regions where the Naqshbandiya have flourished most successfully are Anatolia, Central Asia and the Indian Subcontinent. In the nineteenth century it enjoyed official Ottoman patronage after the suppression of the Bektashi order, which had distinct Shi'ite leanings. It was in the forefront of opposition to the Tanzimat reforms which sought to modernize and strengthen the Ottoman state bureaucracy in the face of the empire's growing subservience to the European powers. In 1925, after the abolition of the caliphate, two Naqshbandi *shaikhs*, Sa'id and

'Abdullah, led a Kurdish-backed rebellion against Attaturk's secular-izing policies. After Attaturk had abolished the *tariqas* they continued to thrive underground. Recently the order has seen a revival in the so-called 'Nur Sect', or 'Followers of Light', founded by Sa'id Nursi (1873–1960), a Kurdish *shaikh* from eastern Turkey. The Nur group has published a number of popular works on science and technology. After forming an alliance with the National Salvation Party led by Necmettin Erbakan, which stood for a fundamental reversal of secularism and a re-Islamization of Turkish life, the group switched its allegiance to the Justice Party, which was much more closely identified with Turkish nationalism.

In Central Asia the success of the Naqshbandiya among Turkic tribes was evidenced by the popularity as a place of pilgrimage of Baha al Din's mausoleum near Bukhara. From the fifteenth century, Tartar tribesmen had grafted Naqshbandi *silsilas* on to their lineages, which facilitated the spread of the order west into Anatolia and south into India. Members of the order were largely responsible for evangelizing the Uzbeks, who brought it as far east as Xinjiang (Chinese Turkestan). Outside Persia, where a Naqshbandi sub-group led by the self-styled *mahdi* Nurbakhsh (1393–1465) converted to Shi'ism, the leaders of the independent states which arose in the wake of the Mongol conquest favoured the order, honouring its *shaikhs* by building mausoleums for them and *khanqas* for their dervishes. With important centres at Samarkand, Merv, Tashkent and Bukhara, from the eighteenth century the order played a leading part in resisting the Russian advance. In the Caucasus it was the mainspring of resistance to Tsarist attacks, from the time of Shaikh Mansur at the end of the eighteenth century to the final capture in 1859 of the Dagestani leader Shaikh Shamil after a series of campaigns lasting three decades. In Central Asia the order organized the Andijan revolt of 1898; after the Bolshevik revolution it supplied most of the leaders of the Basmachi revolt which the Soviets only finally succeeded in putting down in 1932.

For all its tradition of militancy in Central Asia and the Caucasus, the Naqshbandi order has survived in the Soviet Union precisely because it is well adapted to undertake 'underground' Islamic activity. Whereas the Qadiriya, the other leading order active in the Soviet Union, is liable to attract attention by its ecstatic rituals, the Naqshbandiya offers a form of private religious activity which successfully escapes official attention. As a whole the *tariqas* offer a 'parallel religion' to the official Islam backed by the Soviet authorities, with its carefully chosen, party-approved *mullahs* and licensed mosques. Since only the chosen few are given exit visas to attend the Hajj, local pilgrimages to saintly tombs are encouraged by the 'alternative' religious leadership as a way of keeping religion alive. Although the facts are necessarily hard to come by, there is evidence that 'alternative' or 'parallel' Islam is as alive in the Soviet Union as such 'unofficial' and heterodox versions of Christianity as Baptism and Pentecostalism. Thus, according to recent (1979) official figures, about half the 'believing' Muslims (estimated at between 50 and 60 per cent of the population) in the autonomous Caucasian republic of Chechens and Ingushes belong to the *tariqas*, giving the latter a membership of between 150,000 and 180,000 (compared with about 60,000 in the same territory before the Revolution). In Azerbaijan (1977) official Islam counted 16 mosques, compared with an estimated 300 clandestine ones.

Although Soviet officialdom periodically inveighs against the *tariqas* as 'anti-Soviet, anti-socialist reactionary fanatics', there are few signs that their allegiances are diminishing, or that the measures taken by the authorities to counter their appeal are particularly successful. As the least visible of the orders, the Naqshbandiya is certainly the most difficult to persecute. A member of the order has explained to this writer that a *wird* can easily be said without a rosary, by using an ordinary wristwatch as a counter. Secret gatherings, consisting of as few as three persons, can be arranged by word of mouth. Where *shaikhs* or their deputies have only a handful of followers each, secrecy and anonymity are fairly easily maintained, especially since the cultural solidarity of Muslims enables them to protect themselves against Russian infiltration. (Inter-marriage, even in metropolitan areas, is relatively rare, and national feeling against 'Great Russian chauvinism' is still a factor in promoting Muslim solidarity where religious opposition to official Soviet atheism is absent.) Despite the order's involvement in the Basmachi revolts, members of the Naqshbandiya are said to have made a practice of joining the Communist Party since the 1920s, possibly with the aim of shielding their membership. Naqshbandi sources maintain that there are also members of the order in the Komsomol (Communist Youth) and the KGB. While for obvious reasons it is impossible to prove or disprove such claims, they are not implausible given the order's tradition of collaborating with state power whenever circumstances seemed to make this desirable.[50]

The Naqshbandiya's reformist influence and activities have been most extensive in the Indian Subcontinent. Here, as in Africa, the gradual proselytizing undertaken by other Sufi orders had led to the development of forms of religious syncretism in which Islamic practices had become intermixed with local Hindu and Vedantic cults and beliefs. Hinduism, however, is far removed from African paganism. Though 'polytheistic' in the sense of recognizing a multiplicity of forms through which the divine may manifest itself, it belongs to the tradition of an advanced and ancient civilization upheld by a literate and highly cultivated caste of Brahmins whose knowledge of the world and its arts was in no manner inferior to that of their Muslim conquerors. In terms of the prevailing values underpinning the two systems, a clash was inevitable. Whereas the thrust of Islam is towards social equality and religious conformity, that of Hinduism is towards social hierarchy and 'spiritual anarchism'.[51] Whereas the logic of Islam, as of other western monotheisms, propels it towards an intolerant rejection of alternative formulations of religious truth, the trend in Hinduism has been towards a universal acceptance of other faiths within a hierarchical order which links, however tenuously, the rarified speculations of the intellectuals with the superstitious fetishism of the masses.

Despite this fundamental incompatibility between Islamic and Hindu world-views, the Mughal ruler Akbar (1556–1605) made a serious effort to harmonize relations between his Muslim and Hindu subjects by according to the latter a degree of toleration that placed them on a level of equality with the dominant Muslims. Proclaiming his own right as an absolute *mujtahid*, he set about changing those aspects of the Shari'a which conflicted with the rights of his Hindu subjects. Thus Hindus were exempted from paying the *jizya* tax which symbolized their status as *dhimmis*; disabilities impeding their employment in the army and bureaucracy were removed. More controversially, Akbar forbade Hindu girls from converting to Islam in order to marry Muslim men, thereby extending to Hindu families the same protection enjoyed by Muslim families against their daughters marrying out of the faith. In an effort to further standardize social practice, Akbar forbade Muslims to marry their first cousins and discouraged child-marriage among Hindus. He opposed slavery and tried to abolish *suttee* – the practice whereby high-caste Hindu widows were burnt along with their dead husbands – and gave permission for them to re-marry, like Muslim widows. Eventually he and his entourage became vegetarians, partly, no doubt, in order to discourage cow-slaughter and so avoid offence to Hindus.

In extending a religious toleration that increased the power of the state by strengthening the allegiance of his non-Muslim subjects, Akbar was drawing upon several traditions within Indian Islam. Under Hindu rulers the Indus and Ganges regions had long been a haven for religious refugees, including Jacobite Christians, Jews, Zoroastrians and Isma'ilis, who enjoyed relative freedom from persecution within the Brahmanic caste-system. After the Muslim conquest forcible conversion was rare, as was active proselytizing. Lower-caste Hindus tended to be naturally drawn to Islam, since conversion enabled them to escape their degraded status and acquire education and employment in government service. Inter-marriage between Muslim men and Hindu women had further encouraged natural conversion, though it also brought Hindu cultural influences into Muslim families. Of those who undertook conversions, the Sufi *pirs* were by far the most successful. Acquiring reputations as individual holy men, they were closer to the illiterate classes than the *'ulama* and fitted inconspicuously into local traditions. More decisively, they were tolerantly prepared to accept non-Muslims as probationary disciples, gradually absorbing them into Islam by personal precept.

This contact between the two religious traditions produced not only syncretic developments at a popular level, but a theosophical synthesis at the highest. Kabir (1440–1518), an outstanding popular teacher and poet, rejected the rituals of both religions, proclaiming a universalist theism that transcended both of them. His disciple Guru Nanak (1469 –1539), under the combined influence of Kabir's ideas and Sufic and Hindu theosophy, launched the Sikh movement in the Punjab, which, from being a strict if eclectic monotheism, developed into a separate religious community affirming a predominantly anti-Muslim group identity.

The Emperor Akbar patronized both Sikh *gurus* and Sufi *pirs*, especially those of the Indian Chisti order, who were notable for their universalist tendencies. But court ritual departed increasingly from Indian Sunni tradition. In 1581 he promulgated his famous 'Divine Faith' (*Din Illahi*), a monotheism based on reason and asceticism. Imitation (*taqlid*), the unreasoned following of traditional exegesis and *fiqh*, was condemned. Quranic concepts such as devils, jinns and angels were given rationalist interpretations. Sensuality, lust, misappropriation and deceit were prohibited. The Sufi virtues of piety, devotion, gentleness and 'yearning for

God' were extolled. The cult, which amounted to an aristocratic court *tariqa* with the Emperor as its *shaikh*, combined Ibn al 'Arabi's mystic doctrines with courtly flattery. Despite his lack of formal education, Akbar seems to have had a genuine concern for the disinterested pursuit of religious and philosophical truth and an intelligent awareness of his duty as head of a multi-religious empire. He was a man far ahead of his time.

Inevitably there were both Muslims and Hindus who found Akbar's reforms intolerable and sought to retreat into their separate traditions. The Shari'a norms often ran directly counter to the pluralistic traditions embedded in Indian society. A Muslim ruler could, like Akbar, achieve a certain balance by abandoning the Shari'a's claim to universality, reducing it to one form of religious observance among others. But by so doing he reduced his Hindu and Muslim subjects to a common level, depriving the latter of their special sense of historic mission as the final and most faithful bearers of God's messages to mankind. No rarefied theosophical speculation, no spiritual despotism, however morally earnest or enlightened, could compensate for the sense of betrayal felt by ordinary Muslims at the cultural fusion implied by Akbar's reforms. Given the traditions into which the Shari'a had crystallized by the sixteenth century, the reaction that followed was inevitable.

The Naqshbandi order became the spearhead of this reaction. A relative late-comer to India, it had gained a foothold at court during the latter years of Akbar's reign, through the influence of one of its *shaikhs*, Khawaja Baqi-billah. It gathered momentum during the reign of Akbar's successor, Jahangir (1605–27), under the leadership of Baqi-billah's disciple Shaikh Ahmad Sirhindi. At the beginning of his career Sirhindi showed signs of a mystical megalomania not unlike that of Akbar, claiming to have surpassed Abu Bakr himself in gnosis and to have elevated the 'reality of Muhammad' to the 'stage of Abraham'. However, the extravagance of Sirhindi's claims earned him a reprimand from Baqi-billah – and a salutory spell in prison from the Emperor. On his release the *shaikh* appeared somewhat chastened, and set about formulating a role for India's Muslims leading to communalism and ultimately to separatism.

Sirhindi's campaign had ideological and social dimensions. As a Naqshbandi reformer, or *mujaddid*, he attacked those esoteric aspects of Sufism which he saw as facilitating the mixing of Islam and Hinduism at both aristocratic and popular levels. Thus he attacked Ibn al 'Arabi's ontological monism (*wahda al wujud*, 'unity of being') or, rather, the versions of it transmitted by Indian commentators believing, rightly enough, that it could be harmonized with Hindu pantheism. The idea that God alone is existent makes physical objects into mere 'flashes' or 'appearances' which can be worshipped as manifestations of the divine will. In Sirhindi's view, if such syncretic possibilities remained unchecked, Indian Islam must inevitably dissolve into the polymorphous structures of Hindu society. The *tariqas*, which were largely responsible for popularizing Ibn al 'Arabi's doctrines, would have to be firmly subordinated to the Shari'a – in line with the Naqshbandiya's well-known principles. Like Ghazali, Sirhindi believed that the mystic experience must be made to conform with the *zahir*, or outward forms, of Islam if they were not to become contaminated by heterodoxy or disintegrate into personal whimsicality. The alternative theosophy he proposed has been described as 'phenomenological monism' (*wahda al shuhud* or 'unity of witness'), a doctrine which, while seemingly little different from Ibn al 'Arabi's, preserves an absolute and unbridgeable distinction between the Creator and his creations. Reality is not (as in Ibn al 'Arabi) the mirror through which God contemplates himself: rather, it is his reflection, which must never be confused with the original. This distinction, however subtle, opened the way for a complete re-affirmation of the Sh'ari'a: the *'ulama* must be supreme, both in the sphere of outward observance and in that of profound inner speculation.

The supremacy of the *'ulama* over the *pirs* had fundamental consequences for the community: Islam and *kufr* (disbelief), which in the Indian context meant Hinduism, were rigidly, irreconcilably opposed to each other. The honour and security of Islam were dependent upon the humiliation of the unbelievers. Whoever held infidels in affection and esteem or kept company with them, dishonoured his own religion. A good Muslim was expected to avoid contact with non-believers even in daily business.[52]

The influence of Sirhindi and his successors has been incalculable. As Ahmed remarks, it checked the process of Indian Islam's disintegration into syncretic heresies, and gave it 'the rigid and conservative stamp' it bears today. The intellectual leaders of modern Muslim India, including Sayyid Ahmed Khan, Muhammad Iqbal and Abu'l Ala Mawdudi were all, in various ways, indebted to Sirhindi.

The immediate result of Sirhindi's campaign was, however, to push the community towards communalism. By insisting on the irreconcilable character of the two faiths, and that the Muslims must at all costs preserve themselves from contamination by Hinduism, he abandoned Islamic universalism for Shari'a particularism. With Muslims a numerical minority, this was to prove a disastrous ideological base for a multi-confessional empire. When Sirhindi's teaching had finally borne fruit, becoming official policy during the reign of Aurungzeb (1658–1707), it provoked numerous Hindu revolts, bringing Muslim power to the verge of extinction and opening the way to British intervention and, ulti-mately, to colonial rule.

Sirhindi's intellectual successor, Shah Wali Ullah of Delhi (1703–62), was another Naqshbandi *shaikh* who continued the work of bringing Sufism firmly into line with the Shari'a. The son of a Naqshbandi *mujaddid*, he retained a qualified admiration for Ibn al 'Arabi. Wali Ullah was a contemporary of Muhammad ibn 'Abd al Wahhab, and there are definite similarities between them. Both sought to discard the super-structure of the *fiqh* and to return directly to the Quran and the Sunna as advocated by Ibn Taimiya. Both stressed the need for constant *ijtihad*. However, whereas Ibn 'Abd al Wahhab's fundamentalism, applied in the relatively homogeneous environment of Arabian Islam, led to a Khariji-style division of the world into 'us' against 'them', identifying all who failed to conform to Wahhabi tenets as 'infidels' liable to attack, Wali Ullah's occurred in a world where non-Muslims were numerous and powerful. So, while maintaining the momentum of the Naqshbandi campaign against syncretism, he took a much broader view of Islamic allegiance. In theosophy he sought to reconcile Sirhindi's phenomeno-logical monism with the ontological monism of Ibn al 'Arabi; in theology he tried to blur the distinction between the Mu'tazili and Ash'ari posi-tions; in Shari'a, he sought to harmonize the differences between the four *madhhabs*, taking the tolerant view (diametrically opposed to the narrow puritanism of the Wahhabis) that anyone who had once pro-fessed themselves a Muslim remained one, whatever their sins or failings. Confusing the two movements, the British described Shah Wali Ullah and his supporters as 'Wahhabis'.

As an Indian, Shah Wali Ullah had to develop a much more sophisti-cated and less literalistic understanding of the scriptural imperatives than that of his Arabian counterpart. Whereas for the Najdi *'alim*, *ijtihad* meant determining the law by referring back to sources in his own language and formed in the same cultural milieu, for the Indian it involved a striving to discover the Shari'a's underlying purpose and intentions. Najdi fundamentalism involved a restoration, pure and simple, of the supposed conditions of the Medinese caliphate – a restoration which still seemed feasible in the eighteenth century, since in the Arabian heartland things had changed little since the days of the Prophet, while the *jahiliya* which the Wahhabis discerned around them corresponded closely to the descriptions in the Quran and *hadiths*. In the crumbling feudalism of the Mughal decline in India, fundamentalism meant a search beyond the letter of the Shari'a to its spirit – an attitude of mind that led, not only to the reactionary archaism of thinkers like Abu'l Ala Maududi, but to the progressive modernism of Sayyid Ahmed Khan and Muhammad Iqbal, and to those other modernists who saw, and continue to see, in *ijtihad* Islam's necessary response to growth and change in human society.

The seeming paradox that both progressive and reactionary modernist movements in Islam draw upon the 'fundamentalism' of Ibn Taimiya is grasped more clearly if the different environments of his two leading apostles, Ibn 'Abd al Wahhab and Shah Wali Ullah, are taken into account. The latter's position is only deceptively similar to the former's. In spirit, as in doctrine, Wali Ullah is closer to the Berber 'fundamentalism' of Ibn Tumart. Like Ibn Tumart, Wali Ullah opposed the *'ulama* of his day, recognizing that their knowledge of Arabic gave them a monopoly of access to the scriptures and hence of religious authority and social power (making them, in the Indian context, 'Muslim Brahmins'). Again like Ibn Tumart, Wali Ullah took the radical step, against the opposition of the *'ulama*, of translating the Quran into the vernacular tongue – in his case Persian, the language of the average educated Indian Muslim. In 1743 he founded his own school for the study of the Quran and *hadiths*. Two of his sons furthered his religious propaganda by making translations of the Quran into Urdu, the demotic language of Indian's Muslims.

With the collapse of Muslim power and the growing encroachment of the British and the Hindu Marathas, Wali Ullah's Naqshbandi reformism developed into militancy, culminating in the *jihad* launched against the Sikhs by Sayyid Ahmed Barelvi in 1831. This was a crucial development for Indian Islam, for it heralded the end of communalism: Barelvi's attempted *hijra* from infidel British rule to the *dar al Islam* he tried to create on the Afghan frontier foreshadowed the massive and bloody *hijra* in which half a million people were to die in 1948.

Barelvi was a disciple of Wali Ullah's son and successor, Abdul Aziz.

Like his predecessors, he militated against Hindu accretions in certain ritual practices, while showing considerable tolerance towards different religious and theological currents within the Islamic fold. Under Barelvi's leadership, however, the reform movement moved away from its institutional connections with the Naqshbandiya, merging its own *tariqa* with those of the other leading Indian orders – the Qadiris and the Chistis – and subsuming them all within renovated Shari'a orthodoxy which Barelvi called the Tariqa-i-Muhammadiya, the Way of Muhammad. This movement, a forerunner of such twentieth-century reform movements as the Muhammadiya movement of Indonesia, founded in 1907, or the Muslim Brotherhood of Egypt, founded in 1928, combined Sufic discipline with Shari'a norms, as it were making the Sunna into a *tariqa*. In a non-Arab milieu where the majority of people had no access to the scriptures, the *tariqa* structure, with its authoritarian leadership and organized self-discipline, provided the means by which Shari'a orthodoxy protected itself against the continued encroachments of Hindu society. In 1826, following the hallowed path from 'Mecca' to 'Medina', Barelvi tried to emigrate to a region along the North-West Frontier where he could found an Islamic state on liberated territory. Unfortunately this region, though inhabited by Muslims, was under Sikh control. Barelvi's *jihad* against the Sikhs was a dismal failure: the Pathan tribesmen on whose support he depended proved unreliable, especially when Barelvi tried to impose Islamic taxes on them, and deserted in large numbers. He was finally defeated and killed by the Sikhs at Balakot in 1831. The Tariqa-i-Muhammadiya, however, remained a militant Islamic movement in India, and its supporters played a leading part in the great rebellion of 1857. Thereafter they remained a thorn in the side of the British Raj, not being finally suppressed until the 1880s.

In the Far East, the Naqshbandi order, expanded by pilgrims returning from the Hajj, played a prominent part in stimulating resistance to the Dutch in Acheh (Northern Sumatra) and contributed to Muslim militancy in the Southern Philippines. In China it was instrumental in creating the so-called 'New Sect', a movement which led to an unprecedented assertion of Muslim identity in a country where the community had long become assimilated, culturally and politically. Though scholars are still in dispute about many of the details surrounding the New Sect, their original Naqshbandi provenance is not in doubt.

Islam was originally established in China by Arab, Persian and Indian traders. As early as the eighth century there were Muslim communities with their own *qadis* in Canton and Chuan-chow (named Zeitun by the Muslims). In addition to these coastal communities, subsequent centuries saw a substantial influx of Muslim immigrants from Central Asia, including bureaucrats and soldiers imported by the Mongol Yuan dynasty (1279–1368). The social and political pressures on Chinese Muslims led to a superficial acculturation. Having become ethnically Chinese (through intermarriage with Chinese women), the Muslims adopted the Chinese language and Chinese dress. Mosques were built in the style of pagodas, the muezzin making the call to prayer inside the courtyard. Knowledge of Arabic was confined to the imams or 'akhunds', although as with other non-Arabs, the use of Arabic greetings became a Muslim shibboleth. Nevertheless, observance of ritual and dietary laws ensured that the Chinese Muslims retained a separate identity as a religious community. The Hui, as they came to be known, were regarded as foreigners by the majority of Han Chinese. The situation persists to this day, Muslims being recognized as a national minority with their own 'autonomous region' in Ning-Hsia (Kansu), though they are widely distributed elsewhere. Before the emergence of the New Sect the Hui attitude was summed up in the phrase, 'Muslims indoors, Chinese outdoors'.

The Islamic revival in China dates from the late eighteenth century, when a number of Naqshbandi *shaikhs* led a *jihad* against the Chinese Emperor from Khokand (Uzbekistan) and found support among the Muslims in Xinjiang. In response to the sinicizing policies of the Manchu emperors in the nineteenth century, the Chinese Muslims became increasingly assertive of their identity. The New Sect appeared after the return from the Hajj of Ma Ming Hsin, a *shaikh* of the Jahriya branch of the Naqshbandiya, which traces its spiritual descent from 'Ali and practises the vocal *dhikr*, which increases group self-consciousness and solidarity. The New Sect and its affiliated branches appear to have been behind every Muslim rebellion in China down to the present century, including two major revolts which shook the Manchu empire. The first, led by Ma Hua Lung, lasted from 1862 to 1877 and affected most of Kansu and Shensi provinces; the second, led by Tu Wen Hsin, who took the Muslim name Sultan Suleiman, established a Muslim state which ruled half the province of Yunan. One of the leaders of the Yunan rebellion, Ma Te-hsin, was the first scholar to translate the Quran into Chinese.[53]

*

The record of the Naqshbandiya, combining inner spirituality with an outward, political, posture ranging from acquiescence to militancy, according to circumstances, should warn us against characterizing Sufism as a purely mystical or quietist dimension of Islam. The *tariqa* organization, whether built into a kinship system or acting as a kinship surrogate, could be transformed from contemplative to militant activity without change to the structure. The ties of allegiance between a *shaikh* and his *murids*, based on rigorous discipline and absolute obedience, could cement group loyalties as firmly as the *'asabiya* of the tribesfolk. The group's ideology – whether focused on extreme Shari'a rectitude like that of the Wahhabi Ikhwan, or tending towards mahdism as in the movements of Ibn Tumart and Muhammad Ahmad in the Sudan, almost invariably had a Khariji aspect, in that nominal or cultural Muslims tended to be anathematized as infidels. The revolutionary potential of such movements sprang from the underlying psychological processes. The individual Sufi's rejection of the 'world' is a necessary prelude to his attempt to transform it, while the sense of brotherhood and comradeship fostered by the common ritual lends him the courage to wage the *jihad*. Indeed, the personal or 'inner' *jihad* against evil furnishes the preparation for the external *jihad* which aims to destroy evil in the world.

The revitalizing force of Islamic spirituality is something that will always find political expression when the occasion demands it. Like all other central Islamic traditions, its legitimacy derives from the Muhammadan paradigm. The examples contained in this chapter should have made it clear that this latent militancy can be directed against any social or political order perceived as threatening the wellbeing of the community. From the eighteenth century, however, the danger to Islamdom appeared to be coming increasingly from Europe, which, because of its overwhelming economic power and military superiority, demanded a much more radical response than a spiritual renewal or reaffirmation of Islamic militancy. Before the Muslims could hope to fight off the European threat with any chance of success they would have to undergo an intellectual revolution that would enable them to re-state the message of Islam in modern terms. This was the problem that would exercise the most fertile Muslim minds from the mid nineteenth century, when the hegemony of western civilization seemed most assured.

7 ✤ Challenge from the West

The casual visitor to modern Cairo will at first sight see little to distinguish it from other cities which have succumbed to the utilitarian ugliness of the twentieth century. Apart from the river Nile, whose gleaming surface cuts a shimmering swathe through the geometrical patterning of blocks and tenements, it is a noisy, dirty, smelly place, a cacophanous confusion of pedestrians and automobiles, where the sensible tourist usually remains in the cool of a hotel lobby, only venturing out in an air-conditioned bus to visit the dozen or so sights recommended by the tour operators. One of the places on the tourist agenda is the bazaar area known as the Khan al Khalili: a covered *suq* or traditional Arab market, where enterprising shopkeepers offer hand-crafted souvenirs for several times the price they fetch a few streets away. The customary bargaining rituals, according to which buyers and sellers arrive at an agreed and fair price, depend, of course, on a common knowledge of the market – something the tourist cannot hope to acquire in three days. The foreigner who wants to pick up a good bargain must take along an Egyptian companion.

Visitors who are not easily put off by the importunities of shopkeepers and who keep calm in the face of endless demands for *bakshish* from small children may soon begin to notice some interesting paradoxes. In the older quarters of the city around the Khan al Khalili, where most of the men still wear the *galabiya* and women always cover their heads if not their faces, the attitude people display towards foreigners conveys a confusing mixture of friendliness and hostility. At one moment you can be inundated with offers of tea and coffee, and plied with friendly questions about your national origins and family situation; at the next you sense an undertone of menace as someone collides with you in a way that is obviously not accidental, or explodes into irrational fury if you take a perfectly innocuous photograph. The one response that seems to be lacking is the normal urban indifference of the western city: it seems impossible, if you are a foreigner, to avoid being noticed. This applies especially to females. European women invariably complain about being molested – sometimes in a manner so crude that indignation must give way to Rabelaisian laughter. Yet to be treated like a whore seems extraordinary in a society that sets such store by the chastity of women and the hospitality accorded to strangers. Sometimes, of course, the behaviour of foreign women invites the approaches of which they frequently complain. I myself once watched, with fascinated embarrassment, as a tall young woman, possibly American, bra-less and clad in a sleeveless shirt, wearing shorts which exposed the upper portions of her thighs, purchased some mangoes from a stallholder, a dignified young peasant clad in the traditional *galabiya*. This woman – I reflected – is sexually assaulting the man, though she may not realize it. Her garb was a systematic violation of all the sartorial codes governing male–female relations in traditional Islamic society. Only the extreme boorishness of super-power arrogance could produce such a display as this. The mango-seller remained resentfully polite – this was Maadi, a residential suburb much patronized by foreign families, and it would be more than his livelihood was worth to create a fuss here. But in less affluent parts of the city this woman would have encountered the outright hostility her appearance unwittingly invited.

Such extreme gaucherie is, however, still the exception, even in countries like Egypt that have come under increasing American political and cultural influence. If European women find themselves molested, it is not because of the behaviour of a few of their ignorant or foolish peers, but rather because they are seen to conform to stereotypes derived mainly from cinema and advertising, stereotypes full of potent images of European female sexuality. Even where local laws forbid female display in advertising and severely censor movies available for cinema and television, young men returning from the fleshpots of London or Paris, and the growing business of smuggling 'blue' video-tapes for private consumption, ensure that the stereotypes retain their sharpness. The response among the unsophisticated, who know little of European customs and habits, is an almost equal mixture of attraction and repulsion: fascination at the sexual opportunities supposedly on offer, repulsion at the thought that such delectable temptations have so obviously been planted by the devil.

Encounters of this kind, multiplied a thousandfold, are the raw data which make up the tortuous and often agonized discourse of relations between Muslim societies and the West, a discourse that has ebbed and flowed over the past century with the flux and reflux of Western political and cultural hegemony. Because of its intimate and personal character, the arena of sexuality is one of its most emotive battlegrounds. Few things have traditionally more incensed the defenders of *dar al Islam* than the thought that the corruption and promiscuity they perceive in European society may spread to their own, undermining and ultimately destroying the cherished family values which hold them together. But there are many other areas of mutual incomprehension and conflict. Militarily, politically, economically and culturally dominant, the West has come to pose first a challenge and finally a threat to the Islamic world. Since the end of the eighteenth century the problem of the dominant West, whether perceived as Christian, secular or atheist, has been the major preoccupation of thinkers and activists, and indeed of all those Muslims who have tried to work out the relevance of the Quranic message for their generation. The West – like its women – has been a simultaneous source of attraction and repulsion: admiration for its institutions and for the technical prowess that has enabled so many of its citizens to enjoy undreamed-of freedoms and opportunities; disgust at its vulgarity, its seeming callousness and spiritual emptiness, combined with a deep sense of unease that Allah, whose Way has been shown for all mankind in the Holy Quran and the Sunna, should have permitted infidels to violate all but the innermost chambers of the House of Islam. Unlike Christianity, which experienced persecution during the first three and a half centuries of its existence and learned to survive, even to flourish, under non-Christian governments, Islam is a religion 'programmed for victory'. Broadcast to the world on the triumphant wings of the Arab conquest, its formative period occurred at a time when its political hegemony seemed assured. The experience of defeat and failure *vis-à-vis* non-Muslims (if we except the temporary set-back of the Battle of Uhud) was something for which no Prophetic precedents were available: even the Imams of the Prophet's House, whose Christ-like betrayals and sufferings nurtured the Shi'ite faith, had been persecuted by nominally Muslim rulers.

Muslim defeat at the hands of Christian powers had occurred long before the nineteenth century, when most of *dar al Islam* came under European domination. Sicily and Spain had been lost to the West, while from the sixteenth century the Russian state began to expand over Muslim lands in Central Asia and the Caucasus. Arguably, a more serious threat to Islamic civilization came from the Mongol invaders, who finally destroyed the 'Abbasid caliphate and disrupted the eastern trade routes. But in the west neither the Mamluk state in Egypt nor the Ottoman empire based in Anatolia, which finally took Constantinople in 1453, was able to arrest the long process of Islamic decline *vis-à-vis* the Christian powers, which reached its nadir during the first quarter of the twentieth century. There were economic and political reasons for this decline, some of which have a religious dimension. In Western Asia the destruction of Baghdad by the Mongols facilitated the development of the Sufi *tariqas*, fostering a spiritualizing and anti-rationalist approach to Islam in what had once been the centre of the empire. During the same period in Europe the hegemony of the Church was coming under increasing pressure from the forces of humanistic rationalism which culminated in Protestantism and the Enlightenment. In Islam the tyranny of custom enshrined in *fiqh* created a climate hostile to technical innovation. At a time when Europeans were transforming their economies by means of such revolutionary devices as heavy-wheeled ploughs and horseshoes, substantially increasing the agricultural surplus available for investment, Middle Eastern societies were exhibiting a lack of mechanical inventiveness within a much more conservative 'policy of provision'. Agriculture, always more limited because of the aridity of the region, declined as insecure rulers devoted less and less energy to such vital areas of investment as irrigation. Whereas in the West the Roman law which came back into use after a long period of eclipse from the thirteenth century upheld the legal status of corporate groups such as urban guilds and private companies, fostering the development of a vigorous, ambitious and self-confident bourgeoisie, in the Muslim world both the rulers and the Shari'a itself prevented the emergence of independent, expanding centres of power within society.

Inevitably the rise of a dynamic western Europe in conflict with a stagnating Muslim world created a situation in which most of *dar al Islam* came under Europe's economic and political domination. According to a famous, if apocryphal, irony, it was one of the greatest Arab seafarers, Ibn Majid, who piloted Vasco da Gama's squadron in the Indian Ocean, after the latter had rounded the Cape of Good Hope in 1498, thereby ending the Muslim monopoly over the monsoon trade routes which had contributed so much to the wealth of Baghdad and later of Cairo. After capturing Hormuz in 1508 the Portuguese were strong enough to impose restrictions on traders from the Gulf to the Malabar coast.

In India the British expanded their influence following the death of Aurungzeb and the weakening of the Mughal empire in the Maratha wars. By 1818 their hegemony extended, by either conquest or treaty, over most of the Subcontinent, except for the Indus valley. In 1857, after the collapse of the 'Mutiny' led by Indians still loyal to him, the British deposed the last Mughal ruler. Nineteen years later the British Prime Minister Benjamin Disraeli provided Queen Victoria with a new title, 'Empress of India', thereby making members of the world's most numerous Muslim community nominal subjects of a Christian woman ruler. British naval power, expanding westwards from India, took in the varied shaikhdoms of the Persian Gulf, where local rulers were obliged to sign treaties for the suppression of slavery and 'piracy'; in 1839 the British occupied the Port of Aden in Southern Yemen in order to create a coaling station for future fleets.

In the Far East the Dutch replaced the Portuguese as the leading colonial power following the founding of Batavia (Djkarta) in 1619. After the Javanese War of 1825–30 they instituted increasingly direct forms of colonial rule both in Indonesia and in the Malaysian archipelago which they opened up, in competition with the British, for the production of cash crops for the European market. As in tropical Africa, the improved communications led to an expansion of Islamic activity and increasing Shari'a orthodoxy which militated against both foreign rule and local Hinduistic syncretism.

In Central Asia the Russians began displacing Muslim peasants from the Volga basin from the sixteenth century. By 1813 they had taken over most of the Caucasus; by the 1870s they had conquered most of Turkestan, leaving a handful of autonomous sultanates, including Bukhara, surrounded by Russian territory. In their wars with the Ottoman Empire they broke the Turkish monopoly in the Black Sea, annexing territory around the Sea of Azov. In the 1870s they would have gained complete control of the Dardanelles, had other European powers not intervened on behalf of the Sultan.

At the western end of the Muslim world, France began its expansion into the Maghreb by occupying Algiers in 1830 and gradually extending its control over the Sahara. In 1881 it occupied Tunisia, establishing a protectorate there. By 1911 the Sultan of Morocco, the only independent ruler left in the Maghreb, was too weak to resist French 'help' in asserting his authority over the 'lands of insolence' in exchange for protected status. Spain responded to this move by occupying a different part of Morocco allotted to it under a treaty in 1904. In 1911 Italy decided to conquer the remaining Ottoman territories west of Egypt. Following the defeat of the Ottoman Empire in the First World War, Britain, which already had a protectorate in Egypt, established Mandates in Palestine (with specific provision for Jewish colonization), Transjordan and Iraq. France likewise administered mandated territories in Syria and Lebanon. By 1920 the only independent Muslim states remaining were Turkey, Persia, Afghanistan, Central Arabia (Najd), the Hejaz and northern Yemen. The rest of *dar al Islam* was either under direct colonial rule or under some form of internationally recognized European 'protection'.

Everywhere the Europeans established two new principles: the freezing of boundaries and the freezing of dynasties. They insisted on demarcating or making permanent territorial boundaries which had been either non-existent or constantly shifting. Henceforth it was to be clear which government would be held responsible for which piece of territory. At the same time they insisted on the principle of dynastic succession (though not necessarily according to the European system of primogeniture): legitimacy of succession would prevent the disruptive disputes that inevitably followed the departure of a traditional ruler. The effect of both these changes was to increase imperialist control. In order to control the marginal lands for which they were now being held responsible, the newly legitimized dynastic rulers were often obliged to accept European help. With the Khaldunian 'merry-go-round' halted, the Muslim countries were even less well equipped than before to resist European encroachments by throwing up new and vigorous military leaderships.

In the Middle Eastern heartlands, European power at first showed itself indirectly, by stimulating the governments of Egypt and the Ottoman Empire to enact the reforms that would enable them to ward off foreign domination. However, the economic measures which accompanied such reforms helped draw these countries into the net of an imperialist system which, in Egypt's case, brought about the very threat it had been intended to avoid – British military intervention. Throughout the region the growing economic influence of local Christian, Jewish and foreign-protected minorities allied to the Europeans inhibited the development of strong national bourgeoisies capable of resisting foreign hegemony. The protected status of *dhimmis* under the Shari'a, consti-tutionally endorsed by the Ottoman *millet* system, according to which Christians and Jews enjoyed autonomous status within the empire, became the Trojan Horse by means of which foreign cultural and economic influence penetrated the region, undermining the relatively homogeneous social system that had always coexisted with military rule and religious plurality.

In 1798 Bonaparte's brief and ill-fated expedition to Egypt brought about the collapse of the Mamluk system which was replaced from 1805 by the new-style patrimonial autocracy of Muhammad 'Ali, a Turk from Albania who ruled independently of the Ottoman sultan except in name. Having destroyed the last vestiges of Mamluk power by massacring most of their *amirs*, he took direct control over the lands they had enjoyed as tax farmers of the Ottoman sultan, converting the whole of Egypt into one vast personal estate. The new model Egyptian army, led by the Turkish–Mamluk officer class, enabled Muhammad (Mehmet) 'Ali and his successors Sa'id (1848–63) and Isma'il (1863–79) to occupy Syria and the Hejaz and to conquer the Nilotic Sudan as far as the Equator. The achievements of his dynasty included the building of the Suez Canal (completed in 1869), the expansion of agriculture through the construc-tion of new irrigation canals, the progressive control of the Nile's annual flooding by the construction of dams and barrages, and the building upon land thus reclaimed of the new, 'Paris-style' Cairo, a city of fine villas and broad boulevards thoroughly fit for Europeans. These suc-cesses, however impressive, only served in the end to accelerate the country's integration into a world economic system dominated by the imperialists. If the francophile Isma'il's dream of 'making Egypt part of Europe' was indeed realized, it was at the price of making it a European colony. In the short term, Muhammad 'Ali's policy of turning over vast tracts of land to the production of long-staple cotton for the mills of Lancashire yielded new, unprecedented wealth, some of which even filtered down to the wretched *fallah*, who ate meat and bought himself a Nubian concubine. In the long term it proved disastrous, as the collapse of cotton prices following the end of the American Civil War led to bankruptcy and British financial, administrative and, from 1882, military control.

The Ottoman Empire itself scarcely fared better. Faced with the loss of its Christian Balkan provinces, where the nationalist mood had been fanned by western influence throughout the nineteenth century, Sultan

Abdul Mejid (1839–61) enacted a series of reforms collectively known as the Tanzimat (literally, 'regulations'). They built upon changes already imposed by his predecessor Mahmud (1808–39), including the wearing of the fez, a truncated, cone-shaped red felt hat, in place of the turbans and other miscellaneous headgear that had hitherto distinguished *'ulama* from dervishes, merchants from *amirs*, Christians and Jews from Muslims. The Tanzimat gave legal force to the sartorial equality already enjoined on Ottoman citizens. Individuals of all faiths were now to be treated equally before the law. This was a change of doubtful popularity, since Muslims resented losing their superior status, while native-born *dhimmis* had long learned to turn their notionally inferior status to economic and political advantage. Worse still, the foreign *dhimmis* – that is, the Europeans – were exempted from these changes, being entitled under the Capitulations previously signed with various European governments, to have their cases judged before their own consular courts. Naturally the local Christians and Jews, as well as members of other minorities, began to look to their foreign co-religionists for protection. Thus the Tanzimat, in the name of legal rationalization, abandoned one of the cardinal practices of the Shari'a and accelerated that community of interest between the religious minorities and foreign powers which led, among other disastrous events, to the Crimean War (1854–6) and the massacres of Syrian and Lebanese Christians in the 1860s. Plans to establish a secular university foundered on the opposition of the *'ulama;* the foreign missionary schools and colleges originally established to serve the needs of the local *dhimmis* and foreign communities became increasingly popular with the Muslim upper and middle classes. With missionary schools the only available source of modern education, modernization became equated with western cultural penetration and upper-class privilege, both of which were identified in the eyes of the pious populists with a 'Christian' offensive against Islam.

The encroachments of Christian power into *dar al Islam* met with a variety of responses, both military and ideological. Briefly they may be characterized as the archaic, the reformist, the modernist and the neo-traditionalist. The archaic response, exemplified by the revolts of 'Abd al Qadir, the Mahdi Muhammad Ahmad, Dipa Negra and many others, usually occurred in regions far from the metropolitan centres where the classic *hijra–jihad* scenario could be enacted. Modernism may be defined as the response of those who basically accepted the new order introduced by the Europeans and sought to reform or rationalize Islamic thought and institutions in order to bring them into line with the new reality – the point of departure being that present reality. Reformism was more the attitude of those who sought to strengthen Islam by internal reforms, in order to enable it to assert itself more effectively against what they still regarded as an alien and hostile civilization – here the point of departure was the idea of Islam. Whereas the modernist sought to clothe modernity in Islamic dress by proving that the Quran properly understood was no barrier to progress, the reformist sought to provide the Islam he knew and loved with modern clothes, believing that those aspects of modern or Western reality which seemed incompatible with Islamic teaching and practice must be discarded. The neo-traditionalist, like the reformist, aimed to be discriminating about what he accepted and what he rejected of modern western civilization. But, unlike the reformist who looked to the example of the earliest generation of Muslims in order to pare down the inherited body of Islamic lore and practice to an irreducible core of positive teaching and legislation, the neo-traditionalist reaffirmed the later accretions in the face of what he saw as the reformist's modernist backsliding. Naturally, these are fairly loosely defined categories representing positions which often overlapped: my labels are interpretative rather than strictly descriptive. I have, however, tried to avoid using the term 'fundamentalist'. Most of the movements or responses in question, except for the ultra-modernist, which verges on the secular, are 'fundamentalist' in the sense that each seeks to assert what it regards as the essentials – making the term too generalized to be useful. In another sense, 'fundamentalism', being a term borrowed from Biblical literalist movements within Christianity, is inappropriate because literalism or rejection of *tawil* is not necessarily a common feature of the Islamic movements under consideration.

ARCHAIC RESPONSES

We have already seen how in West Africa and the Indian Subcontinent Sufi *tariqa* organization provided the basis for *jihads* against syncretic tendencies of assimilation into non-Islamic cultures. The transformation of an erstwhile quietist *tariqa* into a fighting organization was even more spectacular when anti-Islamic forces were perceived as coming from the Christian enemy, or nominally Muslim infidels controlled by them. During the nineteenth century the modernized government of Ottoman Egypt, as well as the more immediate threats posed by Britain, France,

Russia and Holland, sparked off a number of *jihad* movements inspired by the new activist Sufism, especially in the peripheral regions of Africa and the Far East. One such movement, led by 'Abd al Qadir (1808–83) a *shaikh* of the Qadiriya, followed the French conquest of Algiers in 1830. 'Abd al Qadir established a state in Western Algeria which the French were forced to recognize, giving him time to organize his government on classic Medinese lines, securing regular revenues by collecting *zakat*, administering justice according to the Shari'a and appointing salaried deputies (*khalifas*). However, in 1839 the agreement broke down after the French had attacked 'Abd al Qadir's territory and he resumed the *jihad*. The French, who enjoyed Ottoman support, replied with a ruthless scorched-earth strategy, and in 1847 'Abd al Qadir was finally defeated, captured and driven into exile.

Several other archaic movements in North Africa were led by self-styled Mahdis. All were regionally limited, enabling the French to suppress them bit by bit. The most formidable and celebrated *mahdiya*, however, occurred in the Nilotic Sudan, where Muhammad Ahmad, a *shaikh* of the Sammaniya branch of the Khalwatiya, proclaimed himself Mahdi in 1881, the year before the British occupation of Egypt. The support he enjoyed from the Baqqara tribe and the settled inhabitants of the Upper Nile was prompted mainly by resentment at the Egyptian administration – in particular its heavy taxation, its attempts to suppress the slave trade and its policy of employing European governors such as the Englishmen Sir Samuel Baker and General 'Chinese' Gordon. An early proclamation of the Mahdi blamed the 'Turks' (i.e., the Egyptians, still nominally subjects of the Ottoman Sultan) for introducing non-Shari'a laws and levying the *jizya* (poll-tax) on Muslims:

> Verily these Turks thought that theirs was the kingdom and the command was in their hands. They transgressed the command of God's messengers and of His prophets and of him who comman-
> ded them to imitate them. They judged by other than God's revelation and altered the Shari'a of our Lord Muhammad, Mess-
> enger of God.[1]

Muhammad Ahmad had begun his career by acquiring an exceptional reputation for piety and asceticism at Aba Island in the White Nile. His decision to declare himself Mahdi may have been prompted, as in Ibn Tumart's case, by the urging of his chief disciple, 'Abdullahi. Both men were no doubt aware of the mahdist expectations surrounding the end of the thirteenth *hijra* century (November 1882) among the Sudanese tribes. To his close associates, however, Muhammad Ahmad confided the secret that the mahdiship had been conferred upon him by the Prophet in a vision. In the classic manner he made the *hijra* (to Jabal Qadir in the Juba mountains) before launching his *jihad* against the 'Turks' at El Obeid, which surrendered in January 1883. Thereafter the mahdists (who called themselves the Ansar) found themselves in direct confrontation with the British, who had taken control of Egypt and its dependencies after the collapse of Colonel Urabi's nationalist movement in September 1882. An expeditionary force of 8,000 men under Hicks Pasha, a retired Indian Army officer, was ambushed and annihilated at Sheikhan (Hicks himself was killed, and there were only 250 survivors). The following year Gordon, instead of sticking to his instructions to evacuate the garrison at Khartoum, tried to 'smash up' the Mahdi with extra money and Indian troops. The rest of the story is well known. In October 1884 the Mahdi left El Obeid, besieging first Omdurman, which fell in January 1885, and then Khartoum. The relief expedition from Egypt came too late for General Gordon, who died a Christian martyr's death, leaving the Victorian public with a thirst for revenge. On Friday 30 January 1885, the Mahdi made his triumphal entry into Khartoum in time to lead the noon-day prayer in the congregational mosque. Six months later he was dead, probably from typhus, though rumour had it (as with the Prophet's untimely death soon after his greatest victory) that he had been poisoned by one of his concubines.

Having challenged – and humiliated – British power in a strategic and increasingly sensitive region of Africa, the mahdist state was doomed. Like the first Islamic state, it would have needed to expand continuously in order to maintain its momentum and prevent internal collapse. In the late nineteenth century British power was sufficient to contain it within the relatively poor region of its origin. The agriculture of the Gezira was insufficient to support the military machine, even though peasant cultivators were expropriated to make room for Baqqara tribesmen. The population declined drastically and popular discontent with unruly military governors grew apace. In 1898 the Khalifa's forces were almost completely destroyed at Omdurman, the Mahdi's tomb was desecrated and all but one of his offspring massacred.

The failure of 'Abd al Qadir and the Mahdiya pointed to the futility of the archaic response. European power had proved too overwhelming to resist directly: the *hijra–jihad* scenario was no longer practicable in a world of machine-guns, soon to be supplemented by mechanized transport and air-power. Similar revolts in the peripheral areas, such as the *jihad* against the Dutch in Java led by Dipa Negra, were doomed unless they came to terms with the realities of European power. Thus the Senusiya in Cyrenaica maintained their network of beduin-based *zawiyas* by recognizing Ottoman authority, paying taxes to Turkish officials and refraining from any overt acts against the Sultan. Although they disliked the Turks, they recognized them as being the only independent Muslim power capable of withstanding the pressure from Europe. When the Italians invaded in 1911, the beduin continued their resistance under Senusi auspices. Despite Italian attempts to destroy it, the order maintained sufficient authority to provide the main source of resistance to the Fascist occupation. The victorious allies duly rewarded the order by establishing a Senusi monarchy in Libya in 1945.

Another reformed *tariqa* which survived into recent times was that founded among the Swat Pathans of India's North-West Frontier by a Naqshbandi *shaikh*, the Akhund Abdul Ghafur, in the 1870s. The Akhund avoided encroaching on British territory, which persuaded the latter to recognize his government. Such restraint was, however, relatively rare. In general, the European presence and growing cultural and economic influence had the effect of activating the political dynamic latent in *tariqa* organization: 'The colonizing European presence is the one crucial variable determining the conversion of peaceful religious organizations into militant "nationalist" ones.'[2]

THE FAILURE OF THE OTTOMAN CALIPHATE

Given the realities of European power, the archaic responses were obviously inadequate. Yet the effort to modernize and revive the metropolitan Sunni polities on the traditional basis was to prove equally futile. The nineteenth century saw one military disaster after another for the Muslims. The collapse of the Indian 'Mutiny' in 1857 ended any hope of achieving a reversal of British power by armed revolt. The failure of Colonel Urabi's movement in Egypt in 1882 yielded a similar conclusion. Thereafter Muslim aspirations focused on a revival of pan-Islamic power under Ottoman leadership. This mood was astutely exploited by Sultan Abdul Hamid II who recognized in 'Islam' the only source of prestige and authority capable of holding his crumbling empire together. To compensate for the loss of his territories to Christian rulers, he revived the ancient title of caliph, persuading the European powers that this gave him a quasi-papal spiritual authority over Muslims everywhere. This claim, which was linked to Ottoman occupancy of the Hejaz and guardianship of the Holy Cities, met with some approval from the more traditional classes, who needed a figurehead around which to rally in order to resist European encroachments. Its most tangible benefit was the construction of the Hejaz railway from Damascus to Medina, ostensibly to facilitate the pilgrimage, which was paid for by subscribers from all over the Muslim world. Its true purpose, however, was to enable the Sultan to improve his military grasp over the Peninsula.

However, the revived caliphate proved no more able to revitalize a demoralized Umma than the Mahdiya, or the other 'archaic' rebellions. Abdul Hamid's call for a *jihad* against Britain and France in 1914, following his decision to join in the war on the side of Germany and Austria, proved a dismal failure. The British and French had no difficulty in finding *'ulama* to counter the *jihad* declaration with *fatwas* urging loyalty to the colonial governments. The British successfully played the 'Arab' card against the Ottomans by encouraging the Sharif of Mecca to rebel against his Turkish overlords in the hope of establishing a revived Islamic empire under a Quraishi caliphate. Though the Sharif's action merely succeeded in paving the way for his more astute rival, 'Abd al 'Aziz al Sa'ud (Ibn Saud), his sons Faisal and Abdullah eventually acquired puppet kingdoms in Iraq and Transjordan. After the defeat of the Ottoman empire in 1918, the Khilafat Movement, a popular agitation of Indian Muslims backed by the Mahatma Gandhi, campaigned for peace terms that would allow the Sultan-Caliph to retain control over the Holy Cities. In the event, however, the movement was outflanked by the actions of the Turks themselves, under their military commander, Mustafa Kemal (known as Attaturk). Having saved Constantinople from a British landing on the Dardanelles, Attaturk managed to keep the bulk of the Ottoman armies intact, preventing an allied invasion of the Anatolian heartland. Backed by a new National Assembly, he accepted the loss of the Arab provinces, while repulsing and eventually over-turning a Greek attempt to occupy the mainly Greek-inhabited Aegean littoral. In so doing he established a state based on the idea of Turkish nationhood rather than on Islam. The Turkish nation, which was deemed to have existed long before the coming of Islam, was to embody the people, as in Britain, France, Italy or Germany. In 1922 the last Ottoman sultan was sent into exile; in 1924 the caliphate was formally abolished. The Sharif of Mecca's announcement that he was now caliph met with practically no support, and was in any case soon overtaken by 'Abd al 'Aziz's conquest of the Hejaz. Henceforth the destinies of the Muslim peoples were to be entrusted to national governments arising from the rubble of the Ottoman collapse or under the auspices of the colonial powers.

The nationalist thinkers who influenced these developments remain for the most part outside the scope of this study. There was, however, a specifically Islamic contribution which helped pave the way for the emergence of secular nationalism and the traditionalist reaction provoked by it.

INTELLECTUAL MODERNISM: SAYYID AHMED KHAN

The first of the modernist thinkers to have a substantial impact upon the Muslim world at large was Sir Sayyid Ahmed Khan (1817–98), founder of the Muhammadan Anglo-Oriental College at Aligarh in India, where European arts and sciences were taught, in English, alongside traditional Islamic studies. The aim was to produce an educated elite of Muslims able to compete successfully with Hindus for jobs in the Indian administration. A Sayyid of Persian ancestry whose family had enjoyed close connections with the Mughal court, Ahmed Khan's experience of the 'Mutiny' had convinced him that the 'archaic' struggle against foreign rule was hopeless. The only hope for survival lay in modernizing Islamic institutions by progressive educational policies in the context of loyalty to Britain. In fact Ahmed Khan's analysis of the causes of the 'Mutiny' – a century of exploitation and misrule by the East India Company – was fairly close to that of the British reformers in India who persuaded the government to transfer responsibility for the Subcontinent's affairs to the British parliament.

Ahmed Khan's decision to collaborate with Britain led him towards addictive anglophilia. In 1868 he adopted a 'Western' life-style. On a journey to England the following year he attended Dickens's last public reading, met Thomas Carlyle and visited Cambridge, which became the model for Aligarh, a seminary for producing Indian Muslim gentlemen. British rule in India, he once told the Viceroy, Lord Lytton, was 'the most wonderful phenomenon the world has ever seen', loyalty to which sprang 'not from servile submission to foreign rule, but from genuine appreciation of the blessings of good government'.[3] Ahmed Khan's loyalism was consistent and was duly rewarded. In 1887, the year he advised Muslims not to join the National Congress, he became a member of the Viceregal Legislative Council; the following year he became a Knight Commander of the Star of India.

Ahmed Khan's emotional attachment to Britain was of a piece with his liberal and rationalizing religious outlook. Seeking to reconcile the contradictions between Islam as traditionally understood and the modern sciences he so much admired, he set about reinterpreting the Qur'an, drawing heavily on both the reformism of Shah Wali Ullah and the speculative rationalism of the Mu'tazilis and Ikhwan al Safa. Comparing the nineteenth century with the ninth century, when Islamic thinkers first grappled with the challenge of Greek philosophy, he wrote:

> Today we are as before in need of a modern 'ilm al kalam by which we should either refute the doctrines of the modern world or undermine their foundations, or show that they are in conformity with the articles of Islamic faith.[4]

In interpreting the divine text, Ahmed Khan accepts the right of unrestricted personal ijtihad, based on an accurate understanding of the Arabic idiom of the Prophet's time. Individual passages may be understood literally or symbolically: like the classical philosophers he accepts the principle that different levels of understanding might be achieved by the masses and the educated elite. Thus he argues that the punishment stories were related, as in the Old Testament, not as historical verities, but as morality tales using a popular legendary framework. Angels are 'properties' of things or conceptualizations of the divine moral support which encourages man in his endeavours; jinns are projections of evil desires. A fundamental distinction has to be made between details of revelation (furu') referring to specific historical situations and the general principles (usul) underlying them. In principle God's laws are identical with the laws of nature: as the Final Cause or Creator, his laws, which he maintains as the disciplines of creation and existence, determine the causal relationships governing all material and non-material things. All human morality and social ethics derive from these natural laws. Thus in principle the Shari'a is rooted in natural law; in practice it reflects the ideas and attitudes of the first generation of Muslims. In questioning the Sunna as an infallible source of law comparable to the Quran, Ahmed Khan criticized the methodology of the early hadith collectors, including Bukhari and Muslim, in terms very similar to those subsequently employed by Ignaz Goldziher and Joseph Schacht, the first western orientalists to cast serious scholarly doubt on the historical basis of the Sunna. Using the same rationalistic and historical arguments, Ahmed Khan declared several traditional Muslim institutions, including polygamy, slavery and concubinage, to be forbidden. All laws, according to Ahmed Khan, were subject to change according to circumstances. The only exceptions were the 'ibadas, religious duties, which were absolutely perfect and immutable. This attitude had important political implications: so long as the British guaranteed Muslims the right to perform their religious duties, namely the 'five pillars', rebellion against their government would be illegal.

Ahmed Khan's modernism inevitably incensed the more traditionalist 'ulama, whom he tried to placate by placing them in charge of Islamic studies at Aligarh. In one respect, therefore, his attempt to bridge the gap between science and religion resulted in failure, for by making concessions to the traditionalists he introduced into his system of education the very dualism against which he militated in his writings. His dilemma was the same as that which faced most of the reformers who came after him. The gap between scientific and religious truth could only be bridged by abandoning literalistic interpretations of the divine texts, or even, in the case of hadiths, by challenging their authenticity, thus leaving much of the law open to changes which, in the circumstances, facilitated western domination and cultural penetration. This dilemma persists to this day and can only be resolved when the tide of western power recedes sufficiently to allow an autogenic development of the Shari'a.

PAN-ISLAMIC ACTIVISM: JAMAL AL DIN AL AFGHANI

The most outspoken and vigorous attack on Ahmed Khan's ideas came from outside India and from an unexpected quarter: Sayyid Jamal al Din al Afghani was, despite his name, a Persian Shi'ite, born at Asabad near Hamadan in 1838 or 1839. A passionate advocate of the need for the Umma to unite in the face of the European threat represented especially by Britain, he concealed his origins in order to avoid arousing the hostility of his Sunni auditors. A man of action before he was a thinker, Afghani was a born intriguer and polemicist. An extreme ascetic, he once threatened to castrate himself when the Ottoman Sultan urged him to marry. Following a traditional education in Iran, he went to Afghanistan, where he claimed to be a Turk, concealing his Shi'ite origins. Here he urged the military ruler of Qandahar, Azam Khan, to make an alliance with the Russians against the British. However, after Azam was ousted by his half-brother, Afghani was obliged to leave for Istanbul, where he joined a group of Tanzimat reformers in urging the Muslims to emulate the 'civilized' nations of the west. Having been appointed to the reformist Council of Education he offended the *'ulama* by giving a public lecture in which he referred to *batini* ideas that had long been deemed heretical by Sunnis. In 1871 he was expelled and went on to Cairo, where his attacks on the Khedive Isma'il and his British patrons made him popular in nationalist circles. It was in this period that he found his leading disciple, Muhammad Abduh, with whom he had a relationship similar to that of a Sufi *pir* and his *murid*. A supporter of Colonel Urabi's nationalist movement, Afghani was expelled in 1879 for his inflammatory anti-British speeches. Several of his followers, however, participated in Urabi's government before its overthrow by the British in 1882.

From Egypt Afghani went to Hyderabad in India, where he associated chiefly with the followers of Ahmed Khan. In 1881 he made his celebrated attack on Ahmed Khan, in a pamphlet entitled *Refutation of the Materialists*, in which he accused the Sayyid and his like, who included materialists from Democritus to Darwin, of opening the 'gates of bestiality', thereby inviting the 'perpetration of shameful deeds and offensive acts'. In this pamphlet Afghani deliberately misrepresented Ahmed Khan's ideas: the latter did not, as he claimed, deny transcendence. The true motive for his attack was political rather than religious. He sought to present Ahmed Khan's collaboration with the British Raj as resulting from religious turpitude, in order to discredit the reformer who was gaining ground with the Indian *'ulama*. Two years later, in a rejoinder to a lecture by Ernest Renan attacking Islam for being hostile to science, Afghani strongly criticized the 'Muslim religion', as currently practised, for stifling free thought and progress – which shows that he had not shed his liberal ideas.

In Paris, where Abduh joined him in 1884, Afghani published a periodical in Arabic, *Al 'Urwa al Wuthqa* ('The Strongest Link'), which attacked the British and supported Abdul Hamid's pan-Islamic pretensions while outlining his essentially liberal and reformist attitudes. In 1885 he went to Tehran, but failed to persuade Nasr ul Din Shah to enlist further Russian support against the British. He then spent two years in St Petersburg intriguing against the British before returning again to Persia, where he agitated against the sale of concessions to foreigners. After getting wind of the Shah's plans to expel him, he took sanctuary in a shrine near Tehran. The Shah was forced into violating *bast* before Afghani would consent to remove himself, first to Iraq and then to London, where he continued to agitate against the concessions in speeches, pamphlets and messages addressed to the Shi'ite leaders. His propaganda was a significant factor in the Tobacco Boycott of 1891. In 1892 he returned to Istanbul at the invitation of Abdul Hamid, where he surrounded himself with a somewhat heterodox group of pan-Islamists, including some Iranians who could scarcely be described as Muslims at all. In 1896 one of his acolytes, Mirza Reza, shot and killed Nasr ul Din Shah in Tehran. The Sultan refused Iranian demands for Afghani's extradition, although three of his Persian associates were sent back and duly hanged for their complicity. The following year Afghani died, from cancer of the chin.

The apparent contradictions in Afghani's thinking and the seeming duplicity of his actions are largely explained in terms of his overriding concern to unite the Umma against the West. He was shrewd enough to see Britain as a greater threat to Islam than Russia, because of its more advanced economic system and its active political involvement in Egypt and India. While sharing many of the ideas of Ahmed Khan and the Tanzimat reformers, he turned against them viciously once he perceived the dangerous fissures their doctrines and activities opened up beneath the surface. He failed to realize that the reforms he believed in could not be won without a severe internal struggle in which unity must be the first casualty. The 'Islam' he sought to defend was a civilization, a faith and an allegiance, rather than a carefully formulated religious doctrine. He wanted simultaneously to close the gates against the West and replace the crumbling medieval edifice behind the city walls with a bright new building on classical foundations. Such a double objective was far beyond the capacity of the demoralized leadership of his day, and he died an embittered and disappointed man. But his vision remained, for all who sought a change for the better in the Muslim world, whether through a return to the roots of faith, through governmental reform, or a combination of both. He was thus the intellectual progenitor of both pan-Islamic nationalism and the reformist Salafiya movement.

SALAFI REFORMISM: MUHAMMAD ABDUH

The chief exponent of Afghani's ideas, Muhammad Abduh (1849–1905) was a man with a very different temperament. Born into a peasant family in Egypt his attachment to his country of origin brought him, like Ahmed Khan, to collaborate with the British, rejecting Afghani's pan-Islamic militancy. Early in his career he had come under the influence of a Sufi *shaikh* who had freed him from the 'poison of ignorance' and the 'bonds of literalism'. This influence later merged with his reading of European authors, especially Tolstoy and Herbert Spencer, with whom he was personally acquainted, to create a broad-minded liberalism not far removed from that of Ahmed Khan. Lord Cromer, the British Consul General in Cairo and effective ruler of Egypt from 1882 to 1908, regarded Abduh as an 'agnostic' – a reflection of the extent to which he identified 'Islam' exclusively with the traditionalism current in his day. While Abduh never went so far as Ahmed Khan in adopting a European life-style, he visited Europe whenever possible in order to replenish himself spiritually.

During his collaboration with Afghani on *Al 'Urwa al Wuthqa*, Abduh tended to justify Islam in its social rather than its theological aspects. Like Ibn Khaldun and Ibn Rushd, he saw it as an essential ingredient of social happiness. His main concern was to interpret it in a manner that would release its liberating spirit, enabling Muslims to take their place scientifically and culturally alongside the nations of Europe. For this the political problem would have to be shelved: Afghani's attempts to rouse the Muslims to action through their rulers were doomed to failure and would only provoke the wrath of European powers. In 1888, after the collapse of *Al 'Urwa al Wuthqa*, Abduh returned to Egypt – a momentous decision which implied his acceptance of the reality of British power. Thereafter he concentrated his efforts on legal reform and education. He entered the legal service and rose to become first a judge and eventually the Mufti of Egypt in charge of the whole system of Shari'a law. In his legal rulings he adapted from the Maliki school, in which he had been trained, the principle of *maslaha* (public interest) allowing the law to be changed according to modern requirements: 'If a ruling has become the cause of harm which it did not cause before, then we must change it according to the prevailing conditions.'[5]

Another principle adopted by Abduh, previously employed by the Indian reformer Shah Wali Ullah, was *talfiq* (literally, 'piecing together'), whereby rulings could be given by systematically comparing the views of the four *madhhabs*, and going behind them to the Quran, *hadith* and principles of the *salaf al salih* (pious forebears). In his official capacity as Mufti of Egypt Abduh was bound to give rulings according to the

Ottoman Hanafi code. His influence as a reformer derived from the private *fatwas* he gave on demand, and from his miscellaneous writings and lectures which were collected and published in the periodical *Al Manar* ('The Lighthouse') by his disciple Rashid Rida from 1897 to 1935. Rashid Rida, a Syrian Naqshbandi who, unlike Abduh, never visited Europe or learned its languages and was therefore much less influenced by foreign ideas, emphasized the Salafi aspect of Abduh's work, making it more acceptable to conservatives or fundamentalists than it would otherwise have been.

In his theology Abduh followed Afghani, trying to maintain a balance between reason and revelation. He could not accept the possibility of a contradiction between God's spoken truth in the Quran and his Truth as revealed in nature. He did not, however, go so far as the Mu'tazilis in subjecting God's power to the principle of justice. Instead he side-stepped the issue by assimilating ethics to aesthetics:

> Voluntary actions may also be distinguished as beautiful or ugly according to the idea of their utility or harmfulness. [This distinction] can be discovered by human reason and the senses without the aid of revelation.[6]

The purpose of revelation was therefore not, as the traditionalists maintained, to arbitrarily endow certain acts with the character of good or bad, 'but to help fallible reason by defining some of the good and bad acts on the basis of the utility principle'.[7]

Abduh's ideas were consistent with his position as a man attempting to reconcile the conflicts of his time. Like Afghani he saw that the overwhelming power of the West lay in the vastly superior scientific knowledge at its disposal. The Muslims must free themselves from *taqlid* ('imitation') of traditional authority if they were to benefit from this power and to acquire the capacity to resist those who were using it against them. This could be achieved without sacrificing the basic truths of Islam, since the rational truth of science and the truth of revelation must, in the final analysis, be identical.

This belief that the truths of religion and science could be harmonized, integral to the whole modernist viewpoint, was naive in one aspect, since it was based on the essentially medieval premise that science, like scripture itself, is a finite body of knowledge awaiting revelation, rather than a dynamic process of discovery subject to continual revision. In Egypt, as in India, the establishment of non-religious institutions of learning, encouraged by Abduh, opened the floodgates to secular forces which threated Islam's intellectual foundations.

A similar conflict had, of course, occurred in the Christian West, especially during the latter part of the nineteenth century. Like Abduh and some of his followers, Christian thinkers had tried to maintain the absolute authority of revelation by discovering in scripture intimations of scientific phenomena or laws subsequently revealed by experiment. In the West, however, this process of accommodation between the scientific and religious outlooks had been going on for centuries, and had been leading towards conclusions very different from any that most Muslims were as yet prepared to accept. Liberal theologians from Schleiermacher in the eighteenth century to Tillich in the twentieth have developed a subjective or existentialist view of revelation which centres on its meaning for man, culturally, historically and personally, while leaving science to discover the objective laws governing the universe. Such a theology, however, implies the de-throning of revelation from the category of absolute to that of relative truth – and, ultimately, to that of a particular mode of discourse within a culturally determined symbolic framework.

Elements of this approach can be inferred from the writings of Ahmed Khan, Afghani and Abduh, all of whom were especially aware of Islam's historic importance as a source of culture and civilization. As competent Muslim scholars, they had no need to borrow the exegetical tools of Western analysis if they wished to give their scripture a symbolic interpretation: the whole *batini* tradition, from the writings of the Ikhwan al Safa to the theosophy of Ibn al 'Arabi can be adapted to his purpose, not to mention the work of Mu'tazili exegetes such as Zamakhshari. Their problem was twofold: firstly, in Islam the divine is believed to have manifested itself primarily in the form of a text, so that any scientific or linguistic analysis which casts doubt on that text's integrity must threaten the central citadel of faith.*

The second, related, problem facing the modernists was that the Quran and such portions of *hadith* as must be salvaged to maintain the Quran's authenticity contain a core of positive legislation which, though rooted within the culture of a particular time and place – seventh-century

---

* Hence the furore caused by the publication in 1926 of a book on pre-Islamic poetry by the Egyptian writer Taha Husain which cast doubt on one of the main sources of Quran and *hadith* interpretation.

Arabia – cannot be given a relativistic or symbolic interpretation without abandoning the cultural and social norms which it sanctifies. A Western-ized, philosophically inclined elite can observe Quranic prohibitions in the breach, drinking alcohol, failing to observe Ramadan, indulging in unlicensed sex and disregarding those aspects of Islamic law and prac-tice that it finds uncongenial without necessarily rejecting the higher religious truths enshrined in the divine text; but in so acting it is always vulnerable to the charge that it is failing in its duty of 'enjoining the good and forbidding the evil'. Muslim religiosity has both politically radical and socially conservative consequences. It is radical because it is pre-pared to challenge authority when those in power are seen to be departing from Islamic norms of behaviour. It is conservative because, in the last analysis, the social rituals embodying these norms cannot be abandoned without inviting the accusation of infidelity. The history of post-modernist reform since the time of Abduh shows a tendency to slide from liberalism to traditionalism as the conservatives demonstrate a greater capacity to mobilize mass support in times of crisis.

The swing from liberalism back to traditionalism has been shown most clearly in two regions sharing prolonged exposure to Western influences – the Arab East, including Egypt, and the Indian Subcontinent. Iran, with its distinctive Shi'ite national tradition, is in many respects a special case; while landlocked Afghanistan, still largely tribal, is only now experiencing the kind of upheaval that Egypt and Turkey underwent a century or more ago. In the peripheral regions of Africa and the Far East, traditional forms of Islam may be reasserting themselves, but here Islam is often a badge of racial or ethnic identity, and demands for an Islamic state or stricter observance of ritual may have nationalist or particularist overtones.

EGYPT AND THE ARAB WORLD

EGYPTIAN AND ARAB NATIONALISM

In Egypt the reformist liberalism represented by Abduh opened the way for a secular nationalism which sought to relegate religion to the sphere of private belief, enabling a new, Western-educated elite to take control of the country's affairs and to create a national state on the European model. The religious establishment, always subservient to political power in Sunni countries, capitulated to this development. The Islamic reaction was led by the more conservative reformers, notably Abduh's disciple Rashid Rida and his spiritual heir Hasan al Banna, founder of the Muslim Brotherhood.

Abduh's return to Egypt in 1888 and his quarrel with Afghani over the pan-Islamic question showed that he had begun to recognize that henceforth the future of Islam must lie within the geographical frontiers upheld by the colonial powers and recognized in international law. The term *watan* ('homeland'), a word without pedigree in classical Islamic political thought, appears with increasing frequency in his writings as the unifying factor around which Islamic activity should coalesce. The collapse of the Ottoman empire little more than a decade after his death proved him right. Two of his close associates, Ahmed Lutfi al Sayyid and Sa'ad Zaghloul became the intellectual and political leaders of modern Egyptian nationalism. Lutfi al Sayyid argued that, since three millennia of ancient history had endowed the Egyptian personality with a 'pharaonic core', no amount of borrowing from the West would threaten its identity. Zaghloul led the agitation which resulted in Egypt's becoming a constitutional monarchy under indirect British control in 1922.

Although it failed to satisfy the demands of the nationalists, Egypt's limited independence represented the first victory of the Arab national state over the Umma. Article 1 of the 1923 Constitution (adapted from the Belgian Constitution) declared the country to be a 'sovereign state, free and independent'. Submission to any Islamic super-state was precluded by insisting that this sovereignty was 'indivisible and inalienable'. Article 3 granted all Egyptians equal rights, duties and equality before the law regardless of race, language or religion, thereby abolishing the old Shari'a distinction between Muslims, *dhimmis* and unbelievers. Article 12 declared that 'freedom of conscience is absolute', implicitly contradicting the Shari'a, which prescribes the death penalty for apostates, though Article 13 added the proviso that 'the state protects the free exercise of all religions and creeds in conformity with the usages established in Egypt'. Article 23 recognized that 'all powers emanate from the nation', whilst Articles 24 to 28 gave parliament full power of legislation unhindered by any reference to Islamic law. Clauses dealing explicitly with religion were limited to Article 149, declaring Islam to be the religion of the state, while Article 153 entitled the state – through the person of the King – to appoint religious leaders and to control other religious institutions through a ministry of *waqfs*. Thus in Egypt, as in

Turkey, a secular state had come into being, embodying the nation. Similar constitutions, effectively placing Islam on a similar footing to the churches in Western countries, were established in most other Muslim states when they came to independence after the colonialist retreat.

The creation of the national state made it possible for an emerging native elite to aspire to the Westernized life-style adopted by the European and *dhimmi* upper classes. However, this only widened the gap between the traditional classes, both rural and urban, who wore traditional costume, punctiliously observed Ramadan and other Muslim festivals, and the westernized elites, who wore European dress and often took to such habits as drinking alcohol and attending mixed social gatherings.

In Egypt this situation persisted even after an intermediate class, consisting mainly of native-born army officers, technicians and government employees, came to power in 1952, setting a trend that would be imitated in those Arab states most closely exposed to Western cultural influences. Though the traditional classes, activated by the Muslim Brotherhood, had played their part in bringing Gamal Abdul Nasser and his Free Officers to power, the new nationalist elite soon discarded their former supporters, governing the country instead by a combination of police methods and bureaucratic controls. Nasser and other Arab military rulers who followed his path effectively coopted the religious establishment, which found in Abduh's use of *ijtihad* and *maslaha* the instruments by which they could produce *fatwas* legitimizing almost anything their masters cared to ask for – reforms that often offended the traditional classes by changing the status of women, or limiting private property or the jurisdiction of the religious courts. With the official *'ulama* playing second fiddle to reforming officers and bureaucrats, the opposition among the traditional classes turned increasingly to the radical alternatives offered by the Muslim Brotherhood and its affiliates.

ACTIVIST REFORMISM: THE MUSLIM BROTHERHOOD

The Society of Muslim Brothers, founded by Hasan al Banna in 1928, became one of the main sources of political radicalism in Egypt once Sa'ad Zaghloul's party, the Wafd, had become too closely identified with the colonial interest. (The Communist Party enjoyed a certain amount of support among the small industrialized proletariat and partly westernized intelligentsia, but its appeal was too limited to compete seriously with that of the Brotherhood.) A schoolteacher by training, Banna had begun preaching his reformed doctrines in mosques, schools, and private homes away from the watchful eyes of the authorities. Theologically, Banna's views were fairly close to those of Abduh and his Salafi disciple, Rashid Rida. He attacked the *taqlid* of the official *'ulama*, insisting that only the Quran and the best-attested *hadiths* should be the sources of the Shari'a. Some of his followers were considerably more radical, challenging even the canonical *hadith* collection of Bukhari and Muslim: they were fond of quoting an anti-*hadith hadith* according to which the Prophet is supposed to have said: 'Take from me only the Quran.' They were defensive about the *hadd* (Quranic) punishments, using the classic modernist argument that the thief should have his hand amputated only when the perfectly just Islamic society, in which there was no want, had been realized.

Where Banna and his followers differed from Rida and Abduh was in their determination to create the Islamic society by positive social, political and in some cases military action. While endorsing most of Abduh's modernist positions, they utterly rejected his acceptance of the colonial reality. In this respect their political position was closer to Afghani's, though like Afghani they often found themselves making compromises with the existing political power. Both Banna and his successor Hasan al Hudaybi claimed at various times that Egypt's existing constitutional framework could be adapted to satisfy the requirements of an Islamic state. Islam was an ideal to be worked for, comparable to the ideals of the French and Russian Revolutions: within its framework, development was not only possible, but also desirable and necessary. The Shari'a, however, must reign supreme: its *de facto* replacement by imported European codes had symbolized the rejection of 'God's law', destroying the essence of Muslim society.

At first, Banna aimed to build his Muslim polity within the framework of Egypt. A combination of neo-Sufic *tariqa* and political party, the Brotherhood attracted members from all social groups, including civil servants and students, urban labourers and peasants, artisans and merchants. Members were arranged into units called 'families', families into 'clans', clans into 'groups' and groups into 'battalions'. Members met for prayer, including nocturnal vigils. Much stress was placed on athletics for the young – in order to keep their minds off sex. Members were enjoined to observe religious duties assiduously, and to avoid the evils of gambling, drinking, usury and fornication. Stress was placed on the 'Islamization' of home and family, and loyalty to Brotherhood leaders. Each 'family' was collectively responsible for its members' actions. Banna once described his Brotherhood as 'a Salafiya message, a Sunni way, a Sufi truth, a political organization, an athletic group, a cultural-educational union, an economic company and a social idea'.[8] In his own estimation, however, the reformist aspect, tinged with Sufism, seems to have been paramount. In 1943, convinced of British plots to kill him, he wrote a 'farewell message' in which he stated:

> My Brothers, you are not a benevolent society, nor a political party, nor a local organization having political purposes. Rather you are a new soul in the heart of this nation to give it light by means of the Quran . . . to destroy the darkness of materialism through knowing God.[9]

Despite this disclaimer, the size of the Brotherhood made it a force to be reckoned with. It was alternately wooed by the Palace, which saw in its support a means of improving its pan-Arab image, especially during the mounting struggle for Palestine after the Arab revolt of 1936; and by the left, which sought its support in industrial and political strikes. Its momentum grew even greater with the swell of anti-British feeling after the Anglo-Egyptian treaty of 1936. Throughout this period Banna deftly maintained his independence, earning the hostility of the left and the suspicion of the establishment. In 1948 a group of Brotherhood volunteers fought in the Palestine War, alongside the Egyptian army, where they came into contact with the Free Officers, the nationalist group in the Egyptian army which was to overthrow the monarchy in 1952. After the widespread disturbances following Egypt's defeat in the war the government dissolved the Brotherhood. In December 1948 Nuqrashi Pasha, the Prime Minister, was assassinated by a Brotherhood member. Banna repudiated the murder, arguing that since its dissolution the Brotherhood could no longer be held responsible for the actions of individual members. The following February, however, he himself was assassinated, with, it is thought, the complicity of the incoming premier. In the trials of Nuqrashi's assassins, the prosecution failed in its bid to prove that the whole Brotherhood was implicated in the murder: while accepting that the Brotherhood had been involved in 'murder and destruction', the court rejected prosecution claims of a 'revolutionary conspiracy' and passed relatively lenient sentences on the accused.

The dissolution of the organization led to the emigration of many Brothers, who spread its message to Palestine, Transjordan, Syria and even Pakistan. Hudaybi, the new leader, cultivated a respectable image, repudiating the Brotherhood's terrorist wing, the so-called 'secret organization'. 'There is no secrecy in the service of God,' he said, 'no terrorism in religion.'[10] In 1951, when Nahas Pasha, the Wafdist Prime Minister, unilaterally abrogated the Anglo-Egyptian Treaty, the Brotherhood came out in open support of the government, calling for a *jihad* against the British, while members were trained and armed by sympathizers in the army. The massacre by the British army of more than a dozen auxiliary policemen at Ismailiya in January 1952 brought matters to a head. The following day, 'Black Saturday', much of Cairo went up in flames. The role of the Brotherhood in the disturbances was evident from the symbolic character of the targets selected – foreign clubs and hotels, bars, cinemas and restaurants: establishments where foreigners and Muslim *kafirs* congregated. In July the Free Officers led by Gamal Abdal Nasser placed General Neguib, an army officer acceptable to the Brotherhood, at the head of a junta which forced King Farouk to abdicate and disbanded all political parties. In the 'honeymoon period' after the revolution, the Brotherhood was offered three government posts, but Hudaybi declined. He disagreed with the Revolutionary Command Council's policy of agrarian reform and may have feared that the Brotherhood's image would be tarnished by the responsibilities of office. Nasser and Neguib made a much publicized visit to the tomb of Hasan al Banna.

The honeymoon, however, was not to last. The RCC, still trying to remove the British from the canal zone by negotiation, accused the Brotherhood of secretly acquiescing in the British presence. Hudaybi countered by accusing the government of backing dissidents in his organization. In 1953 the RCC declared the Brotherhood a political organization and therefore subject to the law abolishing political parties. Hudaibi was accused of blocking the land reforms and of aiming to 'overthrow the present form of government under cover of religion'. The Communists welcomed the Brotherhood in the common struggle against Nasser, whom they regarded as an 'Anglo-American stooge' after his negotiation of the Anglo-Egyptian agreement. Sayyid Qutb, the brotherhood's leading intellectual, took charge of liaison with the Communists. The 'secret apparatus' was revived and planned Nasser's assassination. The attempt was made in November 1954. Its failure provided Nasser with the opportunity of crushing the organization completely. In a series of show trials, backed by confessions extracted under torture, the whole leadership was implicated in the plot. Seven were sentenced to death, including Hudaybi and Nasser's would-be assassin, Mahmud 'Abdal Latif. Hudaybi's sentence was, however, commuted on grounds of age and health. The hangings produced a shocked reaction in Egypt, and were greeted with angry demonstrations in Jordan, Syria and Pakistan.

After the débâcle of 1954, the Brotherhood remained quiescent for a decade, with most of its 4,000 activists either in prison or in foreign exile. The nadir of its fortunes was reached in 1965 when, following the discovery of an alleged plot to overthrow him, Nasser arrested another 1,000 members and placed 365 of them on trial. Several were executed, including the activist leader, Sayyid Qutb, who had only been released from jail the previous year. There seems to have been a Saudi connection, with King Faisal playing the 'Islamic card' against Nasser, with whom he was contesting the leadership of the Arabs in Yemen and elsewhere. Faisal and his ally King Hussein of Jordan began giving succour to Nasser's enemies in the Brotherhood, providing them with influential university posts or even coopting them into government. Nasser's catastrophic defeat in the June 1967 war against Israel further discredited his brand of secular nationalism, despite the well-orchestrated pleas from the Egyptian masses that he should not resign. Israel's unilateral annexation of Jerusalem, followed by the burning of the Al Aqsa Mosque, Islam's third-holiest shrine, in 1969 inflamed religious feelings everywhere. Pan-Islamic sentiments were further exacerbated by the Jewish state's creeping annexation of the Occupied West Bank, and by the tacit support its policies received from the West, particularly the United States.

After Nasser's death in 1970 his successor, Anwar Sadat, sought to present a more Islamic image for his regime by frequently having himself televised at prayer and by peppering his monologues with Quranic references. He cautiously encouraged the growing Islamic mood by releasing all Brotherhood prisoners and promising to bring Egyptian law more closely into line with the Shari'a. After his 'corrective coup' against former Vice-President Ali Sabri and other leftists in the leadership in 1971, Sadat actually encouraged the formation of Islamic committees in the universities, in order to counter leftist influence. By the late seventies most of the student committees had come under the control of the Brotherhood and its affiliates.

After expelling his Soviet military advisers in 1972 and winning a partial victory over Israel the following year, Sadat opened the doors of the Egyptian economy to the West, hoping to attract a massive injection of foreign capital. The effects of this policy, both economic and cultural, served to strengthen support for the Brotherhood and its affiliates. Culturally, the relatively straight-laced puritanism of the Nasserist era gave way to a new permissiveness in which Alexandria and Cairo once more became the leading Middle Eastern 'fleshpots', attracting thousands of visitors from Saudi Arabia and the Gulf. Economically, the '*infitah*' exacerbated social divisions, as rents rocketed, food prices rose sharply and local manufacturing capacity was decimated by cheap foreign imports. Inevitably the extremist groups among the Brotherhood's affiliates became the most active opponents of the *infitah* and the Westernizing influences unleashed by it. In 1974 a small band calling itself the Islamic Liberation Group mounted an armed attack on the Military Academy at Heliopolis in which 11 people were killed and 27 injured. Another group, calling itself Takfir wa'l Hijra* played a leading part in the sacking of dozens of nightclubs along Cairo's Pyramids Road during the food riots in January 1977. Six months later the same group kidnapped and assassinated the former Minister for Waqfs, Shaikh Muhammad Dhahabi, when the government refused to release 60 of their comrades. 410 of the group's members were arrested and 23 executed, including the group's leader Shukri Ahmed Mustafa. Other extremist militant groups included the Mukafaratiya ('Denouncers of the Kafirs'), the Jund Allah ('God's Soldiers') and the Jama'a al Jihad ('Jihad Society'). Altogether membership of the extremist groups was said to exceed 4,000.

Sadat's response to these developments was to encourage the moderate Brotherhood leaders, isolating the militants. Two leading exiles, Umar Talmasani and Said Ramadan, were allowed to return to Egypt, Talmasani to take over the editorship of the Brotherhood's principal organ *Al Da'wa*, Said Ramadan to lead a group of nine Brotherhood-affiliated deputies in the Egyptian parliament. (The Brotherhood was not permitted to campaign openly in the parliamentary elections, but no one can have been in much doubt as to who its representatives were.) For a period this strategy succeeded. Sadat's policy of making peace with

---

* *Takfir* means 'denunciation' (as an infidel): the group's name thus carried clear Khariji overtones – first denounce one's fellow-Muslims as infidels, then make the *hijra* separating oneself from them.

Israel, launched after his spectacular visit to Jerusalem in November 1977, was popular with the Egyptian *fallahin* who had provided most of the canon fodder for successive Arab wars against Israel. Despite considerable outrage provoked by his visits to Jerusalem, where he was televised worshipping in the Al Aqsa Mosque (implying *de facto* recognition of Israel's sovereignty), Sadat obtained the support of the official Azhari *'ulama*, and even, tacitly, that of moderate Brotherhood leaders, for his policies.

The failure of the Camp David agreement to provide a settlement acceptable to the Palestinians (and therefore to most of the other Arab states), as well as the increasingly deleterious effects of Sadat's economic policies (which, like those of the Khedive Ismail, seemed to involve wholesale capitulation to Western interests without yielding any proportional benefits, save to a small minority of speculators and profiteers), eventually drove even the Brotherhood moderates into more open opposition alongside Sadat's Nasserist and left-wing critics. In September 1981, reportedly under pressure from Menachem Begin, who warned him that Israel would not withdraw from Sinai so long as open criticism of Camp David was tolerated in Egypt, Sadat rounded on the opposition, arresting more than 1,500 dissidents, mostly Islamic militants. The army was purged of 200 officers thought to be too friendly to the Brotherhood, all independent mosques and religious societies were closed down and all preachers were obliged to register with the Ministry of Waqfs. Just over one month later, Sadat was assassinated while reviewing a military parade to mark the anniversary of the October 1973 war. The chief assassin, Lieutenant Khaled Islambouli, was the brother of one of the Takfir wa'l Hijra suspects arrested on 3 September.

Sadat's successor, Husni Mubarak, judiciously dissociated himself from the more flamboyant aspects of Sadat's Westernizing policies, as well as from the late President's more notorious associates, including his widow, Jihan, and his brother, Esmat, both of whom had been thought responsible for much of the corruption and black marketeering surrounding the President. Esmat had amassed a vast personal fortune, while Jihan, who was insensitive to the point of arrogance, had outraged traditional Egyptian prejudices by publicly embracing US President Jimmy Carter in front of the world's television cameras.

Throughout most of its career the Muslim Brotherhood has been a fluid mass movement, rather than a well-structured political organization. This has been the source of both strength and weakness. Its mass character and relatively inchoate structure has enabled it to survive successive waves of persecution. At the same time, lack of firm organization and effective political leadership have made it virtually impossible for it to commit itself to a coherent set of policies capable of being translated into action. As a result it has usually succumbed to the twin perils facing any loosely organized radical movement: a tacit compromise with the status quo on the one hand, precipitating a reactive extremism on the other. Doctrinally its attitudes have generally been in line with the reformist approach of Muhammad Abduh and Rashid Rida, casting aside the dead weight of *taqlid* and *fiqh* and benefiting from the liberating impact of *maslaha* and *ijtihad* to create an up-to-date Islam suited to modern conditions. In practice, however, both its membership, consisting largely of urban petit bourgeois and rural immigrants, and the symbols around which it coalesces, give the Brotherhood a more positively traditional character. Since reformism has been coopted, not only by secularists in power but by the official *'ulama* whose task it is to legitimize their actions, the Brotherhood has become emotionally, if not always intellectually, traditionalist.

Despite its reformist pedigree, the Brotherhood has tended to develop in a conservative direction, being the only available outlet for those whose religious and cultural sensibilities had been outraged by the impact of Westernization upon their society, in which both the secularizing reformers and the official *'ulama* had collaborated. For example, the feminist movement inspired by Abduh's disciple Qasim Amin, and Huda Sharawi, wife of a Turkish pasha, eventually became the banner under which upper-class women imitated the style and fashions of European women. Once emancipation and Westernization had become inextricably intermingled, the defence of Islam became bound up with the preservation of masculine privileges. Today the Brotherhood finds many of its supporters among young men from traditional families who find it difficult to cope with meeting females on terms of relative equality when they arrive at university. Women's education, however, is an irreversible process; in the universities where the Brotherhood and its affiliates have taken control of student bodies, women have responded by adopting a nun-like style of dress in line with the presumed injunctions of the Shari'a. This garb, the so-called 'lawful dress', may be represented as symbolizing a 'return to Islam'; but is really a form of protection which gives its wearers, who may be unused to mixed social gatherings, a sense of security. I myself have observed that young women so dressed seem immune from the unwelcome attentions of men even if they are alone in a public place. The sartorial message is stated clearly enough: to touch *me* would be an act of *fitna*, an offence against the Shari'a.

Politically, the Brotherhood's career forms an interesting parallel to the role of the pious opposition during the early centuries of Islam, including those who remained loyal to the 'Alid cause. Both proved highly effective at mobilizing opposition to unpopular governments during times of crisis. But when it came to providing an alternative government with a specific set of policies, neither movement had the capacity, or perhaps even the desire, to take on active responsibility. The very inchoateness of the movements made them umbrellas for differing, sometimes opposing, tendencies.

Throughout the 1970s and early 1980s the Muslim Brotherhood remained the principle vehicle for Sunni political activism, not only in Egypt but also in Syria, where it enjoyed the support of the Iraqi and Jordanian governments. The domination of the Regional Command of the Ba'ath Party by a group of 'Alawi sectarians led by Hafez el Asad had given some plausibility to the accusation that Syria had fallen into the hands of an ''Alawi dictatorship'. While there was no evidence that Nusairi religious ideas had penetrated the thinking of the Ba'ath Party ideologists, sectarian *'asabiya* was undoubtedly the true source of their political power.

The Arab Nationalism of the Ba'ath party, like that adopted by Nasser after he discarded the Brotherhood in 1954, represented the ascendancy of the Arab 'nation' over the Islamic Umma, though it was felt that the two concepts could be harmonized. Nasser's initial efforts – notably unsuccessful – were directed towards creating unity at state level in order to give expression to an aspiration, strongly felt during the 1950s and 1960s, that the Arabs constituted a nation (*qawm*) on the basis of common language and culture. This theory had been latent in the thinking of the reformers: Rashid Rida, for example, had sought to revive, in theory at least, the idea of an Arab Caliphate, though he never found a suitable candidate for this office. It was also an unstated assumption in the ideology of the Muslim Brotherhood: Banna, among others, had regarded the transfer of power to non-Arabs after the first four 'Rightly Guided' caliphs as the true reason for the decline of Islam.[11] Only Arabs, because of their language, could taste the real Islam. For the majority of Arabs, Islamic and Arab identities merged imperceptibly: the two were not, as in Turkey, in opposition, particularly if the cultural and 'civilizational' aspect of Islam, as distinct from its religious or legal content, were emphasized.

While the Egyptian Copts, who saw themselves as true descendants of the ancient Egyptians, could take refuge in 'Pharaonic nationalism', for Syrian Christian Arabs the problem of nationality was more delicate. Even before the demise of the Ottoman empire many of them had suspected that the Arab 'nation' might exclude them. Those who, unlike the Lebanese Maronites, wished to dispense with foreign 'protection' tended to give 'Arabism' a more secular character or even sought in Marxism a way out of their difficulties. One of the most influential Arab nationalist writers was Michel Aflaq (b. 1910), co-founder and ideologist of the Ba'ath Party. Born into a Greek Orthodox family, he had lived for a time in Paris before returning to Syria in 1936. His étatist brand of socialism bore the hallmarks of the Popular Front. For Aflaq, as for the Turkish ideologist Ziya Gokalp, the nation pre-dated Islam: however, whereas for the Turks this assumption led logically to a complete separation of religion and politics, for Aflaq and other Arab nationalists 'Islam' was the supreme embodiment of 'Arabism'. In 1943 Aflaq wrote:

> Europe is as fearful of Islam today as she has been in the past. She now knows that the strength of Islam (which in the past expressed that of the Arabs) has been reborn and has appeared in a new form: in Arab nationalism.[12]

For this reason, he concluded, Europe befriended 'traditional' Islam, with its 'superficial worship, vague and colourless values', in order to Europeanize it.[12]

Aflaq's Ba'athist ideology (the word *ba'th*, 'rebirth', appears in Quranic verses about the resurrection) appealed across the sectarian divisions of Syrian and Iraqi society in the name of an 'Arab' common denominator able to include Sunnis and Shi'ites, Isma'ilis and Druzes and the various Christian communities. The major grouping excluded by the Ba'athist ideology was the non-Arab Kurds, concentrated mainly in the mountains of northern Iraq, but also settled in Syria. The universalist and egalitarian appeal of Ba'athism made it attractive to army officers who came to power in Syria and Iraq during the early 1960s, while its organizational structure, modelled on the one-party socialist states of Eastern Europe, made it a suitable vehicle for extending the power of the state, and the welfare patronage at its disposal, throughout society.

Formerly impoverished outsiders compared with the Sunni who dominated the cities, the 'Alawis (Nusairis) had risen to power through the political and military committees of the Ba'ath Party, maintaining their own cohesion while dividing that of their opponents. This was not so much a pre-planned policy of 'entryism' as the result of ordinary politicking, in which individuals greedy for power tended to recruit supporters from their own families and communities and pack them into influential committees. Paradoxically, a party such as the Ba'ath which is formally committed to secular aims and does not recognize *a priori*, sectarian or other group allegiances, is probably more vulnerable to this form of manipulation than a formation which assumes the existence of alternative group loyalties. In Syria, as in most Arab countries, the army plays a decisive role in political life, and the disproportionate number of 'Alawi officers has become a powerful source of Sunni resentment. In June 1979 Brotherhood militants, aided by the duty officer at the Aleppo military academy, massacred sixty cadets, all of them 'Alawis. Subsequent reprisals by the regime for this and other acts of terror committed by the Brotherhood or its affiliates (membership of which is now a capital offence) included the massacre of 400 prisoners at Palmyra in 1980 and the virtual destruction in February 1982 of the city of Hama, a traditional Brotherhood stronghold where there had been a rebellion. The onslaught on Hama resulted in the loss of an estimated 10,000 lives. At the time of writing the spiral of terror and counter-terror had abated somewhat, with the Brotherhood temporarily cowed after the Hama massacres.

Another major centre of the Muslim Brotherhood's activity has been the Sudan, where, since independence in 1954, it has campaigned for the adoption of a permanent constitution based on the Quran and the Sunna. During the 1960s, however, this demand was frustrated by the traditional political parties connected with the *tariqas*, as well as by leftists and Nasserists entrenched in the universities and trades unions. An attempt by the progressive young leader of the Umma party, Sayyid Sadiq al Mahdi, who was also heir-apparent to the leadership of the Ansar, to forge a reformist alliance of Islamic forces was frustrated by Colonel Ja'far Numeiri's Communist-backed coup in 1969. However, after the Communists themselves tried to oust Numeiri in 1971, he removed the leftists from his government and gave their posts to leaders with *tariqa* connections. A new constitution adopted in 1973 proclaimed that 'Islamic law and custom shall be the main sources of legislation'.

Islamization was carried a stage further when, in 1977, Numeiri set up a commission for the revision of Sudanese laws, to bring them more closely into line with the Shari'a. This opened the way for government participation by the moderate wing of the Brotherhood led by Dr Hasan al Turabi, who in 1978 accepted the post of Attorney-general. Relying on the principle of *maslaha*, Dr Turabi allowed members of the Brotherhood to stand as candidates for the Sudan Socialist Union, the only official party allowed by Numeiri. By the autumn of 1980 they had gained a number of seats in the new People's Assembly.

Turabi's compromise with military government was not, however, to the taste of the Brotherhood's more militant members, or to the progressive wing of the Umma party led by Sayyid Sadiq el Mahdi. Sayyid Sadiq, an Oxford-educated scholar who briefly held the premiership in 1968, is impatient at the extent to which the current Islamization programme compromises with – and sanctifies – outdated social customs. He believes very strongly, in line with his family's mahdist tradition, that each generation must interpret the Quran anew in accordance with the needs of the age.

In September 1983, faced with a growing economic crisis and a serious erosion in his political base, President Numeiri suddenly announced that Islamic law was to be introduced in its entirety and that the Quranic penalties would be imposed for *hadd* offences. There were popular demonstrations in support of the President, who, in a much publicized gesture, inaugurated the total ban on alcohol by initiating the pouring of thousands of bottles of beer, wine and spirits into the Nile. Most political observers saw his Quixotic gesture as an attempt to curry favour with the Saudis in order to obtain desperately needed economic aid to shore up his crumbling regime. Even the Muslim Brothers appeared unimpressed by this effort to outflank them by appearing 'more Islamic than thou'. In a veiled attack on the regime's economic policies, Sayyid Sadiq told his followers, during Friday prayers on Aba Island, that the *hadd* penalty for theft should only be applied when no one was driven to steal by reason of want. He was duly arrested, with more than a hundred of his followers, and held in Kobeh prison, where he was still languishing when this book went to press.[13]

INDO-PAKISTAN

If Egypt, with its proximity to Europe, became the intellectual powerhouse of Western Islam, India, subject to Hindu, Persian and Anglo-

Saxon influences, became in the late nineteenth and early twentieth centuries a source of religious and intellectual vitality of equal import-ance for the Muslim world. As in the West, the growing impact of modernization and occidental influence produced an evolution from progressive liberalism to reactive traditionalism. However, in Indo-Pakistan, as in some other non-Arab regions, the process took on a much more combative and urgent character. Faced with the spectre of Hindu domination, whether appearing in the guise of religious orthodoxy or that of a secular modernism imposed by an elite of pandits and tech-nocrats, a substantial number of Indian Muslims made their *hijra* to Pakistan, converting *dar al harb* into *dar al Islam*, where their leaders fiercely debated the ideal Islamic state. Their vision was, however, markedly different from that of the Arab reformers. The Islamic state envisaged by their most articulate spokesman, Abu'l Ala Maududi, was not so much an ideal Medinese polity reinterpreted to suit the conditions of the twentieth century as a recreation of an idealized Muslim society as it was deemed to have existed in India before its destruction by the British Raj. This way of thinking bore some resemblance to that of the ultra-orthodox Ashkenazi Jews who settled in Israel only to preserve the garb and social customs of the eighteenth-century Polish Diaspora.

SPECULATIVE MODERNISM: MUHAMMAD IQBAL

The seminal thinker of modern Indian Islam is unquestionably Mu-hammad Iqbal (1875–1938), poet, mystic, philosopher and intellectual founder of Pakistan. More learned and subtle in his thinking than Muhammad Abduh, he combined the mystical rationalism of the Persian tradition in which he was reared with an understanding of Western modes of thought unsurpassed by any Muslim writer before or since. Whereas Ahmed Khan had exhibited in his career an overwhelming desire to be accepted as an 'Anglo-Indian gentleman', Iqbal, like his Hindu contemporary Tagore, belonged to a generation for which such a position could be more or less taken for granted. Each was free to explore, from a position of intellectual if not of social equality, the *Zeitgeist* of his particular community, and to present it in terms which Europeans could understand.

After a traditional Islamic education Iqbal came under Western in-fluence first at Lahore and then at Cambridge, where he studied from 1905 to 1908 before going on to complete a doctorate in Persian metaphysics at Munich. His earliest poems were written in Urdu, but following his sojourn in Germany he became more romantic and mystical, writing increasingly in Persian. The Quran, he believed, reflected an essentially dynamic outlook, one which was linked directly to the principle of *ijtihad* in the Shari'a, fixing the position of man within an evolving cosmos. Aziz Ahmed has summarized this aspect of Iqbal's thought:

> The movement of the individual self is directly related to the principle of movement in the universe, from chaos towards a pattern of order. Universe as well as life are involved in a process of continuous becoming; and man, who stands at the peak of evolution, can maintain, in himself and in the society to which he belongs, the momentum of this primeval movement by ever-new conquest of the forces of nature.[14]

Iqbal's mystical humanism reflected his reading of Bergson and Nietzsche, as well as ideas developed from the traditions of Islamic neoplatonism. Nietzsche's 'superman' and Ibn al 'Arabi's 'Perfect Man', Bergson's *'élan vital'* and Rumi's evolutionary spiral, merge in his thinking, along with perceptions drawn from Hegel, Whitehead, Russell and Einstein. The work of modern metaphysicians, mathematicians and physicists has not only destroyed the self-subsistent materialism of classical physics: it also serves to refute the Ash'ari view of time as absolute and ultimately indivisible. Thus the 'unseen world' (*al ghaib*) referred to in the Quran is 'not something foreign to the world of matter, but permeates it through and through'. While the Prophethood of Muhammad is located in history, his Message is only 'final' in the sense that it is eternally valid, its aim being 'to awaken in man the higher consciousness of his manifold relations with the universe'.[15] Prophesy is a special mode of mystic consciousness, a 'mode of economizing individual thought and choice by providing ready-made judgements, choices and ways of action' – a mode of understanding appropriate to the childhood of the human race:

> With the birth of reason and the critical faculty, however, life, in its own interest, inhibits the formation and growth of non-rational modes of consciousness . . . The Prophet of Islam seems to stand between the ancient and modern world. In so far as the source of his revelation is concerned he belongs to the ancient world; in so far as the spirit of his revelation is concerned he belongs to the

modern world . . . The birth of Islam . . . is the birth of inductive intellect. In Islam prophesy reaches its perfection in discovering the need of its own abolition.[16]

Theologically, Iqbal affirms the dominance of free will without having recourse to Mu'tazili rationalism: only as an 'ever-growing ego can [man] belong to the meaning of the universe'. There are no pleasure-giving and pain-giving acts, only ego-sustaining and ego-dissolving ones. Resurrection is therefore not an external event, but the 'consummation of a life process within the ego'.[17] Heaven and Hell are states, not localities: Heaven the 'joy of triumph over the forces of disintegration', Hell a 'corrective experience which may make a hardened ego once more sensitive to the living breeze of Divine Grace'.[18]

Using Bergson's distinction between 'time' and 'duration', Iqbal frees the Quranic ideal from its historic setting. The ideal Islamic state has never been fully realized, and should not be confused with the government of the Orthodox Caliphs, as is done by most Muslim revivalists. It is still dormant in the conscience of man. Political activity should therefore not be directed towards the restoration of an idealized Islamic past but towards a future in which the concept of Caliphate or 'vice-regency' is equated with the service of humanity:

> In this ideal state man's vice-regency of God would fulfil itself and honour its trust, by acknowledging that the ownership of all land vests in God and by accepting that man's duty is to produce wealth for the benefit of all humanity.[19]

This ideal is not incompatible with socialism. Marxism, however, gets bogged down in the negative side of the *tahlil* formula ('There is no god . . .') while failing to emerge into the creative and positive one (' . . . but Allah'): 'The religion of that God-ignoring prophet [Karl Marx] is based on the equality of all stomachs.' Communism therefore has much in common with western imperialism. 'Both are dynamic and restless. Both ignore God and betray man. One does this by revolution, the other by exploitation. Between these two millstones, humanity is ground to dust.'[20]

Iqbal came to the conclusion that, as a step towards the realization of the ideal Islamic state, the Muslims of India must have a state of their own:

> The religious order of Islam is organically related to the social order which it has created. The rejection of the one will inevitably

involve the rejection of the other. Therefore the construction of a polity on Indian national lines, if it means a displacement of the Islamic principles of solidarity, is simply unthinkable to a Muslim . . . The principle of European democracy cannot be applied to India without recognizing the facts of communal groups . . . I would like to see the Punjab, North-Western Frontier Province, Sind and Baluchistan amalgamated into a single state . . . the formation of a consolidated North-West Indian Muslim state appears to me to be the final destiny of the Muslims at least of North-West India.[21]

Iqbal, who died in 1938, did not live to see the bloody birth-pangs of Pakistan. It was left to Muhammad Ali Jinna, leader of the Muslim League, to act as its midwife. Iqbal had forseen that a Muslim state dominated by upper-class Westernized Muslims like Jinna would not of itself satisfy the ideal of Islamic government; but he believed that if Islamic law were properly applied 'at least the right of subsistence' would be secured to the Muslim masses: 'For Islam the acceptance of social democracy in some suitable form and consistent with the legal principles of Islam is not a revolution but a return to the original purity of Islam.'[21]

If Iqbal's political thought became the main inspiration of the Pakistan movement, it was left to his disciples to work out what a 'return to the original purity of Islam' meant in practical terms. Few Indian Muslims shared his breadth of culture. The liberalism of his outlook commended itself to the anglicized upper classes, while his charismatic reputation, enhanced by his fame as a poet, made him the popular idol of the masses. But, as with Abduh, none of his successors was strong enough to maintain both positions at once. At first the liberals established a parliamentary oligarchy which paid lip-service to Islamic principles – an Indian version of British Toryism which complemented the upper-class Fabianism of Nehru and his daughter in India. When this foundered it was replaced by a Western-oriented dictatorship of the Punjabi officer class under Brigadier-General Muhammad Ayub Khan. Disillusioned with the empty rhetoric of a cosmetic Islamic state which fell far short of Iqbal's ideals, opposition generally ran through more secular channels. The Awami League in the East and Zuflikar Ali Bhutto's Pakistani People's Party in the West became the principal forces of organized political activity both before and after the crisis over Bangladesh.

Having been coopted by a discredited upper class, reformist Islam in

Pakistan never developed into a mass movement comparable to the Muslim Brotherhood in Egypt. This was partly because, in the Indian environment, survival rather than planning the future had become the principal issue facing the Muslim communities. Distributed throughout the Subcontinent in a variety of mainly urban settlements, there was in reality no common consciousness or consensus of experience upon which progressive reformers could build. After Pakistan's traumatic birth in 1947, the problem of its relations with India and the difficulty of keeping its two halves together were rather more pressing issues than problematic debates about the content of an Islamic constitution. Apart from the political question, there was no way in which a Salafi movement, involving a return to first principles, could develop a popular character in a society where even the literature had no direct access to the Quran and the Sunna. In such an environment, Islamic religiosity crystallized around the formal symbols of Indian Muslim identity – a Pharisaic observance of ritual, dress and social custom, combined with a deep distrust, not just of the West which had ceased to be the burning issue, but of modernity as such, in all its forms. Unlike the Arab world, where (outside the Arabian Peninsula) even the most reactionary *faqihs* had been painfully educated into accepting most of the cardinal points of the modernist rubric, the Indian *'ulama* had retained all the defensive inwardness of the ghetto, fearful that any loosening of the gates of *ijtihad* would lead to an inrush of Western and Hindu influences, destroying both their religion and their distinctive identity. The parallels with attitudes to be found in the East European Jewish communities are compelling.

SYSTEMATIC NEO-TRADITIONALISM: SAYYID ABU'L ALA MAUDUDI

The man who tried to bridge the gap between the ultra-traditionalist *'ulama* and the liberal elite was Sayyid Abu'l Ala Maududi (1903–79), described by Wilfred Cantwell-Smith as 'much the most systematic thinker of modern Islam'.[22] Maududi's thought is rigid and conservative; but it aspires to be both comprehensive and self-contained. His basic premise is that Islam is entirely self-sufficient and does not need to explain itself in terms other than its own. He is not interested in harmonizing his Islamic ideology with other systems. For Maududi, Islam is perfect and needs no justification. Instead he endeavours to expound, by an idiosyncratic combination of *ijtihad* and literalist exegesis, the Islamic dogma as he sees it, covering every field of human activity from politics to the sexual life. He interlards his exposition with polemics attacking a West which he finds morally repulsive and, fundamentally, incomprehensible. Largely ignorant of Western high cultural and intellectual traditions, his views are mostly picked up, second hand, from reading articles in newspapers about various social problems. He never applies the same canons of criticism to contemporary Muslim societies: the perfection of 'Islam' is forever compared with the actual imperfections of Western society: like is not compared with like.

Maududi articulates the narrow outlook of the traditionalist Muslim middle class in India and elsewhere, a class which feels its identity and values increasingly threatened by western economic and cultural encroachments. He defends these values by moving in to the attack: the west is morally decadent and corrupt and must be resisted. There is no necessity for an agonizing reappraisal of Islam in the light of modern reality. All that needs to be done is to modernize the *fiqh* to suit new situations. The only real difference between Maududi and the traditionalist *'ulama* is that, whereas they tend to be out of touch with reality, concerning themselves with arcane and usually irrelevant questions, Maududi has the courage to confront modernity with the whole of the traditional Shari'a edifice. In his hands 'Islam' becomes much more than a succession of hair-splitting legal judgements emanating from an archaic social system. It is a full-blown 'ideology' offering answers to every human and social problem. It is mainly for this reason that, despite his rigidity, Maududi is widely admired by Muslim radicals from Egypt to Malaysia. He is one of the very few non-Arab writers on Islam to have been widely translated into Arabic. Along with Sayyid Qutb, he is the most widely read theoretician among young Sunni activists. The strength of his system is that particular aspects (such as his insistence on traditional *purdah* for women) can be discarded without damage to the structure of the whole.

Theoretically Maududi's system is more radical than the way he applies it in practice. With Ahmed Khan, he holds the view that Islam is 'the natural religion of man, the religion that is not associated with any person, people, period or place'.[23] But, whereas this attitude led Ahmed Khan and other modernists towards an acceptance of religious pluralism, Maududi insists uncompromisingly that the Shari'a must be applied to the whole human race:

> The Quran does not claim that Islam is the true compendium of rites and rituals, and metaphysical beliefs and concepts, or that it is

the proper form of religious (as the word religion is nowadays understood in Western terminology) attitude of thought and action for the individual. Nor does it say that Islam is the true way of life for the people of Arabia, or for the people of any particular country or for the people preceding any particular age (say the Industrial Revolution). No! Very explicitly, for the entire human race, there is only one way of life which is Right in the eyes of God and that is al-Islam.[24]

'Not a single injunction of [the Quran] can be suspected as having been addressed to a particular people,' insists Maududi.[25] Like the traditionalist 'ulama, Maududi regards all six canonical hadith collections and the Quran (which he interprets in a very literalistic manner) as the supreme sources of the Shari'a. He also accepts much of the dogma contained in the four schools of fiqh: 'the differences that appear in the four schools are but the natural outcome of the fact that truth is many-sided.'[26]

While he accepts ijtihad and qiyas as flexible elements in the Shari'a, he has little use for them in practice, at least in the areas of social and family life. His traditionalism is most evident in his general attitude to women, and, in particular, in his defence of purdah, the complete veiling and segregation of women as practised in India. He attacks all the modernists who claim that the Quran and hadiths are free from purdah injunctions: 'The most one could differ in the matter was whether the hands and the face were to be covered or left uncovered.'[27] He concludes, with impeccable logic, that women should be completely covered outside the home (where they should always remain, except when absolutely necessary) because the face is the most attractive part of the human body. If the object of the Shari'a is – as it must be – to 'curb indecency and obscenity, then nothing can be more unreasonable than to close all the minor ways to indecency [i.e., by covering the other parts of the body] but to fling the main gate wide open.'[28] Similarly, birth control is condemned by the Shari'a in all but the most exceptional circumstances because it involves a 'rebellion against the laws of nature'.[29] He rejects the view that the world is becoming over-populated, arguing instead that pressure of population leads to economic development. Men should not be deterred from breeding by the 'phantom of scarcity'.

Like Iqbal's, Maududi's doctrine of khilafa – man's 'vice-regency' – is thus in no way taken to mean that because the world's resources are finite, humans should exercise caution and moderation in exploiting them. On the contrary, though sovereignty over the universe and over the whole world belongs to God, we have the right, even the duty, to exploit them for the benefit of humanity. Private wealth and property are permissible, provided they are employed in the service of 'virtue and public welfare', through payment of *zakat* and other religious taxes. The evils of capitalism result from the moral shortcomings of the rich who refuse to recognize the needs of the poor; they are not caused by the system of private ownership as such. Thus, while Maududi claims that Islam, unlike other systems of East and West, is uniquely placed to solve man's economic problems, his remedies (apart from the prohibition of *riba*, which he interprets to mean lending at interest regardless of profit) do not differ substantially from the welfare capitalism of New Dealers and social democrats.

Maududi's primary aim is to present 'Islam' as an absolute and self-sufficient ideology, completely distinct from and opposed to both the Western way of life and its Eastern socialist equivalents. 'The fact . . . is that Islam and Western civilization are poles apart in their objectives as well as in their principles of social organization.'[30] Western humanism he often characterizes as 'man-worship', a form of *shirk* which he contrasts with Islamic *tawhid* (God's unity). Like Abduh (and unlike Iqbal), he holds the essentially medieval view that 'science' consists of a 'systematized body of knowledge',[31] whose discoveries can be appropriated for the benefit of Islam without causing an epistemological upheaval that must lead to a radical revaluation of Islam's intellectual premises as understood by the traditionalists – a revaluation that must affect all traditional formulations of the Shari'a.

As well as being an ideologist, Maududi was the creator and leader of a militant Islamic organization, the Jamiat-i-Islami. He originally opposed the creation of Pakistan because he feared the liberalism of its founders and the British-trained administrators who would be required to run it.

> All persons who have been trained for running the affairs of a secular state . . . are totally unfitted for an Islamic state which requires human beings of a very different character for its citizens, voters, councillors, office-bearers . . . It requires men who have the fear of God in their hearts; who feel a sense of responsibility towards God; who prefer the next life to the present; in whose eyes moral gain or loss is much more important than worldly success or failure . . .[32]

Abandoning his revolutionary programme for the conversion of the whole of India to Islam, as a first stage in the conversion of the whole of humanity, he accepted the reality of Pakistan, opting for a gradualist approach towards the Islamization of its law and constitution, though he had previously condemned the Muslim League for taking a similar line. He accepted that the *fiqh* would have to be modernized in certain areas of constitutional, international and criminal law, and accepted Pakistan as a *de facto* national state. Thereafter his efforts were concentrated on making Pakistan a 'theo-democracy' based on the Shari'a which would enforce, among other things, the abolition of interest-bearing banks, sexual segregation and veiling of women, and the *hadd* penalties for theft, adultery and other crimes. He admitted that his Islamic state would bear a certain resemblance to Communist and Fascist states, being based on an all-embracing ideology. However, he vigorously denied that its implementation would lead to human rights abuses. Pakistani non-Muslims would enjoy the rights Islam accords to minorities. He accepted the rulings of the medieval *faqihs* regarding the rights and disabilities of *dhimmis*: they would have the 'same freedom of conscience, expression and opinion' as Muslims and would be subject to the same penalties for theft and other crimes. They would be debarred from holding certain key offices in the Islamic state, but not otherwise discriminated against.[33]

The Jamiat-i-Islami became the spearhead of the movement to transform Pakistan from a Muslim homeland into an Islamic state. In the Constituent Assembly's discussions on the Constitution in 1951, Maududi, who had been jailed for his oppositional activities, joined hands with the traditionalist *'ulama* in outlining 22 Basic Principles of an Islamic state. They included the demand that all existing laws contrary to the Quran and the Sunna should be gradually phased out, and that the state should be based on 'the principles and ideas of Islamic ideology'.[34]

The *dhimmi* question came to the fore in the anti-Qadiyani agitation in 1953. The Qadiyanis, a faction of the Ahmedi sect, were followers of Ghulam Ahmed of Qadiyan, who had advanced claims to prophethood in the late nineteenth century. Though many of his followers, who shared a modernist outlook, interpreted these claims metaphorically, Maududi and the traditionalist *'ulama* believed that the Qadiyanis had formed themselves into a separate Umma by designating non-Qadiyanis as *kafirs*, by prohibiting intermarriage with other Muslims, and by praying separately from them. Under the Raj they had been treated as Muslims: indeed, the support they received from the British was the real source of resentment against them, since Ghulam Ahmed's claims were scarcely more blasphemous than those advanced by Muhammad Ahmad and other African *mahdis*. There was also a strictly political motive in the agitation: Muhammad Zafrullah Khan, the Foreign Minister, was a Qadiyani, as were other influential figures. The attack on the sect was thus directed at individuals in the government as well as at the easy-going liberalism of the secularists who were prepared to take a broad view of the question: 'who is a Muslim?'. The agitation led to serious rioting in the Punjab which was only quelled after the imposition of martial law. The report produced by Mr Justice Munir in the aftermath of these disturbances squarely faced the issue that had been fudged in the discussions over the Constitution: an 'Islamic State' as defined by the Maududists and the *'ulama* was incompatible with democracy in the modern sense of the term. A 'lack of bold and clear thinking, the inability to understand and take decisions', had brought about 'a confusion which will persist . . . until our leaders have a clear concept of the goal and of the means to reach it . . . Opposing principles, if left to themselves, can only produce confusion and disorder, and the application of a neutralizing agency to them can only produce a dead result.' The report concluded:

> . . . as long as we rely on the hammer when a file is needed and press Islam into service to solve situations it was never intended to solve, frustration and disappointment must dog our steps. The sublime faith called Islam will live, even if our leaders are not there to enforce it. It lives in the individual, in his soul and outlook, in all his relations with God and man, from the cradle to the grave, and our politicians should understand that if Divine Commands cannot make or keep a man a Musalman, their statements will not.[35]

Maududi was sentenced to death for his part in the Qadiyani agitation, but the sentence was commuted to 14 years' imprisonment, of which he served only two. Disregarding Munir's advice, in 1956 the Constituent Assembly approved the first Pakistan Constitution – a document which persisted in trying to square the circle of having an Islamic Constitution in a multi-confessional state. The Jamiat-i-Islami declared itself satisfied with the lip service paid to Islam in this document, hoping to achieve its real implementation by political pressure and agitation. In fact the political anarchy resulting from the electoral collapse of the Muslim

League led to the imposition of martial law in 1958, sweeping away the Constitution. 'Islamic' was dropped from the name of the Republic. Ayub Khan, who established a presidential cabinet in 1962, left the traditionalist 'ulama to their own devices, though he incurred their hostility by introducing a reformed Family Law which restricted divorce and polygamy in accordance with a liberal Hanafi ruling. The Jamiat-i-Islami played a prominent part in the agitation which brought about the downfall of Ayub's government in 1969; but it made a poor showing in the elections the following year, winning only eight seats from a field of 488 candidates. It continued to agitate over the Qadiyani question, eventually pressuring the government of Mr Bhutto into declaring the Qadiyanis a non-Muslim minority.

The Jamiat also played its part in bringing about the downfall of Bhutto in 1977; and, though Maududi had once declared military rule of any kind to be 'un-Islamic', he enthusiastically supported General Zia ul Haqq during the early months of his rule. With the Jamiat's backing, Zia made Islamization the ideological cornerstone of his government: hadd penalties, including flogging and amputation, were introduced for alcohol consumption, zina (illicit sex), qazf (false accusations of zina) and theft. Though amputations were rare, public floggings became a popular spectator sport, this punishment being inflicted for 'hoarding and profiteering' as well as for hadd offences. Shari'a benches empowered to revise existing laws and sentences were introduced in each of the four provincial High Courts: 'Islam' was thus being permitted to challenge the existing legal and constitutional system. Late in 1979 a retired judge brought a case before the Lahore High Court which effectively challenged the legality of Pakistan's suspended democracy, arguing that the Islamic terms amir (commander) and shura (consultation) were not representational. The previous year General Zia had already deferred promised elections by creating a new system of separate electorates for Muslims and dhimmis, a move long advocated by the Maududists and one which would effectively reduce the status of dhimmis to that of second-class citizens. In October 1979 the elections were again deferred, allegedly because of the confusion created by the new rules governing the registration of political parties, which were now required to satisfy a government commission that their views accorded with Pakistan's official Islamic 'ideology'.

Latterly, General Zia has spoken in essentially Maududist terms of creating a 'new political system', in which only 'practising' Muslims of established honesty and competence could be nominated as candidates for elections. The economic changes introduced by him include obligatory *zakat* deductions from savings (including bank deposits, company shares and insurance policies) – a measure which ran into opposition from the Shi'a community, which collects *zakat* voluntarily for the use of its own establishment. From 1979 house-building loans became available on a rental rather than an interest basis, and it was announced that two government corporations, the National Investment Trust and the Investment Corporation of Pakistan, would henceforth operate on the lines of profit-sharing or equity participation. In the purely religious sphere, the government has coerced Pakistani Muslims into observing their duties: fasting during Ramadan has been strictly enforced, with shopkeepers arrested for selling food during daylight hours. Government officials have to set aside time for daily prayers, while General Zia himself has personally dispatched shiploads of pilgrims for the Hajj.

Despite General Zia's determination to Islamize Pakistan, Islamic radicals, including members of the Jamiat-i-Islami, have expressed scepticism about the efficacy of his measures. Although advised by an 'Islamic Ideological Council', he has tried to implement his reforms through a reluctant judiciary and bureaucracy committed to a more secular outlook. As a military man he is deeply distrustful of populist demands by the Jamiat and other activists to transform mosques into centres for mobilizing the local administration, as in Iran. Like the Muslim Brotherhood in the Sudan, the Jamiat appeared less than wholly impressed by General Zia's Islamization measures and his continuing postponement of promised elections.

In 1983, faced with a prolonged and unprecedented opposition campaign, spearheaded by the Movement for the Restoration of Democracy, in which more than 4,000 people were reported arrested, the Pakistani ruler began holding talks with right-wing political parties, including the Jamiat. In contrast with its earlier collaboration with the military government, the Jamiat now demanded the restoration of press freedom, the release of political detainees and prisoners, the restoration of political freedoms and the holding of elections by March 1984, with a view to ending martial law and transferring power to the people. It was by no means clear whether this was a tactical change of front, intended to facilitate collaboration with other parties, or whether it represented a genuine conversion to a more pluralistic view of 'Islamic democracy'. A Jamiat spokesman confined himself to saying that he would support the participation in the elections of all parties which believed in the 'ideology of Pakistan'. Whatever their long-term strategy, the Jamiat leaders were clearly anxious to distance themselves from a regime of growing un-popularity, despite the fact that the government had adopted a substantial part of their programme.

General Zia, for his part, appears to have turned away from the Maududists towards the more moderate reform movement led by Maulana Abu'l Hasan Nadwi of Lucknow. An admirer of Iqbal and Banna, Nadwi follows Abduh in recognizing a need for the separation of religious and political spheres. Nadwi stresses the importance of education and Islamic da'wa (evangelism), and criticizes the Maududists' preoccupation with the political struggle, which, he believes, can only foment strife among Muslims and could even pave the way for the emergence of a Muslim sect devoid of spiritual values. 'The Iranian revolutionaries', he says, 'are more influenced by the French and Russian revolutions than the revolution of Makkah, which alone is the font of Islamic revolution.'[36] Members of the Jamaat Tablighi, a reformist group committed to Nadwi's principles, are prominent in Pakistani officer circles and are now said to be receiving official encouragement.[37]

THE ISLAMIC REVOLUTION IN IRAN

The origins and cause of the Iranian revolution can only be dealt with briefly here. To summarize a complex situation crudely, the Shah of Iran was brought down by a combination of economic and political factors, mostly of his own making. Unlike the Ottoman dominions and Egypt, which had long been exposed to Western influences, Iran remained comparatively isolated until the end of the nineteenth century. (Before the opening of the Suez Canal in 1869, Iran lay 11,000 miles from Western Europe by the sea-route which carried most of the trade.) The Qajar Shahs who eventually inherited Safavid power ruled over a loosely structured polity in which the Shi'ite 'ulama disposed of considerable social power. In the 1890s they succeeded, partly under Afghani's inspiration, in mobilizing a vigorous and successful national protest against the tobacco monopoly granted by the Shah to an Englishman, Major Talbot. The Tobacco Agitation proved to be the dress rehearsal for the full-blown, but remarkably peaceful Constitutional Revolution of 1905–6, when a section of the 'ulama united with the business community to force the Shah into granting a Constituent Assembly that would protect them from unfair foreign competition. The 'ulama who backed the revolution argued that, in the absence of the Twelfth Imam, it was important to impose constitutional checks on the arbitrary power of rulers similar to those in force in Europe. Their opponents, led by Shaikh Falzollah Nuri, insisted that the true constitution was the Quran and the Sunna, and that European constitutional ideas were basically inimical to Islam. Nuri managed to introduce an amendment into the constitution ensuring that no laws were passed by the Majlis (assembly) till approved by a board of 'ulama.[38]

The National Assembly was successfully defended against an attempted counter-revolution by Muhammad 'Ali Shah in 1908; but the divisions inevitable in this fragile coalition between liberal modernists and the more traditionalist 'ulama opened the way for the Anglo-Russian intervention – a situation complicated by the establishment of a Soviet republic in Gilan after the Russian Revolution. The conflict was shelved – but not resolved – by the rise to power of Reza Khan, who, like Mustafa Kemal in Turkey, came up through the ranks of the army. At first Reza's modernizing nationalism enjoyed the support of some of the 'ulama and the conservative reformers in the Majlis. However, once he had achieved absolute power, taking the crown and title of Shah in 1926, he instituted draconian changes which struck at the roots of the old pluralistic, tribal society. Not only was a new centralized bureaucracy created, but ethnic solidarities were broken up by the manipulation of tribal animosities. Traditional costumes were banned and European dress, including the wide-brimmed felt hat, were forcibly introduced. Though officially registered mullahs were exempted from the latter rule, the new hats were specifically designed to interfere with the rule of prayer. Women's emancipation was imposed by force: the veil was outlawed, as was the traditional chador covering women from head to foot. Government employees, from ministers to road-sweepers, were ordered to parade their wives in public, though women were still denied the right to vote. Like his Qajar predecessors, the Shah made some generous concessions to foreign companies. Thus, under an agreement signed in 1933 with the Anglo-Iranian oil company and intended to last until 1991, Iran was to receive only between 10 and 20 per cent of its oil revenues. Like Attaturk (whom he greatly admired), Shah Reza created a new, Western-educated intelligentsia to run his bureaucracy. Unlike Attaturk, however, he never tried to consolidate his government by means of a nationally organized modern political party and took to governing increasingly by means of military and police repression.

In 1941 the British and Russians, fearing a pro-Axis coup by army officers, deposed Shah Reza and placed his son, Muhammad Reza, on the throne. The weak and vacillating young monarch was almost unseated in 1952, when he was forced to appoint Muhammad Mussadeq, a popular nationalist leader, as his Prime Minister. Mussadeq, supported by the Communist Tudeh party, which was active among the oil workers, nationalized the Anglo-Iranian Oil Company; however, the following year he was overthrown in a military coup engineered by Britain and the United States on behalf of the young Shah. From 1953 the Shah, backed by the army, ruled in a manner very similar to that of his father. Many areas of the economy were modernized, new roads and factories were built and the army, equipped with the latest US weaponry, became the second most powerful local force in the region. (The most powerful, that of Israel, provided the Shah with military advisers and experts in counter-insurgency.)

The rise of OPEC during the 1960s and early 1970s emboldened the Shah to push for higher oil prices, and for a period the higher revenues made the country appear very wealthy – at least on paper. In social terms, however, Iran presented a very different picture. Partial land reforms in the countryside, the exploding development of the cities and rural migration created a restless class of deracinated peasants who eked out a miserable livelihood in the shanty-towns surrounding Tehran and other conurbations. Though oil and other factory workers benefited from the rise in oil revenues, the economic infrastructure was inadequate to permit much of the new wealth to filter down into the community. Galloping inflation and a massive rise in urban rents ensured that only a minority of the Westernized middle class, particularly those with foreign connections, enjoyed the fruits of the country's exports. Corruption in court circles became an open scandal, as it became known that the Shah and his family had siphoned off millions of dollars into foreign bank accounts, and had appropriated much of the national product through such institutions as the Pahlavi Foundation – ostensibly a charitable organization – which owned a controlling interest in a chain of mines, hotels, factories and agri-businesses. Like his father, who had made himself the country's largest land-owner and employer, the Shah turned a considerable slice of Iran's economy into a personal fiefdom.

No doubt many people benefited from the Shah's reforms: considerable improvements were made in health and education under the so-called 'White Revolution' launched in 1963, in which some 1.6 million peasant families obtained land. However, agricultural stagnation, rising rents and general inflation meant that by the mid 1970s more and more people felt themselves to be worse off. This was especially the case in great cities like Tehran, where between 1967 and 1977 (the decade of the oil boom) the proportion of urban families living in one room actually increased, from 36 per cent to 43 per cent.[39]

The Shah finally sealed his fate by sheer political ineptitude. Belatedly, in 1975, he tried to broaden his power-base by creating a single political party, the Rastakhiz or 'Resurgence' Party, on the East European totalitarian model. Two areas of society previously untouched by the regime – the *bazaari* merchants and the religious establishment – were suddenly encroached upon. The party took over all the ministries and public media. Branches were opened in the bazaars and donations forced out of small businessmen: suddenly, instead of tolerating indifference or passive opposition, the regime was demanding active support. The *'ulama* were explicitly attacked. The Shah was declared to be a 'spiritual leader'; the *mullahs* were denounced as medieval 'black reactionaries'. The religious calendar was abolished and a royalist calendar (dating from the supposed foundation of the ancient Iranian monarchy) was substituted. By means of the Party, the state encroached upon the autonomy of the *waqfs* (from which the Shi'ite *'ulama* derived most of their livelihoods), in what was clearly seen as a first move against the independence of the religious establishment. The 1967 Family Protection Law – which had raised the minimum age of marriage for girls to 18, contrary to the Shari'a – was, for the first time, rigidly enforced. Girls who expressed their opposition to the regime by wearing the traditional *chador* were banned from universities and government offices.

This attack on the religious establishment might have succeeded if the Shah had not simultaneously alienated the secular middle-class groups. In 1977, however, he launched a massive 'anti-profiteering' campaign, blaming them for the high rate of inflation. A number of leading industrialists were arrested. Naturally this infuriated the business community, whose members were perfectly aware of the goings-on at court, and the wealthier among them followed the Pahlavi example of transferring their capital abroad. The smaller *bazaari* businessmen, who had always had close ties with the *'ulama*, had already been alienated by the Shah's campaign against the religious establishment. The final element in the formidable coalition the Shah was ranging against himself was the industrial proletariat itself. Premier Amouzegar sparked off a whole chain of strikes in the oil and manufacturing industries by carrying out deflationary measures which included the cutting of bonuses.

The events leading immediately to the Shah's downfall in 1979 (the burning of an Abadan cinema, repeated cycles of demonstrations, shootings and mourning processions) are well documented and need not be repeated here. The important fact is that the monarch succeeded in alienating every significant group in the country – the 'Westernized' business community, the salaried middle class, the *bazaari* merchants, the factory workers, the service workers and the armies of unemployed, under-employed and semi-employed *mustazafin* ('*les misérables*') who lived in the shanty-towns, as well as a section of the rural population. The question that concerns us here is how and why 'Islam' came to play its decisive ideological role in the revolution.

Basically, three aspects of Iranian Shi'ism contributed to the triumph of the revolution: the revisionist neo-Shi'ite ideology of the intellectuals and left-wing activists; the traditional religious hierarchy of Qum and Najaf (Iraq), led by the impressive, charismatic and uncompromising figure of Ayatollah Khomeini; and the popular Shi'ism of the 'Husseiniyat' – the culture of *rawzehs* and passion plays, imported from the villages into the shanty-towns and other districts inhabited by the *mustazafin*.

Shi'ite modernism is a comparatively recent development compared with the reformed Sunnism of Abduh and his followers. One reason for this was the backwardness of Iran in the nineteenth century compared with Egypt and India. Another, paradoxically, is that the 'High Shi'ism' represented by the seminaries of Qum and Najaf was philosophically and legally more adaptable than the *fiqh* dispensed by the traditionalist *'ulama* in Sunni countries. The victory of the *usulis* over the *akhbaris* in the nineteenth century and the principle that only a living *mujtahid* may interpret the law made it possible to introduce many aspects of modernization without encountering opposition from the *'ulama*. It was partly for this reason and partly because of their independent social power that a large section of the Iranian *'ulama*, unique among Muslim clergy, were able to join hands successfully with the liberal constitutionalists in 1905–9. Nevertheless, the stresses between the *'ulama* and the government remained, becoming more acute as a new technocratic elite, trained in Western ways and adopting many Western mannerisms, established a commanding position in society. To the social resentment of those who felt themselves excluded from the benefits of the oil wealth was added the opposition of those *'ulama*, led by Khomeini, who considered that Shaikh Nuri had been right in predicting that 'constitutionalism would be a meaningless trick allowing more, not less, European domination'.[40]

SHI'ITE NEO-TRADITIONALISM: SAYYID RUHALLAH KHOMEINI

Khomeini, a Sayyid from Arak who, like many *mujtahids*, had studied and taught at the famous Fayzieh *madrasa* (college) in Qum, first came to political prominence in 1962–3, during the protests against the Shah's 'White Revolution' – a programme which partially broke up the large estates, distributing land to the peasants, nationalized forests, denationalized state-owned factories, extended the vote to women and established a rural literacy corps. The reforms were evidently aimed at creating support for the Shah among the entrepreneurial middle class and the peasantry without antagonizing too many big land-owners. The Shah organized a national referendum which, according to the government, demonstrated 99.9 per cent 'approval' for the programme. The opposition, which included an alliance of *bazaari* merchants, clergy, public employees and Mussadeq's former supporters in the National Front, responded by organizing a wave of public demonstrations during the month of Muharram (June 1963) which left many hundreds of dead in Tehran, Qum, Isfahan, Shiraz, Mashad and Tabriz. As with the Constitutional Revolution and Mussadeq's movement, the opposition was made up of widely disparate elements. Khomeini maximized its appeal, however, by concentrating on the government's misdeeds rather than on the specifics of his own programme. In only one of his proclamations, for example, did he join with the traditionalist *'ulama* in opposing the franchise for women; on the other hand he vigorously denounced the Shah's regime for 'living off corruption, rigging elections, violating the constitutional laws, stifling the press and political parties, destroying the independence of the universities, neglecting the economic needs of merchants, workers and peasants, undermining the country's Islamic beliefs', and generally capitulating to the West.[41]

For his part in the agitation Khomeini was deported, first to Turkey and thence to the Shi'ite centre at Najaf in Iraq. Here he was to prove much more dangerous than when he was inside the country. Whereas the clergy who remained in Iran could be virtually silenced, expressing their opposition only in Delphic ambiguities, the Iraqis, who had their own quarrels with the Shah over the Kurdish question and over navigation in the disputed Shatt al Arab, were not averse to allowing Khomeini a political voice so long as he refrained from attacking the regime in Baghdad. From Najaf, Khomeini openly denounced the Shah, comparing him to Yazid, murderer of Husain, and urging the faithful to overthrow his satanic regime. At the same time he set forth, in a series of lectures to religious students, a radical programme for Islamic government entitled Velayet-i-Faqih ('the Jurist's Trusteeship'), in which he broke completely with traditional Shi'ite quietism and urged that the government should be entrusted directly to the 'ulama:

> Islam is the religion of militant individuals who are committed to truth and justice. It is the religion of those who desire freedom and independence. It is the school of those who struggle against imperialism . . .[42]

> Present Islam to the people in its true form so that our youth does not picture the akhunds as sitting in some corner of Najaf or Qum, studying the questions of menstruation or childbirth, instead of concerning themselves with politics, and draw the conclusion that religion must be separate from politics. This slogan of the separation of religion and politics and the demand that Islamic scholars should not intervene in social and political affairs have been formulated and propagated by the imperialists; it is only the irreligious who repeat them. Were religion and politics separate at the time of the Prophet (peace and blessing be upon him)? Did there exist, on one side, a group of clerics, and opposite it, a group of politicians and leaders?[43]

In the lectures, which contain polemical attacks on the 'imperialists, the oppressive and treacherous rulers, the Jews, Christians and materialists', Khomeini reverts to Nuri's argument that Islamic government is constitutional, not in the sense of being subject to laws decreed by a majority of the people, but because 'the rulers are subject to . . . conditions . . . set forth in the Noble Quran and the Sunna'.[44] Islam knows not monarchy: 'There is not the slightest trace of vast palaces, opulent buildings, servants and retainers, private equerries . . . and all the other appurtenances of monarchy that consume as much as half of the national budget.'[45] Above all, the ruler who adheres to Islam as well as being of a high personal moral standard must necessarily submit to the *faqih*, asking him about the laws and ordinances of Islam in order to carry them out. This being the case, the true rulers are the *faqihs* themselves, and rulership ought officially to be theirs – entrusted to them, rather than to those who are simply obliged to follow them on account of their own ignorance of the law.[46]

Khomeini's message, delivered to theology students in Najaf, was unambiguous. To a classic, Afghani-style appeal to the faithful to defend Islam against imperialist attacks, Khomeini added the specific corollary that the *faqihs* – that is to say the clerical establishment – must be entrusted with the full responsibility of government. His doctrine was simultaneously revolutionary and ultra-conservative, calling for militant activism, yet demanding that the religious establishment, of which he himself was an important member, had the right, even the duty, to govern the state. This was indeed a radical departure, not only from his previous positions (in 1941, for example, he had stated: 'We do not say that government must be in the hands of the *faqih*; rather we say that government must be in accordance with God's law . . . with the *super-vision* [emphasis added] of the religious leaders'[47]), but from the whole Shi'ite tradition of *de facto* acceptance of political authority which had grown up since Safavid times.

If Khomeini's real position had been fully known and understood, it is doubtful if he would ever have acquired a following massive enough to bring down the Pahlavi monarchy. But, in addition to his role of religious firebrand, Khomeini was a highly astute politician. In his public pronouncements he carefully avoided reference to the *vilayet e faqih*, confining himself, as in 1963, to generalized attacks on US and Israeli imperialism, violations of the constitution, discrepancies of wealth, palace corruption, the waste of national resources on luxuries and weaponry and the evils of SAVAK, the Shah's secret police, whom Khomeini's followers accused of murdering his son Mustafa in 1977. Indeed, up to the time he came to power in 1979, Khomeini continued to argue for a restoration of the 1906 Constitution. A traditionalist *mullah* masquerading as a new Afghani, he might have been convincing to the impoverished folk of the shanty-town if they had known about him, and he had his supporters within the religious establishment, most of them former pupils from Qum. These included Ayatollah Hossein Montazeri, a teacher of *fiqh* at Qum; Ayatollah Muhammad Beheshti, an astute political operator who managed to get SAVAK to approve his being placed in charge of the government-financed mosque in Hamburg; Ayatollah Morteza Motahari, the most intellectual and liberal-minded of Khomeini's followers; Hojjat al Islam Akbar Rafsanjani; and Hojjat al Islam Ali Khamenei: all would play leading parts in the Islamic Revolution. But in itself Khomeini's message cannot have had much appeal for the most active opponents of the Shah's regime – the liberals of Mussadeq's old National Front, remnants of the communist Tudeh party, and the 'new left' movements, inspired by similar developments among Palestinian and Latin American youth, that had mushroomed in the wake of SAVAK repression.

The task of bringing the nationalists, modernizers, leftists and miscellaneous radicals into the ranks of Khomeini's followers fell to the Islamic leftists led by Sadeq Gotzbadeh and Abu'l Hasan Bani Sadr, acting under the inspiration of the guru of the Shi'ite modernists, Dr Ali Shariati. Without Shariati's immense reputation among the Iranian youth, and without the crucial support lent to Khomeini by Gotsbadeh, Bani Sadr and the leftist guerrillas in the first weeks of the revolution, it is doubtful whether the coalition of disparate elements that brought down the Shah would ever have come together.

SHI'ITE SPECULATIVE MODERNISM: ALI SHARIATI

Born in 1933 in a village in Khurasan, Shariati received his early education from his father, Aqa Muhammad Taqi Shariati, a free-lance *mujtahid* who, though not a trained *mullah*, founded in Mashad the Centre for the Propagation of Islamic Truth, an evangelical institution devoted to modernist Quranic exegesis. After learning Arabic, Shariati trained as a teacher. He gave an early indication of his socialist leanings by translating a biography of Abu Dharr al Ghifari (subtitled 'The God-Worshipping Socialist') by the Egyptian novelist Abdal Hamid al Sahar. The book described how, after the Prophet's death, Abu Dharr denounced the first three caliphs, supported 'Ali and, after the latter's defeat, withdrew into the desert in order to keep alive the radical Islamic tradition of supporting the poor against the worldliness of the rich.[48] After graduating from Mashad University in 1960 Shariati won a state scholarship to Paris, where he obtained a doctorate in sociology and Islamic studies. This was the heyday of student radicalism and the beginning of the Third World movement heralded by the Cuban and

Algerian revolutions. Shariati attended lectures by Louis Massignon as well as popular Marxist professors, and undertook translations of Sartre, Camus, Guevara, Giap and, notably, Fanon. While translating Fanon Shariati wrote the French West Indian writer several letters complaining about his hostility to religion. The 'Wretched of the Earth', Shariati believed, could not resist Western imperialism unless they regained their cultural identity, which was closely bound up with religion.

Shariati's sojourn in Paris coincided with an upsurge in the activity of the Liberation Movement, the Islamic-orientated wing of Mussadeq's National Front led by Mehdi Bazargan, an engineer, and Hojjat-al-Islam (later Ayatollah) Mahmud Taleqani, a leading religious supporter of Mussadeq who had been forced into retirement after the Shah's coup. The Liberation Movement's Paris branch, with its affiliated Islamic Students' Society, was presided over by Gotzbadeh and Bani Sadr. Shariati joined the Front, editing and writing for its various publications and rapidly becoming the most influential voice among the oppositionists. In 1965 he returned to Iran with his wife and two children. After spending six months in jail for his opposition activities he was allowed to return to his native Khurasan, where he taught in an elementary school and, for a time, at Mashad University. His classes were suspended, however, when the authorities decided they were becoming too popular, and in 1967 he moved to Tehran, where he began teaching history and sociology at the famous Husseiniya-i-Ershad, a religious foundation supported by veterans of the Liberation Movement. Barzargan taught thermodynamics there, and Motahari (Khomeini's ex-pupil) and Taleqani taught theology.

Shariati became immensely popular. His claim to be developing a new 'Islamic sociology' attracted both secular and religious students. Notes and tapes of his lectures were soon circulating, not only in Tehran but also in the provinces. The Islamic terminology of his discourse not only protected him from official repression, but also made his message more accessible to students from traditional family backgrounds. In 1973, however, SAVAK finally moved against him, closing down the Husseiniya, arresting Shariati and banning his works. He remained nearly three years in prison until a petition from the Algerian Government secured his release. After being kept in home detention for two years he was allowed to leave for England, where he died suddenly in 1977, aged 44. Shariati's supporters claim he was murdered by SAVAK, but the British coroner reported a massive heart attack as the cause of death.

Those of Shariati's writings so far available in English are somewhat sketchy and eclectic, exhibiting an idiosyncratic approach to Islam and a general, if superficial, familiarity with Left Bank political writing. In one of his better-known works, *Marxism and Other Western Fallacies*, he takes on Marx and Sartre, both of whom are condemned for their misunderstanding and rejection, presented as typically Western, of religion. There is no consideration of the ideas of Weber, Durkheim, Kirkegaard, William James or other important Western writers on religion. Shariati's approach was intuitive rather than scholarly. He gives no references to the authorities he cites and at times appears to misrepresent them. His attitude towards Marxism seems to have more to do with its popular appeal for the student left than with its value as a methodology or style of analysis. Nevertheless his grounding in Islamic intellectual traditions gave him a base from which to evaluate Western culture and society in terms which Westerners and, more importantly, the partly Westernized youth of Iran, could understand.

In line with his own political commitment, much of Shariati's writing presents an activist approach. Islam, he claims, 'is the first school of thought that recognizes the masses as the basis, the fundamental and conscious factor, in determining history and society'. In support of this proposition he cites the favourite modernist verse from the Quran:

> Verily God does not change the state of a people until they change the state of their own selves.[49]

Unlike most religious writers, he refrains from accusing Marxists of *kufr* (disbelief):

> Examine carefully how the Quran uses the word *kafir*. The word is only used to describe those who refuse to take action. It is never used to describe those who reject metaphysics or refuse to accept the existence of God, the soul or the resurrection.[50]

Shariati's quarrel with Marxism is two-fold. Sociologically, he claims, Marx failed to distinguish between the forms of ownership, class relations and the tools of production on the one hand, and the structure of domination between rulers and ruled on the other. This failure had its outcome in Leninist and Stalinist industrialism. By assuming that the superstructure of domination arose out of relations of production, the communists thought that public ownership of the means of production would put an end to the dehumanizing exploitation of capitalism.

Actually, all they succeeded in doing was to create a different version of bourgeois society: '. . . the difference between Marxism and the western bourgeoisie [*sic*] is that [the latter] promotes a bourgeois *class* and [the former] a bourgeois *society*'. Here Shariati's critique of Soviet and Chinese communism is in line with that of other 'new left' critics; he follows Fanon in urging that the Third World countries can never recover the self-confidence necessary to modernize their societies until they have first 'returned to their roots' in the popular culture:

> When the intention is to deny the West, to resist it, Marxism is considered the most effective weapon against it; whereas it is seldom realized that Marxism itself is utterly a product of the history, social organization and cultural outlook of this same West. This is not simply because its founders and leading figures are all Western, but rather, to employ a Marxist analysis, the ideology itself must be accounted a mere superstructure resting on the social infrastructure of the bourgeois industrial system of production in the modern West.[51]

Marxist models, Shariati argues, are not simply inappropriate for Islamic societies – though, in common with other critics, he recognizes how unsuccessful Marxist ideas and parties have been in Muslim countries – they are contradictory and wrong in themselves. By denying the autonomous and absolute character of human values they reduce men and women to creatures of production. Whereas Marx's philosophy takes human beings out of the realm of necessity and into history, his sociology puts them back into the mechanistic world of nature. The philosophy is therefore clearly at odds with the sociology: the language in which Marx condemns capitalism is loaded with values derived from western humanism – values whose autonomy he denies: 'Assuming a mystical tone, he speaks of humanity as self-aware, truthful, proud, free, knowing, endowed with moral virtues . . .'[52] In a sense, therefore, Marxists are really idealists masquerading as materialists. Having established the non-material basis of ethical values, Shariati goes on to attribute them to the divine in man, a 'bi-dimensional being', a 'compound of mud and the divine spirit'. This dualism is internal to man, not part of nature. Its uniqueness to man is symbolized by the Quranic story of the angels prostrating themselves before Adam. Humanity's role as God's vice-regent is a function of human free will. The human being's relation to the divinely ordained laws of the universe is analogous to that of the agriculturalist who has the 'freedom' to cultivate trees and plants in accordance with the pre-existing laws of nature. The prophets 'have discovered the divine norms existing in society and nature and, through the exercise of their will in conformity with these norms, they have perfected their mission and attained their goal' of building new societies, civilizations and histories. In Shariati, voluntarism is vindicated and attributed directly to the divine in humanity acting in conjunction with revelation.[53]

The radical political implications of this doctrine become most explicit when Shariati identifies 'God' with 'the People'. Two classes, the rulers and the ruled, have stood opposed throughout history: 'In the class society, Allah stands in the same rank as *al nas* [the people] in such a fashion that whenever in the Quran social matters are mentioned Allah and *al nas* are virtually synonymous.'[53] In the same way, the statement that 'property belongs to God' means that capital belongs to the people as a whole. These are the principles that Abel son of Adam, 'Ali, Abu Dharr, Salman al Farisi and the Imam Husain stood for against Cain, Mu'awiya and the Umayyad dictators. They represent *tawhid* (unity) against *tawlid* (production) and *shirk* – that is, the disintegrative forces of class and nationalism, the 'world-view that regards the universe as a discordant assemblage full of disunity, contradiction and heterogeneity, possessing a variety of independent and clashing poles, conflicting tendencies, variegated and unconnected desires, purposes and wills'. Islam, the religion of *tawhid*, finds its ideal society in the Umma, whose social system is based on equity, justice and common ownership – that is, the classless society. Its perfect representative is the 'theomorphic man' in whom the spirit of God has overcome the half of his being that relates to *iblis*, to clay or sediment.

> [This] ideal man passes through the very midst of nature and comes to understand God; he seeks out mankind and thus attains God. He does not bypass nature and turn his back on mankind. He holds the sword of Caesar in his hand and he has the heart of Jesus in his breast. He thinks with the brain of Socrates and loves God with the heart of Hallaj . . . Ideal man has three aspects: truth, goodness and beauty – in other words, knowledge, ethics and art. He is a theomorphic being exiled on earth: with the combined wealth of love and knowledge, he rules over all beings. In front of him the angels prostrate themselves. He is the great rebel of the world.[54]

Shariati's mystical humanism owes something to Marx and to Sartre, but rather more to the Shi'ite philosophical tradition of Ibn Sina, Mulla Sadra and High Sufism. His 'theomorphic man' is a blend of Camus's *'homme revolté'* and Ibn al 'Arabi's 'Perfect Man'. Shariati is versatile enough in Quranic exegesis to recognize that 'the language of religions, particularly the language of the Semitic religions in whose prophets we believe, is a symbolic language'. It is a 'multi-faceted language, each aspect of which addresses itself to a particular generation and class of men'.[55] The *ayas* (signs) of the Quran are allegorical; the signs of God revealed in nature, however, contain 'positive scientific worth'; they are not mere 'illusions or veils covering the face of truth'. Unlike Ibn al 'Arabi, Shariati is a phenomenological rather than an ontological monist. He regards the Quranic view of nature as being 'closer to the approach of modern science than to that of ancient mysticism'. In a passage reminiscent of Iqbal he argues that Einstein's theories point the way to an 'invisible and unknowable essence that sometimes shows itself in the form of matter, and sometimes in the form of energy'. Science can render knowable the *zahir* or outer manifestations of reality. The 'unseen' reality (*al ghaib*) is hidden because it is unknowable: the Quranic division of the world into *shahada* and *ghaib* 'is an epistemological one, not an ontological one'.[56]

Shariati's approach offers radical possibilities, not only of action, but of interpretation, with consequent implications for religious leadership:

> We have to clarify that we want the Islam of Abu Dharr, not that of the royal palace; of justice and true leadership, not that of the caliphs, class stratification and aristocratic privileges; of freedom, progress and awareness, not of captivity, stagnation and silence. We want the Islam of the fighters, not that of *ruhani* [spiritual leaders]; the Islam of the 'Ali family, not that of the Safavi family.[57]

It would be the intellectuals rather than the traditional clergy who would bring about this return to the radical Islam of 'Ali and Abu Dharr, Shariati explained in a pamphlet which, coincidentally or not, bears the same title as Lenin's famous call to action: *What is to be Done?* They, rather than the *mullahs*, would be the genuine exponents of the 'dynamic revolutionary Islam'.[58]

Understandably the *'ulama*, even those who worked in the progressive establishment at the Husseiniya, found this aspect of Shariati's message highly objectionable. In 1968 Ayatollah Motahari, one of Khomeini's closest disciples, resigned from the Husseiniya in protest against Shariati's anti-clerical lectures. The more conservative 'ulama found his views even more offensive, issuing statements condemning his theological 'errors'. Khomeini, however, demonstrated his characteristic political astuteness by refusing to condemn Shariati. Moreover, without referring to him by name he continued to use phrases borrowed from Shariati, such as 'mustazafin' ('the wretched'), 'the rubbish of history' and 'religion is not the opium of the masses', thereby creating the impression that he substantially agreed with Shariati's views.[59] The young intelligentsia who idolized Shariati concluded that Khomeini was much more liberal in outlook than they would have done had they carefully read the Najaf lectures. By tacitly supporting Shariati, Khomeini established the basis for the combined leadership of the Shi'ite 'ulama and the 'Shi'ite Ph.D.s' which placed itself at the head of the anti-Shah movement and which fell apart almost as soon as power had been achieved.[60]

URBAN GUERRILLAS AND POPULAR SHI'ISM

The Islam of Khomeini and Shariati, the populist and the revolutionary, could never have established itself without a combination of military force and popular mass support. The military arm of the revolution was supplied by the guerrilla movements, which were broadly divided into two groups – the Marxist Fedayeen and the Islamic Mujahidin. The Fedayeen were mostly the children of the secular-minded Westernized middle classes. The Mujahidin, with many fewer women, were mostly the sons of the 'religious' classes – merchants, bazaar traders and clergy.[61] Shariati's influence was greater among the Mujahidin, although by the mid 1970s part of the latter's leadership had veered towards Marxism. In political terms the military activities of the guerrillas were less effective than the repression they provoked. Like the urban guerrillas in certain Latin American countries, they presented a challenge which converted an authoritarian government into an outright military dictatorship. The repressive measures employed by SAVAK did much to discredit the Shah's regime at home and abroad. Executions – often illegal – and the use of torture, assassination and other acts of state terrorism helped to undermine support for the Shah among the traditional and Westernized middle classes, while the publicity these atrocities received in the US adversely affected his image there, contributing to his downfall. After Jimmy Carter's presidential victory in 1976, on a platform that included a general commitment to human rights, the Shah came under pressure from his closest ally to modify his repressive policies at a stage when discontent could only have been met by the further use of force. As with Louis XV in 1789, political liberalization at this juncture was the worst possible course of action the Shah could have taken in his own interest.

If the guerrillas made their contribution to the fall of the Shah by helping to discredit his regime, the *mustazafin* of the densely crowded tenements and shanty-towns finally brought him down. Here the Islamic frame of reference developed by Shariati and Khomeini was to prove decisive. Both thinkers, unlike the more traditionally minded clergy, were prepared to exploit the popular Shi'ism of the masses. The revolutionary or ''Alid' Shi'ism which Shariati had contrasted with the institutionalized or 'Safavid' Shi'ism of the official clergy may have been pitched at radically minded intellectuals, but it could also be harmonized with the popular religious culture of the illiterate rural immigrants who sought to reproduce, in their new and unfamiliar urban environment, the reassuring traditions and customs of their villages.

The 'villagization' of urban culture is a phenomenon that has been observed by many sociologists and is easily understood. The familiar religious festivals help to mitigate urban anomie, often taking on a more strenuous character in compensating for feelings of insecurity experienced in the new environment. In Egypt and North Africa this popular religious feeling is expressed in Sufi *dhikrs*, *hadras* and *zar* cults, as well as in the more orthodox festivals such as the Id al Adha and the Prophet's birthday. In Iran, with its special tradition of folk Shi'ism, mass piety is focused upon the rituals and *rawzehs* associated with the martyrdom of Husain at Karbala, along with the messianic expectations implicit in the doctrine of the Imamate. During the months leading up to the revolution, the 'Karbala paradigm' – to borrow a phrase from the anthropologist Michael Fischer – was fully exploited by Khomeini, both before and after his return from exile in Paris in January 1979. At about the same time, the Mujahidin and Shariati's followers helped to fan popular messianic expectations by putting it about that Khomeini was, in effect, the expected Imam (a blasphemy of which the traditional leadership would never have been guilty). Although Khomeini never explicitly referred to himself as the expected Twelfth Imam, the fact that he allowed himself to be called 'Imam' by his enthusiastic supporters amounted to deliberate exploitation of this concept.

At the popular *rawzehs* in the shanty-towns and poorer districts of Tehran the Shah had often been compared to Yazid, murderer of Husain and arch-tyrant of Shi'a mythology. The Muharram mourning ceremonies had once before been exploited by the opposition, during the protests against the 'White Revolution' in 1963. In November 1978, following a day of serious rioting caused by the shooting of several student demonstrators in Tehran, the Shah imposed a military government under General Azheri. The opposition called for a general strike and there were three days of disturbances in Tehran and other major cities. In December General Azheri banned the traditional 'Ashura marches commemorating the Karbala massacre. A senior *ayatollah*, the liberal Shariatmadari, replied that no one needed permission to take part in a religious procession. From Paris, where he had gone after his expulsion from Najaf the previous October, Ayatollah Khomeini proclaimed that torrents of blood might be spilled at 'Ashura, but the Blood of Husain would triumph over the Sword of Yazid. Good Muslim soldiers should desert if ordered to fire on their brothers and sisters. On the eve of 'Ashura (9 December) the senior *ayatollah*, Mahmud Taleqani, marched at the head of a procession in Tehran numbering about half a million people; on 'Ashura itself (10 December) some two million people shouting 'Death to the Shah!' gathered near the Shahyar monument, built by the Shah with money extorted from the *bazaari* merchants to celebrate 2,500 years of monarchy. On 28 December the Shah tried his last gamble and appointed Dr Shapur Bakhtiar, a member of the National Front, Prime Minister. Bakhtiar persuaded the Shah to 'go on holiday', thereby probably forestalling a military coup. Khomeini condemned the Bakhtiar government, and the Prime Minister was expelled by his colleagues in the National Front. On 19 January, the traditional 'Arbain or Fortieth Day after the Death of Husain, Khomeini called for a massive demonstration against the Bakhtiar government which was attended by more than a million people in Tehran alone. On 1 February, after Bakhtiar had realized that resistance was hopeless, he rescinded his orders to the troops to close the airport, and Khomeini returned to a welcoming crowd of some two million ecstatic people. As Shariatmadari observed somewhat caustically, 'No one ever expected the Hidden Imam to return in a Jumbo Jet.'[62]

Thus, by uniting a disparate group of political forces around

Khomeini, the Islamic Revolution actualized the latent eschatological expectations of Imami Shi'ism and activated the 'Karbala paradigm' for political ends. Never since the Second World War had there been such a massive popular movement as that which brought down the Shah's regime. Naturally enough the events in Iran provoked much re-thinking, not to say soul-searching, in the West. Was this really a new 'upsurge' of Islam, one that would soon overflow the boundaries of Iran and sweep through the Middle East, once again endangering the world's oil supplies?

At the time this book went to press, the question remained un-answered. The Gulf War, after four years of bitter fighting, was still in stalemate. The Khomeini regime was still in power, having consolidated itself by methods which made the Shah's despotism seem mild in comparison. In the long and bloody power-struggle between the hard-line *mullahs* of the Islamic Republican Party and the Islamic modernist forces led by Bani Sadr, Gotzbadeh and the Mujahidin, the *mullahs* emerged victorious. The Islamic Republic's first president, Bani Sadr, was disgraced and forced into exile; Gotzbadeh was executed; and thousands of young Mujahidin of both sexes were executed, murdered, and subjected to tortures as cruel as any conceived by SAVAK. Con-fident in the rewards of martyrdom, hundreds of thousands of young men joined or were drafted into the army; to become cannon fodder for the Iraqi artillery.

However, there was little to suggest that the revolution would be successfully exported beyond Iran's frontiers. The Shi'a communities in Iraq and the Gulf were too carefully supervised, insufficiently discon-tented or too disillusioned with the course of events in Iran to want to throw in their lot with the Iranians. Only in Lebanon, whose impover-ished Shi'ites (known locally as Mutawalis) had become radicalized in the course of a decade of violence, dispossession and destitution, was the revolutionary flame still burning. There it took hold amongst a section of the Shi'ite militia, 'Amal. The offshoot thus created, which had come under the influence of Iranian volunteers in the Biqa' valley, appeared to have been responsible for the suicide bombing attacks which claimed the lives of more than 300 French, American and Israeli servicemen in Beirut and Tyre in the autumn of 1983. Even these actions, however, appear to have been controlled or manipulated by more machiavellian interests. The bombings were thought to have been carried out with Syrian connivance, with the aim of weakening the

resolve of the United States and its allies in propping up an unrep-
resentative and unpopular Maronite government. By the spring of 1984 it
seemed that the Syrian strategy had worked. The United States and its
European partners in the Multinational Force had abandoned any
attempt to shore up Christian Maronite power, and the Lebanese Christian community was forced, as in the past, to turn to Syria for protection.
Locally the victors had been the Druze and Shi'ite militias, the former
benefiting from the 'asabiya of their sect, the latter inspired partly by
Khomeini, but mainly by the example and memory of their former
leader, the charismatic Imam Musa Sadro, who had 'disappeared', in
Shi'ite fashion, after a dispute with the Libyan leader Colonel Qadhafi.

With militant Shi'ism ascendant in Lebanon, some observers saw the
makings of a new revolutionary 'Islamic international', capable of fan-
ning sectarian tensions much further afield. The evidence for this,
however, was very doubtful. In the struggle between revolutionary
Shi'ism and the interests of existing Muslim states, the advantage still
seemed to lie with the incumbents. The attraction of Khomeini's brand of
Islamic radicalism diminished with proximity. Early in 1984, students
and agitators in Tunisia and Morocco who were credited with responsibility for organizing riots against sudden price rises claimed to have been
inspired by the Iranian example; and the governments of both these
states, keen to blame outsiders for their troubles, eagerly pointed the
finger at Khomeini. But there was nothing, beyond a few tracts and
pamphlets using the vocabulary of militant Islam, to show that there
were any organizational links between the Iranian Ayatollah and the
Maghrebi malcontents. Where revolutionary Shi'ism posed a more
serious threat to the status quo, among the Shi'ites of Iraq, the appeal of
Khomeini seemed to be on the wane, as the people rallied to the support
of a government which, however tyrannical, was seen to be defending
the national homeland against the alien invader. Arab and Persian
national identities were proving more effective rallying-points than
revolutionary Islamic solidarity; or, as Ibn Khaldun might have had it,
the reality of *mulk*, the power-state, was triumphing over *khilafa*, the
dream of a universal caliphate.

8 ⚜ Conclusion

Every year as the world grows smaller the Muslim countries are drawn closer together. For all the diverse and multiform ways in which the Divine Idea has manifested itself in their societies, they share a common heritage, and, what is more important, the consciousness of this. Their number includes some of the world's wealthiest as well as poorest populations. Yet in the Quran and the Sunna they share a set of common cultural references and a doctrine which lays particular stress on social justice and communal solidarity. The Quran is a sustained polemic both against the kind of tribal particularism we would now call nationalism and against social and economic inequalities.

The Medinese polity founded by the Prophet attempted to realize the values of Islam in this world. Although the ultimate moral reckoning, so far as the individual was concerned, was postponed, as in Christianity, until the Day of Judgement, Islam was built, like Judaism, on the premise that the experience of living in the good society – that which enforced the laws decreed by God – greatly improved the individual's chance of salvation. Just as the good society of Medina came into existence through the sum of many individuals' rejections, following the Prophet's example, of the Meccan *jahiliya*, so the solidarity of the Medinese Umma, the supra-tribal polity owing allegiance to God and his Prophet, provided the social assurance for the individual's after-life. Where the average Christian would be driven by the Gospel's antinomian and fundamentally subversive doctrines into seeking salvation through a strenuous search for personal moral rectitude in a world he despised or rejected, the Muslim could live reasonably securely within the conventions of his society until he was persuaded that these had departed so far from the norms laid down by God that his own salvation – and that of his family – was imperilled. Then, following the Prophet's own example, he would be inspired to rebel against the existing order, and to try, using the means at his disposal, to recreate the Medinese order. The means, as the Muhammadan model exemplified, was not infrequently the military power of tribalism allied to the ideological motivation of religion. Thus, running through the diversity of historical traditions in the world of Islam there was nevertheless a common thread: the constant creative tension between the ideal and the practical, the dream of the Medinese Utopia and the actuality of the Muslim state.

That the two have always been in conflict has been one of the underlying themes of this book. The Prophet of Islam set his followers the impossible task of realizing the ideals of Islam in a violent and wicked world, using the available sources of political power. A statesman as well as a teacher, he consciously manipulated the dynamics of tribalism to create a supra-tribal polity, inveighing against the older forms of 'asabiya in order to forge the new solidarity of the Muslims under the leadership of the Quraish. Thus the tension between the ideal and the real, the absolute claims of God and the exigencies of human political power, was present from the first. The Prophet himself had recognized the need to compromise between the two principles when he brought Abu Sufyan, Mu'awiya and Marwan into the leadership of the Umma, thereby creating the basis of the Umayyad despotism. For all that, the triumph of pragmatism would never be permanent. The universalist claims of Islam – the demand for greater social justice and equality for all Muslims – were behind the agitations which led to the Umayyad downfall, to successive Shi'ite revolts and to the numerous *jihads* of later ages. The utopian aspirations of primordial Islam, though never fully realized, never ceased to activate discontent and to provide the ideological fuel for generations of Muslim revolutionaries. Given the existence of this Islamic activist tradition, it is hardly surprising that the Marxist revolutionary rhetoric has made comparatively little headway in the central Muslim lands.

The ideal Islamic state was probably never more than a pious fiction. What little we know of the Medinese Caliphate suggests that power politics, assassination, war and plunder played the part they had always done in Arabian history – only now they were focused on a more ambitious end: the aggrandizement of the Umma, a supra-tribal community bound by a common allegiance to God, his Prophet and the Caliphs. It is the actual success of this venture, as much as the utopian promise conveyed by it, that has worked on the imagination of Muslims down to the present. For the social disciplines taught by the Quran and the Sunna, sustained by the idea of a universal, supra-tribal deity, provided the ideological cement which served to unite segmentary formations, enabling them to control much larger territories and eventually to enjoy the benefits of a city-based civilization.

Islam is an urban religion conceived in a pastoral milieu. It is the ideology that accompanies the perennial movement of herdsmen into the settled regions, facilitating their integration into the more cosmopolitan world of the city. However, in encouraging the movement from the periphery to the centre and breaking down the communal allegiances that have kept the tribesfolk apart from each other, Islam also serves to erode urban solidarity. By proclaiming uncompromisingly that the allegiance of man is due to God alone, it inhibits the development of that distinctively urban patriotism which, taking root in Europe, accompanied the formation of social classes and enabled corporate and class allegiance to transcend the biological ties of kinship. The impact of Islam upon society was therefore paradoxical: while proclaiming its hostility to kinship solidarity, it also militated against the emergence of alternative sources of allegiance. Neither city nor monarchy, nation nor 'people' – or their representatives – were endowed with the kind of legitimacy that could enable them to alter the divine law or introduce new laws that could bind the community unconditionally. The decrees of amirs and sultans, the enactments of legislative assemblies, were powerless to introduce social changes which flouted the Shari'a or went against the grain of communal feeling. Power inevitably acquired an arbitrary character – though up till the present century, when the available means of control multiplied, this arbitrary power was less than dictatorial, being conditional upon the duty of upholding the Shari'a, 'enjoining the good and forbidding the evil'.

The failure of Islam's original utopian mission of creating a single united polity bound by the Shari'a was implicitly recognized by Ibn Khaldun, who made an important distinction between the ideal Islamic state (khilafa) and the existing dynastic state (mulk) based on kinship solidarity ('asabiya). Since by his time the Caliphate had ceased to exist, he devoted his analysis almost exclusively to mulk, which he considered necessary both for mankind's social well-being and for Islamic da'wa. Unlike more idealistic thinkers, he recognized 'asabiya as a fact of life, and therefore as a potential source of good. Ibn Khaldun's pragmatism was admired by reformers like Muhammad Abduh and the Maghrebi nationalist 'Allal al Fasi, founder of the Moroccan Istiqlal party, both of whom came to accept the *watan*, or territorial homeland, as the basis for Muslim allegiance within the broader ethnic and geographical diversity of *dar al Islam*. Not insignificantly, Ibn Khaldun was vigorously condemned by the more idealistic reformers, including Rashid Rida and Maududi, who saw in his acceptance of *'asabiya* an argument for compromising with the sin of nationalism.

Theoretically, allegiance to the *watan*, or national state, is incompatible with the supreme loyalty due to the Islamic Umma: it is particularist where Islam is universal; its sovereignty belongs to the monarch or people, where in Islam sovereignty belongs to God alone. The *watan* creates arbitrary frontiers around itself, whereas the Umma exists wherever there are Muslims to engage in communal prayer and to observe the Shari'a. In fact, however, Islam has never failed to accommodate itself to the realities of power – an *ad hoc* process for which thinkers like Al Mawardi and Ibn Khaldun supplied theoretical justification.

A modern example of Khaldunian *mulk* replacing the theocratic imperatives of Islam as the basis of government is provided by Saudi Arabia, whose founder, 'Abd al 'Aziz al Sa'ud, having reached an accommodation with the European powers, began to de-emphasize his Wahhabi title of Imam, calling himself a king and giving his state an overtly dynastic character. For the purists, the Saudi compromise was a betrayal of the movement's Islamic ideals – a feeling which Saudi Arabia's enemies such as Iran and Libya endeavour to exploit in their radio propaganda. The response of the Al Sa'ud family, however, has been to insist that in their country it is the Shari'a that governs all, including the King. Their adoption of the Hanbali system rather than any other allows them to sustain this position most effectively, since the absence of a *fiqhi* superstructure makes it easier to introduce changes in areas not specifically mentioned in scripture. Saudi power is, however, fundamentally arbitrary, being based on conquest and the *'asabiya* of the ruling clan, which has enormous patronage at its disposal.

'Kin patronage' politics (which is what *mulk* plus *'asabiya* amount to in modern terms) are far from exclusive to the Saudis, even though the Al Sa'ud, having the self-confidence of wealth and power, are among the few to proclaim openly the dynastic basis of their government. Thus the real structure of power in Syria and Iraq, if we look behind the facade of Ba'athist organization, is both arbitrary and informal, being based on the *'asabiya* of a handful of 'Alawi families in the case of Syria, and on that of a closely knit group of Arab Sunnis from Takrit in the case of Iraq.* Like the Soviet Communist Party under Stalin, the institutions of Ba'athism serve mainly as one-way channels of command and patronage, enabling the ruling group to consolidate its hold on society. The difference between Ba'athist and Saudi *mulk*, however, is that whereas the former, like Nasserism, has taken upon itself the task of reforming Islam, thereby altering the ideological basis of the state, the latter is content, for reasons already given, to leave Islam alone.

Elsewhere, the problem of modernization has proved more difficult, as the Muslim state has moved further away from its historic origins. Given the arbitrary character of Muslim power, it was perhaps not surprising that modernizing autocrats, from Muhammad 'Ali to Nasser, having tried unsuccessfully to impose reforms on the *'ulama*, took over religious institutions or developed alternative ones. In most Sunni countries the rigidity of a *fiqh* tied to literalist interpretations of scripture and integrated into a traditional pattern of living made innovation difficult, though not impossible. This was especially so in Egypt, where the spiritually liberating aspects of Sufism had become divorced from the legalist mainstream, and Shaikh Muhammad Abduh's efforts to re-integrate the two came too late to supply the new national polity with an 'Islamic' character acceptable to the masses. Superficially speaking, religion had become separated from politics: in Egypt, as in some other countries, the new national state was 'secular', based on religious equality, popular sovereignty and nationally democratic forms of government. Education was modernized – that is to say, imported – and Islam relegated to the status of a religion like Christianity.

Politically and ideologically, however, the experiment was less than successful. Parliamentary democracies can function on the basis of competing party bureaucracies or kinship allegiances when these are appropriately balanced. In most Muslim states, however, the party bureaucracies have a nebulous existence, since the ideas around which such organizations crystallize belong to the Westernized few, while the masses remain largely attached to more traditional – that is to say, Islamic – modes of discourse. Traditional patterns of kinship and patronage are usually to be found behind party labels, and military government of one form or another becomes the principal avenue of reform. Para-

---

* The majority of Sunnis in Iraq are Kurds. Arab Sunnis amount to only about 20 per cent of the total population.

doxically, perhaps, the reformism of army officers (who must have a 'modern' education in order to master the latest military technology) can become the ideological cloak for the new, up-to-date kinship groups which provide the contemporary version of *'asabiya*.

Almost everywhere in the Muslim world the secularism of the elites, whether overt or concealed by Islamic labels, coexists uneasily with the traditional world-view of the masses – a world-view that must needs express itself in Islamic terms. In recent years throughout the Muslim world there has been an apparent resurgence of Islamic activity. This is partly real, in the sense that the rising elites are using Islam as a means of proclaiming their identities; but it is also illusory in so far as Islam is still, as it has always been, the *Weltanschauung* of the traditional classes. What has really happened is that modern communications technology has brought within the purview of politics, the mainly illiterate masses, whom the rising elites are able to mobilize to a degree that would have been unthinkable a few generations ago. The 'Islamic revival' is not so much a return to archaic modes of discourse as an aspect of modernization comparable to the electrification of villages and the building of highways.

Modern methods of communication reach over the heads of traditional hierarchies, enabling national leaders to communicate directly with the masses. This media revolution, which considerably diminishes the political value of literacy, can operate in opposing ways. It can strengthen government, increasing the support available to national leaders, especially charismatic ones like Nasser or Khomeini; or it can enable opposition to circumvent the controls of censorship by means of pirate or foreign-based radio transmissions, or by the large-scale dissemination of tape cassettes. To be successful, political campaigns, like commercial advertising, must draw on popular culture by monitoring and projecting back images relevant to, and activating, the aspirations of the target groups. The present 'resurgence' of Islam in the Muslim heartlands and in parts of the periphery has the same two-sided character as the media revolution. Within certain limits, the rhetoric of Islam can be used to uphold the existing leadership or to attack it, to legitimize or to delegitimize the state. The ambiguity of the Islamic political stance makes it less of a revolutionary force than many people supposed in the days immediately following the fall of the Shah. In countries with high illiteracy where the modernist outlook is limited to a relatively small, Westernized elite, it can be used to mobilize social and economic resentment against the government. By the same token, however, a government can equip itself with Islamic symbols, obtaining *fatwas* to justify its policies, forbidding sales of alcohol, enforcing prayer-time for civil servants or introducing Quranic punishments for *hadd* offences. Since opposition tends to mobilize around Islamic symbols, it can be bought off fairly easily by cosmetic changes. The positive political, social or economic aspects of Islam have not, as yet, become the subjects of a broad enough consensus among contemporary Muslim thinkers to be formulated into a coherent platform around which the masses in all Muslim countries could be mobilized.

None of this means, of course, that a new Islamic consensus is not in the making. On the negative side, the resentments of Muslims against the existing world and domestic orders are growing, and there exists in Islam an authentic vocabulary with which these feelings can be articulated. In the Middle East the continuing humiliation of the Arab states at the hands of Israel and the United States has been given a specifically religious dimension by the Israelis, who have shown themselves utterly insensitive to Muslim feelings over Jerusalem. It is not insignificant that the Islamic Conference, one of the leading Saudi-fuelled vehicles of pan-Islamic activity, was established as a direct result of the burning of the Al Aqsa mosque by a deranged Australian in 1969. Pro-Palestinian, anti-Israeli sentiment is now strong among Muslim activists outside the Arab world, indicating that Israel's continuing occupation of Arab territory is seen increasingly as an Islamic rather than a purely Arab matter.

The failure of either super-power to effect a solution to the Palestine problem has been added to the disenchantment generally felt about their respective economic doctrines. For most Islamic and Third World countries, capitalism means not the development of locally based free enterprise, but its destruction by foreign competition, while socialism, in the versions imported along with Soviet and Eastern Bloc aid, is often perceived as involving an unacceptable level of bureaucratic control, disruption of the traditional small-trading sector and the introduction of costly, inefficient industrial plant. 'Islam', suitably interpreted, offers a middle way between these extremes, a philosophy of the free market tempered by social responsibility, a doctrine which permits private property provided it is put to positive social benefit. In many Muslim countries, experiments in interest-free banking are proving popular, not least because they offer the possibility that petro-dollar surpluses may be invested in socially useful projects while enabling small investors from the traditional trading sectors to release their savings for profitable use. The 'social capitalism' being advanced by Islamic economists may not differ greatly from varieties of cooperative banking or investment tried in the West; but it is one area where insistence on conforming to the Shari'a has proved a stimulus to creative innovation. It is likely to be taken increasingly seriously as the conventional world banking system falls further into disarray or collapses completely. At the moment, however, the movement is in its infancy, and it is ironic, though perhaps not surprising, that the Saudis, who control so much real money, are proving to be among the Muslim rulers most reluctant to allow the introduction of the system into their country.

The middle way of Islam has obvious attractions for a Third World caught between super-power rivalries on the one hand and the progressive impoverishment of the South *vis-à-vis* the North on the other. Islam is authentically Afro-Asian. Its colour is brown rather than white. It enjoys the prestige of both antiquity and modernity. It is untainted by any associations with European domination, since its influence was established in much of Africa and Asia long before the coming of the white man. Yet it is modern because Arab oil wealth can buy in the latest technical marvels, like the new Hajj terminal. Such wealth concentrated in the hands of the rulers of the Hejaz is seen by many of the more naive Muslims in the marginal regions not as the result of geological accident, but as a special manifestation of God's bounty conferred on a family which, unlike so many others, has not abandoned the faith of its ancestors and strives to live by the Law.

Islam also offers the middle way out of the tortuous cultural schisms that have beset so many developing societies torn between the desire to emulate a successful and expanding western civilization and feelings of resentment against it. For a rising generation of university-educated intellectuals, it offers a bridge to the unlettered but vocal masses: it is not insignificant that many of those on trial in Egypt for the Sadat killing and the disturbances afterwards were doctors, engineers, technicians – people whose talents would, a generation earlier, have gained them admission to Nasser's technocratic elite. For many young women, too, Islam can paradoxically offer a middle way in the direction of greater personal freedom: for those living in over-crowded cities the new-style 'lawful dress' covering the body from head to foot, leaving only hands and face exposed, represents a new maturity. It is both a positive rejection of the false coquettishness that characterized earlier gener-ations of 'westernized' Muslim women, tyrannized by cosmetics and expensive hair-dos, and a way of securing relief from the unwanted attentions of men in a milieu where many men, fresh from the country-side, see Western dress as a harlot's uniform.

Islamic reassertion is thus a bridge as well as a sword, a means of healing the social and cultural fissures resulting from the imposition of western culture as well as the source of a vocabulary that can be used to dethrone rulers or justify their assassination. In Iran its revolutionary potential was demonstrated to maximum effect. But there was no certainty that Khomeini's movement would spread far beyond Iran's own frontiers or escape from the Shi'ite sectarian ghetto. Though many Sunni Muslims sympathized with the revolution's aspirations and ap-plauded the overthrow of the Shah, few outside the Shi'ite communities would strive actively on its behalf. For one thing, the reformism of Shariati and Bani Sadr, which might have found a response in Sunni hearts, was replaced by the reactionary neo-traditionalism of Khomeini and his fellow *mullahs*: no Sunni activists were likely to take kindly to a doctrine insisting that only the established *faqihs* should have political power. For another, despite many threats to overthrow the 'Satanic' regime in Baghdad, the revolutionary government had barely succeeded in crossing the international frontier: if God, the architect of all victories, was indeed on the side of the Islamic revolution, he was taking an inordinate amount of time to reveal His Will in the matter. Finally, it was not unnoticed among people who might otherwise have sympathized with Khomeini, that he remained allied to the Syrian leader, Hafez el Asad, the 'Alawi sectarian who had butchered 10,000 Muslims in Hama and many others elsewhere. Indeed the Iranians had often publicly accused the Muslim Brotherhood of being agents of US imperialism, Zionism and so forth. For those inclined to read these signals in religious rather than political terms, Shi'ite solidarity overrode any serious com-mitment by Tehran towards wider pan-Islamic revival.

At the time of writing, the revolutionary elan of the Iranian Islamic republic appeared to be exhausting itself in an increasingly futile and costly struggle with Iraq. But the revolution had sounded a warning to the Muslim states and the rest of the world. The vocabulary of Islam and its symbols would continue to exercise a powerful attraction over people's minds so long as there were large bodies of believers who remained unintegrated in the political process. The Quran's attacks on social injustice and the abuse of wealth, combined with the Prophet's activist example, can always be invoked to mobilize opposition to Muslim governments perceived as corrupt or unjust, especially those which fail to equip themselves with convincing Islamic credentials. To that extent Islam seems set to remain on the political agenda for many decades, until such time as it becomes absorbed like other religious traditions into some pluralistic international culture of the future. After that, it may be expected to flow once again in the more diffused and less rigid channels of high Sufism, whose liturgical disciplines and free-ranging theosophical outlook provide it with a universalism less parochial than Judaism and less anthropocentric than Christianity. Freed from the Pharisaic rigidity which makes so much contemporary Islamic activity seem culturally sterile (when compared, for example, with sophisticated variants of the Hindu-Buddhist traditions), Islam could prove a highly congenial faith for a scientific age, and one with an important message. For beyond the admonitions to the faithful to create the good society by observing the Law, there is a message addressed to the whole of mankind. It is a message that proclaims the Eternal Transcendent, and man's special responsibility as guardian of this planet. It is a message which calls on men and women to show gratitude for the world's bounty, to use it wisely and distribute it equitably. It is a message phrased in the language and imagery of a pastoral people who understood that survival depended upon submission to the natural laws governing their environment, and upon rules of hospitality demanding an even sharing of limited resources. In a world increasingly riven by the gap between rich and poor nations, and in constant danger of nuclear catastrophe, this message has an urgent relevance and it is one that we ignore at our peril.

References

All Quranic quotations are from The Message of the Qur'an, *translated and explained by Muhammad Asad (Gibraltar, 1980). Asad follows the text of the recension of Hafs ibn Sulayman al Asadi as it appears in the so-called 'Royal Egyptian' edition published in Cairo in 1337 H.*

Chapter 1 (pp. 23–48)

1. Quran 22:27–8
2. Muhammad Asad, *The Road to Mecca* (Tangier, 1974), p. 357
3. Hafiz Wahba, *Arabian Days* (London, 1964), p. 129
4. James Buchan, 'Secular and religious opposition in Saudi Arabia' (paper delivered to Symposium on Saudi Arabia held at Exeter University, July 1980). There is a condensed version of Buchan's account of the Siege of Mecca in David Holden and Richard Johns, *The House of Saud* (London, 1981), pp. 511–27
5. BBC Summary of World Broadcasts ME/7129/A/1f.
6. ibid.
7. *Guardian* (14 Sept. 1982)
8. Ali Shariati, *Hajj*, trans. Ali. A. Behzadnia and Najla Denny (Houston, Texas, 1978)
9. *Muslim*, London (January 1969), pp. 77–80
10. Asad, *Road to Mecca*, p. 367
11. Genesis 21:13
12. Asad, *Road to Mecca*, p. 355, cf. Genesis 21:12–21
13. *Encyclopaedia of Islam*, 2nd edn (Leiden, 1955), entry under 'Ka'ba'
14. A. Guillaume, *The Life of Muhammad*, translation of Ishaq, *Sirat Rasul Allah* (Oxford, 1955), pp. 35–6
15. Quran 6:74–9
16. Ali Shariati, *One and an Eternity of Zeros* (Tehran, n.d.)
17. Shariati, *Hajj*, pp. 31–2

18. *Muslim*, loc. cit.
19. Shariati, *Hajj*, p. 41
20. ibid., p. 69

ADDITIONAL WORKS CONSULTED

Ezzedine Guellouz, *Mecca, the Muslim Pilgrimage* (Tunis, 1979)

Mohammed A. R. Khan, 'On the meteoritic origin of the Black Stone of the Ka'bah', *Popular Astronomy*, XLVI, no. 7 (Aug.–Sept. 1938)

Encyclopaedia of Islam, 1st edn (Leiden, 1913), entries under 'Ka'ba', 'Mahmal', 'Mecca', ' 'Umra'

Encyclopaedia of Islam, 2nd edn (Leiden, 1955), articles under 'Hadjdj', 'Hanif', 'Hidjaz Railway', ' 'Ibrahim',' ' 'Id al 'Adha', ' 'Isma'il'

Z. Badawi and Z. Sardar, *Hajj Studies* (London and Jedda, 1979), vol. 1

Russel King, 'The pilgrimage to Mecca: some geographical and historical aspects', *Erdkunde*, XXVI (Feb. 1964), pp. 1231–43

A. S. Tritton, 'A pilgrimage from Morocco', *Islamic Studies*, Karachi, V, no. 1 (March 1966)

Abdullah 'Ankawi, 'The pilgrimage to Mecca in Mamluk times', *Arabian Studies*, London, 1 (1974), pp. 116–66

Richard Burton, *Personal Narrative of a Pilgrimage to Al-Madinah and Meccah* (London, 1855–6; facsimile reprint of 1893 edn, Dover Publications, New York, 1964)

The Autobiography of Malcolm X (Harmondsworth, 1970)

Movement Studies 1978 (film), directed by Mick Czaki for the Hajj Research Centre, Jeddah

Mimar: Architecture in Development, Singapore, 4 (April–June 1982)

Chapter 2 (pp. 49–100)

1. *Hamasa* of Abu Tamam, 506, trans. R. A. Nicholson in *Literary History of the Arabs* (London, 1930), p. 136
2. Quran 96:1–5
3. Maxime Rodinson, *Mohammed* (Harmondsworth, 1973), p. 77
4. C. G. Jung, *Psychology and Religion* (Yale and Oxford, 1938), p. 99
5. Quran 82:19
6. Quran 104:2–3
7. Quran 89:17–20
8. Quran 80:1–2
9. Quran 75:37–40
10. Quran 10:28
11. Quran 8:17
12. Quran 33:32–3

13. See Muhammad Asad, *The Message of the Qur'an* (Gibraltar, 1980), n.218 at Quran 2:229

14. Quran 24:31

15. Quran 3:130

16. Quran 17:33

17. F. Donner, *Early Islamic Conquests* (Cambridge, Mass., 1982), p. 9

18. Quoted in Muhammad Asad, *The Principles of State and Government in Islam* (Gibraltar, 1980), p. 32

ADDITIONAL WORKS CONSULTED

Ernest Gellner, *Muslim Society* (Cambridge, 1981)

W. M. Watt, *Muhammad at Mecca* (Oxford, 1953)

W. M. Watt, *Muhammad at Medina* (Oxford, 1956)

Charles Issawi, *The Arab World's Legacy* (Princeton, 1981)

Ibn Khaldun, *The Muqaddimah*, trans. F. Rosenthal, 3 vols (Princeton, 1967)

Muhammad Zafrulla Khan, *Muhammad, Seal of the Prophets* (London, 1980)

Tor Andrae, *Mohammed: The Man and his Faith* (London, 1936)

J. S. Trimingham, *Christianity among the Arabs of Pre-Islamic Times* (London and Beirut, 1979)

Chapter 3 (pp. 101–140)

1. Thomas Carlyle, *On Heroes and Hero Worship* (orig. pub. as *Heroes, Hero-worship and the Heroic in History*, 1841), edn with *Sartor Resartus* (London, 1914), p. 299

2. Quran 24:35

3. Quoted in Helmut Gaetje, *The Qur'an and Its Exegesis*, trans. A. T. Welch (London, 1976), p. 201

4. ibid., p. 199

5. ibid., p. 58

6. Quran 3:7

7. Quoted in Gaetje, p. 56

8. Quran 19:16–22

9. Quoted in Gaetje, pp. 121 ff.

10. Jonathan Raban, *Arabia Through the Looking-Glass* (London, 1979), p. 19

11. Toshihiko Izutsu, *God and Man in the Koran: Semantics of the Koranic Weltanschauung* (Tokyo, 1964), p. 13

12. Quran 29:61

13. Quran 10:66

14. Quran 68:9
15. Quran 25:18
16. Izutsu, *God and Man*, p. 95
17. Muhammad Asad, *The Message of the Qur'an* (Gilbraltar, 1980), n. 2 at Quran 1:2
18. Quran 39:46
19. Quran 33:63
20. Quran 24:45
21. Izutsu, *God and Man*, p. 120
22. e.g., Quran 23:80, 85
23. Quran 2: 23–4
24. Izutsu, *God and Man*, p. 151
25. cf. Quran 2:70, 75
26. Quran 12:2
27. Quran 41:44
28. Quran 14:4
29. Quran 5:48
30. Al Asha al Akbar, *Diwan*, ed. Muhammad Hussein (Cairo, 1950), 33:32–4
31. Quoted in Izutsu, *God and Man*, p. 174
32. Asad, *Message*, p. iv
33. A. J. Arberry, *The Koran Interpreted* (London, 1956), 79:1–5
34. A. Yusuf Ali, *The Holy Qur'an – Text, Translation and Commentary* (Leicester, 1978), 79:1–5
35. *The Diwans of Abid Ibn al Abras of Asad and Amir ibn al Tufail*, etc., ed. and trans. Sir Charles Lyall (Cambridge, 1913 and 1980), p. 31
36. Quran 57:20
37. Quran 41:39
38. *The Times*, 2 April 1976
39. Asad, *Message*, n. 106 at Quran 20:120
40. Genesis 3:16–17
41. Quran 20:122
42. Quran 7:10
43. Mohammed Iqbal, *Six Lectures on the Reconstruction of Religious Thought in Islam* (Lahore, 1930), p. 117
44. Quran 22:35–6 and cf. 8:12
45. Quran 49–13
46. *Diwan al Hamasa*, 713:4, quoted in Izutsu, *God and Man*, p. 237
47. cf. Quran 2:257
48. cf. Izutsu, *God and Man*, pp. 57–8
49. Quran 14:7
50. *Sahih* of al Tirmidhi (Cairo, 1950), II, p. 157, cited in Izutsu, *God and Man*, p. 55

51. *Diwan al Hamasa*, 762: 1, quoted in Izutsu, *God and Man*, p. 206
52. Quran 12:33
53. Quran 3:110
54. cf. Toshihiko Izutsu, *The Structure of Ethical Terms in the Koran* (Tokyo, 1959), p. 218
55. Quran 6:39
56. Genesis 20:30–38
57. Michael Fischer, *Iran: From Religious Dispute to Revolution* (Cambridge, Mass., 1980), p. 72
58. Exodus 14; Quran 7:136ff.
59. Quran 53:38, 6:164, 17:15, 35:18, 39:7
60. Quran 17:15
61. Quran 17:4–5
62. Asad, *Message*, n. 7 at Quran 17:5
63. Quran 34:19
64. Quran 4:79
65. Quran 4:40
66. Quran 2:216
67. Quran 81:1–14
68. Quran 84:7–12
69. Quran 18:29
70. Quran 56:41–4
71. Quran 18:31
72. Quran 56:15–38
73. Asad, *Message*, n. 15 at Quran 32:17
74. Yusuf Ali, *Holy Qur'an*, n. 5240 at Quran 56:35
75. Jalal al Din al Suyuti, *Kitab al Anwar* (Tunis, n.d.), p. 26, quoted in Abdelwahab Bouhdiba, *La Sexualité en Islam* (Paris, 1979), p. 94
76. Quran 75:22–3
77. Suyuti, *Kitab*, p. 38, quoted in Bouhdiba, *Sexualité*, p. 98

ADDITIONAL WORKS CONSULTED

Patricia Crone and Michael Cook, *Hagarism* (Cambridge, 1977)
John Wansbrough, *Koranic Studies: Sources and Methods of Scriptural Interpretation* (Oxford, 1977)
Richard Bell (ed.), *The Qur'an*, 2 vols. (Edinburgh, 1937, 1939)
Richard Bell, *Introduction to the Qur'an* (1953), ed. and rev. W. M. Watt (Edinburgh, 1978)
Kenneth Cragg, *The Event of the Koran* (London, 1972)
A. J. Arberry, *The Koran Interpreted*, 2 vols. (London, 1955)
Encyclopaedia of Islam, 2nd edn. (Leiden, 1955), article under 'Al-Kur'an'

Chapter 4 (pp. 141–180)

1. Sayyid al Aweis, *Letters to the Imam el Shafei* (Cairo, n.d.)
2. ibid.
3. J. Schacht, *Origins of Muhammadan Jurisprudence* (Oxford, 1950), 1959 edn, p. 140
4. M. G. S. Hodgson, *The Venture of Islam* (3 vols, Chicago, 1974), vol. I, p. 327
5. Quoted in Schacht, *Origins*, p. 135
6. Muhammad ibn Isa al Tirmidhi, *Sahih*, cited in Muhammad Asad, *The Principles of State and Government in Islam* (Gibraltar, 1980), p. 38
7. Imad al Din ibn al Shamma, quoted in F. Rosenthal, *The Herb: Hashish versus Medieval Muslim Society* (Leiden, 1971), p. 101
8. Jalal al din al Suyuti, *Al Jami' al Saghir*, quoted in Asad, *Principles*, pp. 48, 106
9. N. Coulson, *A History of Islamic Law* (Edinburgh, 1964), p. 124
10. Asad, *Principles*, p. 12
11. Coulson, *Islamic Law*, p. 2
12. Abu Muhammad ibn Ali ibn Hazm, *Al Muhalla* (Cairo, 1347 H) vol. I, pp. 62–4, quoted in Asad, *Principles*, pp. 13–14
13. A. Bouhdiba, *La Sexualité en Islam* (Paris, 1979), p. 72
14. *Al Fatwa al Hindiya* (Bulaq, 1310 H), vol. 1, p. 47, cited in Bouhdiba, *Sexualité*, p. 67
15. Quran 2:282
16. cf. Quran 4:34
17. Muhammad ibn Isma'il Bukhari (1810–1870), *Sahih* (Cairo, 1312 H), vol. 4, p. 91, cited in Bouhdiba, *Sexualité*, p. 144; see also A. Guillaume, *The Traditions of Islam* (Oxford, 1924), pp. 125–6
18. Edward Lane, *An Account of the Manners and Customs of the Modern Egyptians* (London, 1836; facsimile of 1860 edn, Dover Pubs., New York, 1973), p. 82
19. ibid., pp. 63, 82
20. I Corinthians 7 *et seq.*
21. Quran 24:32
22. Bouhdiba, *Sexualité*, pp. 112, 113
23. Muhammad ibn Isa al Tirmidhi, *Sunan* (Medina, n.d.), vol. II, p. 413, Bab. 9, *hadith* 1167, quoted in F. Mernissi, *Beyond the Veil* (Cambridge, Mass., 1975), p. 11
24. Muslim ibn al Hajjaj, *Al Jami al Sahih*, vol. III (Book of Marriage), p. 130 quoted in Mernissi, *Beyond the Veil*, p. 11
25. Abu Hamid al Ghazali, *Ihya 'ulum al din* (Cairo, n.d.), p. 50
26. ibid.
27. Aini, *'Umdat al qari shar'ih al Bukhari* (Istanbul, 1308 H), vol. 9, p. 484, quoted in Bouhdiba, *Sexualité*, p. 111

28. Masud al Qanawi, *Sharh lamiat ibn el Wardi* (Cairo, 1310 H), p. 14, quoted in Bouhdiba, *Sexualité* p. 110

29. Quran 65:4

30. Quran 65:1–6

31. Nawal el Saadawi, *The Hidden Face of Eve* (London, 1980), p. 206

32. Lane, *Manners and Customs*, pp. 180–81

33. Muhammad Asad, *The Message of the Qur'an* (Gibraltar, 1980), n. 218 at Quran 2:229

34. Coulson, *Islamic Law*, p. 138

35. Bouhdiba, *Sexualité*, pp. 138–9

36. Quran 24:30–31

37. Asad, *Message*, n. 36 at Quran 24:31

38. Quran 33:53

39. cf. Bouhdiba, *Sexualité*, pp. 139–40

40. Lane, *Manners and Customs*, p. 296

41. Maxime Rodinson, *Islam and Capitalism* (Harmondsworth, 1977), p. 34

42. ibid., p. 55

43. ibid., p. 57

44. ibid., p. 91

45. Bryan S. Turner, *Weber and Islam* (London, 1974), p. 13

46. ibid., p. 173; Sami Zubaida, 'Economic and political activism in Islam', *Economy and Society*, 1 (1972), p. 324

47. X. de Planhol in *Cambridge History of Islam* (4 vols, Cambridge, 1970), vol. 2B, p. 453

48. ibid., p. 456, citing J. de Thevenot, *Relation d'un voyage fait au Levant* (Paris, 1664), p. 239

49. G. von Grunebaum in *Cambridge History of Islam*, vol. 2B, p. 491

50. J. Schacht in ibid., p. 563

51. C. Cahen in ibid., p. 520

52. Ibn Taymiyya, *Siyasa Sharia* ('Le Traité de droit publique d'Ibn Taymiyya'), trans. H. Laoust (Beirut, 1948), p. 172

53. I am grateful to Jim Piscatori for helping me clarify my argument in this section.

Chapter 5 (pp. 181–226)

1. Ibn Saghir, *Actes du XIVième Congrès des Orientalistes*, trans. A. de Motylinski (Paris, 1908), pt 3, p. 68, quoted in Charles-André Julien, *History of North Africa* (London, 1970), p. 28

2. Julien, *History*, p. 62

3. Gustav Thaiss in N. R. Keddie (ed.), *Scholars, Saints and Sufis* (Berkeley, 1972), p. 356

4. ibid.
5. Clifford Geertz, *The Interpretation of Cultures* (London, 1975), p. 104
6. Bernard Lewis, *Origins of Ismailism* (Oxford, 1940), p. 25
7. Abu Daud, *Sunan al Mustafa* (Cairo, n.d.), vol. II, p. 135, cited in S. H. M. Jafri, *Origins and Early Development of Shi'a Islam* (London, 1979), p. 268
8. M. G. S. Hodgson, *The Venture of Islam* (3 vols, Chicago, 1974), vol. I, p. 304
9. ibid., p. 305
10. W. M. Watt, *The Formative Period of Islamic Thought* (Edinburgh, 1973), pp. 246–7
11. W. M. Watt, *Free Will and Predestination in Early Islam* (London, 1948), p. 139
12. Quran 3:7
13. Sayyid Muhammad Husain Tabataba'i, *Shi'ite Islam*, trans. S. H. Nasr (Houston, 1979), p. 99
14. A. Esmail and A. Nanji in S. H. Nasr (ed.), *Isma'ili Contributions to Culture* (Tehran, 1977), p. 244
15. M. G. S. Hodgson, *The Order of Assassins* (The Hague, 1955), p. 19
16. ibid., p. 5, n. 11
17. See *Mahjubah: The Magazine for Muslim Women*, Tehran, 1, no. 8 (October, 1981), pp. 52–6; Tabataba'i in *Shi'ite Islam*, pp. 227–30; N. Coulson, *A History of Islamic Law* (Edinburgh, 1964), pp. 110, 111

ADDITIONAL WORKS CONSULTED

David Bryer, 'Origins of the Druze religion', *Der Islam*, vol. 52, no. 1 (Feb. 1975)

J. C. Wilkinson, 'The Ibadi imama', *Bulletin of the School of Oriental and African Studies*, vol. XXXIX, no. 3 (1976)

Encyclopaedia of Islam, 1st edn (Leiden, 1913), entries under 'Kharidjites', 'Al-Husayn B. 'Ali B. Abi Talib', 'Karbala', 'Shi'a'

Encyclopaedia of Islam, 2nd edn (Leiden, 1955), entries under 'Alamut', 'Duruz'; 'Isma'iliyya', 'Karmati'

M. G. S. Hodgson, 'How did the early Shi'a become sectarian?', *Journal of the American Oriental Society*, vol. 75 (1955)

John Townsend, *Oman: The Making of a Modern State* (London, 1977)

Chapter 6 (pp. 227–286)

1. Quran 23:116
2. Quran 6:151
3. Quran 41:46

4. Quran 4:59
5. Quran 13:15
6. Quran 42:29
7. Quran 50:16
8. Quran 53:5–9
9. Muhammad Asad, *The Message of the Qur'an* (Gibraltar, 1980), p. 996
10. Quran 57:20
11. *Encyclopaedia of Islam*, 1st edn (Leiden, 1913), entry under 'Tasawwuf'
12. A. J. Arberry, *Sufism* (London, 1968), p. 33
13. ibid., p. 34
14. ibid., p. 42
15. *Encyclopaedia of Islam*, 1st edn, entry under 'Rabia al Adawiya'
16. Margaret Smith, *Rabi'a the Mystic and Her Fellow-Saints in Islam* (Cambridge, 1928), pp. 102–3
17. Michael Gilsenan, *Saint and Sufi in Modern Egypt* (Oxford, 1973), p. 137
18. ibid., p. 14
19. A. J. Arberry, *Revelation and Reason in Islam* (London, 1957), p. 99
20. ibid., p. 98
21. Arberry, *Sufism*, p. 58
22. ibid., p. 60
23. Louis Massignon, *La Passion d'Hallaj* (2 vols, Paris, 1922), vol. I, p. 303
24. W. M. Watt, *The Faith and Practice of Al Ghazali* (London, 1953), p. 20
25. ibid., p. 56
26. ibid., p. 60
27. ibid., p. 133–40 *passim*
28. Ibn al Arabi, *The Wisdom of the Prophets* ('Fusus al Hikam'), trans. Titus Burckhardt and Angela Culme-Seymour (Aldsworth, 1975), p. 24
29. R. A. Nicholson, *Rumi, Poet and Mystic* (London, 1950), p. 24
30. Jallal al Din Rumi, *Mathnawi*, trans. R. A. Nicholson (6 vols, London, 1929–37), vol. i, 1–5
31. ibid., vi, 1454–60
32. ibid., iv, 3637ff.
33. Edward Lane, *An Account of the Manners and Customs of the Modern Egyptians* (London, 1936; facsimile edn, Dover Pubs., New York, 1973), p. 241
34. E. E. Evans-Pritchard, *The Sanusi of Cyrenaica* (Oxford, 1949), p. 2
35. Louis Massignon in *Encyclopaedia of Islam*, 1st edition, entry under 'Tasawwuf'
36. Gilsenan, *Saint and Sufi*, p. 5

37. J. Spencer Trimingham, *The Sufi Orders in Islam* (Oxford, 1971), p. 241
38. Gilsenan, *Saint and Sufi*, p. 33
39. ibid., p. 43
40. ibid., p. 72
41. A. J. Arberry, *Sufism*, p. 75
42. Quran 33:41–2
43. Frithjof Schuon, *Understanding Islam*, trans. D. M. Matheson (London, 1976), p. 123
44. Trimingham, *The Sufi Orders*, p. 195
45. Gilsenan, *Saint and Sufi*, p. 168
46. I. M. Lewis, *Islam in Tropical Africa* (Oxford, 1966), p. 311
47. ibid., p. 60
48. cf. Vincent Crapanzano in N. R. Keddie (ed.), *Scholars, Saints and Sufis* (Berkeley, 1972), p. 342
49. J. F. P. Hopkins in *Encyclopaedia of Islam*, 2nd edn (Leiden, 1955), entry under 'Ibn Tumart'
50. A. Bennigsen and S. E. Wimbush, *Muslim National Communism in the Soviet Union* (Chicago, 1979), p. 6; Serif Mardin, 'Religion and Politics in Modern Turkey' in J. Piscatori (ed.), *Islam in the Political Process* (Cambridge, 1983), pp. 138–9
51. Aziz Ahmed, *Islamic Culture in the Indian Environment* (Oxford, 1964), p. 75
52. ibid., p. 185
53. Raphael Israeli, *Muslims in China: A study in Cultural Confrontation* (London and Malmö, 1978)

ADDITIONAL WORKS CONSULTED

Hamid Algar, 'The Naqshbandi Order' (unpublished typescript kindly lent to me by Professor Albert Hourani)

M. Molé, *Les Mystiques musulmans* (Paris, 1965)

Albert Hourani, *The Emergence of the Modern Middle East* (London, 1981), ch. 5

A. J. Arberry, *The Doctrine of the Sufis*, translation of Abu Bakr al-Kalabadhki, *Kitab al-Ta'aruf li-mathab ahl al-tasawuf* (Cambridge, 1935, 1977)

Majid Fakhry, *A History of Islamic Philosophy* (London and New York, 1983)

Chapter 7 (pp. 287–352)

1. P. M. Holt, *The Mahdist State in the Sudan* (Oxford, 1958), p. 34

2. A. S. Ahmed, *Millennium and Charisma among the Pathans* (London, 1976), p. 9

3. Aziz Ahmed, *Islamic Modernism in India and Pakistan 1857–1954* (London, 1967), p. 33

4. *Encyclopaedia of Islam*, 2nd edn (Leiden, 1955), entry under 'Ahmed Khan'

5. Zaki Badawi, *The Reformers of Egypt – a Critique of Al-Afghani, 'Abduh and Ridha* (London, 1976), p. 46, citing *Tafsir al Manar*, IV, p. 350

6. Muhammad Abduh, *Risalah al Tawhid* (Cairo, 1346 H), pp. 73–80, cited in Nadav Safran, *Egypt in Search of Political Community* (Cambridge, Mass., 1961), p. 67

7. Richard Mitchell, *The Society of Muslim Brothers* (London, 1969), p. 14

8. ibid., p. 14.

9. ibid., p. 29

10. ibid., p. 88

11. ibid., p. 210

12. Quoted in Hisham Sharabi, *Nationalism and Revolution in the Arab World* (New York, 1966), p. 112

13. A. S. Cudsi in J. Piscatori (ed.), *Islam in the Political Process* (Cambridge, 1983), pp. 51–2; author's interview with H. E. Sayyid Sadiq al Mahdi, January 1980; press reports, October 1983; information kindly supplied by Mr Graham Thomas

14. Ahmed, Islamic Modernism, pp. 142–3

15. Muhammad Iqbal, *Six Lectures on the Reconstruction of Religious Thought in Islam* (Lahore, 1930), pp. 11, 12

16. ibid., p. 176

17. ibid., p. 165

18. ibid., p. 170

19. Ahmed, *Islamic Modernism*, p. 159

20. ibid., p. 159

21. From Iqbal's letters to Jinna quoted in Ahmed, *Islamic Modernism*, pp. 160, 162

22. W. Cantwell Smith, *Islam in Modern History* (Princeton, 1957), p. 234

23. Sayyid Abul Ala Mawdudi, *Towards Understanding Islam* (London, 1980), p. 20

24. Mawdudi, *The Religion of Truth* (Lahore, 1967), pp. 3, 4

25. Mawdudi, *Towards Understanding*, p. 81

26. ibid., p. 104

27. Mawdudi, *Purdah and the Status of Woman in Islam* (Lahore, 1979), p. 20

28. ibid., pp. 197, 198

29. Mawdudi, *Birth Control* (Lahore, 1978), p. 73

30. Mawdudi, *Purdah*, p. 23
31. Mawdudi, *The Religion of Truth*, p. 23
32. Mawdudi, *The Process of Islamic Revolution* (Lahore, 1979), pp. 15, 16
33. Mawdudi, *The Islamic Law and Constitution* (Lahore, 1977), pp. 270f.
34. ibid., pp. 316–18
35. Munir Report (1954), p. 229, cited in Ahmed, *Islamic Modernism*, p. 242
36. *Arabia: The Islamic World Review*, London, no. 11 (July 1982), pp. 38–9
37. ibid. no. 10 (June 1982), pp. 14–19
38. See Michael Fischer, *Iran from Religious Dispute to Revolution* (Cambridge, Mass., 1980), pp. 149–50
39. Ervand Abrahamian, *Iran Between Two Revolutions* (Princeton, 1982), p. 447
40. Fischer, *Iran*, p. 151
41. Abrahamian, *Iran*, p. 425
42. Ayatullah Ruh Allah Khumayni, *Islam and Revolution*, selection of speeches and writings trans. and ed. H. Algar (Berkeley, 1981), p. 38
43. ibid., p. 28
44. ibid., p. 55
45. ibid., p. 57
46. ibid., p. 60
47. ibid., p. 170
48. Abrahamian, *Iran*, p. 465
49. Quran 13:11
50. Quoted in Abrahamian, *Iran*, p. 465
51. Ali Shariati, *Marxism and other Western Fallacies*, trans. H. Algar (Berkeley, 1980), p. 49
52. ibid., p. 23
53. Ali Shariati, *On the Sociology of Islam*, trans. H. Algar (Berkeley, 1979), p. 116
54. ibid., pp. 123–4
55. ibid., p. 71
56. ibid., p. 84
57. Abrahamian, *Iran*, p. 470
58. ibid., p. 471
59. ibid., p. 479
60. cf. Ernest Gellner, *Muslim Society* (Cambridge, 1981), p. 43
61. Abrahamian, *Iran*, p. 492
62. See M. H. Heikal, *The Return of the Ayatollah* (London, 1981), p. 177

ADDITIONAL WORKS CONSULTED

Albert Hourani, *Arabic Thought in the Liberal Age 1798–1939* (Oxford, 1962)

Middle East Journal, Washington DC, 37, no. 1 (1983), articles by Mangol Bayat, Yvonne Haddad, Bassam Tibi

Edward Mortimer, *Faith and Power: The Politics of Islam* (London, 1982)

E. I. J. Rosenthal, *Islam in the Modern National State* (Cambridge, 1965)

Hamid Enayat, *Modern Islamic Political Thought* (London, 1982)

V. S. Naipaul, *Among the Believers: An Islamic Journey* (London, 1981)

Michael Gilsenan, *Recognizing Islam: An Anthropologist's Introduction* (London, 1982)

Mohammed Ayoob (ed.), *The Politics of Islamic Reassertion* (London, 1981)

H. A. R. Gibb, *Modern Trends in Islam* (Chicago, 1950)

Janet L. Abu Lughud, *Cairo: 1,001 Years of the City Victorious* (Princeton, 1971)

J. Piscatori (ed.), *Islam in the Political Process* (Cambridge, 1983)

John L. Esposito (ed.), *Islam and Development* (Syracuse, New York, 1980)

G. H. Blake and R. I. Lawless (eds.), *The Changing Middle Eastern City* (London and New York, 1980)

Suggestions for Further Reading

Titles marked with an asterisk are highly recommended.

A. J. Arberry, *The Koran Interpreted*, 2 vols. (London, 1956). The most elegant translation in modern English.

Muhammad Asad, *The Road to Mecca* (Tangier, 1974). Personal account of a Jewish intellectual's conversion to Islam.

* Muhammad Asad, *The Message of the Qur'an* (Gibraltar, 1980). Arabic text, literal English translation and scholarly, modernist *tafsir* make Muslim scripture accessible, for the first time ever, to the Western general reader.

Cambridge History of Islam (4 vols, Cambridge, 1970). A scholarly compendium of a high standard, scandalously lacking an index.

Fred Donner, *Early Islamic Conquests* (Cambridge, Mass., 1982). Excellent on interaction of tribalism and religion in the first great Arab–Muslim movement.

John L. Esposito (ed.), *Islam and Development* (Syracuse, New York, 1980). Papers by leading US academics on religion and socio-political change in the Middle East.

E. E. Evans-Pritchard, *The Sanusi of Cyrenaica* (Oxford, 1949). Study of a reformist Sufi *tariqa* by one of the masters of modern anthropology.

Majid Fakhry, *A History of Islamic Philosophy* (London and New York, 1983). An excellent introduction which places Muslim philosophers in their theological setting.

H. A. R. Gibb, *Modern Trends in Islam* (Chicago, 1950). Important account of Islamic modernism by Britain's best-known Islamic scholar.

Michael Gilsenan, *Saint and Sufi in Modern Egypt* (Oxford, 1973).

* Michael Gilsenan, *Recognising Islam* (London, 1982). An anthropologist's introductory guide to popular forms of Islam in Egypt and the Levant.

Alfred Guillaume, *Life of Muhammad* (Oxford, 1955). Translation of Ishaq's *Sirat Rasul Allah* which gives a real flavour of the original Islamic movement.

* Marshall G. S. Hodgson, *The Venture of Islam* (3 vols, Chicago, 1974). Most ambitious attempt to place Islamic history in a world context by outstanding American scholar.

* Albert Hourani, *Arabic Thought in the Liberal Age* (Oxford, 1962). Classic study of intellectual backgrounds of Islamic modernism and nationalism in the Middle East.

* Ibn Khaldun, *The Muqaddimah: An Introduction to History*, trans. F. Rosenthal, ed. and abridged by J. Dawood (London, 1978). Still, after six centuries, the best introduction to the history of the Middle East.

* Mohammed Iqbal, *Six lectures on the Reconstruction of Religious Thought in Islam* (Lahore, 1930). A sincere and partly successful attempt at bridging the conceptual gap between Islamic and Western philosophical outlooks by the century's most outstanding Muslim writer.

Toshihiko Izutsu, *The Structure of Ethical Terms in the Koran* (Tokyo, 1959), and *God and Man in the Koran: Semantics of the Koranic Weltanschauung* (Tokyo, 1964). A Japanese scholar's linguistic analysis yields a scientific insight into the Muslim scripture and its relationship with the literature of its time.

Jalal al Din (Rumi), *Mathnawi*, trans. R. A. Nicholson (6 vols, 1929–37, London). Encyclopedic Persian epic poem translated literally by one of the great British Persian scholars. Unfortunately for the Philistine reader, the salacious passages have been rendered into Latin. For an introduction to Rumi with poetically translated selections, see R. A. Nicholson, *Rumi, Poet and Mystic* (London, 1950).

N. R. Keddie (ed.), *Scholars, Saints and Sufis: Muslim Religious Institutions since 1500* (Berkeley, 1972). A collection of papers of a generally high standard examining both official and popular versions of Islam in the Middle East and North Africa.

* Edward Lane, *An Account of the Manners and Customs of the Modern Egyptians* (1836; facsimile of 1860 ed., Dover Publications, New York, 1973). Classic ethnographic study of Cairene life.

Louis Massignon, *La Passion d'Hallaj* (2 vols, Paris, 1922). A Catholic vision of Sufi mysticism focused on the martyrdom of the famous mystic.

Richard Mitchell, *The Society of Muslim Brothers* (London, 1969). The only scholarly account in English, essential reading for anyone interested in modern 'fundamentalism'.

Edward Mortimer, *Faith and Power: The Politics of Islam* (London, 1982). Well-written account of modern Islamic politics by Middle East specialist of *The Times* (London), somewhat lacking in sociological background.

V. S. Naipaul, *Among the Believers: An Islamic Journey* (London, 1981). Personal encounters with 'fundamentalists' and others by one of the foremost writers in English, full of insights but without scholarly underpinning.

J. Piscatori (ed.), *Islam in the Political Process* (Cambridge, 1983). Papers of a generally high standard on Islamic politics in various countries.

Fazlur Rahman, *Islam* (Chicago, 1979). Best one-volume summary in English of Islamic beliefs and practices by a leading Muslim scholar.

Maxime Rodinson, *Mohammed* (Harmondsworth, 1973). A highly readable and plausible account of the Prophet's career by one of France's leading scholars.

Edward Said, *Orientalism* (London, 1978); and *Covering Islam* (London, 1981). Lively polemics by Palestinian literary critic against scholarly and journalistic distortions of Islam and the Middle East.

W. Cantwell Smith, *Islam in Modern History* (Princeton, 1957). An account of modernist movements in Islam by an outstanding Canadian scholar.

Frithjof Schuon, *Understanding Islam*, trans. D. M. Matheson (London, 1976). Sufistic view of Islam by a Western convert, much admired by T. S. Eliot.

W. Montgomery Watt, *Islam and the Integration of Society* (London, 1961). A venture into sociological analysis by a prolific scholar of classical Islam who is also a professing Christian. Much his most interesting work.

Glossary

'ABD: 'Servant' or 'slave'; commonly used as a name when coupled with one of the names of Allah. See also *'Ibada*.

AHL AL BAIT: 'People of the household', specifically used of the Prophet's household.

AHL AL HADITH: 'People of the tradition', or traditionalists, for whom the Prophet's example was supreme, even as against Quranic injunction. See also *Hadith*.

AHL AL KALAM: 'People of debate'; rationalists who upheld the supremacy of the Quran rather than that of the *hadith*.

AHL AL KITAB: 'People of the book'; originally referred to Muslims, Jews and Christians but came to include Zoroastrians and other groups possessing sacred texts.

AHL AL SUNNA: 'People of the Sunna' (Sunnis); those who uphold customs based on the practice and authority of the Prophet and his companions, as distinct from the Shi'ites and Kharijis. See also *Sunna*.

AL: Clan or 'House', as in Al 'Imran (3rd Sura of Quran), Al Sa'ud, etc. Not to be confused with *al* (short 'a'), the definite article.

'ALAWI: Member of extremist (*ghulu*) Nusairi sect in N.W. Syria which venerates 'Ali.

'ALID: Descendant of 'Ali, cousin and son-in-law of the Prophet.

'ALIM: See *'Ulama*.

AMIR: 'Commander'; originally military commander but subsequently applied to rulers and members of their families. *Amir al Muimin* ('Commander of the Faithful'): a title held by caliphs and some sultans.

ANSAR: 'Helpers' of Muhammad native to Medina, as distinct from the Muhajirin who accompanied him from Mecca.

'ASABIYA: 'Tribal or group solidarity'; a term used by philosopher Ibn Khaldun in his theory on state formation in North Africa.

'ASHURA: The 'tenth' of the month Muharram, when Shi'ite rituals are held commemorating the death of the Prophet's grandson Husain.

AYA: 'Sign' or 'miracle'; used for verses of the Quran.

BAB: 'Gate'; term applied to representatives of the Shi'ites' Hidden Imams.

BARAKA: 'Sanctity' or 'blessing' vested in and available from holy people, places or objects.

BAST: Twelver Shi'ite institution of sanctuary in mosques and other holy places.

BATIN: 'Inner', 'esoteric' or 'hidden' meaning of a religious text, especially the Quran.

BAY'A: 'Contract' or oath of allegiance binding members of an Islamic sect or Sufi *tariqa* to their spiritual guide.

BID'A: 'Innovation', as distinct from custom and law legitimized by the Shari'a.

CHADOR (Pers.): Traditional Iranian garment covering women from head to foot. See also *Hijab*.

DA'I: 'Propagandist' or missionary, especially in Shi'ite Isma'ili movements. See also *Da'wa*.

DAR AL HARB: The 'realm of war' or those lands not under Muslim rule, where, under certain circumstances, a war or *jihad* can be sanctioned against unbelievers.

DAR AL ISLAM: 'Realm of Islam'; originally those lands under Muslim rule, later applying to lands where Muslim institutions were established.

DA'WA: Esoteric 'propaganda' or mission of the Shi'ite Isma'ili sect.

DERVISH (Pers.): 'Mendicant'; member of a Sufi *tariqa*.

DHIMMI: Non-Muslim peoples afforded security of life and property (*dhimma*) under the Shari'a on payment of a poll tax (*jizya*).

DHIKR: 'Mentioning' or 'remembering'; specifically used for Sufi rituals designed to increase consciousness of God which include the repetition of his name(s).

DIN: 'Religion', 'belief', as opposed to *dunya*, 'worldly existence'.

FALLAH (pl. *fallahin*): Peasant farmer.

FANA: The 'extinction' of individual consciousness, and thus union with God, in Sufism.

FAQIH: Exponent of *fiqh*.

FAQIR: 'Pauper'; term applied to ordinary member of Sufi *tariqa*.

FATWA: Legal decision of a *mufti*.

FEDAYEEN (sing *fidai*): Soldiers prepared to sacrifice their lives in the cause of Islam. Now used for guerrilla fighters.

FIQH: 'Understanding' (of Shari'a); the system of jurisprudence based on the *usul al fiqh*.

FITNA: 'Temptation' or 'trial'; the name given to the civil wars which broke out within the expanding Muslim empire during the first 200 years after Muhammad's death.

FUTUWA: Young men's clubs, sometimes similar to guilds.

GHAIB: 'Unseen' and 'transcendent'; hence *al ghaiba*, the 'occulthation' of the Hidden Imams in Shi'ite doctrine.

GHULU: 'Exaggeration'; the over-emphasis of one aspect of doctrine to the point where the whole edifice of the Sunna is undermined. Hence, *ghulas* or extremists.

HADD (pl. *hudud*): 'Boundaries'; divine statutes and punishments contained within the body of the Shari'a.

HADITH (pl. *ahadith*): 'Tradition' or report of a saying or action of the Prophet. One of four roots of Islamic law. See also *Shari'a, Usul al fiqh*.

HADRA: 'Presence' [of God]; Sufi ceremony.

HAJJ: The annual pilgrimage to Mecca. One of the five duties (*rukns*) of Islam, required of every believer once in his life if possible.

HALAL: That which is 'permissible', particularly foods which comply with Islamic dietary rules.

HANAFI: Referring to the Sunni legal *madhhab* ascribed to Abu Hanifa.

HANBALI: Referring to the Sunni legal *madhhab* ascribed to Ahmad ibn Hanbal.

HANIF: 'True believer'; a term used to describe those Arabs who were monotheists before the revelation of the Quran.

HARAM: A sanctuary; 'that which is forbidden' by the Shari'a.

HIJAB: 'Screen'; veil traditionally worn by Muslim women in public; always covers the head, but not necessarily the face and hands.

HIJRA: 'Emigration' of Muhammad from Mecca to Medina in 622CE, the base year of the Muslim calendar.

HIYAL (sing. *hila*): 'Artifices' or 'tricks'; legal methods to circumvent general prohibitions.

'IBADA: Religious worship.

'ID AL ADHA: 'The festival of the sacrifice' on the last day of the Hajj.

'ID AL FITR: 'The festival of breaking the fast' at the end of Ramadan.

'IDDA: Legally prescribed 'period' during which a woman may not remarry after having been widowed or divorced.

IHRAM: 'State of ritual consecration' during Hajj, when pilgrims wear white garments. See also *Haram*.

I'JAZ: An elliptical quality of beduin speech.

IJMA': Consensus of the Muslim community or scholars as a basis for a legal decision. Shi'ites interpret it as a consensus of Imams.

IJTIHAD: Individual judgement to establish a legal ruling by creative interpretation of the existing body of law. See also *Mujtahid*.

IKHWAN: The 'Brothers', soldiers of 'Abd al 'Aziz, founder of the Saudi dynasty, and adherents of the Hanbali reformer 'Abd al Wahhab.

IKHWAN AL MUSLIMIN: Muslim Brotherhood, a society founded in 1928 by Hasan al Banna; originally aimed at re-establishing a Muslim polity in Egypt.

IKHWAN AL SAFA: 'Brothers of Purity', a group of Isma'ili-influenced thinkers based in Basra in the tenth century.

'ILM: 'Knowledge'; in particular religious knowledge of '*ulama*.

IMAM: 'One who stands in front' to lead the *salat*, hence the leader of the Muslim community. In Shi'ite tradition, 'Ali and those of his descendants considered to be the spiritual successors of Muhammad.

IMAN: 'Faith' or religious conviction.

INFITAH: The 'opening up' of the Egyptian economy to the West in 1972, in the hope of attracting foreign capital.

INSAN: 'Human being', from the root meaning 'to be companionable, agreeable or genial'.

ISLAM: 'Self-surrender' or 'submission'; reconciliation to the will of God as revealed to Muhammad. See also *Muslim*.

ISNAD: 'Support'; chain of authorities transmitting a *hadith*, thus guaranteeing its validity.

JA'FARI: Referring to the sole Shi'ite *madhhab* ascribed to the Imam Ja'far al Sadiq.

JAHL: 'Ignorance', hence *jahiliya*, 'period of ignorance', or pre-Islamic times.

JIHAD: War against unbelievers in accordance with Shari'a. Also applied to an individual's struggle against baser impulses.

JIZYA: Poll tax levied on *dhimmis* in a Muslim-ruled society.

KA'BA: Cubic building in Mecca containing the Black Stone, believed by Muslims to be a fragment of the original temple of Abraham. Focus of prayer (*salat*) and the Hajj. See also *Qibla*.

KAFIR: 'Disbeliever', or infidel who has rejected the message of the Quran.

KAHIN: Traditional shamanistic soothsayer in Arabia at the time of Muhammad.

KALAM: 'Debate' on matters of Muslim theology and cosmology. See also *Ahl al kalam*.

KATIB: 'Writer', specifically secretary in government office.

KHALIFA: Caliph, the 'deputy' of God on earth. In the Quran applied to

Adam, and hence to all humanity in relation to the rest of creation; specifically applied to the early successors of the Prophet as leaders of the Islamic state or *khilafa*, and to the successors of founders of Islamic states or Sufi *tariqas*.

KHANQA (Pers.): Sufi hospice, mainly in areas of Persian influence.

KHARIJIS (Arabic pl. 'Khawarij'): 'Those who go out'; members of a group of puritanical Muslim sects during Umayyad and early 'Abbasid times.

KHUL': 'Renunciation', or divorce initiated by the wife, according to the Shari'a.

KHUMS: 'Fifth'; a tax of one fifth of all trading profits, payable to *mujtahids* in Shi'ite areas.

KISWA: Black 'clothing' or covering of the Ka'ba, renewed annually.

KITAB: 'The book', or religious scriptures. *Umm al kitab* ('Mother of scripture'): divine *ur*-text of which the Quran is part.

KUFR: 'Disbelief', an ungrateful rejection of Islam. See also *Kafir*.

KUTTAB: School at which the Quran is taught.

MADHHAB: 'Adopted policy'; specifically applied to five recognized systems of *fiqh* (jurisprudence).

MADRASA: 'College', especially for religious studies.

MAGHRIB: 'Sunset', hence the prayer or *salat* at sunset; also Muslim 'occident', i.e., N.W. Africa, Morocco, for which the French transliteration 'Maghreb' is commonly used.

MAHDI: 'Awaited One'; a Messiah and reformist leader who aims to restore the original purity of the Islamic faith and polity. In Shi'ite tradition the Twelfth Imam.

MAHR: Dowry given to a woman on marriage and retained by her if she is divorced by her husband.

MAKRUH: Acts designated as 'distasteful' or 'undesirable' under Islamic law; there is merit in abstaining from them, but no sin in committing them.

MALIKI: Referring to the Sunni legal *madhhab* ascribed to Malik ibn Anas.

MA'RUF: 'Known'; term used in the Quran for familiar and approved custom; hence, generally, 'the good'.

MASHRIQ: 'Sunrise'; Levant.

MASLAHA: That which is 'beneficial'; term used for the principle of public interest in the Maliki *madhhab*, adopted by modern legal reformers.

MAULID: 'Birthday'; festival celebrating the anniversary of a religious figure.

MAWALI (sing. Mawla): 'Associates' or 'clients'; status at first given to non-Arab converts to Islam.

MILLET: Non-Muslim religious community within the *dar al Islam*.

MUBAH: Acts 'allowed' under Islamic law, commission or ommission of which are not sins.

MUFTI: Expert on the Shari'a qualified to give rulings (*fatwas*) upon questions of law.

MUHAJIRIN: Those who emigrated from Mecca to Medina with Muhammad. See also *Hijra*.

MUJAHID (pl. Mujahidin): Soldier fighting a holy war or *jihad*.

MUJTAHID: Religious scholars sanctioned to make individual interpretations to determine points of law, especially among Shi'a.

MULK: 'Dominion' or existing Muslim state as distinct from the ideal Islamic state (*khilafa*).

MUNKAR: 'Unknown'; term used in Quran for wrongful action as distinct from *ma'ruf*: hence evil generally.

MUQRI: 'Reciter' of the Quran.

MURID: 'Aspirant', or follower of a Sufi master.

MURSHID: Sufi master.

MUSLIM: One who has submitted to God; a follower of the religion revealed to and established by Muhammad. See also *Islam*.

MUSTAZAFIN: The wretched, '*les misérables*'; impoverished inhabitants of Iranian shanty towns.

MUT'A: Shi'ite legal institution of temporary marriage contract.

MUTAWWIF: Guide caring for pilgrims in Mecca. See also *Tawaf*.

MU'TAZILIS: 'Those who stand aloof'; theologians belonging to the rationalist school which introduced speculative dogmatism into Islam.

MUWAHHID (pl. Muwahhidin): 'Unitarian'; one who believes in God's unity (*tawhid*). Term used by Wahhabis and Druzes (among others) to describe their beliefs.

NASS: Designation of a successor, in particular a spiritual successor in the Shi'ite tradition.

PIR (Pers.): Sufi master.

QADI: Judge administering Shari'a.

QARI: 'Reciter', particularly of the Quran.

QIBLA: Direction of the Ka'ba to which Muslims turn while praying, hence the recess in a mosque which shows it.

QIYAS: 'Analogy'; the principle in jurisprudence used to deal with new situations not mentioned in the Quran or Sunna.

QURAN (Koran): 'Discourse' or 'recitation', the immutable body of revelations received by Muhammad.

RA'I: 'Opinion' or personal judgement of *faqihs* in interpreting Quranic rules.

RAWZEH (Pers.): Recital of the martyrdom of Husain, the Prophet's grandson, performed at religious gatherings in Iran. *Rawzeh-khan*: professional narrator.

RIBA: 'Usury', as prohibited in the Quran.

RIBAT: Sufi hospice.

RIDA: 'Satisfaction'; stage through which a Sufi progresses in his search for God.

RISALA (pl. *rasail*): 'Report' or 'epistle'.

RUKN (pl. *arkan*): 'Pillar'; one of the five religious duties prescribed for Muslims: Hajj, *salat*, *sawm*, *shahada* and *zakat*.

SADAQA: Voluntary contribution of alms.

SALAF: 'Predecessors'; appellation of the first generation of Muslims. *Salafi*: term describing the twentieth-century reform movement inspired by them.

SALAT: Ritual worship performed five times daily, one of the 'five pillars' (*rukns*) of Islam.

SAWM: Annual fast and daylight abstinence during the month of Ramadan, one of the *rukns* of Islam.

SAYYID: Descendant of 'Ali's son Husain. *Sidi* (local usage in the Maghreb) is applied to members of saintly lineages.

SHAHADA: Profession of faith whereby a Muslim declares his acceptance of God and his Prophet; one of the *rukns* of Islam.

SHAIKH: 'Elder'; head of a tribe or Sufi master.

SHARI'A: 'The path to a water-hole'; a name given to the sacred law of Islam which governs all aspects of a Muslim's life. It is elaborated through the discipline of *fiqh*.

SHATH: 'Roaming' or 'straying', whereby a mystic addresses his audience as though he were God.

SHI'A: 'Party' of 'Ali, comprising those groups of Muslims who uphold the rights of 'Ali and his descendants to leadership of the Umma.

SHIRK: 'Association' of partners to the divinity; idolatry.

SILSILA: 'Chain' of inherited sanctity (*baraka*) or kinship connecting the leaders of Sufi orders to their founders.

SUFI: Follower of Sufism (Arabic *tasawwuf*), the Islamic mystic path, from *suf* ('wool') garments worn by early adepts.

SUNNA: Custom sanctioned by tradition, particularly that of the Prophet enshrined in *hadith*.

SUNNI: See *Ahl al Sunna*.

SURA: Chapter of the Quran.

SULTAN: 'Authority' or 'power'; actual holder of power, as distinct from the *khalifa*; later common term for sovereign.

TAFSIR: 'Commentary' on the Quran.

TAHLIL: Prayer – 'la ilaha illa Allah', 'there is no deity but God' – particularly used in Sufi rituals.

TA'IFA: Organization of a Sufi order, as distinct from its spiritual path.

TALAQ: Declaration of divorce by the husband according to the Shari'a.

TANZIMAT: Administrative decrees; reforms instituted by the nineteenth-century Ottoman sultans.

TAQIYA: Dissimulation of one's beliefs in the face of danger, especially among Shi'ites.

TAQLID: 'Imitation', or the basing of legal decisions on the existing judgements of the four Sunni *madhhabs*.

TARIQA: 'Path' of mystical and spiritual guidance; a term which also came to be applied to the organization through which a *tariqa* extends itself in Muslim society.

TASAWWUF: See *Sufi*.

TAWAF: Ritual circumambulation of the Ka'ba by a pilgrim during the Hajj or 'Umra.

TAWHID: 'Unity' of God. Central theological concept of Islam.

TAWIL: Esoteric or allegorical interpretation of the Quran, predominant among Shi'ites.

TA'ZIYA: Shi'ite passion plays depicting the death of Husain.

TEKKES (Turk.): Sufi centres in Turkish-speaking areas.

'ULAMA (sing. *'alim*): 'Learned men', in particular the guardians of legal and religious traditions.

UMMA: Community of believers, in particular the community of all Muslims.

'UMRA: Lesser pilgrimage to Mecca which can be performed at any time of the year.

USUL AL FIQH: 'Roots' or foundations of jurisprudence. In the Sunni *madhhabs* they comprise: the Quran, the Sunna, *ijma'* (consensus) and *qiyas* (analogical deduction). See also *Fiqh*.

WAHY: 'Inspiration' or 'revelation' of the Quran.

WALI: 'One who is near God'; a saint in popular Sufism.

WAQF (pl. *awqaf*): Pious endowment of income originally for a charitable purpose; sometimes used as a means of circumventing the Shari'a's inheritance laws.

WATAN: 'Homeland' or 'nation', a concept borrowed from Western nationalism.

WAZIR: Administrator or bureaucrat appointed by the ruler.

WIRD: Private prayer in addition to the *salat*.

ZAHIR: 'Manifest' aspects of God, as distinct from the hidden or *batin*; hence literal or exoteric meaning of Quran or *hadith*.

ZAKAT: 'Purity'; term used for a tax of fixed proportion of income and capital (normally 2½%) payable annually for charitable purposes; one of the *rukns* of Islam.

ZAR: Exorcism ceremonies.

ZAWIYA: 'Corner'; building for Sufi activities.

ZINA: Sexual relations outside marriage, including both adultery and fornication, prohibited in the Quran.

Index

Figures in italics refer to map numbers.